# Cicely's Lord Lincoln

# Cicely's Lord Lincoln

## A Story of King Henry VII

Sandra Heath Wilson

buried
river
press

© Sandra Heath Wilson
First published in Great Britain 2014

ISBN 978-0-7198-1362-7

Buried River Press
Clerkenwell House
Clerkenwell Green
London EC1R 0HT

www.halebooks.com

Buried River Press is an imprint of Robert Hale Ltd

2 4 6 8 10 9 7 5 3 1

Printed in Great Britain by Clays Limited, St Ives plc

# Chapter One

October 1486

'No, HENRY TUDOR, you will *not* turn me into your mistress!'

The angry words were uttered to thin air by Lady Cicely Plantagenet, now Lady Welles. Hooded and cloaked to hide her identity, she stood alone on the windswept stairs from the Thames to the palace of Westminster. She was seventeen, and her large grey-brown eyes were bright with anger and defiance, for she was nothing if not spirited, and for some reason, today was the last straw.

It was early afternoon, the palace was relatively quiet because the court was at Greenwich, and she had been summoned for another secret assignation with her unwanted lover, King Henry VII, who forced her to his bed by threatening those dear to her. He was not worthy of the throne he had stolen through treachery from King Richard III, the uncle she had always loved far too much.

Well, today Henry would *not* have his own way! Being made to lie with this Lancastrian usurper, even in secret, was one thing, becoming his publicly acknowledged mistress was quite another. But that was what he was demanding of her, and if she went to him, there would be a bitter confrontation.

She was the daughter of a Yorkist king, Henry's aunt by marriage *and* the sister of his queen, and would *not* submit to further shame. She felt immense guilt already, because her exceedingly sensual nature let her down. Henry was a far more exciting, skilled and considerate lover than his cold exterior suggested, and she despised herself for finding a great deal of pleasure with him. It disgraced her, but she could not help it. She told herself that least she was protecting those she loved, which provided an undeniable reason for submitting to this king. But she was not as averse as she ought to be, and loathed herself as a consequence.

Last month there had been a salacious scandal at Winchester, where the court had gone for the christening of Henry's son, Prince Arthur. Henry had embroiled her in an unmistakably intimate kiss that, to her unutterable mortification, had been witnessed. Her husband had left her because of it, and she had fled back to London. But Henry continued to impose upon her. Well, today he could go to Hades. He blighted her life, and this time she would brave his uncertain temper and disquieting moods by returning to her husband's residence in the heart of London. But it was an empty place without Sir Jon Welles, who, although Lancastrian and Henry's half-uncle, was much loved by his fiercely Yorkist wife.

Head held high, Cicely went back down the steps to the unremarkable skiff that had conveyed her so anonymously to Westminster. Still hooded, her face in complete shadow, she sat down and wrapped her fur-lined cloak tightly around herself. She was dark-eyed and dainty, with a curving, small-waisted figure and a mass of thick, deep chestnut hair that was at present hidden beneath a headdress as well as her hood. Too resentful to care what Henry might or might not do on account of her defiance, she sat stiffly and proudly. She was a highborn lady of the House of York, a princess, and Henry Tudor should *never* forget it!

The autumn air was chill, low clouds scudded and the breeze made the river choppy as the little craft sped downstream on the fast-ebbing tide, jolting on wavelets and strong cross-currents. Vessels of all sizes crowded the water, from the smallest fishing boats to the most elaborate gilded barges of the nobility. There were modest coastal vessels, lighters, ferries and rafts, large and small, all capable of passing beneath London Bridge. Larger seagoing craft stayed downstream of the bridge. The tall steeple of St Paul's Cathedral rose from the summit of Ludgate Hill on the north bank, above the tumble of the city's tightly packed roofs, winding streets and numerous churches. On the south bank was Southwark, and the cathedral with its great square tower.

Cicely was glad when Three Cranes wharf appeared ahead, where she would alight to make her way uphill to the Welles town house, Pasmer's Place in St Sithe's Lane. The house was named after its owner, Master John Pasmer, a member of the Skinners' Guild and the Calais Staple. He was a fat, jolly man who owned many properties in the city, of which Pasmer's Place was easily the finest. Cicely liked him, because she sensed that his political sympathies lay with the House of York, the rightful reigning House of England. *Her* House.

The wharf was where wine was loaded and unloaded by the three sturdy wooden cranes from which it took its name, and there was an immense crush of vessels and on the quay itself many people, horse-sleds and wagons. Only one skiff was at the foot of the steps, having just conveyed the young gentleman who now stood at the top, flirting unconscionably with a pretty whore, who seemed likely to waive her charges for one such as him.

Like Cicely's, his hood was raised against the cold, and as the breeze billowed his rich cloak, she saw he wore costly thigh boots. She knew those boots! They belonged to her favourite cousin, Jack de la Pole, Earl of Lincoln. Her craft nudged the steps and she alighted. Jack remained unaware as she paid the boatman and went up towards him.

The future Duke of Suffolk was in his twenties, handsome, charming, and one of the most inveterate flirts in the kingdom. King Richard III—Jack's uncle as well as hers—had informally indicated this nephew as heir-presumptive to the crown of England. If Richard had not died at Bosworth Field, Jack would still be heir to the throne, and if Richard had remained widowed and childless, Jack would have eventually become King John II of England. Instead, Richard had been hacked to death, and his crown stolen by Henry Tudor.

For looks, Jack took after his father, the present duke, with long dark curls, dark eyes and a fine figure, but his smile and character owed nothing to his humdrum sire and everything to Jack himself. Dashing, irrepressible and engaging, he was also strong-minded, shrewd and discreet, and always kind and sympathetic. She loved him immensely, more than anyone else in her living family— only Richard still mattered more, but he would *always* be peerless. Jack was one of two men she protected with her body; the other was her husband, Sir Jon Welles.

She halted right behind him. 'How now, sir?'

He whipped around and she put a finger to her lips. No names in front of the whore, that finger said. Leaving his hood raised, as did Cicely, he looked back at the young woman, drew a coin from his purse, placed it in her palm and closed her fingers over it. She tossed her head haughtily at Cicely and then hurried away towards Thames Street.

Cicely smiled. 'Do you *ever* stop playing the gallant, Lord Lincoln?'

He grinned. 'I was about to pay you an unannounced visit, Coz.'

'In broad daylight? Are you mad?'

'Well, I thought it safer than calling after dark, which

*would* raise Tudor's hackles.'

Jack knew why she went to Henry and hated it, but she had made him promise not to do anything rash on her account. Jon did not know that the king, his half-nephew and brother-in-law, was *forcing* her into frequent adultery, and the kiss at Winchester would have confirmed his belief that she went to Henry more than willingly. Jon now wished no more to do with her. But to her he remained her cherished lord, and she would continue to shield him. She honoured him too much not to.

She was reproachful with Jack, however. 'You know you should not try to see me at all.'

'Plague take it, Cicely, I will *not* stay away from my dearest cousin simply because Henry Tudor might choose to misinterpret. Did you know he has been having one of his creatures follow me everywhere? I half expect the fellow to watch when I have a shit! So today, on the assumption that even Tudor's spies have functioning cocks, I paid one of the Bishop of Winchester's pretty Southwark geese to keep him busy.'

'I hope she earns her money, or he will already be on your trail again.'

'He last saw me on the south side of the Thames, and will need a bloodhound to find me here. I am more likely to be discovered because Henry is having *you* followed.' Jack studied her. 'And where have you been, without even your maid? To his bed?'

She told him of her decision, and he was taken aback. 'You take a risk, sweetheart. Henry is not used to being disobeyed.'

'I really am too angry today, with him and myself. Can you imagine the Yorkist outrage if I were to be set up openly as Henry's mistress? Yet *he* does not seem concerned. He makes so much of claiming to have united York and Lancaster by marrying my sister, thus ending decades of bloody civil war, and yet he would do this. It is the sort of thing that might provoke a resumption of conflict. The daughter of Edward IV, humiliated by being set up as Henry's official mistress? He is mad!'

Jack smiled. 'Sweetheart, I doubt there is another woman on earth more able to arouse a man as you do. Tudor is no different. He will do *anything* to have you to himself. But he is not fit to kiss your feet, let alone any other part of you.'

She returned the smile. 'Oh, Jack, you make me feel good.'

'One day you will learn exactly *how* good I could make you feel.'

'I am tempted.' She so enjoyed such silly jesting with him that it suddenly made her sad. Tears came to her eyes and she had to press her lips together.

Jack put his arm quickly around her shoulder. 'Come, I will take you home.'

His clothes were scented with thyme. How it suited him, and how gratifyingly good it was to be so close to him. Too good sometimes, she thought.

'It is not a *home* now, because Jon has gone. I have not heard from him since Winchester. He took himself off to Lincolnshire and ignores all my letters. No doubt he is being influenced by Henry's lizard of a mother.'

Born a Beaufort, the illegitimate line descended from John of Gaunt and specifically barred from the throne, Margaret was now the Countess of Derby. She was Jon's older half-sister, sanctimoniously pious and mealy-mouthed, and she wielded immense influence over Henry, upon whom she doted to the point of being fanatical. Henry's claim to the throne came solely from Margaret, which was why Henry declared himself king by conquest, not by blood right. To Margaret, the fault for Winchester lay solely with Cicely, the adulterous Yorkist strumpet. Her dear Henry was pure as the driven snow.

Jack's arm tightened and he rested his head to hers. 'Jon will return, sweetheart. Come now, a measure of his close-guarded favourite wine will restore you. And me.'

'What if he never wishes to see me again?'

'Jesu, lady, where is your confidence? I would return to you even if you spread yourself beneath Tudor a thousand times.'

His arm remained around her as they walked, hooded and unidentifiable, across the wharf and up into an alley that gave way to the various narrow streets that climbed towards St Sithe's Lane. She hated it there without Jon, but had nowhere else to go. Except to Henry, which was what he wanted, but she would *never* do!

Her mother, the Queen Dowager, was in virtual seclusion near Sheen palace, with her three youngest daughters, and anyway also blamed Cicely for Winchester. Cicely's older sister, Bess, now Henry's uncrowned queen and the mother of his baby son and heir, was justifiably jealous and angry, for it was not only *this* king who had come between the sisters, but his predecessor as well.

The love of their fascinating uncle, Richard III, was what Bess had always wanted most of all, but his heart had been given to Cicely, who surrendered hers in return. She had now been loved by two very different kings.

The first-floor parlour at Pasmer's Place was wainscoted and comfortable, and a good fire danced in the hearth. Outside, the racing clouds now began to thread over the London sky, and several shafts of pale sunlight swung across the room, illuminating tapestries, paintings and rich furnishings as Cicely poured two glasses of Jon's best Rhenish wine. There was no place for servants when she wished to speak privately with her cousin.

Divested of his cloak, gauntlets and hat, Jack was revealed to be of athletic build with broad shoulders, lean hips, and his full share of easy Plantagenet elegance and appeal. His legs were well shaped, and he possessed loins ample enough to turn most female heads. His face was aristocratic and rugged at the same time, and his smile was as devastatingly engaging as Richard's had been. And, like Richard, he could speak volumes with a glance. Those glances conjured unerring thoughts of sharing his bed.

His clothes were rich—furred indigo velvet, stitched with the silver leopards' heads of his family—and there was a fine single amethyst on the fourth finger of his right hand. His legs were tightly encased in grey hose and his thigh boots seemed calculated to concentrate female attention upon his generous manhood. Not that female attention needed encouragement. His shoulder collar was not lavish, merely silver studded with modest sapphires and pearls, and his dark curls tumbled loose and long, requiring frequent pushing back from his fine-boned face. When he did this, the amethyst ring flashed to deep purple.

'It is not often that I am waited upon by a king's daughter,' he said, accepting a cup of wine as they stood in front of the fire.

'Then you should bask in the privilege while you can, sir.' She smiled, her mood suddenly lightening. 'Oh, Jack, you bring *such* memories with you.'

He raised his glass to her. 'We only saw each other last month at Winchester, and I hardly imagine *that* is what you think of so fondly.'

'Certainly not, for I cringe to remember it. So, clearly, I think further back than Winchester.'

'And I know to whom.' Jack sipped the wine, which was very good. 'You still love Richard, but what of Sir Jon? You are very fond of him, I can tell that.'

'But he is no longer fond of me. You did not see the kiss. I am a leper to him now. To *everyone* now.'

'Not to me, and certainly not to Henry,' Jack observed, glancing at the gown she had chosen for the abandoned assignation. It was made of rich plum-coloured brocade, elaborate and seductively beautiful, with a low bodice and pendulous sleeves that were lined with silver satin. A gown in which to enchant a king. And this earl, he thought.

He studied her. Her father, Edward IV, had been well over six feet tall, exceedingly handsome and engaging, with auburn hair and blue eyes, but this daughter was his opposite. Her sisters took after their father. Cicely was the only dark one, and she had an allure that men could not resist. She certainly attracted Henry Tudor, whose desire for her showed no sign of abating after a year, and whose stifled emotions were sometimes so delicately balanced as to be barely controlled.

'So, Coz, the kiss at Winchester was *that* shocking? Jesu, lady, what were you doing? Rolling Henry on the floor, stark naked?'

'No, but . . .' She glanced at him, a little shamefaced. 'I am rather talented with kisses, Jack. Richard taught me so much and I learned with such eagerness. You cannot imagine.'

Jack lowered his cup. 'Sweet God, Cicely, you almost have me standing with anticipation. Are you telling me Richard was really that good?'

'Oh, yes. He knew how to caress every sense, and turn earth into heaven. No one will *ever* compare. Not even you, which certainly says a great deal of him,' she added with a little smile.

'I am insulted.' Jack set his wine aside. 'So, he imparted all this to his sweet, innocent little niece? Shame on him.'

'It was not like that, Jack. Never, ever think such a thing of him. I ceased to be innocent the moment I realized what my love for him really was. He did not seduce me from my purity, *I* seduced him from all his principles. *I* was the one who took advantage.'

'Cicely, he was twice your age.'

'You think that mattered? He was thirty-two, I was sixteen and older than my years. What is so terrible about that? I was certainly of a proper age to part with my chastity if I so chose. And it happened because *his* guard was lowered for a second, not mine. He touched my hair, took a small lock and parted it between his finger and thumb. Oh, Jack, the sweetness devastated me, because I suddenly understood my feelings for him. It was like a flash of lightning that passed into every part of me. And so *I* kissed him, Jack, and I did so with such honesty and passion that he was unable to resist. He tried to, because he did not want to break faith with his responsibilities as my uncle and my king, but I would not let him. I can be so very persuasive when I try. And I tried, believe me. I so wanted him to kiss me that I had no innocence at all.'

The ghost of a smile played upon Jack's lips. 'Cicely, you tempt me simply by drawing breath, so I understand him. But then some might say I have no principles from which to be seduced in the first place.'

'Yes, you do, Jack, you have a great many principles, and I admire them all.' She glanced away again. 'I am my own enemy, Jack, because I was born to make love. It is so much a part of me that I cannot ignore it. My character is to be naturally wanton.'

'Then there are two such in this room.'

'You are male, Jack, it is *expected* that you should be a rampant stallion, whereas women become whores or bitches. I have lain with Richard, and—once—with his illegitimate son, John of Gloucester. I have lain with my husband, and now with Henry. It is so easy for me, because it is my nature. I am the way Almighty God made me.'

Jack gazed at her. 'I knew you were . . . warm . . . but had not realized exactly how warm.'

She smiled ruefully. 'Well, you do now. And a teacher like Richard Plantagenet could only make me even more abandoned and needful. I was a greedily eager pupil, and could have made love with him from sunrise to sunset, and then into the night. There was never any lessening of the reward, never any dimming of our kisses. Jack, I would not have shrunk from *anything* with him. If it was

14

possible, then we did it. No limits, no boundaries, no rules that could not be broken. I loved him so much. So very much.' Her voice caught.

Jack shifted his position. 'How in God's own name do priests stay celibate when they hear such confessions?' he muttered.

'Do you wish me to stop?'

'No, sweetheart, because I think you need to say it all, and if I am the one who is here to hear you, then I will hear everything. You know that. You would do the same for me, I think.'

'Yes, I will always be here for you, Jack.'

'I know it.' Jack smiled, but his eyes were darker than before.

'Richard and I were put on earth to be together. Do you understand?'

He cleared his throat. 'I begin to, sweetheart.'

'I know I was young—I still am, and many would say I cannot possibly know what I am talking about—but I have always seemed older than I am, always forthright and curious, and men find me interesting because of it. Richard always had time for me, always talked to me, answered my questions and laughed with me, never at me. He teased, yes, but it was always gentle and never unkind. He was such a man. Such a man. I had no intention of letting that unimaginable joy slip through my fingers, and so I seized it. And he was mine for those short weeks, Jack. He belonged to me.' Tears stung and her voice was uneven. 'A niece cannot love her uncle that way and retain innocence. I do not know if you have ever loved to distraction, but that is how it was with Richard and me. It was so beautiful, so perfect and untarnished that it was neither sinful nor shameful.'

'It is clear you would not have changed anything.'

'I would have refused to leave him at Nottingham, before Bosworth, when he sent us—all his heirs—to

15

Sheriff Hutton for safety. I should have stayed, outfaced all the scandalized whispers and been openly at his side. For him I would have done all the things I will not do for Henry Tudor. The last bones of my reputation would have been gladly consigned to the scandalmongers, but Richard would not let me. And now I feel that I deserted him when he needed me most. If I had stayed, we would have been together that last night before battle. He would not have been alone, and I would have seen to it that he slept in my arms and awakened invincible. Henry would have been vanquished and we would still have the rightful king on the throne of England. Richard would have been a great monarch, Jack, truly great, but two short years were not enough.'

Jack put his hand to her cheek. 'I am envious, sweetheart. Not because Richard had you, but because I have never known a love like that. I certainly do not find it within my marriage, nor does my wife. I think it is fair to say that never were two people less compatible, except perhaps Henry and your sister Bess. My wife feels it no less than me. We are happily estranged. As for finding true love . . . I have bedded by far too many women, but have yet to find what you shared with Richard.'

'You will find her, Jack. You are so very desirable, in every way, that I know there is someone worthy of you waiting to be found. I certainly find you very attractive indeed, and being with you is always a pleasure.' Such a pleasure, she thought a little guiltily, because Jack de la Pole had always stirred her blood. Not that she would let him know, of course.

'But not attractive and pleasurable enough.'

She met his eyes. 'That is as may be, Cousin, but as I was saying before I indulged in the whys and wherefores of my love for Richard, I was not sharing a polite peck on the cheek with Henry at Winchester. It was not a kiss I sought, but . . .' She hesitated to admit the truth. 'But he can be

16

astonishingly seductive. I can see by your face that you find that difficult to believe, but it is true. He has an uncanny charm. I know how dangerous he is, but he knows how to be gentle and amusing, and how to make love, so in his case, appearances are very deceptive. That is why I understand well why Jon has gone away as he has. I should have told him why I went to Henry, because now I have lost him. And I do so want him back.'

'Your heart has room for him?'

She smiled. 'Oh, yes. That is something else Richard told me, the need to keep Jon separate, in a special place in my heart.'

It was an important slip. Jack looked at her. 'That, sweetheart, is pure crud. How could Richard say anything to you about Sir Jon Welles, mm? If I am not mistaken, Richard died before Jon entered your life. And do not repeat that you lay with Jon at Nottingham in June 1485, because I know damned well it is a fabrication, in which Sir Jon connives, to legitimize your child by Richard.'

# Chapter Two

FOR A MOMENT Cicely's tongue was tied in dismay. 'Maybe Richard said it of someone else and I just guessed what he would say of Jon.'

'Now you give me a discourteously lame explanation.' Jack continued to look at her and then took her cup and set it aside with his. 'Crud is crud. So there is something you are not admitting.'

'Please, Jack . . .'

'I know the power of grief. Strange things happen because of it, do they not?'

She gazed at him.

'We share blood, Cicely, and maybe we do not only share wantonness. You do not know this, but I had a daughter, Jillian, not by my wife. I was fifteen and so was her mother, who died in childbed. Jillian lived to be five, when she died after being bitten by a rabid dog. She had come to live with me, because it was what I wished, and I loved her. After her death . . .' He paused to put a hand to Cicely's cheek. 'After her death, I sometimes thought I was with her again. It seemed so very real, and yet I knew it was not.' He tilted her face. 'Am I right in thinking this is happening to you?'

Tears wended down her cheeks. 'Yes,' she whispered. 'I know Richard is not real, I *know* it, Jack. But I cannot help calling him to me when the pain becomes too much. For a little while I have him again.'

Her matchless, beautiful Richard, irreplaceable, unforgettable, exquisite. She shared his hair, long, heavy, and the same deep shade of chestnut that glinted with copper in the sun. His eyes were a clear, dark-rimmed grey, wide, arresting, quick, warm . . . He was a god to her. He always would be.

Richard III had been the slight, dark Plantagenet of his generation, as she was of hers. Despite being a little below medium height, slender and almost fragile, with a barely discernible sideways curve to his back, he was actually formidably strong. Certainly he had been a skilled fighter and shrewd military leader, and but for betrayal would almost certainly have killed Henry single-handedly at Bosworth. But away from the battlefield, Richard's manner had always been informal and yet regal, and he had such presence and charm, such effortless grace and authority, that he outshone all around him. Justice and loyalty had been his creed, fairness and honesty the principles he valued. He had been the perfect man, king and lover.

Cicely knew he had gone, but could not accept it, and so he lived on in her thoughts and dreams. Her imagination made him breathe again, so she could touch him, kiss him, talk to him, laugh with him and love him. Common sense told her he was not real, merely a phantasm created by her intolerable grief, but she did have a truly tangible memory of him, a son, hidden safely away from Henry.

It was a very dangerous secret because, illegitimate or not, Leo was a Yorkist boy with Richard III as his father, Edward IV as his grandfather and Cicely Plantagenet for his mother, and as he grew older he would draw dissatisfied Yorkists—of whom there were many under Henry VII. If that eventually happened, Henry could soon find his realm in a state of full rebellion.

Jack claimed her attention again. 'It can be a comfort to

conjure these imaginings of Richard, sweetheart, but not if you let them take over. Richard would not want that, and nor do I. If I remind you of him, then listen to me as if I *am* him. Do not feed on the past. He has gone and cannot return. I *do* know how you feel, truly, so take notice, I implore you.'

He went to the window to look down into St Sithe's Lane. 'Do you want Jon to return?' he asked suddenly.

'Yes. Why do you ask?' She was taken unawares by the question.

'Because, after hearing what you have said about Richard tonight means that when I look at you now I know you are able to teach Old Nick new delights of the flesh. Henry clearly knows it as well, and wants more and more of you, so make use of your power in order to get what you want out of him—his summons to Sir Jon to return. Imply a reward of immeasurable carnal bliss, enough to exhaust the royal cock.' He glanced around, smiling. 'I know you are quite capable.'

'I am to be dandelion leaves to a starving royal rabbit?'

He laughed. 'You would get whatever you wanted out of *this* bunnykin, and that is a fact. Henry will not hold out for long if you show him your great big eyes, floppy ears and pretty little fluffy tail. In a manner of speaking, of course.'

She smiled, but was then serious again. 'Do you think Henry would let me see John of Gloucester if I pleaded in the same way? So far he refuses to countenance it.'

Jack turned. 'He is right. His torture destroyed John's mind.'

'I have to see John. We were so very close, and might well have married. I feel I have failed him. I deserted Richard, and now I desert his son.'

'John will not even recognize you. Please leave this. He would not wish you to flay yourself on his account. You know it. Henry's guilt will not allow it anyway. John is Richard's son, and your love for your uncle is the whole

20

crux of it with Henry. He is jealous to the point of madness because he does not know the truth of it, but he strongly *suspects* you and Richard were incestuous lovers. He cannot bear the thought of it, and yet it excites him as well. Henry Tudor does not like his own reactions, sweetheart.'

'I know it.'

Jack paused. 'You have not told your husband how Tudor blackmails you, but you did not hesitate to tell me. Why?'

'Because Jon might do something rash. His own nephew puts horns on him. And I told you because . . . I can say things to you that I could not possibly say to anyone else. I feel close to you in a way that is entirely different.'

'Please do not tell me I am like a brother to you.'

'No. Definitely not.' But the knowledge confronted her. She felt physical desire when she looked at Jack de la Pole so it was most certainly not as a brother she saw him. How could any warm-blooded woman *not* feel desire for him?

'I am relieved to hear it.' He smiled as their eyes met, but then he spoke of Henry again. 'I should stick a dagger in this usurper for what he does to you; instead I stand by my word and cravenly let you give yourself to him for my sake.'

She felt guilty, and forgot her desires as she went to take his hand. 'I give you no choice, for I have made you promise. You are vital to the House of York, Jack, its leader because Richard chose you to succeed him. Who else can there be for York? Your next brother, Edmund? Saints preserve us, for he is not only too young at sixteen, but obnoxious and loutish as well, from all accounts. So let me help by doing what I do best—lie on a bed and make love. I would do *anything* to protect you. Do you not see?'

'Oh, Cicely . . .' His voice was tight with emotion.

'You will not change my mind on this, Jack. Truly.' Too conscious of him, she went to pour a little more wine into their cups.

'Cicely, I came here today to discuss something with you.'

She anticipated him. 'About this Lambert Simnel plot in Burgundy?'

'You sense my thoughts almost before I know them myself.' He smiled again. 'The *plot* may be in Burgundy, but Simnel is now in Dublin, which is knowledge for you alone, sweetheart.'

'He is claiming to be my brother Dickon, and seems set to challenge Henry for the throne, but is he genuine? Henry clearly fears he may be. Tell me, Jack, is this Simnel my brother, or is he an imposter?'

Her brothers—Edward, now almost sixteen, so briefly King Edward V, and the little Duke of York, thirteen, whom they all called Dickon—had been placed in the royal apartments at the Tower for safety after her father's unexpectedly early death in 1483. Then undeniable proof had suddenly been put before Richard—Lord Protector at the time—that her parents had never been lawfully married, and thus all the children of their union were illegitimate. This meant that Richard himself became the next legitimate heir to the crown. His sense of duty and justice obliged him to be king. He could not have done anything else.

Now Henry had reversed everything, and made Edward IV's children legitimate again. He had to, because the only reason he had gained such support at Bosworth had been his promise to unite York and Lancaster by marrying Edward IV's eldest daughter. But by legitimizing Bess, he also legitimized her brothers, both of whom had a far superior claim to the crown than his own. But the boys had disappeared, and there were wild stories that Richard had done away with them. He had not harmed them, but had sent them to safety with his sister, the Duchess of Burgundy. Henry knew that much, but not if they still lived. If they did, they were a grave danger to his throne.

Jack's voice interrupted her train of thought. 'You say I

comfort you, Cicely, but you have no idea how I value your loyalty. It is to seek your unswerving support that I have sought you today. You are the one I can always rely upon, but if I tell you about Lambert Simnel, I will involve you in high treason. Knowing that, do you still wish me to answer your question?' A beam of weak sunlight struck his dark curls as he pushed them back from his forehead.

She nodded. 'But know that I may see it as a hopeless cause, and try to dissuade you,' she warned. 'And I *will* if I think you are about to risk your life needlessly. So, what is so important about this Simnel? *Is* he one of my brothers?'

'I have no idea where your brothers are or if they still live. This boy is the Earl of Warwick, son and heir of our other uncle, George, the late Duke of Clarence.'

'*Warwick?*' She was thunderstruck. Clarence had been the middle brother, between her father and Richard, and always dissatisfied and less loyal. He had eventually gone too far with his treason, and had paid the ultimate price at her father's bare hands. 'But that cannot possibly be so, Jack. Warwick was with us at Sheriff Hutton, and is now in the Tower after being captured by Henry. You know it, because you and John of Gloucester were sent to the Tower with him. You are the only one to be freed again. And anyway, Warwick is barred from the throne by his father's attainder.'

'Make no mistake of it, this boy *is* Warwick. Attainders can be reversed, so if Henry parades the boy from the Tower as proof of Simnel's imposture, he, Henry, will be the one guilty of falsehood. The boy sent with us to Sheriff Hutton, and who now languishes in the Tower, is *not* Clarence's son, nor as it happens any blood relation of ours. The name Lambert Simnel is a conceit. The real Warwick is in Dublin, helping to raise Irish support. Before that he was in Burgundy, under the protection of our aunt—*his* aunt—the duchess. He knows nothing of your brothers, and if the duchess had them, she no longer does. She takes

23

the precaution of refusing to say what happened to them, so their whereabouts remains a mystery.'

He held her astonished gaze. 'Sweetheart, Clarence had learned of your father's previous marriage contract long before it became public and Richard was forced to act upon it. Clarence even knew that your father's first wife had been Lady Eleanor Boteler, born Talbot, daughter of the first Earl of Shrewsbury. She died four years *after* your father biga-mously married your mother. So Clarence realized that you, your brothers and sisters were illegitimate. This meant that if your father died, Clarence and his son, being next in line, before Richard, were the rightful heirs to the throne. Your father had to be rid of him to ensure that your brother Edward inherited the crown.'

Jack drew an expressive finger across his throat at the word 'rid'. 'Little Warwick was sent to Burgundy late in 1477, when he was two, and his place taken by another boy, whose parents were paid very well for giving him up. Clarence, who feared your father's intentions, was exe-cuted secretly weeks later, so his action had been timely. Your father did not find out about the changeling, nor did Richard, who was an innocent party anyway. It can all be confirmed, because the duchess has documents bearing Clarence's signature and seal, describing a small birthmark on his son's left ankle and requesting her to protect him. The boy in the Tower has no such mark, but I am informed that Lambert Simnel most certainly does. Cicely, Clarence felt his son was as much at risk from your father as you now believe yours is from Henry.'

She *did* fear what Henry would do if he discovered her son's existence. They had pretended that her son – supposedly Jon's – had died after birth. But he had lived, and was now Master Leo Kymbe, cared for at Friskney in Lincolnshire, close to Jon's lands. He was protected by the Kymbe family, and in particular by Tom Kymbe, who was not only the brother of Cicely's devoted maid, Mary, but one of Jon's most loyal supporters. Friskney was Jack's manor, but not even he knew Leo's whereabouts, only that he lived.

Speaking of her uncle Clarence's death brought a more recent, very unpleasant memory. 'Jack, Henry made me go to the room in the Tower where Clarence died. He said my father killed him in person, and a witness left a record that was found when Henry had the Tower searched for evidence of my brothers after Bosworth.' She drew a heavy breath. 'Richard told me my father had made a fool of him about the first marriage, and he was tricked about Clarence's death as well. Richard did not know of it until afterward, when the deed had been done.'

'Richard's support was always invaluable, Cicely. He had no secret ambition of his own, but merely saw his role as the loyal brother. And that was exactly what he was. Latterly, your father could not have done without him. Richard was an exceptional man, and I was proud to not only be his nephew, but be considered his heir when his legitimate son died so tragically. But now he has another son. Where is Leo, Cicely?' The question was asked quietly.

She hesitated. Dared she tell even Jack?

'There is no need to hesitate, Cicely. You already have my word that I will not impose my ambitions upon him. He has more Yorkist blood than anyone, but his illegitimacy means he can never be king. Although, I suppose, it is not unknown. William I was William the Bastard, as I recall. I suppose I dare not hope Richard married you?'

'He did not.' But he *had* mentioned it . . . 'Jack, Leo is at Friskney where, at Richard's command, you took my brothers from the Tower in 1483, after my husband's ill-advised attempt to "free" them when Richard ascended the throne so unexpectedly.'

'My, my, how fate runs in circles,' Jack murmured, glancing away a little oddly. 'Yes, I left your brothers in the care of Thomas Kymbe, one of Richard's staunchest allies, until they finally came to join the rest of us at Sheriff Hutton.'

'Thomas Kymbe has passed away, and it is his son, called only Tom, who cares for Leo now. Tom Kymbe is my husband's adherent,' she added reluctantly.

Jack was startled. 'Lancastrian? Jesu, Cicely! So, this Tom Kymbe sits like a cuckoo in *my* manor, but supports the red rose? That is not what I like to hear.'

'He is a good man, Jack, and I trust him. Friskney is a safe place for Richard's son.'

He became quiet suddenly, avoiding her eyes by looking at the window, from where another moving shaft of wintry sunlight shone briefly. The change in him was palpable.

'What is it, Jack? What's wrong?'

'Do you believe in premonitions, Cicely?'

'I . . . think I do. Why?'

'If my whereabouts should be unknown, or if there is any doubt of my continued existence, remember Friskney.'

She gazed at him. 'You frighten me.'

'I have a strong feeling I will have to go there one day. And no, it will not be anything to do with your son.' He cleared his throat briskly. 'But we digress, do we not? I must tell you that Lord Lovell and Sir Robert Percy are already in Burgundy, lending their support.'

Friskney was forgotten. 'Francis and Robert? They are with you in this?' The two men were Richard's oldest friends, and had been party to his love for her. He had even sent Robert to bring her to him that last time in the hunting tower. She knew that only months ago Francis had survived and escaped after leading an ill-fated uprising against Henry, but there had been no word of Robert. Until now. It was good to know they were both safe in Burgundy.

'Cicely, do you imagine either of them would ever miss an opportunity to restore the House of York to the throne? If plans come to fruition, my aim is not only to see Warwick become King Edward VI, but myself as Lord Protector during his minority. Francis and Robert will enjoy the ascendancy and influence they had under Richard.'

'But *you* are Richard's heir! Warwick is barred from the throne by his father's attainder!'

'I have already said that attainders can be as easily undone as they are done. Cicely, any claim I might have now, in this new climate, will be viewed as purely through my mother and therefore secondary to a claim through the male line. If we are to gain the measure of support we need, it has to be Warwick, who if nothing else is legitimate and of a more senior *male* branch of the family than me or even Richard. Warwick is now the only one with the necessary rank and blood. I hold second place, I fear.'

She gazed at him. 'Presumably you will do away with Henry?'

'As he would do away with me in the same circumstances.'

'Do not think you have the measure of him, Jack. He is a very clever man, and he has the luck of the Devil. He will not be easy to defeat. And another thing . . . if this should lead to battle, which it must, you know that you and my husband will be on opposing sides?'

'Maybe.'

'Of course you will. He is Henry's half-uncle, which will matter in the end, no matter what the bad feeling at the moment.'

'Sir Jon Welles is not only Henry's uncle, he is *your* husband, whom you love and who loves you. Why else is he protecting your son? He risks everything for you, and after Winchester do not take it for granted he will side with Henry against me, because I do not believe it is a foregone conclusion. But if he and I *were* to face each other in hand-to-hand battle, we have already discussed it and decided we would thrash the very excrement out of each other.'

'I cannot believe Jon would desert Henry.'

'You underestimate yourself, sweetheart. And him.'

'Perhaps you are *overestimating* this whole business,' she

pointed out.

'I sought you today to clear my mind, and I have.'

'Your choice had already been made. My advice is to abandon this plot, because I believe it is better left for a while.'

'And permit Henry more time to sink his filthy Tudor talons into England? And into you? No.' His fingers curled around hers, and the sensuousness with which he did it sent shivers through her entire body. 'Now is the right time,' he said softly. 'We will easily raise the army we need. With Warwick as our claimant, the support is there for the taking.'

Tears came to her eyes. 'But will you be able to trust it? Richard could not at Bosworth, and look how he died. I do not want you to die like that too. Please, Jack. Desist from this right now.'

'How heartening you are,' he said, without his usual humour.

'Because I love you, Jack, and do not want to have to seek you at Friskney. Please, Jack. Do not go on with this.'

'I think I had better go.'

'Please, Jack,' she said again.

'I realize it is a little late in the proceedings to say that I pray with all my heart you are not closer to Henry Tudor than you say.'

'Oh, Jack.' Reproach choked her voice.

He closed his eyes. 'Forgive me for that. Forgive me. I know that you, above all, would never betray me.' He caught her hand and then pulled her into his arms.

The embrace was not quite that of cousins, because she was suddenly acutely aware of him as an incredibly attractive and loving man. Jack de la Pole was like a soothing breeze on a stiflingly hot day, and she wanted to inhale him, take him into herself ... make love to him. Sweet images passed through her mind ... and sweeter sensations spread through her body. She should pull away, stop it before it began in earnest, but the way his thumb moved softly against her bare shoulder was fleshly imprisonment.

'My poor Cicely, you have had so much to bear,' he whispered.

She could not speak, and hid her face against his shoulder. Craving overwhelmed her, and it was *such* craving. Desire ran wildly through her veins. It would be so easy now to press closer to him, to steal some reward from his body. She only had to press to his hips, for he was aroused, she knew that. He could not hold her this way, caress her this way, whisper this way, and be indifferent.

Her eyes closed and her senses stirred as they should not, and for a moment she almost raised her lips for a kiss. It was so natural, so obvious a thing to do, but she knew it would change their friendship forever, and she did not want to forfeit such a precious thing. Jack de la Pole was the lover she must *never* have. She did not care about Lambert Simnel or the Earl of Warwick, she cared about Jack de la Pole. He was already in danger from Henry, and if she became his lover, he would be in even more danger.

And so she made herself draw away—but her heart was racing and she knew there was colour in her cheeks. Jesu, she *so* wanted him! Jack de la Pole was too attractive and caring, too tactile and kind . . . too virile and tempting. And she was suddenly far too responsive to everything about him. She was lonely, unhappy, and in need of physical comfort from someone she loved and who understood everything. Such comfort was within reach now, here, in the room with her.

'Cicely?' He reached to touch her cheek, but she stepped swiftly away.

'No . . .'

'Have I upset you?'

She gazed at him. 'No, Jack, you know you have not.'

There was such a silence, such a charge in the atmosphere. She wanted so much from him, but knew she must fight her fleshly weakness. It would be so very easy. She had only to touch him for him to know. He knew anyway. Yes, of course he did, but he would not make the first move, not with her. There were unspoken words in the air, not just a scattering of them, but pages, and they could both read them. But this was a moment for sense, not sensuousness.

Yet the tension was there between them, in the open at last, if still silent. For her it was like that first insight with Richard. A sudden realization, the opening of her eyes to a blinding truth. She had always loved Jack de la Pole, but now that love invaded her body as well as her heart. There was a need to hold him, caress him, explore him and know him. A need to share everything with him, every breath and waking moment. She wanted to experience every intimacy with him, as she had with Richard. It was that shocking and forceful a feeling. But she did not dare do anything at all, for fear of Henry's vengeance.

Jack's lips parted to speak, but she prevented him. 'Do not say it. Please. We both know, I think. Things are no longer the same between us.'

'I have been at fault in this for some time now.'

'But you said and did nothing, except to tease. Today, perhaps because of the carnal things of which I have spoken, everything has changed. I should not have said them, but I did, and for that I apologize.'

'Jesu, Cicely, do you really think it is because of *today*? I have wanted you ever since I saw you part from Richard at Nottingham. There, I have said it anyway, because to leave it unspoken is wrong. It needs to be said, and no, it will not change my behaviour towards you, if that is what you fear.'

'I fear for you, Jack. Henry is—'

'Plague ravage him!' Jack broke in. 'If you only knew how astonishingly affecting it was to see you take your leave of Richard. You were both so close to tears, but he had to show an unconcerned face to his supporters. He was the king, and his heart was breaking because he had to send you away. And then again, at Sheriff Hutton, when he rode to that hunting tower from Nottingham, just to be with you for a few hours. I encountered you as you returned from him. Do you remember?'

'Yes, I remember.'

'Jesu, how you glowed with the aftermath of lovemaking, and your unhappiness at being away from him again could have been sifted from the air around you. I was so moved, so filled with feeling for you, so aware of everything about you that I actually thought of *making* you come with me when I obeyed Richard's instructions to leave for Burgundy with *all* his close heirs. Instead I took only your brothers and our little "cousin" Warwick, because *Bess* would not leave. That meant you stayed with her, and John felt honour-bound to protect you both.' Jack paused. 'I wanted you to be with me, Cicely. With *me.* That is one of the reasons I so dislike your sister.'

He paused emotionally, and then continued, 'But for her, John of Gloucester's mind would not have been destroyed by Tudor's barbarity, and you certainly would not be coerced into his vile bed, or married to his fool of an uncle, who does not know he has been blessed with the most exquisite woman God has ever created. Yes, Cicely, you are in my heart, and you always will be.'

'Jack, I want you as you want me, but if Henry were to realize this, he would make sure of your death. I was angry with him today, but I *will* go to him again and be everything he wishes—except his mistress—because I want you and Jon to be safe. I am thankful I can find pleasure with him, because it makes it tolerable.'

'I need to kiss you.'

She closed her eyes. That closeness again, that yearned-for closeness, and the exciting knowledge that he awaited a signal, any sign at all that she wished him to go further. Surrender beckoned, and when he held out his hand, all restraint fell away. She whispered his name, and gave in to the intensity of her blinding new love. The desire engulfed her completely, flaming between her legs and clutching her heart. And so she went into his arms, raised her mouth, and found his.

It was a gentle kiss, almost a quivering of their touching lips, but it loosed wild, almost enervating sensations that were totally unlike anything before. She was caught up by it, as if upon a current that flowed through her whole body, but especially through those inner muscles that always gave such pleasure. Her breasts tightened, her skin was flushed and she kissed him with such lazy sensuality that it was almost as if she tasted nectar. She moved her mouth luxuriously against his, relishing him. How she wanted to consummate such a wonderful kiss. How she wanted to offer her body to his, and share love with him.

These were moments to dwell upon, to learn from and feel so much, to drift into and upon . . . sweet moments that she had sworn to herself should never happen with Jack. Her resolve was as weak as ever, for she could not resist him. He was so very attractive and beloved, devastatingly so, and she could feel her perfidious body urging her on. She pressed to him, her breath escaping on a long sigh as she felt his arousal. Oh, sweet God above, how good this was. How very, very good. And with Jack.

He brought the spell to a close by gently disengaging her arms. 'No, sweeting, not in Sir Jon's house. I may think him a fool for turning his back on you, but I still like him. Curse him.' He struggled for composure as he kissed her palm. 'Not that I like him enough to leave his wife alone.'

She closed her eyes, caught up in her own struggle. 'I wanted to keep you as my dearest cousin, and not spoil it by taking you as my lover. I even talk of shielding you from Henry, but here I am, yearning to make love with you.'

'And we will make love, I promise.'

She could not meet his eyes. 'Please do not think badly of me.'

'Badly?' He cupped her chin and made her look at him again. 'I am the last person with any right to think badly of you, nor would I anyway. We have just shared a kiss so laden with feeling that it almost broke my soul.'

And mine, she thought. *And mine.*

'Cicely, this is not another passing dalliance. I have never wanted—loved—anyone as much as I want you, and I do not employ the smooth flattery of a practised seducer to say it.' He drew a tender fingertip over her lips. 'Just know that when you need me—want me—you have only to say. I will wait. We will find somewhere to be together, as we need to be. Love can always bide its time.'

He kissed her again, more passionately this time. The first kiss had been warm and rich; this one was edged with fire . . . and the promise of limitless fulfilment.

# Chapter Three

WHEN JACK HAD left, Cicely sat by the fire in the almost dark room, for the October afternoon had faded swiftly as more clouds filled the sky. She thought about what had just happened. She had not anticipated it, nor had she even been aware of the strength of her feelings for him. But suddenly her entire being was in complete chaos.

Jack had always been the one in whom she could confide, the one who understood and comforted her, the one who sensed her thoughts almost before she knew them herself . . . as she anticipated his. They were sensitive to each other, intuitive, and now it had become a binding of selves. Of blood. It came into her, she did not look out at it. And Jack felt the same. They were woven through each other, the warp and weft of a single rich cloth. As it had been for her with Richard.

She leaned her head back to think of the uncle who had changed her life forever. Now she could only imagine him, yet on one occasion in particular he had been so real that even now she could hardly believe he had not really been there.

It had happened one night at Westminster Palace, when her grief for him prevented sleep. He had come to the bedside, in the light of the night lamp, and bent down to kiss her. His hair brushed her skin, his lips were warm and giving, and she got up to go into his arms. He wore the fine grey velvet clothes she remembered so well, the circlet still gleamed against his forehead, and on the curtailed little finger of his right hand was the fine ruby ring Henry had stolen from his corpse at Bosworth. How blessedly solid and real he was. She could even taste the mint on his breath as he kissed her.

But he had come to reprimand her for going to Henry, on her own, simply to try to gain the measure of the new king. How immature and silly she had been, thinking it would be as easy to make Henry trust her as Richard always had.

She remembered his voice, light and yet not. 'Oh, Cicely, you have an incredible capacity to captivate, but you do not yet know how to ration it. Least of all with a man like Henry Tudor. You have to be taught a salutary lesson in what can be done with the gift you use so lightly and that I share. You have no notion at all of its power, but for your own sake you need to be made to understand.'

He had moved away from her, his tread slightly uneven because of the sideways bend of his spine. One shoulder was a little higher than the other, but it made his embrace so intimate and tender that whoever he held felt cherished. Everything about him was sensuous and alluring.

Reaching the wall opposite the bed, he leaned back against it, facing her, arms folded. His lips curved with promise and his eyes were dark and warm. 'Come to me and kiss me. Seduce me.'

She had gone to him joyfully, sliding her arms around him to put her lips to his, but he made no move at all, not even to straighten from the wall. Yet everything about him invited her to intimacy. Again and again she experienced those familiar waves of exquisite pleasure between her legs. He did not respond, no matter what she did, and yet he implied consent . . . although it was behind an erotic barrier that she could not penetrate, however hard she tried.

He dominated her without moving or speaking, and gave such unbelievable gratification that she could neither resist nor desist. She *wanted* him. Desperately. It was intolerably affecting, and he cast such voluptuous sorcery over her that she was helpless. Her kisses had devoured his lips, crushing them with passion. She used all the skills she possessed, remembered all the things she had done with him, tried *everything* she knew, and when he remained unmoved, she wept. It was only when she sank tearfully to her knees and hid her face in her hands that he relented and took her up into his arms. Bewilderment weakened her, understanding was beyond her, and his embrace was all that mattered.

At last he kissed her, raising her mouth slowly to meet his again. The joy of *him,* and his incredible magic, was so arousing that pleasure overwhelmed her. His lips toyed mercilessly with her and plundered what little was left of her strength, and his caresses, seeming so light and gentle, aroused her passion to such a peak that her inner muscles submitted helplessly to a riot of pleasure.

Everything he did was calculated, cruel even, but these were kisses she would remember into eternity, for they finally demonstrated exactly how potent and completely spellbinding he really could be if he chose. It was no mere impression, it was fact. This man could conquer with a smile, confine with a glance, and devastate with a kiss.

But then he withdrew his lips from hers. 'What would you not do for me now, Cicely? Mm? Is there anything?' The last word was barely a whisper, and carried with it the promise of his body. 'Go to Henry Tudor, Cicely, seduce him as you seduce me.' His voice was so very soft and tempting, so very loving, even while he asked her to go to the man who had slain him. His eyes were unfathomable, but compelled her to obey.

Hesitantly, unhappily, she had moved towards the door.

She did not want to, but for Richard Plantagenet she would have done anything. Yet as she reached it, he had come quickly over to seize her hand.

'No, sweeting, no. I do not really wish you to do anything of the sort! I love you, Cicely, and would not force anything like that upon you.'

The spell was deliberately shattered, and she was so overcome that she wept.

'Oh, Jesu, I should not have done it,' he breathed, and held her tightly to him. 'Forgive me, sweetheart, please forgive me.'

She remembered how she had clung to him, hardly aware of what had just happened.

'Oh, my poor, sweet Cicely, I have treated you badly tonight, but I had to make you understand, not me, but *yourself.* I could think of no other way.' He slipped his arm tenderly around her shoulders, and rested his forehead gently to hers. It was such sweet communion that she could almost absorb his love.

'Cicely, I needed to show you what it is in my capacity to do. For those minutes I deliberately misused the gift that I have, and I did not need force, threats or any other such thing to influence you. I made you love and want me more than ever. You *would* have gone to Henry for me. Because you thought it was what *I* wanted.'

'Yes, I would have gone. I would do anything for you, Richard.'

He made her look at him. 'It is not magic, but it *is* enchantment of a sort. *You* have this gift as well, do you understand? *You* can do the things I did, and in your heart you know it. That is why you created this. Yes, sweetheart, it is all your doing, not mine. You create me when you need to confront yourself with things you do not understand or do not wish to acknowledge. Cicely, *never* underestimate your power over men, but use it judiciously. It will come so naturally to you that you will hardly know you do it. Men want you, and you can have whichever one you choose. *Any* man. You could certainly have Henry Tudor if you so wished. And I am afraid you cannot apportion the blame for that to anyone but yourself.'

'No!' she had protested.

'Yes. You used allure that you do not yet know how to properly control. It is *such* allure, my dearest, and all too soon you will know exactly how to use it. Do *not* turn it lightly upon someone as dangerous as Henry Tudor. Be careful with what you have, but never forget it is yours. You are able to make men want you, forgive you, trust you, or anything else you wish of them.'

'That cannot be true,' she remembered saying.

'I was not wise during life, Cicely. I should have used what I knew I had in order to be certain of those around me. If I had, and if I had made calculated political decisions instead of adhering to what I believed to be right and just, there would not have been a Bosworth. Without Bosworth, without so many things, I could subsequently have applied myself to justice and honour. Instead I lost it all. So do not repeat my mistakes. Learn from me, because as God is my witness I am trying to teach you now.'

'Why did you not see that you should use it more?'

'If I had deliberately misused my gift, I would have been a king with truly destructive charm, a user and a schemer, a trickster and a villain, hiding behind endearing smiles and kindly words. A man whose bent back really was an indication of the nature of his character. That is not me, sweetheart, so maybe I *am* a fool. I certainly placed my trust where I should not. I think I was overwhelmed by everything that happened. From being Duke of Gloucester, content to serve your father and rule sensibly in the north, I was suddenly, as if from a catapult, put on the throne itself, where life is anything but sensible. It was not what I wanted, Cicely, but it was what I had to accept. I could have been a good king, but I was not allowed to be.

38

Circumstance overtook me. And so did death.'

*And so did death . . .* The memory faded into the present, and Cicely gazed at the fire through a shimmer of tears. 'Oh, Richard,' she whispered, 'my beloved Richard. I have not paid attention to your warning, because here I am, in bondage to Henry, regretting my separation from Jon, and fully intending to lie with Jack, who is about to be Henry's mortal enemy. Would it be possible to do worse?'

Barely half an hour later, a messenger wearing the queen's livery rode into the yard, and within moments Cicely's maid, Mary Kymbe, hurried in. She was of an age with her mistress, with a fresh complexion and brown curls, plaited and coiled, and had been with Cicely since Nottingham. She was as much a friend as a maid. The sealed letter she brought was direct from Bess, who was still in Winchester, having not yet been churched.

Cicely took it reluctantly. 'Does the messenger await an answer?' she asked.

'No, my lady. He will leave again the moment a fresh horse has been made ready. He returns to Winchester.'

'Very well. You may go. Oh, and see that he receives whatever refreshment he requires.'

'Yes, my lady.'

Mary left again, and Cicely opened the queen's seal with great reluctance. The cheerless opening greeting made her heart sink.

*Lady Welles,*

*It is not my pleasure that you should appear at court from now on. Your presence will be offensive to me, and to my lord the King. You are therefore forbidden to attend. On no account are you to approach unless I send for you specifically.*

*You are to remain at Pasmer's Place. Failure to obey will result in your removal to a place where you will be securely*

*confined. You are not to have any contact at all with the
Queen Dowager, who renounces you, and from whom you
will shortly receive a missive exactly the same as this.*

The signature was as formal and aloof as the rest of the
letter. Bess was punishing her, and it was understandable,
but it could not be true that Henry was in agreement with
his queen. He would never wish his lover to be excluded
from court. He wanted Lady Welles within easy reach of
his bed. At all times.

And if it had not been so sad, it would have been
amusing that Bess pretended to be allied with their mother,
whom she so loathed that all contact had now been severed.
If the *former* Queen of England was ever in need, she would
not receive succour from the *present* queen. Their mother
was not a warm woman, and had never shown love to her
children. Ambition was all, and in its pursuance she had
never baulked at anything. A little like Henry's mother,
Cicely thought wryly. Now, however, the Queen Dowager
had Henry Tudor to deal with, not Richard, and Henry
disliked her as much as she disliked him. He would never
forgive Edward IV's queen for coming out of sanctuary
into Richard's protection at the very time when he, Henry,
vowed publicly in exile to unite York and Lancaster by marrying Bess.

Bess and Cicely had once been very close, sharing everything, but now the elder sister accused the younger of never
having shared anything, and of inveigling all her secrets in
order to laugh at her with Richard. It had not been true, but
Bess would *never* forgive. Never. Richard had been Cicely's
lover and only hers. They belonged to each other so completely that only his death had separated them. Bess was
tied to Henry, never to Richard, but she did not want him.
She loathed him. And Henry knew it, because he loathed
her in return. Instead, Henry followed Richard into the
arms of her younger sister, and Bess had no idea of the true

extent to which he followed.

Cicely looked unhappily at the letter. She did not want to hurt Bess, but Henry's will took precedence in everything. If he wanted Lady Welles at court, then at court she would be.

Not long after that, when darkness was complete, except for lanterns and torches in the courtyard and out in the lane, the yard of Pasmer's Place suddenly rang with horsemen wearing Henry Tudor's green, red and white colours. The king would brook no defiance from Lady Welles, who was to be taken immediately to Westminster Palace whether she would or not. There was no discretion and secrecy now; the world would know he had sent an escort for her. And the world would enjoy drawing scandalous conclusions.

But now that she had kissed Jack de la Pole, and been kissed by him, emotions had been released that she had not known since Richard. The undertow of it sucked safety from beneath her feet, because she would suddenly have to struggle to pretend to Henry what had been easy before. Could she do it? Was she capable of convincing him that nothing had changed? Henry Tudor was not an easy man to deceive. If she failed, then the darker side of him might well lead him to carry out his threats to Jack and to Jon.

'So, Cicely, even with the ruination of your good name and your marriage, you steadfastly refuse to become my mistress?'

'Yes, Henry, I do.' Now more than ever, she thought.

Henry was soft spoken, almost caressingly so when he chose, and there was sometimes a hint of French and Breton in his voice with, maybe once or twice in a conversation, a trace of his Welsh roots. He had spent half his life in Brittany, being hunted in exile by the House of York, and before that, as a boy, in Wales. It was only since invading in 1483 that he had been in England, of which he was so unjustly king. Now it was *his* mission to hunt the House of

York, wherever he found it. No, perhaps not wherever he found it, for he did not wish to hunt the former Lady Cicely Plantagenet, he wished to spend as much time in bed with her as he could.

They were in the candlelit apartments at Westminster that had once been Richard's, and that other king's presence still seemed to be everywhere. If she closed her eyes she could still see him. She knelt before Henry, the plum brocade gown spreading on the floor around her, its decoration shining. The candlelight glowed on the perfection of her shoulders and throat, and the inviting shadow between her breasts was there for him to gaze upon.

Henry was twenty-nine years old, complex and capable of cruelty, and he begrudged the intense, barely disciplined feelings she aroused in him. He wanted so much to be indifferent to her, but could not. Instead, he loved her, and it intruded upon his customary rigid control. He was tall, slender and graceful, not handsome, but very striking, with long, reddish hair, high cheekbones, a narrow chin, thin lips, a large nose, a guarded manner and a hooded gaze. His unsettling eyes—charcoal-coloured, small, the left not always acting in accord with the right—were so like the North Sea in winter that they were a reflection of his chill disposition. He was pale, spare and almost hypnotic when he moved; yet when he was motionless, as now, he was always menacing. He liked to be bleak and remote.

That Henry Tudor was the king could not be mistaken, for his black velvet coat was richly trimmed with ermine, and the heavy gold livery collar across his shoulders bore the new symbol of his reign, the red-and-white Tudor rose. Wearing black had become his habit, because it was an expensive dye, and because it made him seem so stark, no matter how many jewels he wore. Apart from the collar, he had three rings: an enviable emerald, a signet ring bearing a design of his favourite saint, St Armel, with the leashed dragon he had banished from terrorizing a Breton village, and the ruby ring that had been taken from Richard's dead hand at Bosworth. She had 'seen' that ring since then, and on the hand to which it rightly belonged.

He raised Cicely gently by the elbow, bringing with him the faint but pleasant scent of cloves, which was always on his clothes and breath. She could not read him yet, and did not know what to expect, but to her relief he smiled.

'Forgive me, sweetheart, I did not mean to let you kneel to me at all, let alone remain there.'

'I have rather a lot for which to forgive you, Henry.' She relaxed a little, but hid it well. He seemed in a level enough mood, she thought, although she would be unwise to rely upon it. Certainly she knew that when he was like this, he liked her to stand up to him. And she liked to do it. He called it 'sparring', and so it was.

'You do not shrink from censuring your king to his face?' he asked.

'Why do it behind his back? It is the looking at his face while I do it that provides the satisfaction.'

'Well, that is what I would expect of you.' He assisted her to a chair close to the fire. 'Cicely, I would have thought my offer preferable to the state in which you now find yourself,' he said then.

'The state into which *you* have consigned me,' she replied. 'I am already humiliated, and will *not* be disgraced completely by becoming your mistress. I am married to your uncle, and—'

'My half-uncle,' he corrected, 'and you are not strictly married to him because you did not have my royal consent. *And* you wed him before the annulment of your first union with Ralph Scrope, who, granted, is now dead, but that does not make your second marriage safe.'

She was stung. 'I was *not* married to Ralph Scrope! That was all a fiction, as you well know, Henry Tudor! And you *did* give your consent for me to marry Sir Jon!'

'Oh, that fire! How I love it.'

'Henry, you *know* the contract was forged.'

'Even though it was drawn up at your dear Uncle Richard's behest *and* bore his signature and seal?' His voice had changed slightly. Jack was right, Henry's suspicion that she and Richard had been incestuous lovers provoked him as nothing else.

He waited for her to respond, but she remained infuriatingly silent. 'Oh, Cicely, I have just pointed a bony, accusing finger at Richard. Have you no vitriolic retort for me?'

She met his gaze squarely. 'Richard had the contract drawn up, yes, but he set it aside on learning I had no wish to marry Ralph. He did *not* append his signature or his seal. Ralph did it because he wanted a Plantagenet bride who he thought would make him royal and bring him wealth and land. *He* forged the contract and then turned traitor to Richard in order to spite me, because I spurned him and accepted Richard's son instead.'

'Do not mention John of Gloucester, Cicely. You know why I did it, and that I regret it.'

There was silence. The incredible cruelty that had been done to Richard's illegitimate son in the Tower could not have taken place without Henry's knowledge or permission, perhaps even his participation. He could be utterly without conscience. Now John had no wits left, and was nothing but a living husk.

'What were you about to say?' Henry prompted, returning to a previous point in the conversation. 'You are married to my half-uncle, and . . . what?'

'And have committed adultery—you and I *both* have. But you are the king, of course, so such a scandal will not hurt you at all.'

'It is not considered exactly admirable for a married king to fuck outside his wife's bed. Not if he is going to be caught, and certainly not with his wife's sister.'

'Fucking outside your marriage does not seem to be much of a consideration if you want to install me as your

44

mistress. Why, I imagine it would do your reputation no end of good, because let us be honest, at the moment you are seen as rather unpleasant, shifty and dull.'

'Such sweet praise,' he murmured.

'Why should I not say what I think? It is because of you that *my* name is now notorious, and I have lost the husband I love. And before him, you took Richard. I will *never* forgive you, Henry.'

His oddly uneven eyes were turned upon her. 'I know my supposed crimes, sweetheart, you do not need to repeat them. So, I gather from all this that you *still* want my bone-headed uncle?'

'Yes, Henry, he is my dear lord, and I have hurt him so much that I can scarce bring myself to *look* at you, let alone become your mistress.'

'You look at me steadily enough now.'

'Do not do that,' she said.

'What?'

'Bestow your best spaniel gaze upon me.'

He smiled. 'I thought I had nasty, squinty little eyes. Is that not how you have described them?'

'If you make me angry enough, I will call them that again.'

'I have no doubt, whereas *your* eyes are always so very beautiful.'

'Is that a real compliment, or is it barbed?'

'My compliments to you are always real, sweetheart.' He paused. 'Did you *really* have to make such a point of coming to the river stairs and then departing again?'

She met his eyes. 'If you know that, you must have been spying on me.'

'Not in person.'

'Then your creature will also have told you that on my way back to Pasmer's Place I encountered the Earl of Lincoln.'

'Lincoln, who evaded my spy in Southwark and then

went to see you? The Lincoln you met on the Three Cranes steps, and who escorted you *into* your house. Yes, I know.'

Nerves fluttered inside her, but she prayed she did not show it. 'We talked, Henry, that is all, and we would not have encountered each other at all if I had not changed my mind about coming to you. When I reached the palace this morning, I realized it would be better if I did not see you.'

'What in God's own name did you imagine I would do to you? Hang a notice around your neck and make you stand on the steps of St Paul's?'

'No, I simply shrank from a confrontation.'

'*This* is a confrontation?' He spread his graceful hands.

'No, because you are clearly in a good mood. But even so, you sent an armed escort to *force* me here.'

'With all due respect, I sent an escort to see you *safely* here. There is a difference.' He regarded her, and then linked his hands together and tapped his mouth thoughtfully with his forefingers. It was one of several little ways he had, and that his mother had as well. 'Cicely, would it assist my cause if I apologized again for the discourtesy you consider me to have shown today? And for Winchester?'

'No.'

'*Cariad*, I was hardly to know my mother and both my uncles would walk in at that particular moment!' The Welsh in him was evident in his slight annoyance.

He had only two uncles, Jon and Jasper Tudor, now Duke of Bedford and married to Cicely's Woodville aunt, Catherine. Henry had never known his own father, Edmund Tudor, who died before he was born, and Jasper, Edmund's younger brother, had always taken care of him, first in Wales, and then in exile in Brittany. It was Jasper's influence—as much as Henry's mother's—that had crippled Henry's emotions and made him the tormented man he now was. Cicely did not like Jasper Tudor, and he did not like her. It was almost virulent.

'Even if you *had* known, Henry, you would still have

46

kissed me. And you had already made a public scene because you learned my husband had made love to me over a table. In private, I hasten to add.'

'*Fucked* you over a table,' he corrected.

'And very good it was too. I am sorry if my marriage is so offensive to you, but it is *my* marriage, not yours. If Jon were here now, I would do it again. Right in front of you.'

'I can believe *that* too. And I can assure you that he would not long be perched on top, because I would finish the job for him. There is nothing I want more right now than to drive into you until your pretty teeth chatter, my lady!'

'I am cross with you, and so would just lie beneath you, like a dead codfish on a slab.'

'No, you would not, Cicely, because you enjoy lovemaking far too much. Even with me.' He changed the subject again. 'What do you know of this pretender in Burgundy? This Lambert Simnel? Is he your brother, the Duke of York?'

If he meant to unsettle her, he succeeded.

# Chapter Four

ALTHOUGH FRIGHTENED, CICELY managed to maintain the spirit she knew Henry liked so much. 'I know nothing, Henry, as I have already told you. But you *had* to make my brothers legitimate again, did you not? How you must be praying they are dead. Instead, in the absence of bodies or any proof of any kind, you have made for yourself two possible challengers with a much better claim to the throne than you. You *have* done well.'

He heard her out. 'And you, sweet Cicely, never miss an opportunity to goad me about it.'

'You surely cannot expect anything else.'

He gazed at her. 'It would do me no good to *expect* anything of you. But I can hope, which is entirely different.' His lips pursed, and then he returned to the matter of Lambert Simnel. 'What of your cousin, Lincoln? Dare I trust him?'

'I am not close enough to Lord Lincoln to be so much in his confidence.'

Henry raised an eyebrow and pursed his lips. 'No? Is he not your dearest Jack?'

'You are my dearest Henry, but you do not tell me your secrets.'

She was rewarded with the ghost of a smile. 'That is true. So, can I trust Lincoln?'

'He may have fought for Richard at Bosworth, but he has sworn fealty to you since then, and he remained at your side during Lord Lovell's recent rebellion.'

'Indeed so, and in return I have been generous to him, considering he was, to all intents and purposes, Richard's heir. How close *are* you to him, sweetheart?'

She met his shrewd, watchful gaze. 'Not in his bed. Nor has he dibbled me against the nearest wall.' She was reminding him of his first encounter with Bess, which had been before he married her and had been an unmitigated disaster, but which had resulted in Prince Arthur, a remarkably large and healthy 'eight-month' baby.

He cleared his throat. 'Well, if Lincoln has not had you yet, he will be thinking about it.'

'He can think as he wishes.' She smiled, using her charm. 'Henry, I do not think my cousin knows whether Simnel is my younger brother or not, nor do I think he cares. I am sure he is your man now.' Lying to this king was always a hazardous exercise, but she had no choice. Jack was now more important to her than ever.

'Hmm.' Perhaps he was convinced, perhaps not. 'The fact that Simnel claims to be your *younger* brother suggests Edward V is no longer with us.' He invited her opinion.

'I have no idea, Henry. Truly I do not. You are the one with the army of spies.'

He began to cough suddenly. Or was he clearing his throat again? Cicely had been puzzled by these coughs for some time, because there was something odd and rather tortured about the way he struggled to quell the spasm. 'Henry, have you consulted your physicians yet?'

'It is nothing.' He put up a hand and after a while overcame whatever it was, but he had gone a little pale, and she knew something was wrong.

'Henry, you are—'

'Enough, *cariad*.' He cleared his throat a last time and then resumed speaking. 'I was about to say, it would seem I have to take this Simnel threat seriously.'

She gazed at him. 'I think you would be very unwise not to. What is wrong, Henry? That is not an ordinary cough.' The possibility that was creeping into her mind was ominous, and she did not like to think of it. Not consumption. Please. Whatever she thought of Henry, she did not want him to suffer such a horrible, lingering death.

He squeezed her hand briefly, naturally, thoughtfully. It was a reminder of how disarming and gentle he could be. 'I am perfectly well, sweetheart. About Simnel. . . ?'

'You will always be beset by such rebellions, and you know it. How can it be otherwise when you have invaded with foreigners, added English and Welsh traitors to them, and killed an anointed king of pure English blood and royal descent, in order to usurp his throne? Most of those who supported Richard at Bosworth will continue to oppose you, no matter how compliant they are on the surface. And no matter how you have sought to unite York and Lancaster by marrying Bess, seeing me married to Jon, and Jolly Jasper married to my aunt.'

He ignored the jibe at Jasper. 'Which means Lincoln will break his word as easily as he breaks wind.'

'Henry, you suspect everyone and everything. You cannot help yourself. It is why you always look so *sly*!'

'Oh, how darling you are.' He paused. 'You will *never* forgive me for Richard, will you?' he asked with another swift change of subject.

'No, I will not.' If Henry VII hoped the carnage of Bosworth had rid him of Richard III, he knew better now, for not only did Richard haunt him as a king and a man, but also as the keeper of her heart.

Henry put a hand to her chin to make her look at him again. 'You should never have come to me that time without permission. Here, in this room. You came simply to assess me, but found more than you bargained. If you had not been so bold and insolent, I might never have begun

50

to want you so much. Might never have so despised every man who comes near you.'

'Insolent? I am a king's daughter, Henry.'

'And I am the king himself, Cicely, and so I eclipse you,' he answered softly.

'You think so?' She bestowed a caressing smile upon him. Yes, Richard was right, using her charm came so easily she hardly knew she did it.

He raised an eyebrow. 'Hmm, well, I suppose I would be wise to leave the point open for discussion,' he murmured, his humour still evident. His strange eyes rested thoughtfully upon her. 'Perhaps I already wanted you, before you came here. I think from that first moment at Lambeth, when I went out to welcome you and your sister at the end of your ride south from Sheriff Hutton. To *my* capital. After the triumph of Bosworth,' he added deliberately.

She did not react. This time he would *not* get the fiery response he sought.

He smiled. 'Oh, please do not fail me, Cicely. I am only happy when I am sparring with you. Or fucking you.'

'Take yourself to Hell, Henry.'

'Ah, you could not resist it! You answered me back. You do it so splendidly that I could almost hug myself. And *please* do not tell me that I am the only one who would want to hug me. Besides, I refuse to go to Hell unless you come with me.' He paused. 'Cicely, I *am* sorry for what happened at Winchester. You wrong me greatly if you really think I would have kissed you anyway on that occasion. It was not my intention to let anyone witness it.'

'No? I do not entirely believe you, Henry, because by forcing yourself between husband and wife, you think you have made the wife needier. Perhaps she will turn to you after all, and become your mistress, bound only to you. Why, you probably have another Rosamund's Bower ready and waiting.'

'A bower? Waste time finding my way around a fucking

51

maze? I think not. When I want you, I *want* you. In a straight line. As for manipulating you into a corner from where there is only one way out, no, Cicely, I had no such plan. I wanted to kiss you, I *needed* to kiss you, and so I did. The outcome was not of my seeking or intention. *Please* believe me.'

'I will not fall prey to *that*, Henry. I know your notion of winsome appeal. How you emphasize the word "please", how you speak so softly and a little regretfully. How sad and *dear-little-puppy* your eyes become. Not in unison, of course, but eventually they focus together.'

'I did not know I possessed any winsome appeal, or that I was seducer enough to lure you into kissing me again. Is that not what you always tell me? That I am totally bereft of redeeming features? You have a way of insulting me, Cicely, a haughty, seductive way that tells any red-blooded man, especially this one, how unbelievably exciting you are in a bed. I vow you are a succubus, and have ravished me in my sleep. There cannot be many men who have looked at you and not wanted you. Even your sainted uncle Richard III.'

'My uncle did not view me as anything other than his niece,' she answered with monstrous dishonesty.

'The child you bore was his, not that of Sir Jon Welles. Admit it, Cicely. The child is dead, Richard is dead, so why will you not tell me you lay with him?'

'Because I did *not* give myself to him, nor did he seek such a thing. It is the truth, but you choose not to believe me.'

His eyes encompassed her again. 'I choose much that I cannot have. I do not care if your sister has given me a male heir, or if she gives me twenty more. I do not like her. I married the wrong sister. She is the eldest, but *you* are the one I want.'

'You could not have married me because when we first met I was already with child by Sir Jon. And since then I have been barren, and therefore not at all suited for the role of producing countless Tudor children.'

'I know.' He touched her cheek. 'Cicely, I also know what I am . . . what I may become. You do not hesitate to point out my faults, and I need that. Every king should have one such as you. You are the only living soul who dares to criticize me to my face, and I love you for it. How else can I say it?'

She looked at him. 'I do not know, Henry, for I am wondering if you have prepared a second little speech should this one not have the desired effect.'

'*Duw*, you can be so damned infuriating, Cicely. By now you should be able to tell when I am being sincere.'

'That Welsh word did not sound very polite.'

'It was restrained, believe me.'

'Well, it is impossible to always tell when you are being sincere, Henry Tudor, because you can entice like the Archangel Gabriel but fib like Beelzebub.'

He laughed. 'I am flattered.'

'I still refuse to be your mistress, Henry. I will *not* be so labelled. I will *not* be demeaned by allowing you to boast that I have sunk to becoming your kept whore.'

'*Sunk? Whore?* I believed it was an honour to be a king's acknowledged mistress. And boasting is not in my nature. I have many failings, but not that particular one.' He was clearly perplexed. 'Cicely, I fail to see why this is so important. You have been in my bed numerous times, and you do not recite a catechism while there, so. . . ?' He spread his hands enquiringly.

Richard would have understood in an instant. But *he* would never have asked this of her in the first place. 'Henry, I have come to your bed, but secretly. To become your mistress will be to screech aloud that I part my legs beneath you. That I am your latest doxy.'

'Latest? Cicely, how many doxies do you imagine I have? There are no doxies at all.'

'Except me.'

'You are not a doxy. *Cariad*, after Winchester, everyone *knows* we are lovers.'

'It was a kiss, Henry. We were not discovered writhing on the floor in the throes of fornication. I have been shamed, but no one can say for certain that I have lain with you. They can think all they wish, but they do not *know*. It makes a great difference to me.'

He touched her cheek again. 'The throes of fornication? Hmm, an agreeable image to keep my right hand busy. Very well, I will not mention the word "mistress" again. I swear it.' He hesitated. 'Now, can you *please* forget Beelzebub and believe in Gabriel for a while?'

'I will keep both in mind.'

He regarded her. 'What is wrong?' he asked then. 'There is a change in you.'

She was a little shaken, having thought she appeared the same, but his question was direct, not teasing. A convincingly reassuring—yet at the same time diverting—answer was needed. 'I . . . I am upset that you continue to think I committed incest with my uncle. Henry, my child was *not* by Richard. He would be as appalled to hear you say it as he was about the false rumours spread concerning my sister's purported feelings for him. It is all untrue.'

And may the saints forgive her. Because of Bess's lack of discretion, the whispering about Richard had become insufferably dangerous and widespread, even to the point of claiming he was poisoning his dying queen, to hasten her to death in order to marry Bess, whom he had already deflowered. He had been forced to deny it all publicly. When he first kissed Cicely Plantagenet, he was a widower, fond of but long out of love with the wife who had already died slowly, but *naturally*, of consumption.

'What did Richard have that was so irresistible, Cicely?'

What a fool she was to divert him from one thing, only to fix him upon something worse. Now she had no choice but to continue. 'He was simply an extraordinarily attractive man, attentive, kind, brave, admirable, thoughtful, cultured, clever and amusing. Shall I go on?'

'So, he was all the things you think *I* am not.'

'Well, *you* said that, not me.'

'I must learn to guard my tongue.'

'Shall I tell you what else there was about him?' she went on, unable to prevent herself. 'Once seen, he could *never* be forgotten, which is why you put his poor, broken body on display after Bosworth. You showed him no honour or respect, Henry, and I still think you so base and unchivalric for it.'

His eyes flickered, and she knew she had touched a nerve. 'Well, Cicely, it was not only his face that was memorable, was it? His bent back and uneven shoulders rather stayed in the mind as well!'

The words whipped her, and her poise was suddenly demolished. In its place was a very unwise, very bitter fury. 'And *you*, Henry, will be memorable for your total lack of honour or scruples ... and your divergent little eyes!' she cried, forgetting everything but the need to defend Richard. 'He was the anointed king, the rightful king in every conceivable way, and so dear to me that I could scratch your eyes from their sockets, because *you* took him from me. From England. Will you be such a king as he? No, of course you will not. You are too begrudging, contorted, scheming and suspicious a man to even come close to him. I wish *you* had died at Bosworth. I wish he had returned triumphant and continued the reign that would have made him one of England's greatest kings, if not the greatest. So do not denigrate him when I am near!'

Her chin was raised challengingly, and her Plantagenet eyes flashed. 'Do you *still* enjoy sparring with me?' she breathed, but already knew how very far beyond the boundaries she had trespassed. Her eyes closed and she bit her lip. Then she sank to her knees. 'Forgive me, Your Majesty.'

He rubbed an eyebrow, taking time before responding.

'Yes, Cicely, I do still enjoy sparring with you, although I am not sure sparring was exactly what you had in mind with that tirade.'

'I showed you no respect.'

He raised her again. 'True, but I provoked you a little too far. Beelzebub, not Gabriel, I fear.'

He forgave her? 'I should not have said those things.'

'Indeed, and in due course I will be expecting a truly grovelling, truly erotic apology.' He smiled.

Oh, those smiles of his. When they reached his eyes, as now, they weakened her resolve. She had come here thinking she would need to *force* herself to respond to him, but he would not let her force herself to anything. He was now making himself so likeable that she knew she would still find pleasure with him. She could not escape her own nature.

He searched her face. 'Why, *why* do you persist in denying your physical love for Richard? You kiss him again and again with every word, and become so passionate, so *savage* when you defend him, and so aglow with emotion you might as well be fucking him in front of me.'

She strove to compose herself again. His calm response to all her insults was almost as unsettling as if he had been furious. 'We were not lovers,' she said. 'We were *not*!'

'I envy him so. He will always be precious to you, because he is framed in time, an eternal portrait. He will never grow old, never fail you, *never* become the fiend you are so sure I will be. Instead he will always be beloved, always have your heart and *never* relinquish it. Sir Jon Welles cannot compete. Nor can I. But he has gone, Cicely. *I* am the king who needs you now.'

'The king who uses me.'

'Because I love you,' he whispered, drawing her close to put his lips to hers.

By now he knew so very well how to coax her, how to tease the response she did not want to give, least of all today, when she had been kissed by Jack de la Pole. What she felt for her cousin was infinitely greater, deeper and more vital than anything she had shared with this king, but Henry was wooing her now, and wanted her to return his kisses. When he wished, he exerted an allure that was close to enchantment. And he wished it now.

Henry's slender fingers pried under her headdress at the nape of her neck. He held her to him, to *all* of him, making certain she could feel the strong erection created by kissing and holding her. His lips were soft and pliable, knowing and gentle, and played temptingly with hers. She had always known that someone had showed him how to use his sensuality, just as Richard had taught her, but she had no more idea now of the woman's identity than she had been when Henry first kissed her. For all those years he had been in exile in Brittany and latterly in France, there had to have been many lovers. But he had learned about exquisite lovemaking from someone in particular; she sensed it as surely as if he had told her.

He moved behind her to take off her headdress and his graceful fingers pushed richly through its warmth, twisting just a little, to find resistance. Only a little, just for the erotic pleasure it imparted.

She closed her eyes as he kissed her shoulder. Tiny shivers passed over and through her as he unfastened her gown and drew it down from her shoulders, until it slipped around her feet in soft, beautiful folds of plum brocade. Now his hands moved over her naked body, cupping her breasts to toy with her nipples until they stood hard and proud, and then he slid his fingers down into the dark hairs at her groin.

'Oh, Cicely, you fill my soul,' he breathed, kissing the crook of her neck. 'I have a mind to enjoy what your husband enjoyed, a fuck over a table.'

'I will do whatever you wish, Your Majesty,' she murmured, leaning her head back as his lips played over her skin. Jesu, he was good . . .

He released her and swept documents, ink and wax from the table that had once been laden with the same things for that other king. 'Your bed awaits, my lady,' he said, lifting her until she sat on it and then he parted her thighs, slipping his fingers delicately towards the apex, where he took time to fondle and please her. Those fingers knew all they needed to know to give her waves of satisfaction. She could not help herself, she was prey to her own self, and he indulged that self as it so needed.

She drew him a little closer, and began to slowly untie the laces that secured his loins. He was rigid, gleamingly, urgently so, and now hers were the knowing fingers, touching, manipulating, stroking and pleasuring so much. She enclosed him, smoothed a soft finger around his tip, and did all the things that could not fail to bring him to a barely containable pitch of excitement. He was so pleasing to watch during these moments. To see Henry Tudor relinquishing himself to his sensuality was to see him come to life. He no longer hid within his cold outer shell, but was there before her, the real man, warm, emotional, filled with desire and need.

His breath caught as she rolled her palm luxuriously over the gleaming head of his erection. 'Oh, what you do to me, lady . . .' he breathed, pulling her closer to enter her at last. She wrapped her legs around his hips, making it easy for him to push into her, and when he was to the hilt, unable to go further, he paused, deliberately flexing himself inside her until she gasped with the delight of it. She hated herself, *hated* herself, but this was so voluptuously satisfying and exciting all she could do was surrender to it.

Oh, the kisses and caresses that followed. They were joined, on fire with desire and need, and they both wanted it to go on and on. He did not move within her, except for those quivers that seemed to find a ripple that spread sweetly through her entire body. But he at last began to withdraw and then enter again—oh, so slowly and richly—and she moved against him, increasing his pleasure as well as her own. It was exquisitely rewarding, and she could not have counted the increasingly satisfying climaxes that made her secret muscles undulate.

His eyes were closed, his hair fell forward, swaying with his motion, and catching against the rich black cloth on his shoulders. So much reward, so much delight. This was Henry Tudor the lover, and there were surely not many women who had ever encountered him. Except that one other.

He met her eyes; she knew he was close to coming. 'Sweetheart?' he whispered, because he *always* waited for her, always made certain they were together in those final ecstatic moments.

She smiled. 'Yes,' she whispered.

He came so violently that he shuddered against her, his eyes closed with the ferocity of it. It was such a shattering peak, unrestrained and sublimely prolonged. His whole body was engulfed by intense pleasure, and as it began to fade at last, he gathered her into his arms to be sure she remained impaled upon him. He sank his hand through her hair, and pressed her mouth to his to kiss her with a passion that almost fused their lips together.

But at last, and with great gentleness, he drew from her, breathing a little shakily as he sought composure. She slid from the table to slip her arms around his waist, rest her head against him and inhale his warmth and the cloves. When Henry Tudor made such love to her as this, she became a traitor to everything she held dear.

How long they stood like that she could not have said, except that she exulted in every sweet second of it. He stroked her hair lovingly, but eventually had to speak. '*Cariad*, if there were to be anything amiss, you would tell me?' The words were muffled because his lips were to her forehead.

'There is nothing wrong, Henry.'

'Oh, yes, there is. I know you, sweetheart. Something has happened that you will not tell me, and I would always wish to help you. Please tell me you know that.'

There was kindness and concern in every word, and her guilt pricked unpleasantly. So she took refuge in using her gift. 'I am thinking of taking the veil, Henry,' she said seriously.

He hesitated, and then laughed spontaneously. 'The veil? *You?* Your vows would be broken so frequently that I hardly dare imagine the sanity of your confessor. There would not be enough Hail Marys to cope.'

'Then maybe I should confess to you, Henry, for *you* to exact punishment.'

'Then *my* confessor would collapse of the shock. You might survive longer in a monastery than a nunnery.'

She laughed. 'Oh, Henry, can you imagine it? All those poor brothers, rushing to defend their virginity.'

'I doubt if many of them remember where they left it,' he answered, then he touched her cheek regretfully. 'I do so love being with you like this, Cicely, but there are so many obstacles, not least our opposing Houses.'

She caught his hand. 'Yes, we are from opposites sides, and yet are the same. Henry, if you were faced with saving your son or your mother, which would you choose?' she asked suddenly.

'I do not know. Must I sacrifice either?'

'Yes.'

'Then I do not know the answer.'

'I will tell you. At first you would keep trying to protect them both, knowing that in the end, there has to be a decision. So how can you expect me to desert York for you? Or turn from Jon? Or pretend Richard did not exist? Or his son? Or my cousin? I am like you, I do not want to give up anyone.'

He searched her face. 'And at second?'

'You would sacrifice your son, because you can have more sons. Arthur is still a baby and has not yet begun to touch your heart with his personality. But you only have one mother, and she cannot be replaced.'

'That is what you believe? Maybe you are right. I will not know until the very moment of decision. Then again, I would sacrifice them *both* for you.'

# Chapter Five

CICELY'S LIPS PARTED with shock. 'You cannot possibly mean that, for I can easily be replaced!'

'I tease, of course.' Henry smiled a little, but in a way that made her suspect it was not teasing after all. 'But it *would* cause a few ripples, mm? A king who would give up his heir for the forbidden woman he loves beyond common sense?'

'You do not love me beyond common sense, Henry. You do not love *anything* beyond common sense.'

'Ah, there you have me.'

She looked at him. 'If only everyone could see you as you are now.'

'Alone with my naked sister-in-law, my cock hanging out to dry? I do not think you *do* wish it, sweeting. I certainly do not.' He straightened his clothes to tie himself into respectability again, but then he had to subdue another cough. This time it was not as easily done. He stepped aside, turning away as the coughing persisted.

She hurried to bring some wine. 'Drink it, please!' she urged, trying to press the gilt cup into his hand.

But before he could take it, the coughing overwhelmed him in earnest. His whole body went into spasms, and small beads of perspiration dampened his forehead. He struggled to catch his breath, and had to lean his hands on the table, head bowed as he continued to cough.

Alarmed, Cicely put the wine aside. He was clearly unwell and she did not know what to do. 'Should I bring someone, Henry? One of your physicians?'

'Just help me to a seat,' he managed to say, still racked with coughs as he stretched a hand to her. Supporting his arm, she ushered him to the most comfortable chair, and when he managed to sit he was ashen, and seemed suddenly older than his twenty-nine years.

'Should I bring someone?' she asked again, smoothing his hair back from his face.

'No! No . . . It will pass,' he managed to reply, but it was a good minute before the spasm relented enough for him to speak again. 'Do not bring anyone, sweetheart,' he said, his voice hoarse and unsteady.

'Henry, I cannot stand by and do nothing!'

'Do as I say, Cicely.' It was the King of England who looked at her now.

She lowered her eyes. 'But, Henry, I spent many hours close to Richard's queen. I know that cough.'

'It is merely something that afflicts me in the colder months, but not every year.' He managed to clear his throat and take a deep breath. 'I will be myself again in a few minutes now. I do not want you to speak of this to *anyone*, Cicely.'

She knelt beside the chair. 'My silence could endanger your life.'

'As if a Yorkist would be bothered about *that* small thing.' He smiled.

'Well, this Yorkist *is* bothered about it.' She gave him an impish look. 'You see, I may get the blame, and that would not do at all.'

He smiled. 'It certainly would not.' His fingers closed over hers on the arm of the chair. 'But I need your word on this, Cicely. If you please.'

'You have my word,' she said at last, 'but know that it is given with great reluctance.'

'If there is reluctance, then I want you to swear upon Richard's honour.'

'On *Richard's* honour?' She sat back on her heels. 'Why? Is my word not good enough?'

'Your word is reluctant, sweetheart, but I know that if *Richard's* honour is drawn into it, you will have no difficulty abiding by your promise.'

'I swear, upon Richard's honour, not to say a word of this to anyone.'

Henry relaxed, leaned his head back and closed his eyes.

'But I can write of it,' she said, needing to tease him into smiling again.

Which he did. 'No, sweetheart, you cannot. Nor can you paint it, stitch it or carve it on a tree in symbols.' He reached for her hand again. 'My indifferent health makes me vulnerable, and there are those in your House who would give much to know it.'

There was faint colour in his cheeks again, but not a great deal, and he seemed very tired. She looked at the sharply defined line where his jaw reached up towards his ear. It made him seem so fragile. *Was* it consumption?

He saw the look on her face. 'It is *not* what you think, sweetheart, and to prove it I will soon get you on the bed and do you justice.' He studied her. 'There *is* something bothering you. Well? What is it?'

She remembered what Jack had said about getting Henry to do what she wanted. 'I . . . well, I wanted to beg two favours, but if I ask now you will think I take advantage of you.'

He was amused. 'I would not hesitate to take advantage of you, sweetheart, so ask me.'

'First, I wish to see John of Gloucester.'

'No.'

'Please.'

'Why do you wish to see him? To remind yourself of what a tyrant I am?'

'Why would I need reminding?'

He paused, amused. 'Damn you, lady. I suppose I must take that answer as I see fit.'

She drew his hand to her cheek. It was the one upon which he wore Richard's ruby. 'Do you not see? I need to be sure, in my own heart, that John no longer knows me.'

He rested his fingers over hers. 'Cicely, you break my heart sometimes. I *strenuously* advise you to forget the whole notion. Richard's son will *not* know you.'

She bit her lip. 'Nevertheless . . .'

'If you are so determined to have your way and ignore all advice, then I will give ground, Cicely. You may see him, but only if I accompany you.'

'You? But—'

'When we are at his door, I will give you one last chance to change your mind, which I think you will. Yes, sweetheart, you will. In the meantime I will see that arrangements are made. It will have to be very private, I trust you understand that?'

'Yes.'

'What is the other thing you wish to ask of me?'

'I wish you to send for my husband.'

He groaned. 'Cicely, he is best left to come around in his own time. *I* should certainly stay well out of it, having been the cause of his distress.'

'Then please let me go to him.' She knew Henry would not wish *that*.

He knew she knew. 'You are artful, my lady.'

'I want my own way,' she answered disarmingly.

'The abject and erotic reward you promised earlier is now mandatory, you know that?'

'I will obey your every whim.'

'My whims are legion, and only stop short at the

physically impossible. Very well, I will send for your husband. But . . . there is a condition. I will send for him to be here for the Christmas season, but until then, you will return to court.'

'Oh, please, no—'

'Yes, Cicely. You will leave Pasmer's Place and take up rooms at Greenwich Palace. That is the condition. Refuse, as you did earlier today, and my numbskull of an uncle can stay in Lincolnshire until he rots.'

Greenwich Palace was on the Thames, downstream of London. Nominally it still belonged to the Queen Dowager, having been a gift from Cicely's father, but now it might as well belong to Henry, who used it as if it were. Rooms were prepared for Lady Welles, well away from the royal apartments and therefore not likely to cause comment.

As soon as Cicely's return became known, Bess, newly arrived from Winchester, sent for her, believing Cicely was deliberately defying her letter. 'You have the nerve to flout my command?' she cried the moment they were alone together. She was twenty years old, with wonderful blue eyes and a faint blush of rose upon her cheeks, and was quite the loveliest of Edward IV's five surviving daughters. She wore sapphire blue, with a pearl-stitched gable headdress, beneath which her shining red-gold hair was completely concealed. Her forehead was shaved, a fashion that many men loathed, including Henry. And Richard.

She was clearly fully recovered from childbirth, for her figure was restored to its former slender-waisted elegance. Her beauty almost glowed, although the pinched line that began to set in around her mouth had never been there while Richard lived.

Cicely knelt, and knew her sister would leave her doing so. 'I have no choice but to return, Your Grace.'

'No choice?' Bess paused, her blue eyes sharpening. Then dull colour suffused her otherwise pale cheeks. 'The

66

king? *Henry* has brought you here?' she breathed.

Cicely kept her eyes fixed upon the floor.

'So, you still have your claws into a king, sister mine?'

There was no answer to give. At least, not one that would not sound the height of insolence.

'I want you to return to Pasmer's Place,' Bess said bluntly, pointlessly.

'I cannot.' Cicely looked imploringly at her. 'Please, I do not do this to hurt or spite you.'

'You do *everything* to hurt and spite me, Lady Welles. I intend to take this up with the king. I will *not* be insulted by your presence.'

Cicely wished her well, for Henry would not give an inch. He wanted his sister-in-law close to him, and nothing his wife said would make any difference. 'I will try to stay well away from you, Bess. Oh, do not reprimand me for using that name. We are sisters and should be close.'

'Close? When you do all in your power to destroy my happiness?'

'Not willingly.'

'So, you are more than kissed by my husband, you are *serviced*! What a very disagreeable experience, to be sure.'

Cicely longed to tell her that Henry Tudor was *not* a disagreeable experience. 'The king takes his pleasure of me, that is all. It means nothing, because *you* are his queen.'

'It means everything to me. He is *my* husband, *my* king! Oh, why are you not dead? I wish for your demise so much, even more than I wish for Mother's. I hate you both, but for such different reasons. She is abhorrently cold and calculating, whereas you ... you are abhorrently *warm* and calculating. You seduce Henry with your tempting caresses and sweet whispers.'

Cicely studied the floor again. Henry Tudor needed no seducing.

'I *will* speak to Henry,' Bess vowed. 'I will tell him I am with child again, and your continued presence will be dangerous to my condition.'

Utterly shocked, Cicely stared at her. 'You would lie to him about *that*?'

'Why not? Love, war, it is all the same.'

'Do not be a fool, Bess. Take the word of one who knows. Henry Tudor may be everything you loathe, and he may be cold and daunting on the outside, but he can be a warm and sensuous man, a good lover and an amusing, engaging companion. He will never send me away, no matter how you plead with him.'

'Get out!' Bess cried, so overcome with fury that she had to steady herself on a chair back. 'Get out of my sight!' Her voice rose on the last word.

Cicely began to obey, but then turned. 'Be careful what you say to him about being with child. You have not yet had time to know for certain, because you have not been back from Winchester for long enough. Lie to him about this, and he will know.'

Then she left.

As if being at Greenwich and subjected to renewed whispering was not punishment enough for Cicely, Jack was absent as well. Whether by design or not, the moment she arrived from Pasmer's Place, he was sent to Sheen to preside over numerous courts and hearings dealing with suspected Yorkist malcontents. Jack had sworn fealty, and Henry made him stand by it. Being behind bars would not benefit the House of York, and so Jack did as he was ordered. No one could have known treason was a word he even understood. This was Jack de la Pole at his most subtle and cunning, smiling and evincing amiability and above all . . . loyalty to the new crown.

Not seeing Jack caused Cicely more pain than anything else. She missed him so much that unhappiness keened through her from morning until night. And when night came, she lay awake, thinking about him . . . knowing that he was thinking of her. Or   perhaps he sought solace in the arms of another? For the first time in her life she was beset by jealousy. Jack had always been a womanizer, and had only to look at a woman to make sure of her. Perhaps he did this now. Perhaps his cousin Cicely was, after all, no more to him than any of the others.

Then at last, one crisp morning late in that same month of October, she saw him again. She was returning to her rooms along the windswept terrace after walking in the gardens, and she was wishing for Jack, when . . . there he was, coming towards her.

He wore a fur-lined cloak over his fine royal blue clothes, and a jewelled brooch flashed in his soft velvet hat as he snatched it off to bow. 'Lady Welles?' He smiled into her eyes.

'My Lord of Lincoln.' She tried to keep the pain at bay, but her wretchedness must surely be plain to him.

And it was. 'Cicely?' He came closer. 'Sweetheart?' He lowered his voice, and almost reached out to her, but prevented himself in time, because there were others nearby, any one of whom might be Henry's spy.

'I . . . have missed you so, Jack.'

'And I you.'

She bit her lip and could not answer. The agony was so much she almost wept there and then. The thought of him with someone else was unsupportable, and yet he had to endure it with her all the time, because of Henry. How could he bear it? How could he understand and support her in all she did?

He decided to ignore the possibility of spies, and put his arm around her shoulder. 'What is it, sweeting? Mm?'

'Nothing. I am being very foolish.'

'I hoped you would be pleased to see me, not reduced to tears.' He smiled and tightened his arm for a moment.

She glanced up at his face, so handsome and animated, so seductively formed, so very, very desirable. But she must not say anything, she could not say anything. She would not be so unutterably weak and foolish. 'I love you so very, very much,' she whispered.

'Not more than I love you, sweetheart.' He searched her eyes, trying to read her. 'Please do not think I have been unfaithful to you,' he said then, so accurately that she might as well have put the question to him.

'I could not blame you if you had been, Jack. You know I lie with Henry, and—'

'And nothing, Cicely. You have to do it, I know that. If you were to lie with someone else, and from choice, well, that would be different.'

'I only want to be with you.'

He put his hand to her chin. 'And I think it is time we confirmed our love, sweetheart. I can only reassure you by showing you how I love you. By proving it. And I will. You need me, I think.'

*You need me, I think.* Richard's words. Tears welled from her eyes, and she bowed her head. Again ignoring anyone who might be watching, he pulled her into his arms and held her tightly. 'Oh, sweetheart, you do my vanity such service,' he said lightly. 'If anyone reports this to Henry, we will say that you needed comfort because of losing your idiot husband.'

He meant to tease and make her smile a little, but she could not. Being without him had been a torture akin to that of being without Richard. She tried to stop her foolishness, because Jack was alive, and he was with her again now. For these moments he was hers, even though she did not know if he had been constant. He said he was, but she had no confidence at all in her own ability to hold such a man.

He turned her to face him. 'Short of pinning you to the wall in front of everyone, there is no more I can say at this moment, except that I love you, that I have not forsaken you for a single moment, and that I never will. Have faith in yourself, sweetheart. You are loved by kings and by this presumptuous earl who has long aspired to your bed. Look at me. Now then, what do you see in my eyes, mm? You see love, pure, unblemished, *true* love. Do not *ever* think I would betray what we have. You dishonour me to think it. I am no longer the rakehell you knew before. Tell me you know so.'

She gazed at him. 'I know so,' she whispered.

'There, that was not so hard, was it? Do you go to Henry tonight?' He made her walk on towards the palace entrance.

'I . . . No, he has a difficult, very late meeting that is likely to go on into the small hours.'

'Good, I hope it strains his brain and incapacitates his dick for a while.' Jack hesitated. 'What is this meeting about?'

'I do not know, except that it is connected with private matters in Brittany.'

'Private matters?'

'That is all I know, Jack. Truly. I'd tell you if I was aware of something that would be of interest to you. He certainly has not told me anything. In fact, he never discusses his time there. He will not even speak of it to Jolly Jasper.'

'Oh?' Jack was intrigued. 'I thought he and Jasper were like this.' He crossed his fingers aloft.

'So did Jasper. There was quite a quarrel, but it was all in Welsh so I did not understand, save that it was quite clearly liberally sprinkled with foul words. I did not need Welsh to be sure of *that*.'

Jack raised an eyebrow. 'Henry has Breton secrets? How interesting it would be to learn them.'

'Do not attempt it, Jack. Please. Do not meddle with Henry.'

'You really do fear him?' Jack searched her eyes.

'I enjoy lying with him, Jack, but yes, he frightens me. He can be so very warm and amusing, and then suddenly, without any warning at all, he changes. That is when he really frightens me.'

'He will not know that I come to you tonight.'

She was shocked. 'Here at Greenwich? You cannot!'

'Why?'

'Is that not obvious?'

'Lady, I have slipped secretly in and out of more bed-chambers than I can possibly recount. I can do it as easily here at Greenwich as anywhere else. We do each other no good at all by staying apart. We need to love.' They entered the palace, where there were unexpectedly few people. He glanced around, and then drew her into a deep window embrasure that was hung with a heavy curtain, which he drew further across to cocoon them from view. There, for a few dangerously exciting stolen moments, they were alone.

He pulled her into his arms again and kissed her. How she welcomed it, and how foolish she felt for her doubts and fears, because as her lips softened helplessly against his, she was caught up again in the comfort of love. She closed her eyes. These were sweet moments, honeyed and piquant, with the fragrance of thyme so clean and fresh on his breath. Reckless need clutched at her. Let them do it now, for she could not bear to wait until the night!

He was tempted into the same foolishness, but then there was a trill of female laughter from the terrace entrance and the sound of dainty footsteps as some of Bess's ladies entered. Dismayed, the secret lovers pressed well back out of sight and waited as the ladies tripped past, giggling over a handsome Breton minstrel who had sung for the queen the evening before. He had come with the party of gentle-men with whom Henry was to have the meeting tonight.

When they had gone, Jack smiled ruefully. 'A moment of complete lunacy blessedly avoided, I think,' he said softly, drawing Cicely's hand to his lips and lingering over it. 'Perhaps it would be best to go our separate ways until tonight?'

She clutched his hand. 'I so look forward to it, Jack.'

'So do I, sweeting, so do I. Now you go on to your rooms and I will come to you when the time is right and Henry is fully distracted. For the moment I will wait here until you are safely gone.' He glanced around the curtain, and after another brief, stolen kiss she hurried away. But she wanted so much to turn around and go back to him. Suddenly she was alive again. The days of miserable doubt had gone, and Jack was here again.

That night, as the first snow of winter fell outside, and the fire glowed in the little hearth in Cicely's bedchamber, she and Jack faced each other at last. The door was locked, and Mary was in the outer room, sewing a little coat for Leo. He was supposedly her nephew, and she loved him as if he were, and so her needle flashed busily as she kept guard while her mistress gave herself so gladly to the Earl of Lincoln. Mary would not have been averse to submitting to Jack de la Pole herself, given the chance. She smiled wistfully, her needle continuing to flash.

In the bedchamber, Cicely gazed at the cousin she desired so much. There was such excitement pounding through her now that she wondered he could not hear her heartbeats and feel them pulsing in the air, and yet he had not even touched her. 'I . . . I am afraid, Jack.'

'Afraid?'

'That I may disappoint you.'

He smiled. 'Being mindful of your praise for Richard's extraordinary talents, I think *I* may disappoint *you*.'

'I feel so green, as if this is the first time.' She also felt so very foolish. This was Jack, whom she had known for so much of her life, and who had suddenly become more precious to her than that same life. She burned with desire for him, but seemed unable to do anything except lack all sophistication. She was a virgin again, unknowing and hesitant, wanting so much and yet afraid to welcome it.

'Oh, sweetheart,' he said softly. So softly. He came closer

73

to unfasten her gown and slide it from her shoulders. He gazed at her. 'You are so beautiful,' he whispered, putting a gentle hand to her chin and tilting it. 'Let us begin with a kiss, that is all.'

Her lips parted beneath his. He did not touch her, except with his fingers beneath her chin. And his kiss. Such a kiss. It enchanted her, beguiled her, *lured* her out of the protective little hiding place she had neither sought nor wanted. Slowly, willingly, she slipped free and returned the kiss. No, she did not merely return it, she gave her whole self to it, holding him as tightly as she could.

His mouth now crushed hers, working upon her, playing with her, drawing more and more wantonness from her. Desire sped dizzyingly through her veins and into every pore. His scent filled her nostrils, his breath was so sweet and fresh, and his kiss so potent and commanding that she allowed her senses to lead her where they would. Where *he* would.

And lead her he did, until she was almost faint with need of him. Her inhibitions had now melted away completely, and she took charge of her own desires, undoing his doublet and pushing it back from his shoulders, until there was only his thin shirt beneath, and soon that had been removed as well. But impatience took over. Neither of them could wait until he was completely naked. He lifted her into his arms and put her gently on the bed, and then undid his laces to release the long, thick erection that so many women had desired before her.

His dark eyes were even darker as he lay with her and looked into her darkened eyes. 'This feeling I have for you is unlike any other I have ever known. I love you, Cicely, and I always will.'

He kissed her again. There was nothing to hold them back now. Nothing at all. At last he pushed into her, and they became one.

# Chapter Six

IT WAS THE eve of All Hallows, a year and a day after Henry's coronation. The night was cold, wet and wind-swept, but there were still bonfires in the countryside around Greenwich, to ward off evil spirits. Wood smoke carried on the gusting wind.

Henry's inner court indulged in a night of merrymaking and disguising, where identities were hidden by hoods, masks and costumes to imitate the supernatural. Minstrels played, acrobats and stilt walkers performed, and there was a hobby horse, covered with ribbons and possessed of savagely snapping jaws that were directed at anyone within reach. A fool was there, supposedly to amuse the king, but the king did not seem particularly amused. Clearly the fool was not enough of a fool.

Cicely thought Henry looked unwell again. She sat at one of the long, crowded trestle tables lining the hall, and was able to observe him. He was very pale, with shadows beneath his eyes, and he seemed withdrawn. His throne was raised above the flanking thrones at the dais. One would have been unoccupied, because Bess was unwell, but Jasper had taken her place.

Jasper Tudor was a swarthy, dark-eyed Welshman with an air of assurance borne of having kept his nephew safe for so many years. He was in his fifties, yet his hair was still virtually black and showed no signs of thinning or going grey. He certainly bore no likeness whatsoever to his royal nephew, who entirely resembled Margaret, Lady Derby, his omnipresent mother.

The new Duke of Bedford's clothes were a rich ruby in colour, velvet trimmed with black fur and a crusting of gold embroidered dragons, with no hint at all of a mask or a costume, but then Henry did not observe the occasion either, save by his presence. There was a permanent scowl on Jasper's face when he was obliged to attend festivities, or indeed most social occasions, and in Cicely's opinion he always looked as if he were chewing upon wasps. The wasps grew larger and stung him even more whenever Cicely caught his eye, because he could not stand even the sight of her. A jolly fellow indeed, she thought.

It was strange that Henry did not wear his favourite black on this of all nights, when the supernatural brushed with the natural. Instead he chose a furred cloth-of-gold sleeveless coat that brushed the floor, and beneath it a grey doublet and hose. The monarch's circlet was around his forehead and he sat very still, watching everything, *his eyes so hooded he resembled the slyest of foxes.* Once, only once, Cicely thought she saw him stifle a cough. Or perhaps it had been a mere clearing of his throat, for it was over in a moment.

There was not a huge gathering, because he had dismissed most of his courtiers to their own lands for Hallowtide. Those who remained were close to him in one way or another, or, like Jack, were being watched. Free and yet not free. He was permitted into London but had to present himself before the king every morning and night. The last thing Henry would do was send the Earl of Lincoln back to his lands, from where he might be easily able to foment Yorkist trouble. From the moment Henry learned of Lambert Simnel, complete liberty had become out of the question for the former heir of Richard III.

Cicely and Jack had been very careful not to draw attention, but the atmosphere between them was always charged, as if a thunderstorm were about to break directly over them. He had come to her on a number of occasions now, always very carefully, and never giving a follower the chance to follow. If they encountered each other during the day, a glance was enough to set Cicely's blood racing and bring colour to her cheeks, but she dared not smile too much at him or linger long in his company. He was not here yet tonight, although she had expected him. His absence made the evening as dull and flat as an overlong sermon by a too-elderly priest.

Henry's lip-reading imp had often watched when she and Jack spoke together. She called the little man an imp because that was how he struck her. He was deaf, but had not been so from birth and thus could read lips and repeat to Henry what he had interpreted. Heaven alone knew what Henry might have learned through him, because no one else at court seemed to know what was being done, right there in front of them. How many unwary remarks had clever Henry been told? She, Jack and her husband Jon knew of the imp, but they appeared to be alone.

Her costume tonight consisted solely of a little veil over her gable headdress, so that the top half of her face was concealed. It was enough of a disguise, she thought, especially as those on the dais had not made any effort at all. Her gown was rich rose-pink velvet edged with grey fur, its pendulous sleeves lined with silver brocade, and she made full use of the veil in order to avoid eyes because the shocks of Winchester still loomed large in memories. As soon as she could slip away, she would, whether Henry liked it or not. He would summon her tonight anyway.

Her attention moved to his mother. Margaret was small, thin, fanatical and deadly, and had schemed and murdered in order to see her only child on the throne of England.

Most of the treachery that had brought Richard down had been at her instigation. She, being Jon Welles' exceedingly fond half-sister, had once formed a pact with Cicely to prevent him from learning of his wife's intimacy with Henry, but since Winchester, to Margaret, Lady Welles had become the Yorkist Whore of Babylon.

Someone wearing sapphire-blue velvet stitched with charcoal, and a rather peculiar costume, leaned over Cicely suddenly. 'How now, Coz?'

Jack! She looked up gladly. 'Why, Lord Lincoln, and without so much as a mask to hide your identity.'

He bent close to her ear. 'Beware, sweeting, Henry's imp has just taken up a position behind him.'

She glanced, and there the fellow was, watching their lips as if his life depended upon it. Which it probably did.

'May I join you?' Jack asked.

'You need to ask?' She made room as best she could, and he squeezed in next to her. She glanced at his lower regions as he made himself comfortable, and hid her mouth from the imp to comment. 'How indecently tight your hose are. Tell me, were you melted and poured into them?'

'I had to pull them on with infinite care.'

'The result is mortal sin,' she said softly, and then glanced curiously at his costume, for he had an animal skin flung over his left shoulder and carried a long scarlet staff that was drawn with magical symbols. 'What *are* you, exactly?'

'Merlin.'

'Indeed? You have need of a wand to cast your spell?'

'You are the best one to answer that,' he replied, smiling warmly.

'And you know the answer. Oh, how I love you, Jack. The more I have of you, the more I want. I am dependent.'

'I am glad to hear it. Why should it all be one-sided?' He smiled again.

Her glance was drawn to the dais suddenly. Henry was

coughing. It was not a spasm as she had witnessed before, but it was enough to concern her.

Jack followed her glance. 'What is it?'

'Nothing of importance.' But she continued to observe Henry. He was now a little agitated. Was that too strong a word? Perhaps, but he was no longer at ease. Certainly he was not himself, because when Margaret turned to speak to him, he had to ask her to repeat herself. Margaret did not seem to notice anything amiss, Cicely thought with some surprise, having expected his doting mother to be alive to every small thing where he was concerned.

Jack could not help but observe her preoccupation. 'Is something wrong with Henry?' he asked suddenly.

'Mm?'

'I *am* still here, you know.'

She looked at him quickly. 'Forgive me.'

He smiled. 'I forgive you everything.'

At that moment Henry got up. Cicely could see how he struggled not to cough or draw any attention to his indisposition as he inclined his head to the hall in general. As he left, he waved the merrymaking to continue.

She looked swiftly at Jack. 'I have to go to him.'

'Why?' He was clearly puzzled.

'His leaving is a signal.' Everything she said these days was a lie of one sort or another. And she did not *want* to lie to anyone. Certainly not to Jack, who was not deceived anyway.

'I will find out what is going on, Cicely. You are quite clearly bothered about him, and he does not seem well to me. Not well at all.'

'There is nothing wrong with him that I know of,' she replied, but the lie was in her eyes.

Jack smiled. 'We are too much alike, sweeting. You cannot fool me. You *will* tell me, for I will get it out of you, whatever it is.'

'Please let it be, Jack.'

He smiled again. 'Go to Tudor, sweetheart. I will see you later.'

'Later?'

'Oh yes.'

Cicely knew Henry would have gone to his private apartments, and intended to approach him uninvited, something he had expressly forbidden her to do. She turned her veil back as she approached the entrance to the royal apartments, but in spite of knowing who she was, the two guards in green and white immediately crossed their spears to bar her way. Their orders were to admit no one, but she caught them unawares by ducking swiftly beneath the spears and into the private rooms beyond. They came after her, of course, but Henry saw and dismissed them with a flick of his hand. He was seated by the fire, and indicated she should not kneel, but then gripped the arms of the chair as he struggled against the urge to cough.

She went to him and put a hand on his forehead. Jesu, he was hot! Even the scent of cloves seemed heated. Yet he also seemed so oddly calm. It was not an ordinary fever, and she was sure he was worse than he himself suspected.

He took a deep, laboured breath. 'I have had enough of tonight, and will be well enough in the morning.'

She was afraid of him and for him. Her secrets were such that he must never know them, and she dreaded that he would, but seeing him like this now still affected her. Perhaps she had enjoyed his lovemaking a little too much. '*Please* let me send for your physicians, Henry.'

'No, *cariad*,' he said again, but weakly, his eyes closed. His lips moved, as if he still spoke, but there was no sound. Then he looked again, and smiled weakly. 'I love you, sweetheart,' he murmured.

He did not even know he said it, she thought, getting up slowly. Her feelings were utterly confused in those seconds. Richard's motto had been *Loyaulte Me Lie*—Loyalty Binds

Me— and if she broke her word on this, she would fail *him* as well as Henry. A true vow should never be broken, least of all if it was made upon the honour of a man like Richard. But she *had* to tell *someone,* because Henry was King of England and he needed attention.

Then she knew what to do. She would not disobey Henry by sending for his physicians, or even his astrologers, but she *would* tell his mother. Let Margaret make any necessary decisions about her son!

She ran out to the guards. 'Tell the king's lady mother that he requires her presence. Urgently!' They hesitated, and so she called upon her formidable Plantagenet lineage. 'Do as I say, or you will rue it! *Now!'*

As one hurried away, she returned to Henry, intending to stay with him until Margaret arrived. She was alarmed to find him slumped in the chair, his head fallen to one side. A strand of his hair clung to one of his cheeks, and she pushed it back anxiously. His breathing was laboured, and his lips moved again, although she was sure he no longer knew she was there.

She knelt by his side again, her hand over his, and that was what greeted Margaret as she swept in like a black thundercloud. 'Lady Welles! How do *you* have the gall to be here?'

'I have the gall because the king is unwell, my lady,' Cicely interrupted, getting up so that Margaret could see fully how Henry had collapsed in the chair.

'Sweet God! Not again!' his mother cried, and hurried forward to feel his burning neck, where the racing of his pulse was easily discernible.

Again? Cicely was startled. The coughing spasms were not the only thing to afflict him? He had actually collapsed like this before? She knew he was not physically strong, not in the way most men of his age were. He was active enough, but did not indulge in jousting or any other truly strenuous, dangerous pastimes. She had thought it was because he took care not to endanger his life, but maybe it was also because he knew he was not vigorous enough. 'He is often ill like this?' she asked.

'It is no concern of yours,' was the ungracious reply.

Cicely was anxious. 'I wanted to send for his physicians, Lady Margaret, but he forbade it, and so I sent word to you.'

'You were correct,' Margaret replied grudgingly.

'Together we can manage him to his bed, my lady', Cicely ventured, 'and loosen his clothes, for he needs to be cool again.'

'Well, it seems you are still accustomed to helping him undress, Lady Welles.'

'Yes, Lady Derby, I am. My closeness to the king has never ceased. Clearly that is something else you have failed to observe.'

'Something *else*?'

'You failed to see he was ill tonight. I saw and I followed him here. He was conscious when I arrived, and he admitted me, so I have not entered these rooms without his permission, should you imagine I did,' she added.

Margaret flushed, and was on the offensive again. 'You have no shame!'

'I have the king's affection, Lady Margaret, and for that I feel no shame.' *Oh, but you do, Cicely Plantagenet, you do!*

'Even though he is your sister's husband?'

'That fact does not seem to concern *him*, my lady.'

Margaret flushed again. 'Men are men, Lady Welles, so the blame lies with you.'

'As it lay with you for consummating your marriage when you were too young? You were a child temptress?'

'How dare you!' Margaret quivered from head to toe.

'I dare while you do, my lady.' Cicely confronted her. 'I had not realized how much of a harlot you are.'

'If lying with your son makes me a harlot, Lady Margaret, then so be it. But now, perhaps we should not claw each other, but help him?'

Margaret simmered, but indicated they should try to raise Henry by supporting him under his arms. It was a struggle, because they were both small women, but he was slender enough, and not too heavy.

He was totally oblivious, and a dead weight as they struggled to get him across to the archway that led into his bedchamber.

'No doubt you have been here with him as well,' Margaret said, gritting her teeth as they hauled him up on to the high mattress.

His breathing was husky, and when he lay there at last, propped against the rich pillows, Margaret gave in to her maternal anxiety, tears filling her eyes as she pressed her hands to her mouth. 'Oh, Henry, my son,' she whispered, the words muffled against her fingers.

'Lady Margaret, it is clear from what you have already said that the king has been like this before. What is it? What illness does he have? I have seen him coughing, but this is not the same.'

'You seem almost concerned, my lady.'

Cicely looked at her. 'Because I am.'

'Why? Do you hope he suffers for the defeat of your uncle and the torture of John of Gloucester?'

'I am not of the House of York in this, my lady. Your son is my lover, and I have given him my word to keep his secret.'

'Since when could the House of York be trusted to keep its word?'

'My uncle was the House of York, my lady, and you could *never* accuse him of dishonour, because honour was one thing he possessed in plenty. You, who know more of deceit than any other of God's creatures, gave Richard III *every* cause to find you guilty of treason, but he never once raised his hand against a woman. You were a Medusa to him. And *you* carp about the House of York keeping its word? You astound me. And is this *really* an appropriate time to resort to such pettiness? I have made a promise to the king, and if it is good enough for him, then it should also be good enough for you.' Cicely was astonished by her own audacity, but she was angry, and dismayed that Margaret of *all* people was failing to act in what was a hazardous situation for Henry.

Too outraged and insulted to reply, Margaret busied herself by unfastening Henry's cloth-of-gold doublet. But then her emotions steadied. 'This distemper has beset him before,' she said, more evenly. 'His lungs are not strong. He is strong enough in everything but this. But, if it *should* be fatal, it will be many years yet before it prevents him from ruling effectively. For now, he is still young and fit in every other way, and it only affects him in the cooler months. Battles are seldom, if ever, fought in the winter, and there is nothing wrong with Henry in the summer. So his illness is not yet of any interest to your Yorkist friends.'

Cicely went to dip a fresh napkin in the water bowl on a side table and returned to wipe Henry's face gently.

Margaret watched her. 'And where does my half-brother rank in your overflowing heart, my lady?'

'As my beloved husband. Oh, do not smirk like that. I do love Jon, very much indeed, but the king matters to me as well.'

Margaret straightened from undoing the many little fastenings of Henry's doublet. 'So, you would have me believe you came here as an angel of mercy, and *not* for a Hallowtide dally?'

Cicely continued to wipe Henry's face, and then his exposed chest, from which she could feel the heat of his fever. She could also hear how he wheezed. 'Lady Margaret, whatever the king may wish, I think you have to send for his physician immediately. He cannot be left without any assistance. You have made no promise to him, so *please* send for whichever physician is considered the most discreet.'

Margaret looked at her son again and then nodded. 'You are right. Master Rogers should come, for he is both physician and astrologer, and I know the king holds him in great trust.'

Trust? That did not sound like Henry, Cicely thought, wishing she could glance down and find his eyes upon her, alight with amusement about some small thing. But his eyes were closed, and he did not move at all, except to breathe heavily.

Margaret looked at her. 'Tell a guard to summon Master Rogers,' she said, asserting her authority.

Cicely did not argue but went quickly to the door and instructed the same guard who had brought Margaret. Then she poured a small cup of wine and returned to sit on the edge of the bed. Putting her arms around Henry's neck, she gently tilted him in order to offer the cup to his lips. 'Henry? Sip this, for it will help make you feel better.'

His lips moved a little and his eyelids fluttered, so she knew he was aware of something. 'Please, Henry,' she pleaded. 'Try for me.'

His eyes opened a little. 'Cicely?'

'Please, sweetheart,' she begged, using the endearment for the first time, and doing so in front of his mother.

'I had to sink to this to drag a loving word from you?' He only just managed to speak, but it was with his endearing humour.

She smiled. 'Do not expect it too often. Now, *please*, take a drink.' She touched the cup to his lips again, and he drank a little. Two mouthfuls, maybe, no more, but then he closed his eyes again.

She laid his head gently back and set the goblet aside. Not caring that Margaret was there, she ran her fingers gently through his hair, to cool his head a little. He was so unknowing and without defence.

Margaret watched. 'Perhaps you should leave now, my lady,' she said coldly.

'As you wish, my lady.'

Cicely started to get up, but Henry seemed to have heard, and roused a little. 'No. Stay.' He did not open his eyes, and his hand moved as if seeking hers. So she linked his fingers. She looked at Margaret, ready to defy her, but Henry's mother did not say anything.

He coughed a little, that dreadful hollow sound that Cicely remembered from Richard's queen.

At last Margaret perceived her anxiety to be no act. 'He recovers each time, Cicely.'

'But is each time worse than the one before?'

'Not as yet. I do not think it is true consumption, just a weakness of his chest.'

Cicely was ironic. 'And to think it was Richard who was so slight and seemingly delicate, yet I do not recall him ever being indisposed.'

Much later, when Master Rogers had attended Henry, who slept comfortably, Cicely returned secretly to her own rooms, candlelit and warmed by the dying fire in the small hearth, and found Jack waiting. Mary had admitted him, and stood nearby anxiously, but Cicely knew it was not the maid's fault. Jack de la Pole could wheedle his way past any woman.

As Mary went to her own bedchamber, Jack smiled at Cicely. 'I promised I would see you again later, sweetheart. And with Tudor clearly indisposed, I thought we should take the chance to enjoy some time alone together. I hardly imagine he is interested in my whereabouts at the moment.'

His smile. She felt its warmth, even its caress, and her loyalty to him was suddenly of too much importance. She had information about Henry that Jack should know, even if it would not help him yet. But she had made a vow to Henry.

'Is something wrong?' Jack looked at her.

She hesitated, divided by conscience. But she was not

divided by love. When it came to love, this cousin was all that truly mattered. 'Jack, if you had made a vow on Richard's honour, would you stand by it?'

His lips parted. 'Of course. What manner of question is *that*?'

'I have made such a vow, Jack. So look at me. Read me. What is it that you wish to know?'

His shrewd dark eyes searched her face.

'Read me,' she repeated softly.

'About Henry?'

She gave the merest nod.

'Now is the time to show how very close we are in every way, mm?'

'Yes.'

He leaned back against a table and folded his arms lightly. His amethyst ring caught the candlelight. 'He is ill?'

She gave a barely perceptible nod.

'Seriously? I hope.'

She pursed her lips.

'Not seriously.'

She held his eyes intently and could feel his concentration.

'So, not yet, but it may become so?'

Again the tiny nod.

'Well, he looks thin and pale, and has certainly lost weight recently. He sometimes seems older than his years, and almost frail.' He studied her again. 'Is it a steady decline? No, I can read not. Possibly progressive? I see I am right. Well, he seems hearty enough in the summer. So, it is periodic. Possibly the cooler months?'

She nodded.

'And when it strikes, it lays him very low?'

Another nod.

He gazed at her. 'When he coughed you were almost scalded, sweetheart. You were close to Richard's queen, and I know how it distressed you. Do you suspect Henry has consumption?'

She looked at him, recalling how she had felt to see Henry so ill. She felt guilty for betraying him.

Jack smiled a little. 'Poor Cicely, you cannot help liking him, can you?'

'I have affection for him, Jack, but I *love* you. Never suspect otherwise.'

'I know, sweetheart. So, Henry has some consumptive ailment that strikes him down in the cooler months, and which *may* be progressive, or may not. Whatever, the winter is when he is likely to be weak. Am I right?' He saw her nod. 'And when it strikes him, he really is incapacitated?'

She nodded again, trying not to picture Henry as he lay on the bed, his hand reaching out in search of hers.

Jack straightened from the table and came to embrace her. 'Oh, sweetheart, you are so torn. Your poor little heart is too soft.'

'But I am of York, Jack, and I will *never* forget it. Henry knows it too.'

'Does he? Then his love for you is clearly very great. I would never have thought Henry Tudor had such intense emotions.'

She pulled from his arms a little unhappily. 'I have broken my word to him, and wronged Richard's memory.'

'Jesu, sweetheart, look at me.' Jack made her face him again and then raised her chin. 'What have you said to me? Mm? Nothing. I merely jumped to conclusions. That is *all*. You have not sullied Richard's name or broken the terms promised to Henry, which, I imagine, were not to tell anyone anything.'

'Or write it, draw it . . .'

'And you have not. Not one betraying word passed your lips, sweetheart. I love you, Cicely, and you love me. Our lineage is close, we are close in spirit and in heart, close in *every* way, and so I was simply able to infer everything. So rest easy, my darling. You have kept faith.'

'But—'

He put a finger to her lips. 'No, sweetheart. No buts. Besides, we waste time now. We are alone, we need to make love, and the bed awaits. Can anything be more important?'

She smiled. 'No,' she answered softly, closing her eyes as he pulled her into his arms to kiss her. Such a seductive and loving kiss. It banished everything. Except him.

# Chapter Seven

ON A WET night late in November, when driving rain stung like ice and water trickled everywhere, riders dismounted in the confines of the Tower. Cicely was among them.

Hooded and cloaked, she was helped down to the shining cobbles, where torches reflected in puddles. Shivering, she watched Henry dismount. He too was hooded and cloaked, and was agile again as he swung his leg over the pommel and jumped down. He should not have come out in such weather, she thought, for he had still to fully recover.

He took her hand and led her down some steps to a small, arched doorway. The night was banished as the door was closed behind them, and the Tower folded over them like a stone shroud. More torches flared within, the flames leaping against the ancient stone walls, and servants hurried forward to take Henry's hood, cloak and gauntlets. He wore black velvet, and tonight seemed taller, leaner and starker than ever. His long hair clung to the velvet, and he flicked it back as he watched the servants attend Cicely.

Then all the servants withdrew, except one, who waited at a discreet distance to conduct them through the warren of passages. Henry turned to Cicely. 'Do you wish me to forbid this, even now?'

'No.' But she knew in her heart that the real John of Gloucester had gone forever, leaving only a living statue.

Henry was aware of her hesitance. 'I am gravely at fault, not only because of my shameful guilt for what has been done to John of Gloucester, but also for giving in to you. Refusing you can be like denying morning the light to follow darkness. You can still change your mind, sweetheart, and I dearly wish you would, for it can only be distressing for you.'

'If I do not see him, I will wonder for the rest of my life if I could have helped him.'

Henry rubbed his eyebrow for a moment, and then nodded. 'So be it.' He snapped his fingers at the waiting man, who bowed low and led them through the great fortress that was built to be a terrifying symbol of Norman power. It was still a terrifying symbol of royal power.

Their steps echoed on the uneven flags, and more bracket torches smoked and fluttered. It was the same part of the Tower as that other room where her father had murdered his brother. She shivered as they mounted winding steps, passing narrow slit windows through which the wind whistled unimpeded.

A jailer waited at a door at the top, and his keys jingled as he fell to his knees on seeing Henry.

'Your Majesty.'

Only then, at the very last second, did Cicely's steps falter and stop. She could see the door at the top, and the candlelight creeping from beneath it, but suddenly could not go further.

'Cicely?' Henry touched her.

The torchlight shone on her tears. 'Please tell me you hold him in comfort, not a room like that other.'

'He is in comfort, in an apartment, as befits his birth.' There was relief in Henry's response as he sensed she could not proceed. 'Illegitimate or not, he is a king's son and grandson. My conscience—and my affection for

91

you—would not permit me to incarcerate him in a cell. What I did at the very outset of my reign I would certainly not do now.'

'Please, take me from here.' She was deeply ashamed of her cowardice. *Forgive me, John. Forgive me, Richard.*

He shook his head at the jailer, and then ushered her back down the steps. He led her well away from the steps before halting to put his arms around her and hold her close. She buried her face against the costly black velvet of his doublet.

He stroked soft skin at the nape of her neck. 'It is the wisest thing, sweetheart.'

She closed her eyes. If it had not been for her, and the effect she had upon this unsettling king, John of Gloucester would still be as hale as Jack.

Henry was affected too, perhaps more than he realized. 'Hate me for what I did to John, sweetheart, but *never* desert me. If you wish to be avenged for my triumph over your House, and for everything else I have done to you, then deserting me is the way to do it. I need you so much that the breaking of my heart would be so very easy for you. I should not confess it to you, but I do, because I know I can trust you. I know that if you are prepared to vow to me upon Richard's honour, then you are true to me. You, of all God's creatures, would *never* be untruthful with his name.'

She felt sick, and when he raised her lips to his, the kiss he gave was so loving and gentle that she hated herself still more. And so she returned his embrace with all the fervour she could. It was a vicious circle, the more her guilt, the more she tried to reassure him, and the more he responded, the more guilt she felt, and so it went on. It would be so very much easier if she felt nothing for Henry Tudor, but she did, and there seemed nothing she could do to prevent it.

She pulled away at last. 'Take me from here, Henry. Please.'

He put a hand to her chin and made her look up at him. 'Where do you wish to go? Back to Pasmer's Place?'

'No, not there. With you. I want to stay with you. *With* you, in every way, until tomorrow. Please.' She needed to have his comfort, and to give hers in return. Atonement? Maybe. Yes . . . probably.

His thumb moved gently against her. 'Then I will take you to Westminster. It will be too crowded and public at Greenwich, and more scandalized whispering is the last thing you—or I—need now.'

'You will be with me?'

'Of course. You should not need to ask.'

He put his lips gently to hers again, a gentle solace that made her weep in earnest. Remorse so engulfed her that she could hardly bear it, but her final loyalty would always be with Jack. It could never be otherwise.

Henry held her tightly for a moment, sensing her distress, but wrongly attributing its cause to John of Gloucester. 'Are you able to leave?'

As she nodded, he took her towards the arched entrance through which they had arrived. Then, having donned their outdoor clothes, they returned to the windswept night, but almost immediately something inexplicable made her turn towards a shadowy corner where there was only one torch. Someone stood there. He stepped forward, into the torchlight, a slight figure with a bearing that affected her even on such a night. She gazed at him. 'Richard?' she whispered.

She saw him so clearly. The rain and wind did not seem to touch him, for his dark chestnut hair fell thickly to his shoulders without blowing. As always, the golden embroidery on his grey velvet doublet glittered in the light from the flames; he was magnetic, bewitching, adored and commanding. His effect upon her was effortless. He was the king, the one true King of England, and she worshipped him.

Henry ceased to matter and the dismal night was of no consequence as she moved hesitantly towards the corner. 'Richard?' Her steps quickened. 'Forgive me for everything!' she cried, thinking she saw reproach in his eyes.

He held out his hand, but as she touched him and breathed the costmary on his clothes, there was suddenly only the rain-swept air and empty night. It was too much. Distraught, and drowning in grief and guilt, she sank to her knees in the rain, her face hidden in her hands. She wanted Richard to still be here. She wanted—begged for—his love and understanding. But tonight he gave her nothing.

Henry did not take her to Westminster with him, nor indeed did he stay with her, but instructed two of his men to accompany her back to Pasmer's Place. He said nothing to her, but his face was set and his manner suddenly very cold. She was not too overcome to be unaware of the severity of the change in him, and as he rode off with the remainder of his horsemen she knew how very much she had alienated him.

She struggled in vain to collect herself. Tonight had been disastrous, and she deeply regretted ever pleading for such a favour of Henry. If only she had listened to Jack, and to Henry himself. Instead, she had persisted until she was actually at John's door. Now she had deeply offended Henry. Deeply. In front of him and those accompanying him, she had reaffirmed her undying adoration for Richard Plantagenet. And just after Henry had confessed so much of himself to her. And made plain his trust.

Emotion still wrapped tightly around her as Henry's men left her standing in the middle of the courtyard at Pasmer's Place. The unforgiving downpour continued, and the wind whined accusingly around the eaves. She did not care, but raised her face to the stormy night, welcoming the sting and cleansing cold of the rain.

It was only then, as she finally turned to enter the

house, that she saw a distinctive white horse tethered in a corner, beneath the low, overhanging thatch of a lean-to shelter, well out of the weather. It was Jack's mount, Héraut, so fine and desirable a stallion that it was well known as his, but even in the windswept darkness she could see that its saddle was very shabby and nondescript. Nor, when she looked again, was the horse itself as well groomed as it should be.

After hastening to her rooms, for Mary to help her out of her wet clothes, she went to the candlelit parlour, looking neat in a cream velvet gown, her hair loose. Jack stood by the fire, a thigh-booted foot on the fender, one hand on the stone mantel, a goblet of Jon's wine in the other. He was gazing into the fire and turned as she entered.

He wore a quilted peach-coloured doublet and dark brown hose, with a gold collar across his shoulders. The amethyst in his ring shone for a moment as he raised his wine to her. 'Greetings, Coz. I fear I have made fast and loose with your husband's best Rhenish.'

She smiled. 'I am sure Jon would not have minded while you were still merely my cousin. Now, however, I believe he would take exception to such a liberty.'

'No doubt. I saw you from the window, left standing in the courtyard by Henry's men. You were—are—upset. I could tell. Why were you simply left there? Why only two guards? Is Henry displeased with you?'

'I did not know I was being observed. Yes, he is displeased with me.' She went to slip her arms around his waist, rest her head against him and tell him what had happened.

He held her. 'Oh, Cicely, why can you not see that *you* raise Richard? He does not really come to you.'

'He simply appeared out of the darkness, and was so very real that I believed it *was* him. And I believed he accused me. I could not help it, Jack, and now I have hurt Henry and maybe he will not forgive it.'

'He will. His cock twitches and swells at the mere thought of you. As does mine.' Jack leaned back a little in order to look at her. 'You cannot be rid of Tudor that easily, dearling, no matter how you wish it.'

She gave a reluctant smile. 'Maybe you are right. I do not know. But yes, he really does love me. I know that now, tonight more than ever. And he *trusts* me. He really believes that because I swore on Richard's honour, I am true beyond doubt.'

'And your conscience has become a great weight? Well, do not permit it to be. Henry Tudor was responsible for Richard's death, *never* forget it.'

He coiled her hair around his fingers and eased her head back until her lips were presented to his. His mouth was tender, adoring, rich and infinitely knowing. He made the moment so erotic and tantalizing that she felt her anxiety melting away into the familiar stirrings of unstoppable desire.

Her hands explored his back through the ornate quilting of his doublet. He had a way of kissing her, a gentle but urgent way, so filled with love and care that she could not help but want to be joined to him again. But not here! Not in Jon's house!

The barrier was suddenly there, and she pulled from his arms. 'No, Jack—'

He closed his eyes and exhaled slowly as he sought to collect himself. 'Your damned fool of a husband, I take it?'

'Yes. Forgive me, Jack, but I cannot betray him under his own roof. Not when I have asked Henry to summon him back to London.'

'I trust irksome Sir Jon will not arrive tonight?'

'No. He is to return for Christmas.'

'And in the meantime, you will commit adultery elsewhere, but not here?' His smile deepened. 'Well, I suppose there is sweet reason in there. Somewhere.'

'You are a man and cannot understand why such things

mean so much to a woman.' She remembered using very similar words to Henry.

Jack took her hand and raised the palm to his lips, dwelling over it for a long moment and then entwining her fingers warmly in his. 'I may not understand entirely, but I respect completely.'

'I do not tease or play games, Jack,' she said anxiously.

'I know.' He released her and went to the window, which was lashed with rain as a new breeze swept up from the Thames. 'The tide is changing,' he murmured absently.

'Why are you here, Jack? Not simply to see me, I know *that.'*

'Now she stamps upon this swain's heart,' he murmured.

'You have brought Héraut, but have made him look as undistinguished as you can, and I do not doubt that tonight's weather suits your purpose for him, whatever it is.'

'I shall have to wear a helm when I am with you, to prevent you from stealing right into my head.' But he smiled. 'I am taking Héraut to the Mermaid tavern.'

'The one in Gough Alley? Between here and Three Cranes?'

'Yes. To be taken north in due course, as a red herring to Henry.'

'What do you mean?'

'Héraut is associated with me, and it suits me to have him out of sight here in London. Closer to the time, I intend to send him north, with a group of "merchants" who are actually my men. They will have money with them, and my white hobby falcon from Sheriff Hutton. To all intents and purposes it will seem that *I* intend to go north as well. In fact I will flee to Burgundy to join Francis, Robert, and numerous others, and thence to Dublin.'

'In support of the Earl of Warwick.'

'The rightful King Edward VI. Yes.'

'And what horse will you ride in the meantime?'

He clearly bit back a witty rejoinder, and she understood it well enough to give him a cross look. 'If you *dare* say that, Jack de la Pole, you may consider yourself to have had the last such ride!'

'Forgive me, sweetheart, but to be fair, I *did* resist.' He came to kiss her cheek.

'Is there still nothing I can say to turn you from all this?'

'I must do it, my darling. The white rose should be restored to the throne.'

She embraced him again. Their lips came together and she hung upon the kiss. She wanted to be with him as she should have been with Richard. She had been parted from Richard against her will, because it was what *he* wanted; now she would be parted from Jack, because it was what *he* wanted. What about the things *she* wanted?

He extricated himself. 'Sweetheart, if you want me to make love to you beneath Jon Welles' roof regardless of finer feelings, you are going the right way about it. Have a little pity, I beg you. I am only human.'

'I love you so much.'

'Then you must wait until we are elsewhere,' he said, smiling. 'And I will have to handle my own problem.'

'Just do not let any whore handle it for you.'

He laughed, but then glanced at the windows as the bells of London sounded midnight. 'It is best I go now anyway, for I have someone to meet.'

'Who?'

'That, sweetheart, is for me to know and you to wonder about.'

'Just be careful.' Suddenly, for no apparent reason, she remembered the poem she had found in one of Richard's books at Sheriff Hutton. 'Jack, there is something I want to say to you. Richard wrote a poem when he was young, and it says everything of how I feel about you:

*To be without you is to fade a little within,*
*To not hear your voice is to lose the sweetness of music,*
*To forfeit your smile is to be plunged into darkness,*
*To never feel your touch is to lose all sense of being,*
*To know you have gone forever is to steal away all joy.*


That is how I feel too, Jack. I would forfeit all joy if I lost you.'

He came to her again and crushed her into his embrace, kissing her hair and then her lips, and when he looked down into her eyes, she saw tears in his. 'Cicely, I return your love tenfold, never forget it. And you will *never* lose me.'

She summoned a bright smile to lighten the moment. 'So, sir, if I had let you dibble me a moment since, it would have been a hasty matter, a brief passing of the time until you go to your meeting? Shame on you.'

'My hasty matters would still take you to paradise, my lady. I do not have my wicked reputation undeservedly. Besides, do I need to remind you that I was here some time, waiting for your return?'

'So it is *my* fault? How did that happen? But I will forgive you anyway.'

'Farewell for the moment, sweetheart. I will see you again very soon, you have my word upon it. Your bed at Greenwich still welcomes me, I think.'

She quelled the urge to again plead with him to be careful, and to clutch his sleeve to prevent him from leaving at all.

# Chapter Eight

WHEN JACK LEFT, Cicely went to the window to watch him cross the courtyard to where Héraut waited beneath the lean-to. He was hooded and cloaked, and might have been anyone. Certainly he did not seem like the Earl of Lincoln, nor did his horse give him away on such a terrible night. Even through the window, and above the racket of the weather, she heard the clatter of hooves as he rode out into St Sithe's Lane and thence towards the Thames. Her heart was heavy as he passed out of sight. He risked so very much in this venture.

She was about to turn away when she saw a stealthy figure hasten past the gates in Jack's wake. The figure's hood fell back, and Cicely recognized the whore who had been with him at the top of the Three Cranes steps. There was something about the girl, the way she glanced furtively back over her shoulder, and then hurried on after Jack. She was following him!

Jack was engaged upon something secret and dangerous, and the whore did not behave as if she followed him simply to complete the consummation interrupted on that other occasion. Had there been an ulterior motive for engaging him then, an attempt to be close to him for something other than a matter of the flesh? Might she be in Henry's pay? Was such a conclusion too much of a leap? Alarm cut jaggedly through Cicely, and she had no intention of taking the chance.

She ran from the parlour, calling for Mary to bring a dry cloak and hood. Within moments, ignoring Mary's anxious protestations, and forbidding the maid to come too, she hurried out into St Sithe's Lane and, looping the train of her gown over her arm for more freedom and to keep it from dragging through the wet and grime of the street, she ran as fast as she could towards Gough Alley and the Mermaid tavern.

The rain stung her face and the wind gusted through the city streets, sucking almost spitefully between the taller buildings. Gutters and drains gurgled as water streamed from eaves, and there were puddles and rivulets everywhere, gradually coming together to cascade downhill in torrents towards Three Cranes and the Thames. Only the most strongly secured lanterns on the corners of buildings managed to defy the elements and stay alight, and there was hardly anyone about, only a detachment of mounted men-at-arms in Tudor livery, riding slowly in the direction of St Paul's. Cicely knew instinctively that they were not involved in anything that might concern Jack, but were simply on their way to whatever ordinary duty they had been allotted.

Crossing over empty Thames Street, where the cobbles were so water-washed they lost all form, she made her way quickly down an overhung street towards the river at Three Cranes. Everything was drenched, and her feet were cold and wet. The downpour soaked through her cloak and hood, but at least she could now see the whore ahead, if no sign of Jack and Héraut. He must already be at the Mermaid.

Reaching a corner, the whore halted to peer into the narrow alley that culminated in the popular Mermaid tavern. As the girl slipped out of sight, Cicely hurried to the corner behind her. Looking around it in the same way, she saw the whore's cloaked figure against the lanterns outside the tavern, from which emitted a great deal of noise and raucous male laughter. Drunken laughter, for the most part, and it seemed inordinately loud, as if the tavern were much closer than its actual twenty-five yards away. It was something to do with the shape of the alley, Cicely thought, astonished that she was actually able to hear fragments of mostly foul-mouthed conversation.

There was no sign of Jack, but she heard a horse whinnying from the stables at the rear of the tavern. Héraut? The whore hid behind a stack of four large tuns against the alley wall, almost next to the doorway. She could only be seen from Cicely's direction, not by anyone who emerged from the tavern.

Cicely was undecided what to do. Wait? Or go into the tavern to find Jack and warn him? That would not be easy, for only a certain type of woman entered such low places, and anyway she had a costly gown beneath her cloak and over her arm, which if observed would immediately arouse unwelcome interest. But even as she deliberated, Jack appeared in the narrow doorway, brightly lit from behind, the hood of his cloak flung back as he turned to the man who emerged with him.

The stranger, cloaked and as yet unhooded, moved into the full light of a lantern, and she saw that he was at least twice Jack's age, taller, with curling shoulder-length grey-blond hair and a short pale beard that merely coated his chin. His bearing was assured and he was well built, although without any of the thickness of middle age. His hair and cloak fluttered as he faced Jack. He was striking if not handsome, with a firm jaw and straight nose, and expressive eyes set beneath unexpectedly dark brows. As his cloak flapped wildly in the wind, she saw he was dressed plainly beneath. Not entirely due to a desire for anonymity, she thought, because he somehow seemed very at home in such clothing. In many ways he was the very opposite of Jack, who was always dashing and flamboyant.

Then, to Cicely's dismay, although Jack spoke quietly, his words were clearly audible above the noise of the tavern.

'So when is it to be, Tal?'

'It needs careful thought, my friend.'

The voice of the man called Tal was soft spoken, with a definite Welsh lilt. Another Welshman, she thought.

'I know we have the support of—' Jack turned away to face the tavern, and whatever he said was suddenly lost amid the other sounds.

The whore was straining to hear, and maybe she *could* from her position! Cicely reacted in a heartbeat. Still holding her gown up from the street, she ran noisily down the alley, calling out loudly. 'My lord! My lord! I knows I'm late, but I'm 'ere for you now!' she cried, disguising her voice.

Jack whirled about, his hand reaching defensively beneath his cloak for his dagger. His companion did the same. Cicely continued to run, and as she flung herself into Jack's arms, her hood fell back and he realized who she was. 'Jesu, Ci—'

She stopped him with a hearty buss, and then stood with her hands suggestively upon her hips, her head tilted saucily. '*Two* of you, sirs? Why, I'll be 'appy to accommodate you both, but I'll charge you twice, make no mistake of *that*!' She beamed at Tal, who looked at her as if she was the spawn of the Devil.

Jack went along with her immediately. 'Well, wench, we were just about to give up on you, were we not?' He gave his friend a reassuring nod.

The other relaxed visibly. 'It is never wise to give up on the fair sex,' he responded, managing a convincingly jocular tone.

He did not look it, but he was definitely Welsh, she

decided, or at least from somewhere along the Marches, and there was an intensity in his sharp eyes—green, she saw now—that quite commanded her attention. The wind sucked ferociously into the alley, dragging his cloak so violently that it lifted sufficiently for her to see that around his neck he wore a long gold chain from which hung a crucifix and a small, richly jewelled wheel of St Catherine. A man of piety?

But now was not the time to assess Jack's stranger. She gave Jack another resounding kiss, and then seized his hand. 'Come, I do not mind being out in the open, sir, but a *little* privacy is best when I go on my knees before you!'

'I am more than ready for such attentions from you, sweetheart,' he replied as she led him deliberately towards the tuns. As they neared, the whore bolted from her hiding place and fled down the alley and out into the street. Jack recognized her.

Relieved, Cicely looked urgently at him and his friend, making sure her back was towards the street. The whore might yet hear what she should not. 'No names! Do not say more in this place, Jack, because it echoes everything. I was at the end of the alley but could hear you quite clearly. The whore certainly could. Come, we must go out into the open, for she may still be listening.'

They moved out of the alley, and the wind and rain buffeted them as they emerged into the street. There was no sign of the whore, but she might be just out of sight in a doorway. The torrential rain sank through their clothes anew, chilling their skin. Their hair clung in rats' tails and their faces gleamed, but at least the lantern on the corner had given up its battle, leaving them in much more shadow.

She could feel the stranger's gaze turn towards her, assessing her as she assessed him. 'May I speak freely, Jack?' she asked, and when he nodded, she went on, 'You recognized the whore from the Three Cranes steps? Well, she followed you from Pasmer's Place. I saw her from the window. Was it a chance encounter that day at the quay? Or was she waiting for you?'

He thought. 'Well, I did not think it at the time, but yes, she was waiting, although how she knew I would go that way, I do not know.'

'You must have told someone. Think, Jack. Who was it?'

He thought again. 'A new page,' he said after a while. 'I sent him to advise my steward that I intended to call upon Lady Welles to see that she was well. The steward I would trust with my life, so it had to be the page. Sweet God, Henry's tentacles have reached into my own household! I would—I *have*—risked my life by trusting those immediately around me. Jesu.' He was clearly shaken, and she knew he was thinking of Richard, who had also trusted unwisely. Fatally. 'Well, the boy will be sent on his way, lucky not to have his hand severed at the wrist.' He caught Cicely close and kissed her on the lips. 'Thank you, sweetheart.'

'Jack de la Pole, if tonight's work is a sample of your discretion and secrecy, you are *not* going to triumph over Henry.'

'Do I not know it! Truly, we will be wiser from now on.'

The other man cleared his throat. 'Jack, are you going to introduce me, or leave me standing here like two left legs?'

Jack was apologetic. 'Forgive me, both of you. Tal, may I present my cousin, Lady Welles, once Lady Cicely Plantagenet, daughter of Edward IV, niece of Richard III.'

Tal removed his gauntlet to bow low over her hand. 'Your servant, my lady.' A particularly strong gust of wind almost snatched his words away completely.

She saw that he wore a handsome dark yellow topaz ring and for a moment she could smell cinnamon, warm and spicy, as she imagined the air of the Holy Land would be. But already the perfume had faded, because he drew away again. Another man to associate with a distinctive scent and a fine ring, she thought, sensing that, because of

Jack, she was going to know this man very well.

Then Jack made the second introduction. 'Cicely, this is my old friend . . .' He hesitated, and then finished, 'Taleisin ap Gruffydd.'

She saw a look of surprise cross Tal's face.

Jack continued, 'He and I are allies in this, so you may speak freely. And Tal, you may always trust this lady, for there is none stauncher to York.'

Cicely suspected that Jack had confided more about her, and felt suddenly defensive. So she addressed Tal rather pointedly. 'Staunch to York and to my cousin of Lincoln, even if I do lie with Henry Tudor.'

Tal held her gaze steadily. 'I know what you do, Lady Welles, and why you do it. Please be at ease in my presence, for I do not censure you.'

She was a little mollified, but no matter what he *said*, she sensed his concealed disapproval. The wearing of the crucifix and the Catherine wheel was indicative of his religiousness. He probably adhered to the very letter of the Bible, she thought, and might even have a prayer book with him now, as Henry's mother always did. What would he say if he knew she had also lain gladly with her own uncle, and borne him a son? She glanced at Jack. Surely he would not have betrayed *that* to this Welshman?

Jack felt the glance and drew her aside. 'Forgive me for telling Tal of your closeness to Henry, my darling, but there may come a time when I will *have* to think of using you to communicate direct to him. Tal is my right hand, and so I have confided your situation to him.' He caught her hand and squeezed it. 'But please, never think I would confide Leo's existence. I hold you in the highest regard, Cicely. If you had not been here tonight, Tal and I might well have given far too much information away. I will hide Héraut somewhere else now. With luck the whore will not have realized he was to be left at the Mermaid.'

He took her back to Tal. 'Tal, please take care of my lady

while I get my horse again. We dare not use this place now.' Then he hurried back into the alley.

Cicely felt awkward with Tal. She was aware of him in an uncomfortable way, not least because although he had a Welsh name and accent, with his blond hair and green eyes he simply did not *look* Welsh. There was something unsettling about him, as if he was not who he claimed to be. Yet Jack clearly trusted him implicitly.

Tal was conscious of her as well. 'What do you think of our venture, my lady?' he asked suddenly, watching her closely.

'I wish I could feel more confidence in it.'

'With all respect, Lady Welles, it is a well-planned rebellion that will put York back on the throne of England.'

'But you are Welsh, sir, how can it be in your interest to turn a Welshman off the throne?'

'Tudor may have Welsh blood, my lady, but he has done Wales no favours. The land of his birth is worse off now than it ever was under the House of York. And both your father and King Richard had higher-born Welsh blood in their veins than this dismal Tudor. There are many in Wales who deeply regret his triumph over your uncle.'

His voice was gentle and measured, and she felt that Taleisin ap Gruffydd was a thoughtful, highly educated man who considered everything very carefully before acting.

He spoke again. 'Please be so good as to call me Tal. It is best, and it saves you from wondering how to address me.'

'Very well. Tal.' She did not like being so familiar with him so quickly. He disturbed her unaccountably. 'Do you reside in London?' she asked, for something to say.

'I have a house here, but my lands and principal residence are in Berkshire. I am seldom there at the moment. It is best you do not know more, Lady Welles, for your sake, not mine,' he replied. 'The less you know, the less you can ever tell.'

'You think I would go to the king?' She prickled.

'No, I meant the less the king's torturers would be able to elicit from you.'

She stared at him.

He met her eyes. 'Forgive me, but if it came to a decision between Henry saving his own neck by being ahead of his enemies, or sparing yours because he loves you, I fear his own worthless carcass would come first.'

She did not say anything more. Hearing this stranger say such things brought the danger of this plot home to her as nothing else. She felt even colder than before, as if her blood had lost its vitality.

The rain chose then to become a cloudburst, and Tal drew her right against the wall and pulled her close, sheltering her as best he could. It was not an affectionate gesture, or one that suggested physical attraction, just the action of a man who wished to shield her as he could.

She was relieved when Jack led Héraut back to them and addressed Tal above the racket of the weather. 'I think we must abandon tonight.'

'Agreed.' Tal moved away from her. 'Second on the list, the day after tomorrow?'

'Yes.'

Tal turned to her. 'I bid you farewell for the moment, Lady Welles. I have a feeling we will see each other again.'

She shared that uncomfortable prospect, but gave him a smile of sorts. 'Farewell ... Tal.' She watched as the Welshman hastened away uphill towards Thames Street, and then disappeared towards the east.

Jack observed her mixed expression. 'What is it?'

'He said something that has made me finally realize how great a hazard you face, Jack.'

Héraut was restive in the storm, and Jack controlled him as he put an arm around her. 'It will end in victory, sweetheart. We cannot fail.'

'Who is he?'

'Tal? A friend.'

'You have never mentioned him. And what did he mean by "second on the list"?'

'It is not your concern, sweetheart.' He put a finger beneath her chin and lifted her lips to kiss her.

For a few seconds the stormy night ceased to matter. They were engrossed in each other, lips joined, hearts beating together. Then he rested his forehead to hers. 'I will take you home now, and then remove myself to the respectability of my own dwelling.'

He had recently taken a house in Gracechurch Street. 'It is a long way on a night like this,' she said.

'Are you offering me a bed for the night?' he asked, smiling.

'No. Having you sleep at Pasmer's Place would offend Jon and incense Henry.'

'Then I must toil my lonely little way home in the cold, wet and dark.' He laughed at her face. 'Oh, dear, I cannot believe you are taken in by such pathetic male whimpering. I am quite capable of hying my hide back to my own bed, in which I will lie totally alone, I swear.'

'There is not much I could say if you went to bed with six whores.'

'The words "well done", and "my God, what endurance!" might suffice.' He lifted her effortlessly on to Héraut, and then mounted behind her, his arm firmly around her waist. He kicked his heels and urged the horse up in the direction of St Sithe's Lane, and she was glad that the rain hid how many tears she wept for this sweetest of cousins, and the increasing danger in which he put himself with each new moment of this plot.

They both glanced back several times, but there did not seem to be anyone following. The weather must have finally driven Henry's creature to ground.

# Chapter Nine

CICELY AWOKE LATE the following morning to find it was still raining, but the wind had lessened to a gentle moan around the eaves. A good fire flickered in the hearth, and when she turned her head towards it she saw Mary seated in the chair, fast asleep.

For a moment she could only think of what had happened with Jack, and the mysterious Tal, but then her thoughts went back to a little earlier the night before, and being with Henry at the Tower. A sinking feeling overtook her, and she curled up tightly in the bed, trying to drive it away. But it persisted, and she was afraid.

'Are you well, my lady?' Mary had awakened and come to the bedside.

'I . . . think so.' Cicely uncurled and pulled herself up as the maid arranged the pillows behind her.

'Perhaps you should not get up at all today, my lady. You were out until so very late, and were so cold and wet. Twice. I fear you may get an ague.'

'I will be well enough, Mary. I am certainly warm and dry now.'

'Yes, my lady.' The maid spoke on an odd note, and Cicely looked quickly at her.

'Something is wrong?'

'A royal messenger came not long since. A spoken instruction from the king himself that you are not to go to court unless summoned.'

Cicely's heart sank still further. 'I see. Thank you, Mary.' Now Lady Welles really was excluded, because defying her sister was one thing, but defying the king's express order was out of the question.

'Do you wish me to bring you something?' Mary asked. 'Something to restore you? A cordial, perhaps? I have one of my aunt's recipes.'

'Mistress Kymbe's recipe?' Cicely smiled, for elderly but deaf Katherine Kymbe was the midwife who had delivered Leo. She was also a wise woman, with knowledge of arts, herbs, poisonous plants and all manner of other things, including restoratives and similar potions. 'Then I am sure it will be just the very thing. And some bread and honey, if you please.'

'Yes, my lady.'

'Please bring my robe. I will sit by the fire.'

'Yes, my lady. Oh . . .'

'Yes?' Cicely sat on the edge of the bed.

'A letter from my brother arrived for me an hour ago.'

'Why are you telling me? Is something wrong with my son?' Cicely asked, alarm igniting in an instant.

'No, my lady, not at all. But Tom does write of him, and wishes me to let you read the letter. I . . . think it is actually for you, although Tom would not presume to actually address it as such.'

'I would not be offended, for I like your brother.'

Mary assisted her with her warmest robe, and ushered her to the comfortable chair by the fire. Then she took the letter from her purse, removed the final page, and gave the others to Cicely. 'I will bring your refreshment, my lady. Is there anything else?'

'Not yet. Thank you.' Cicely smiled at her. 'What would I do without you, Mary Kymbe? You are worth a hundred

111

of the queen's ladies-in-waiting.'

'And you are worth a hundred queens,' Mary replied, smiling as she went out.

Cicely began to read Tom Kymbe's letter, which was written in a surprisingly elegant hand. Although why she should be surprised, she did not know, because Tom Kymbe was a gentleman, and far from being rough.

*My dearest sister. Greetings.*

*I would have you know that all is well here. Our aunt thrives, and has much occupied herself with Leo, who also prospers. He is now nine months old, and a fine boy. He has grey eyes and dark chestnut hair, and so is not at all like the Kymbes. I believe he takes after Felice's uncle.*

Cicely smiled. How carefully Tom Kymbe worded it, telling her so clearly that her son took after Richard. Felice was the mother of Tom's dead son. She had died in childbirth, and her baby soon after. Now Leo had been given the safety of that baby's identity.

*He crawls now, and has a lusty voice when he wishes for something to be done. I believe Felice must have been higher born than she realised, for to be sure her child has imperious moments. But he is also affectionate, loving nothing more than to be fussed and cuddled. I love him dearly, and my only regret is that Felice cannot see and hold him for herself.*

Cicely swallowed. Tom was telling her everything she wished to know, and she was indebted to him for it. She had liked him from the moment they met, and nothing she had heard of him since had changed her mind. The Kymbe family were all, without exception, truly admirable and honest.

*Leo eats well, even though he is small. By that I mean that he is small for his age, but then his mother was as well, and so was the uncle after whom Leo so clearly takes. He will be a handsome boy too. His health leaves nothing to be desired. He simply flourishes in every way. He will be a credit to his parents, of that I am sure.*

*Sir Jon Welles has been here this last week—*

Cicely broke off. Jon was at Friskney?

*—to attend to some negotiation with the Earl of Lincoln's agents concerning a disputed watermill. It is not a truly serious matter, merely an awkward clause that casts doubt upon to whom the miller must submit his dues. Neither Sir Jon nor the earl, both being rich men, will die of starvation if such a small matter goes against him. But the law is the law, and must be adhered to.*

*Sir Jon is perhaps a little thinner than he was, but his temper is even and his humour still sharp. He has shown an interest in Leo. Perhaps he regards him as the boy he and his lady lost. Certainly he is anxious to provide Leo with whatever I may not be able to. He is a very good lord.*

Cicely smiled. Her disloyalty with Henry had clearly not impaired Jon's sense of duty. He had promised to watch over Leo as his own son, and that was what he was doing. Could she have ever expected otherwise? No, because Sir Jon Welles was all honour.

*I cannot speak of Lord Lincoln, who holds Friskney. I have never met or even seen him, although I understand he once dined here with our father. He is of the House of York, of course, which cannot always be a recommendation in these parts, but to my knowledge he has never been unjust.*

113

Cicely paused again, this time to wonder what sort of lord Jack was to those whose wellbeing was in his hands. He was her dear cousin and she loved him in all ways, but she saw a different Jack de la Pole than perhaps the likes of Tom Kymbe. She smiled. It would be very hard to imagine Jack as anything other than a just lord.

She wondered why Tom had gone out of his way to mention Jack. Maybe it was because Jon had mentioned him? Yes, because he liked her cousin, and if Jack held Friskney, Jon was bound to speak of him to Tom. She read on.

*There is one thing I hesitate to mention concerning Sir Jon, and that is—*

To Cicely's annoyance, that was all she could read, because Mary had detached the final page. Why remove it? What, exactly, had Tom written next? Clearly something his sister did not think Lady Welles should read.

Mary chose that moment to return with a tray, and Cicely eyed her immediately. 'What is on the last page, Mary?'

'Oh, only silly family matters, my lady.' But the maid flushed.

'No, Mary, because Tom was about to relate something concerning Sir Jon.'

'It was nothing,' the maid said again, while trying to avoid her mistress's eyes as she set the tray gently on the little table beside the chair.

'Please, Mary. I have to read it. Tom meant me to read it.'

Mary drew a heavy breath and then reluctantly surrendered the final page. 'I am sure it is nothing, my lady. Tom must have misunderstood.'

Cicely took the page and read the final paragraph.

*There is one thing I hesitate to mention concerning Sir Jon, and that is he is not alone here, but has brought*

114

*a lady with him. Perhaps not a lady, exactly, because she is Lucy Talby's younger sister, and you know my opinion of that hag. This woman is named Judith, and is far more beautiful than Lucy. I cannot mistake the nature of her dealings with Sir Jon, for she is clearly his mistress, as her elder sister was before her. They share a bedchamber. Lady Welles should not be in London, for she, I know beyond doubt, would soon see off this unworthy creature. Lady Welles should be with her husband.*

Cicely was stricken, but knew she had no right to be. She had not been faithful to Jon—even less faithful now, with Jack as well as Henry—so why should he not be unfaithful?

But the feeling of unreasonable hurt was intense.

As if that day had not already been hurtful enough, fate now dealt Cicely another blow, this time in the form of an unannounced visit from Bess.

Cicely was trying to write another conciliatory letter to Jon, although it was now more difficult than ever, when the sound of Mary's running footsteps interrupted her. The maid halted in the doorway, clearly disconcerted. 'My lady? The . . . the queen is here.'

Cicely stared at her. 'The *queen*?' She had been so engrossed in her writing that she had not heard.

'Yes, my lady. She wishes to speak with you in private.'

'Then, please conduct her here, Mary. And see to it that suitable refreshment is prepared. The very best quality, do you understand? This is my lord's house and he must not be shamed.'

Mary bobbed a curtsey and hastened away again, leaving Cicely to wonder why on earth Bess would come to Pasmer's Place. Surely she would have enjoyed the authority of summoning her sister to Greenwich? Or perhaps she knew Henry had excluded Lady Welles, and had come to gloat. Yes, that might well be it.

Cicely got up slowly, smoothing her powdery golden velvet gown and praying she looked more composed than she felt. There was no time to think of a headdress. It seemed she stood there an age before footsteps returned. Mary opened the door and stood aside for Bess to sweep grandly into the parlour in a flurry of peacock blue.

Cicely sank to her knees, and remained there while servants brought fresh wine and food. Then, when they had withdrawn, and the door was finally closed, Bess spoke coldly. 'It pleases me that you are once again obliged to skulk away here, Lady Welles.'

There was no answer to give. Cicely kept her eyes upon the floor.

'So, Henry has had enough of you? I believe he has ordered you to stay away from court.'

Cicely did not raise her head, or offer anything that might be construed as insolence.

'What were you and Henry doing at Winchester? Look up at me, curse you! I wish to know the details.'

Surprised, Cicely did look up. 'But . . . you know, surely?'

'I have not demeaned myself by asking others, but now I order *you* to tell me.'

'It was a kiss, that is all.'

'All? Your husband left you because of it, so it must have been far more.'

Cicely shook her head. 'Only a kiss,' she said again.

'Then it was clearly not a mild peck.'

'That is right.'

Bess went to the table to read what Cicely had written to Jon. 'Oh, dear, how you abase yourself. Does your Lincolnshire lordling really mean that much to you?'

'Yes, he does.'

'Then perhaps you should have thought of that before you seduced *my* husband.'

Cicely did not respond.

'Why have you done this, my lady?' Bess asked. 'Why, when you had already had Richard, did you lie with Henry as well? *Henry*, the man responsible for Richard's death!'

'You would not wish to hear my reason. Truly.'

'Oh, but I do, sister mine. I want to know *everything*. Beginning with the kiss that you have yet to explain.'

'Please do not ask me, Your Grace.'

'You will remain on your knees until you obey me in this. You no longer have Henry to hide behind, but are now at *my* mercy. If I show any.' Bess helped herself to some of Jon's wine, and then sat in the chair by the fire. 'Well?'

'You will not like what I say, Bess, so please, be very sure you wish to know.'

'No familiarity, madam, for I am the queen and you my subject.'

'Very well. Henry's kiss at Winchester was passionate, filled with desire, and he wished it to lead to consumma-tion. No, not there in that room, but later, in the bed I often shared with him at Winchester. I have told you before that he is a tender lover, and so he is, and I know so well how to please him. I enjoy his lovemaking, far more than I wish to, but I am a lost soul, is that not what Mother once said of me? Among other even less complimentary things. Oh, I was forgetting, you do not like Mother either, and refuse to have her anywhere near you. My, how difficult it soon will be to find anyone of your blood to be friendly with.'

'You bitch!' Bess leaned forward suddenly and tossed the contents of her cup into Cicely's face. It splashed every-where, dripping from her chin, into her hair, and down between her breasts.

Cicely did not move an inch, and was able to close her eyes in time. 'Well, Bess, you asked me to describe what happened at Winchester, and I did. Do you wish me to go on to tell you why I lay with Henry in the first place?'

Bess gazed at her, and then sat back slowly. 'Yes. Tell me.'

'He threatened to do the same harm to Jack and my husband that he did to John. He said that unless I went to him, their punishment would be on my conscience.'

Bess stared at her. 'I do not believe you,' she whispered.

'Then do not. It is the truth. I have become Henry Tudor's leman because I wish to protect those I love. I would do it to protect you as well, Bess. I cannot help it that men seem to find me so desirable, but they do, and if I am able to use that fact to help those I hold in my heart, then I will. If Henry sends for me again, I will go, no matter what you say or do. I am sorry, Bess, truly I am, but what else would you expect me to have done?'

After a long moment's silence, Bess got up shakily. 'It is a lie,' she said, trying to convince herself.

'No, Bess. Yet I do not think only ill of the king. He is not an easy man, but he is sometimes a very engaging, gentle one. I know him, yes, far more than you, even though he is your husband. I do not seek it, because I *do* want him to be happy with you. It causes me great pain to know how things are in your marriage. If it is my fault, I have done nothing to seek such blame. I would *never* wish to supplant you. My heart is not given to Henry.'

'You are so easy with words, are you not? You can weave sweetness out of the air and present it in tangible form, like a caress. You even reach to me, except that I am wise to your trickery. You *do* seek to supplant me. You want Henry to yourself, as his queen!'

Cicely forgot herself sufficiently as to get up without permission. 'Do not be such a *fool*, Bess! How can I possibly become Henry's queen? I am an adulteress, married to Jon to whom, as far as the world is concerned, I have borne a son, and I have been gracing Henry's bed when I most certainly should not. I am definitely not suitable to be his queen, even if I wished it, which I do *not*! I love my

118

husband. Oh, you may scoff, but I do, and I would never wish to cast him aside, although he may wish to do that to me. I loved Richard, so very much that I cannot think of him without grief. And now I love Jack de la Pole so much that my heart could burst of it.'

'Jack?'

'Oh, yes. He and Richard are the only men for whom I would ever defy every rule and convention, every chapter of the Bible or instruction from the Pope. I would do anything for Jack, and would have done anything for Richard. There are no limits.'

'You are so abandoned?'

'Yes,' Cicely replied frankly.

'You *are* a whore!' Bess cried suddenly.

'And so must you be if you are to win Henry!'

'How dare you!' Bess took several steps and slapped Cicely so hard across the face that she almost knocked her from her feet.

The blow stung and brought tears as Cicely tried to steady herself against the table, and she put a protective hand to her cheek as she faced her sister again. 'Why such rage, Bess? Might it be because you know I am right? You have not loved in the way you must if you are ever to understand me.'

Bess was beside herself, and slapped Cicely's other cheek, this time succeeding in knocking her to the floor. Cicely lay there a moment, biting her lips to prevent herself from uttering the sob that rose so sharply in her throat. Then, slowly, she got up, and faced Bess once more.

'Do you wish to hit me again, Bess? Then do so. Here I am, at your disposal. You are my queen, and I dare not lift a finger to you.'

Bess's eyes brimmed with tears, although whether they were of fury or contrition was hard to say. 'Richard should have been mine,' she said at last. 'If he had returned my love, I would not be as I am now. I would be like *you*! Have you any notion of what it is to feel frozen inside? To so loathe a man's touch that it makes me feel physically sick? Yes, I am jealous, Cissy, so jealous and consumed by it that I cannot bear the sound of your name. I *want* to want Henry, but he treats me as if I am nothing more than a milch cow. How can he possibly be as you describe him? An enjoyable lover? A gentle and engaging man? That is not the Henry Tudor I know.'

'And who is the Bess *he* knows? Well? Is she warm, appealing, playful and amusing? Does she court him, want him and give him all he wants so that he will do the same for her? Bess, you are *hopeless* with him! I want to shake you for your foolishness. Henry would not need me at all if he could turn to you. But if he tried, you would reject him.'

'I despise him,' Bess whispered, turning away, the tears rolling down her cheeks.

'Do you love Prince Arthur?'

Bess turned back in surprise. 'Of course!'

'Well, he is not yours alone, Bess, he is half Henry. You made your child between you. Can you not at least see him like that? Without Henry, there would not be a Prince Arthur.'

'I cannot forgive the manner of his begetting. Against a wall, like a common trollop.'

'You cannot be like this with a man like Henry. He should not have treated you like that, but you anger him so. And was it really as violent and unwanted as you choose to remember now? He says it was not. Yes, I have spoken to him about it, because *he* told me and I was angry that he treated you so. Bess, you are so haughty and superior. It really will not do. Henry does not forgive easily. I believe he probably loathes *me* now, and—'

'Why? What happened?'

Cicely told her. Exactly.

Bess stared at her. 'I ... I do not understand. You thought you saw Richard?'

'I often think it, Bess. I loved him so much, and even though Jack is now in my heart, I still cannot stop loving and needing Richard. He was my first love, and had he lived, would have been my only love. I called out to him in front of Henry at the Tower, Henry was angry, and so I will not be welcomed to his bed again. But if I were, I would not find it a terrible place to be. I would know pleasure awaited. Have you *ever* known physical reward? Have you?'

Bess met her eyes. 'No. At least, I do not think so.'

'Believe me, if you had, you would know. It is such a wonderful, elating feeling, even more so if you reach it together. And Henry will wait, to be sure of it. He is that much of a lover.'

'He is also half mad,' Bess replied. 'One moment he is all smiles, the next he is a monster.'

Cicely lowered her eyes. 'I know. He cannot help it, Bess.'

'Yes, he can. He has as much command of himself as everyone else,' Bess insisted.

'I do not think so. He really cannot keep a tight hold upon his moods. But when he is his true self . . . he is so good to be with. It is communion, Bess, such wonderful, exquisite communion. I knew it with Richard, once with John, and then with my husband and with Henry. Now I know it with Jack, with whom it is almost as sublime as it was with Richard. I know that feeling so very, very well that I am truly sorry you have never experienced it. But you can have it with Henry. You may be the Plantagenet princess, the senior daughter of a king, while Henry is merely an earl's son with some royal blood, but he has the crown of England, and you, like it or not, are merely his unwanted queen. You have to seek his forgiveness.'

Bess went to pour more wine, this time relenting enough to bring some for Cicely as well. 'I feel only revulsion for him.'

'He has to come to your bed to beget another heir, that is

the way of all marriages. Make him want to stay with you. Drink strong wine first, think of all the most disgustingly erotic things you can, imagine he is Richard, make love to *Richard*. You will enjoy Henry, I promise. Hold him, kiss him lingeringly, run your fingers through his hair, caress his body. Follow your instinct. If you wonder what it would be like to do something, then *do* it. Kiss and taste parts of him you are probably shocked to even think about. Yes, that part especially.'

'Did . . . did you do that with Richard?'

Cicely met her eyes. 'Yes.'

Bess turned away, clearly shaken. 'Did he . . . teach you how to do it?'

'I did not need much teaching, Bess. It was so natural to do it, to *want* to do it. Instinct tells you to do it, for your own gratification as well as your lover's. Among all the kisses and caresses, the exploring and adoration, to do *that* is one of the most perfect acts of all. To take him between your lips . . . for those utterly intimate moments, we women have all the power. The man we love is ours, absolutely, and if he should come then . . . Oh, I do not know what else to say, except that I am almost talking myself into rushing to find Jack to get on my knees and undo his laces.'

Bess gave a little smile. 'Well, even *I* can imagine doing it with Jack. I was far more tempted by him at Sheriff Hutton than I ever let him know.'

'I am glad you did not succumb, because now *I* would be very jealous. He is mine, and I want him entirely to myself.'

'He has a wife,' Bess pointed out.

'So has Henry. I tempt husbands from their marriage beds, remember? The Plantagenet harlot. As for Jack, he has a wife who does not want him but prefers the Bible. He has had two children, and lost them both. His wife is certainly not interested in producing another.'

Bess gazed at her. 'Poor Jack.'

'Bess, if you can like the thought of it with him, it means that you actually are excited by the thought of the act itself,' Cicely pointed out.

'Maybe, but not with Henry Tudor!'

'Trust me, you will enjoy it. Excite him to that point, and he will do such things for you as well. You are so beautiful, Bess, and if he sees desire in your eyes, he will make love to you, not simply attend to you as a matter of unpleasant duty. Which is what *you* do to him. Welcome him, and you will never regret it. Gratification is not a solely male preserve, *we* can have it as well. If you do not do these things, he may turn to me again, or to someone else who will not care about *you* in the least. I care about you, I always have and I always will. I like so very much about him, you have no idea, but I *love* Jack. With all my being.'

Bess's lips quivered and she drank the wine, before discarding the glass. 'I cannot give in to my feelings as you do, Cicely.'

'Yes, you can. You had such fantasies about Richard.'

'But . . . I did not ever imagine actually *doing* them. Oh God, I think I will die of wretchedness.' Bess hid her face in her hands.

Cicely gathered her into her arms. 'I am so unhappy for you, Bess.'

'Do you really, truly think I could enjoy lying with Henry?'

'Yes, and he is worth the effort. Just remember that.' Cicely kissed her sister's cheek.

'I came here to be as vile as possible to you.'

'I know.'

'I am sorry for throwing wine over you and hitting you.'

'Twice as I recall.' Cicely smiled.

# Chapter Ten

IT WAS THE morning of the Feast of St Nicholas, 6 December, and Cicely was in a skiff being conveyed to Greenwich, where she had been summoned, not by Henry but by Bess. Henry continued to ignore Lady Welles, except to repeat his order that she was not, under any circumstance, to come to Greenwich. Cicely could not understand it. Henry said one thing, yet Bess apparently contradicted him? Well, Bess's summons was very formal, under signet, signed by Bess herself, and this time Cicely felt that it must have been sent with Henry's knowledge. After an agony of deliberation, weighing going against not going, she decided to obey her sister, but she was careful to take the letter with her. If she had to confront a furious Henry, she would at least be able to show him the reason she had come. She prayed she would not see him at all.

She had continued to see Jack, never at Pasmer's Place but always at his newly taken residence in Gracechurch Street. And always with so much discretion that Jack teased that even *he* did not know when she was under his roof! The page suspected of spying for Henry had been sent away, Jack having relented from worse punishment because of the boy's age, and now the Earl of Lincoln's entire household could be completely trusted.

Cicely was always taken to Jack by a circuitous route, always doubling back along lanes and footpaths, going into shops and then slipping through to alleys behind. Sometimes she rode there, always cloaked and hooded, always led by another devious route that often made them seem to be going in the opposite direction from Gracechurch Street. But she always reached Jack safely, and they were able to spend loving hours together.

Now, at Greenwich in the cold light of the December morning, she alighted reluctantly at the steps. The air was crisp, the sun was shining and there had been a frost overnight. She paused, adjusting the ties of her cloak, beneath which she wore a shell-pink velvet gown with midnight-blue brocade lining and a dark blue headdress. Whatever awaited her inside, she did not want to face it. The urge to get back into the skiff was as strong as the one that had decided her two months ago outside Westminster.

She made herself think of Richard, and then drew upon something he had once said to her. *'All you have to do is think of me, picture me, and what is not clear will become clear. You know me more than anyone else, you know how I would respond to something and what I would do as a consequence.'*

Yes, she knew. He would not condemn her for anything, but would support and love her, no matter what she did, and at this moment he would expect her to show true Plantagenet pride. And so she would. A brave smile came to her lips and she caught up her skirts to mount the steps and go into the palace.

She was conducted to the queen's apartments, where she found ladies, courtiers, luxury and music. Bess was seated with her ladies on the floor around her silver brocade skirts, but Cicely was dismayed to see how pale she was. She had been smiling with her ladies, although forcedly, until Cicely was announced, at which she frowned and dismissed everyone in order to speak to her sister alone.

She prevented Cicely from kneeling. 'How are you?' Her

tone did not invite first names.

'I am well, Your Grace. Thank you. I trust I find you in equal good spirits?'

'I trust you are not too dismayed about your husband's new mistress?'

Where was this leading? 'I know of it, Your Grace, although not that word had also reached court.'

'Everything reaches court. It is not pleasant to have another woman in your marriage, is it?'

Cicely began to understand. 'No, it is not, Your Grace, but there is nothing I can do about it. Sir Jon is free to do as he pleases.'

'And you regard yourself in the same light?'

Cicely looked her. 'Bess? What is wrong?'

'What is wrong is that I tried to do all the things you said, I really tried, and yes, there was some pleasure. Not that he tried very hard, he was simply marginally gentler, but then he left my bed and instructed me to . . .'

'Yes?'

'To summon you to my household. You are to join it in two weeks' time, and will be included throughout the Christmas season.'

Cicely stared at her.

'Oh, do not pretend you are unaware.'

'But I know nothing, Bess. I have not heard from the king, except to be ordered to stay away from here. I did not understand when you summoned me. I actually hoped you and the king were perhaps a little reconciled.'

'Reconciled? I believe he found it amusing to let me struggle to please him. Why else would he insult and crush me by making me send for you?'

'I . . . do not understand, Bess. I have stayed away from court, not sent word to the king, and I certainly do *not* want to hurt you.' Cicely was upset, and angrier with Henry than she believed possible. After all the things she had said to him, and to Bess, *this* was how he behaved!

'I see you are incensed, Cicely.'

'Yes, I am, but certainly not with you.' Cicely had to bite her lip because she suddenly felt tearful for her sister, who was being made so unhappy by Henry Tudor's disagreeable behaviour. 'Have—have you sought Margaret's help? Maybe she can reason with him?'

'I already have, but she is with her dear Henry in this.'

'Then I do not know what I can say. I cannot even go away from London to Jon, not only because he would not have me, but because the king will not let me. I am as trapped in this as you, Bess.'

'Oh, I know, Cissy.' Bess drew a long breath and leaned her head back against the rich tapestry of her carved chair. 'I am so miserably unhappy, and I feel that Henry's loathing for me grows rather than diminishes. I hate him. I truly do. If he were to die tomorrow, I would be overjoyed. Only his death will do.'

Cicely stared at her. 'Oh, Bess . . .'

'It is the truth,' Bess replied quietly.

'Reconciliation will take time,' Cicely reminded her, for Bess herself was not innocent in this. Since meeting Henry, she had been as deliberately disagreeable as she could. It was hardly surprising that he was not going to be easy to win around, but that did not excuse his mean spite now. Or Bess's desire for nothing less than his death.

At that moment the king's approach was heralded. Cicely's heart sank. She really did not want to see him. He entered almost immediately, wearing black, with Richard's circlet around his forehead. He was clearly irritated about something, but halted the moment he saw Cicely making a deep curtsey. For a split second she knew he'd been caught completely off guard, and she could feel his annoyance, both about what had originally spurred him to come to Bess, and to once again find himself face to face with the rejected lover he had forbidden to come to court.

In a moment he was in control of himself again. 'You

were commanded not to come here, Lady Welles,' he said coldly.

To Cicely's relief, Bess, who had also curtseyed to him, came to her rescue. 'I requested my sister's presence. I believe you know why.' No first name, not even a 'Your Majesty'.

His wintry eyes moved to his queen and then back to Cicely, then he inclined his head. 'Ladies.' The word was uttered through clenched teeth. Then he left again, without saying whatever it was he had come about.

Bess rose. 'You see how tender and loving he is?'

'Perhaps I should leave again.' Cicely straightened as well. What a lout Henry could be, and without trying too much. She closed her eyes for a moment, and saw him lying beside her, his hair tangled against a pillow, his lips curved in a lazily seductive smile, his eyes dark with love.

'Cicely, it was *his* instruction that made me send for you. He cannot have it both ways. Although he *is* Henry Tudor, and probably thinks he can. But it all hurts so much more now because I abased myself by trying to seduce him into my bed. I really did try, and for a few minutes his kisses were pleasing. He caressed me as if he really meant to make love to me, not just dibble me as he usually does. But then, suddenly and for no reason that I could perceive, he changed. He took me without consideration, and then left, pausing only to order me to send for you.'

Cicely went to hug her. 'I am so sorry,' she said again.

'I know. Yes, truly I do. I was upset with you when you came, but you are still a comfort to me. I think I must simply accept that Henry wants you, not me.'

'He does not want me.'

'For someone who knows so very much about men, you seem remarkably ignorant when it comes to Henry. Of course he wants you, I could tell in even those few moments. He will not let you simply return to Pasmer's Place when you leave me. You may count upon it.'

128

'I pray you are wrong, for I have no wish at all to be between you and him.'

'*He* is between *us*, Cissy. Well, I have delivered His Majesty's thoughtless command, and so I am afraid you will have to come here. But while you are here now, I must say something to you. It concerns Jack. *Please* urge him to abandon whatever he is dabbling in.'

'I do not know if he dabbles in anything.'

'Come now, Cissy, Jack cannot help himself. He is York, so of *course* he is. I may not have your intimate acquaintance with him, but I still know him well enough. I also know he does not like me now because of what happened at Sheriff Hutton. He is right, of course. I thought only of myself and my unrequited love for Richard. I involved you and John and so we were all captured.' Bess paused. 'What happened to John is therefore my fault.'

'*Yours?* Why do you think that? Henry was the guilty one, Bess.'

'I feel the guilt, Cissy. But it is in the past; what happens *now* is more important. Jack is bound to be deep in this Lambert Simnel foolery and if he does not desist, he will pay the price. Cicely, if you have any influence with him, you will *make* him see sense. Please. Jack may not like me, but I am still very fond of him, and always will be. We all knew each other as children, and he was unfailingly kind and exciting to be with. He could invent such games for us all, and he watched over us. Do you remember how he saved you that time when you fell in the pool in Sherwood? You were seven, I think.'

'Yes, and he was fourteen, or thereabouts.' Cicely remembered. He had ridden past as she lost her footing and fell from an overhanging branch into the deepest part of the pool. Young ladies should not have climbed trees at all! As he was quick to point out afterwards. He had dived in to save her, and had held her close afterwards because she was so shaken and frightened. Perhaps he had claimed her in more ways than one that day in the woods, because he still held her now. Closer than ever.

'Cissy, promise you will do everything you can to keep him from this conspiracy.'

'My promise is given, Bess.'

Later, as Cicely returned through the palace towards the river entrance, she heard scurrying footsteps behind her, and turned quickly to see a page in Henry's colours.

The boy bowed low. 'Lady Welles?'

'Yes.'

'His Majesty commands your presence, my lady. If you will follow me?'

So Bess was right, she thought, nodding resignedly.

She was not taken to Henry's apartments, but to a room on the ground floor, at the rear of the palace, facing on to the walled garden that in summer would be filled with red and white roses. The page indicated the door, and then hurried away.

Was she to simply go in? Or wait? She had no idea, but at last raised a hand to knock. The door was opened, by Henry himself, and he almost pulled her inside and then locked the door so there was no risk of interruption. Cloves were in the air, and she was so uneasy in those seconds— because she feared his anger would lead to violence—that an almost arctic draught seemed to pass over her.

But all he did was prevent her from kneeling, help her remove her heavy cloak, and then move away, placing at least ten feet between them. He tossed her cloak aside and did not meet her eyes. 'I trust you are well?' he said then, as if he did not know what else to say.

'Yes, Your Majesty.' A silence fell that she *had* to break. 'You—you seem well, Your Majesty. I pray you are now fully recovered from your illness?'

'Yes.' He rubbed his eyebrow. 'Our last meeting was not . . . pleasing to me, my lady.'

'I understand that, Your Majesty.'

'Understand? *Do* you?'

'I was very foolish. I thought I saw something that was not really there. Under the circumstances of that evening, it became a little too much for me. I can only crave your understanding . . . and hope for a little kindness.'

'Why did you beg for Richard's forgiveness? For the sin of gracing *my* bed?'

Was now the moment to use her ability to charm and influence? If she did, she knew she risked conveying feelings she did not have for him. But he deserved an answer, and so she would be honest. At least about this. 'Yes, Your Majesty.'

He turned away with an angry sound. 'So, you cease to worry about your husband and cousin?'

It was a verbal punch, and renewed her awareness of him as nothing else. She had to win him again, she had no choice. 'Please, Your Majesty, if I may only finish?'

He signified consent, facing her again.

Now she used her charm, summoning a faint glitter of tears, imploring with those shimmering eyes, and conveying such wretchedness and regret that he would need to be granite to withstand it. 'I—I thought I was face to face with the uncle you had conquered, the uncle whose memory I sullied because I not only lay with you, his most bitter enemy, but I found pleasure in so doing. So much pleasure.' She paused, allowing the reiteration to dwell. 'Of course I begged him to forgive me,' she went on softly. 'I thought I saw accusation and bitterness in his eyes, and I could not bear it. Not after being in the Tower, almost seeing John of Gloucester, and *still* going into your arms. I had even asked you to take me to your bed that night. I *so* wanted to be with you.'

'Did you?'

'Yes. You cannot possibly know how I felt in those moments, nor could I reasonably expect you to. I failed you,

I know that, but I did not mean to. I would never mean to do that.'

He gazed at her. 'Can I believe you, lady?'

'Yes. I would have told you then, had you permitted me. Truly. And if you had shown kindness, I would still have gone more than willingly with you that same night. I wanted to be with you. I wanted it very much.'

'So, you blame my lack of understanding?'

She met his eyes. 'No, for I know how it must have seemed to you, especially when you had just told me . . .' She broke off, leaving his confession silently between them. Then she swallowed, making her lips tremble a little, before looking at him again with lovely eyes. 'If you had only let me explain to you . . .' Her voice trailed away softly, promisingly.

'Well, now you have.' He fell silent.

In those cold moments she wondered what he would be like if he learned of her love for Jack. Then the moments dropped colder still. What if he *did* know?

He changed the subject completely. 'What are your relations with the queen?'

'The queen?' She was rattled, as he meant her to be.

'You *do* know the queen?' The acid was there.

'She is my sister and I love her, Your Majesty.'

'For God's own sake, Cicely, have you forgotten my name?' Irritation flushed over him. 'Are you and she on good terms again?'

'Yes, Your— Henry.'

'So no doubt you have again been regaled with my disgraceful behaviour between the sheets? That would indeed set my cause back by several centuries. Cicely, when I told her to send for you to be in her household, I was not serious, but malicious. And she deserved it.'

'You were cruel, and no, on this occasion she did not deserve it.' She dared to spar.

His eyes were alight. 'So, the secrets of my marriage

132

bed have been laid truly bare? Once again you are so much in someone's total confidence that all the grim details are related in fine detail?'

'You were cruel to her,' she repeated.

'She seemed to think that one small effort—quite clearly to her distaste—would have me lapping from her palm. For what it is worth, I *did* try to respond, but then I saw her face. She loathed every moment of it. So yes, I was cruel, but no more than she always is to me.'

Cicely gazed at him. 'That is not what Bess told me. Yes, she tried hard to be all you wished, but whatever you saw on her face it was not loathing, because she was finding you pleasing. She *told* me so, Henry. Would I lie about such a thing? She is now mortified and will recoil from you again, but if you are kind, I am sure you can still find happiness together.'

'So, yet again Henry Tudor is unworthy?'

'Yes.'

'Thank you. Your audacity never fails.' He moved away, dragging his elegant fingers along a table top. Richard's stolen ruby caught the light from the window, as did its companion emerald. 'As I was saying, I did not intend my instructions to be acted upon, I was merely being obnoxious. Second nature, I know.'

'How is someone else supposed to divine your words when you do not mean what you say?'

His eyes met hers again. '*You* would have known, and I would have felt the edge of your sharpest tongue.'

'You did not say it to me, you said it to the queen.'

'Oh, do I not know it. I will be more circumspect with her in future.'

'If you did not mean it, perhaps you should have informed Lady Derby.'

'My mother? What has *she* to do with it?'

'When the queen sought her assistance, to try again to seek your love, Lady Derby criticized and mocked her, as if you had confided everything.'

He returned to her. 'It would seem you have kept the whetstone to hand, Cicely. Well, my mother has not and will not be party to this delicate little matter. You think I would tell my *mother* what I do between the sheets? Jesu, lady!'

'Nor do *I* wish to know, Henry. I am no longer part of *your* life, and wish to be allowed to proceed with my own.' Which she knew was the very last thing he wished her to do . . . unless he proceeded with her.

'I fear you cannot always have your own way,' he responded.

She used her eyes upon him again, remorseful, heart-broken, yearning and still with that shimmer of tears. 'I have told you everything about that night at the Tower, Henry, so if it pleases you, perhaps I should withdraw?'

'No, Cicely, it does not please me. I must say more about that night, for you have no inkling of what I felt. It was as if Richard really was there. I could almost see him myself, almost perceive him in those shadows. I watched you, Cicely. You were love itself, begging everything from him that I so wanted to give you myself. Never tell me again that your love for him was only that of a niece for her uncle, because you will insult me beyond measure. Please be honest with me now. Tell me the truth. Was Richard your lover?'

'No. Now it is you who insults me.' She was afraid again, because for a man like Henry Tudor, it would be but a short leap to wondering about her son, and whether or not death had really taken him. And who his father might really have been.

Henry was bitter. 'Always you deny it, always I know you lie. And now you are close to your cousin, who has a dagger prepared for my back.'

Somehow she remained unflustered. 'Lord Lincoln is true to you. He has not said or done anything that would lead me to doubt him. And I am close to him because he is my kinsman and I love him as such.'

'Do you?' His eyes seemed to bore into her. 'Is that really all you feel for him? He is everything that women adore, and you, sweetheart, are a very sensuous and loving creature. I would imagine that Lincoln's generous proportions can more than satisfy you.'

'I am sure it could, but he and I are not lovers. So I do not know. I have never been his lover, Henry Tudor, but I *was* yours.' Dear God, how she hoped he was not aware of the nights she spent with Jack. Did he know about Gracechurch Street?

'Yes, you were my lover. I look at you and see my heart's nemesis.'

She realized he did *not* know about those stolen nights. 'Then send me away.' That he would never do. His anger and suspicion were strong, but so was what his heart dictated. She could see it all in those hooded and—on this occasion—tell-tale eyes. She was employing all her wiles now. And they had to be subtle wiles, because this was not a man who would be taken in by anything even remotely obvious. And it was not all artifice, because this clever, talented, mercurial but unsound king exerted a fascination of his own. Beguilement was never far away.

'Send you away? Jesu, Cicely.' He seemed amused.

'Then what do you want of me?'

'Everything.'

'Forget me, Henry, and turn to your queen. Send me back to my husband.'

'Who has a mistress.'

She was startled. 'Is there anyone who does *not* know?'

'It is common talk. Besides, I have him closely watched.'

Her face showed nothing. If he was having Jon watched, what did he know of Friskney? 'Surely you do not suspect Jon of being disloyal to you?'

'He loves you, sweetheart, and so is vulnerable to York!'

'You have fucked me, Henry, does that make *you* vulnerable to York?'

He pursed his lips. 'How to the point you are, as always.'

'You cannot help it, can you? You have little spiders everywhere, all of them scuttling around and then hastening back to the centre of your immense web to tell you everyone's secrets.'

'What a charming analogy.' He smiled sincerely for the first time. 'Such a sharp tongue.'

'You should have the ammunition ready to blunt it.'

He came to put a hand gently to her cheek. 'Oh, those sparks, in your eyes and on your lips. In all of you. You are alight with them.'

'Please do not do this, Henry . . .'

His hand fell away. 'So the rift is to be perpetuated?'

She could smell the cloves, and knew their effect. *His* effect.

He watched her. 'Oh, the nuances on your lovely face, how they intrigue me, but I think they would displease me.'

'Only some of them.'

He smiled, and it was in his eyes as well. 'Oh, Cicely, I have missed you so very much.' He came close enough to take her hands and draw her to him, until their bodies touched. His lips were only inches from hers, the cloves began to filter through her skin as he linked her fingers and stretched her hands down until it seemed they must be torn from his.

Then he swayed just a little—it could hardly to be seen at all—and she swayed with him. He had done this many times before, and it never ceased to be erotic. It was also wistful and moving, captivating, and so imbued with love that she closed her eyes for the magic of it.

# Chapter Eleven

HENRY WAS SO sweetly seductive now that it seemed impossible he could be savage and cruel, but even knowing this, Cicely wanted to kiss again those lips she had kissed so many times before.

She unlinked her hands from his and slipped her arms around his neck to pull his mouth to hers. The scent of cloves was intoxicating as he embraced her, tightly, adoringly, as if he had been parted from her for a lifetime. She could feel him trembling. He was caught up with emotion, and when she drew from the kiss she saw how dark and aroused his eyes were, how filled with feeling, how steady and intent. 'I cannot stop loving you, Cicely. Without you I am so intolerably unhappy that my life is nothing but an existence.'

'Oh, Henry, I—' She broke off as trumpets echoed from the river.

He drew away irritably. 'Devil take the French!' he cried, the words almost exploding from him.

'Henry,' she said gently, 'I can wait for you.'

He hesitated, and then smiled. 'You will wait for your king?'

'Of course.' Yes, she would, because he had twined around her again.

'I cannot ignore the French ambassador, nor the representative of Isabella and Ferdinand, whom I must also receive today. Already I negotiate a marriage for Prince Arthur, but that is the way of it, mm? Catherine, daughter of Ferdinand of Aragon and Isabella of Castile. She is only a year old herself, but if I have anything to do with it, she will one day be Queen of England. Neither she nor my son will have any say at all in the matter. Arranged matches are a despicable institution, are they not? No, do not answer.' He took her face in his hands and kissed her again, gently. 'I must lie with you again, soon. When are you to come to my wife's household?'

'In two weeks.'

'Jesu, I cannot wait that long. You must come immediately, to the same rooms you had before. For the moment I will send someone to see you safely back to Pasmer's Place, but I want you to come here no later than tomorrow. Do you understand? I cannot endure for longer than that. I have so much frustrated desire to surrender to you.'

'What will happen when Jon returns? He has to be here for Christmas.'

'I will still expect you to come to me when I wish. I no longer care what he thinks.' The trumpets sounded again. 'I must go. I will send someone to escort you.'

'I can find my own way.'

'That is no reason for me to permit you to return alone. I have allowed it the past, but no longer.' He paused. 'Cicely, I am sorry for my behaviour at the Tower. I could not see for the redness within me.'

'I know.' She put her hands over his.

His parted lips brushed hers several times before he kissed her again. His arms went around her and his body cleaved so close that he seemed to seek consummation through their clothes. He dwelt upon the kiss, as if drawing enough energy from it to sustain him until they met again. 'Dear God, I do not want to leave you,' he whispered then, resting his forehead to hers, adding words in Welsh. '*Tan yfory.*'

'What does that mean?'

'Until tomorrow.' He left then, his swift steps fading along the passage.

Minutes passed, and she almost decided to leave on her own anyway when more steps sounded, this time approaching. Male footsteps, their swiftness indicative of annoyance. So, she had an unwilling escort. She sighed, envisaging a sullen companion all the way back to Pasmer's Place.

But when the owner of the steps entered, she was astonished—and delighted—to see it was Jack!

His face changed when he saw her. 'Cicely? I had not realized *you* were the reason Henry chose to instruct an earl to be lady's maid.'

He began to close the door, but she shook her head quickly. 'Leave it open, Jack. Wide open.'

He obeyed, before placing his cloak and gauntlets on the table along which Henry had drawn his fingers. Then he came closer. He wore dark wine velvet, aglitter with silver leopards' heads, and there was a large amethyst in the centre of his circular hat brooch. He did like amethysts, she thought.

This room had now seen three very precious rings in the past half an hour: a ruby, an emerald and an amethyst. A fourth, a sapphire, if she included John of Gloucester's little ring, which had been in her purse since the night at the Tower, when she had entertained a brief, futile hope that he might recognize it.

Jack kept his voice very low. 'I thought Henry seemed to be in an inordinately amiable mood. Now I know why. *You* are back in the royal arms. He seemed a little smug when he issued his instruction, and I suspected a hired beauty with secret orders to get me in bed and then wheedle information between fucks.'

'I would wheedle, sir, but for the fucks, not the information.'

'Oooh, lady, say much more and I will not dare to leave this room. It would not do for the Earl of Lincoln to be seen with Lady Welles, a staff protruding from his hose.' He smiled. 'So, let us leave right now, and I will be a chivalrous but very proper escort. I imagine our times together will be curtailed for a while.'

The air was biting as they raised their hoods on the river stairs, where skiffs and barges jostled for position. There were more clouds than before, and a gentle breeze as Jack assisted her into a skiff. They huddled together, as far from the boatmen as possible, and kept their backs towards them anyway.

Jack's long dark curls fluttered across his face as the skiff was shoved away from the steps and then rowed upstream. He removed his gauntlet to take her hand and pull her fingers to his lips. 'Did Henry tell you anything new today?'

'No. Unless you count that he intends to negotiate a marriage for Prince Arthur with Catherine of Aragon.'

Jack gazed at her, his smile fading. 'This is true?'

'I would not invent it.'

He looked away. 'Such a grand international marriage would certainly entrench his bony arse on the throne. He must be farting roses, and I must pray the negotiations fail.'

'Leaving only thorns between his cheeks?' She smiled, but then became serious. 'He will not give up easily. I think I am the only one against whom he does not have a will of iron.'

'An understandable weakness, sweetheart.'

She clung to his hand. 'Jack, Bess is at pains to warn you that Henry is suspicious of your involvement in the Simnel plot. You know it already, of course, but the fact that she has mentioned it makes me feel you may be under closer scrutiny than you realize. She cares about you.'

'Indeed.' He was scathingly abrupt.

'She reminded me of that time at Sherwood when you saved me from drowning.' Cicely smiled. 'I may only have been a child, but I did enjoy being able to put my arms around your neck as you carried me to safety. You had spots, I remember.'

'Thank you. I recall thinking you were pretty. Mind you, at fourteen or so I was hardly much of a judge.'

She dug him with her elbow, and then suddenly asked, 'How is Tal?'

'Well enough the last time I saw him.'

'I saw him when I left you yesterday. In fact, I have seen him several times, although he has always drawn back out of sight in the hope that I have not. He has either been going in or coming out of the court almost opposite your house, where the Earl of Shrewsbury's town residence is to be found.' She glanced at him, but his face gave nothing away. 'He is Welsh, maybe the Marches, which could well be Shropshire.'

'Do not probe, Cicely, because I really will not explain anything to you. Forget where you have seen him. Forget *him*, I beg of you.'

'Taleisin ap Gruffydd is not his real name, is it?'

'Yes, it is, sweetheart. Now, leave it, please.'

'Just tell me if your plans are going as well as you hoped.'

'Yes. We have many friends, and are raising a great deal of money and support. We already have an army in readiness to assemble here in England, to say nothing of the troops we will bring with us when we invade. And false trails are being laid.'

'Héraut?'

'Not yet, but soon.' He smiled.

Tears filled her eyes and she looked away across the Thames, observing a merchantman slide downstream towards the estuary. Its wake slapped against the skiff, and the current gurgled around the splashing of the oars. The seagulls were joined by others, and their racket was deafening.

There were spots of rain in the air, and the first hint of fading light, when Jack finally escorted her into St Sithe's Lane, but hardly had they gone a few yards when something made Cicely glance behind. A young woman stood on the corner, her face shaded by her hood. Realizing she had been observed, she turned to hurry out of sight again, but there was something familiar about the way she moved.

Cicely's fingers tightened over Jack's arm. 'I . . . I think we have been watched. By the same whore as before. How would she be here, just as we pass? Henry *must* have sent her!'

'And it may also have been accidental.'

'No, Jack. He sent you to escort me, and now *she* is here. It is *not* a coincidence.'

'All she will have seen is cousinly friendship, sweetheart. And she may not be following us on Henry's business, but because she is interested in me.' He paused. 'I know how vain that sounds, but it has happened before.'

She gazed at him, so handsome and debonair, so aristocratic and stylish. 'It is not vanity, Jack de la Pole, just a fact of life for you. You turn female heads, including mine.'

'I am your mirror, sweetheart. Never forget it. Come, it is cold out here and the rain is just enough to be discomforting.'

Soon he conducted her through the gates of Pasmer's Place, where torches had already been lit and they were suddenly confronted by a recently arrived cavalcade bearing Jon's yellow and black colours. His horse was there too, capering about in such a way that she knew he had only just dismounted and gone into the house. She faltered uncertainly, for she did not know what to expect, or how she herself would react on seeing him again. Why had he returned so early? She had not expected to see him for another two weeks at least.

Jack glanced at her. 'Do you wish me to come in with you? Or would you rather I took myself away?'

'Stay. Please. I . . . am afraid, Jack. What if he is cold to me?'

'I will be alongside you, sweetheart.' He slipped an arm around her shoulder and ushered her across the thronged yard. As they went, she noticed a lady's palfrey among the horses. It was one she had ridden at Wyberton, Jon's favourite castle.

She glanced at Jack, who had also seen it. He tightened his arm momentarily. 'Do not forget now, you were summoned to Greenwich by the queen. It is the truth, so say it. And Henry instructed me to escort you back here.'

She nodded.

They heard Jon before they saw him. His voice, never usually raised, carried angrily from the great hall. 'Dolt! Take better care!'

On reaching the hall, where the wheel-rimmed candleholders from the roof cast a dim light that would soon need help from the wall torches, they found confusion everywhere. Jon had brought much baggage with him, and men and maidservants scurried, taking things to whatever room they were required. Cicely glanced around for any sign of a two-legged baggage, but saw no one.

Her husband stood by the great fireplace, a mug of ale in his hand as he kicked at the logs, sending clouds of sparks up the chimney. She could see the turquoise ring she had given to him. It had once been her father's, and she was glad he still wore it, for at least he had not rejected *all* of her.

He still looked the same, except . . . Tom Kymbe was right, he *was* thinner. And he did not look his usual hale self, she thought, concerned. He was thirty-seven now, a fine-looking man of bearing and presence, with long, wiry brown hair that was fading prematurely to a great

143

deal of grey at the temples. His was a tall figure, spare and not given to unnecessary movement—not unlike his half-nephew Henry in that respect—and he looked good in his old leather travelling clothes, with a wide, buckled belt at his waist. He wore most clothes well, from the plain and simple to even the most elaborate court robes.

His nose was straight, his lips thin, and neither hard nor set, and his long-lashed eyes were an incredibly vivid blue that was discernible even across the busy, dimly lit hall. The fact that he was Margaret's half-brother was difficult to imagine, for he bore no resemblance to her whatever. He had told Cicely he took after his father, Lionel, sixth Baron Welles, for whom Tom Kymbe had named his short-lived son. Hence Cicely's son by Richard had taken the dead boy's name and identity, and become Leo Kymbe.

Cicely knew her husband to be adroit and very capable, someone to inspire confidence and trust. At least, he had been. She no longer knew how to regard him, for it seemed he had brought his new mistress to the house he shared with his wife. Even so, she wanted to run to him, and for everything to be as it had been before Winchester. Instead, confusion and unhappiness kept her in the doorway.

Jack took her elbow. 'We must go to him, sweetheart.'

'I cannot.'

The servants now realized she was there, and there was a discernible lessening of activity. It was a change that Jon could not help but detect, and he turned, his blue eyes coming directly to her. He neither greeted her nor acknowledged her in any way, he simply looked.

Suddenly she wanted to leave, but Jack prevented her. 'Accompany me to him.'

Reluctantly, but holding her head high, she let Jack conduct her towards the fireplace. The servants parted, and there was whispering. They all knew Sir Jon and Lady Welles had been living separate lives since Winchester, and those who had accompanied Jon south from Lincolnshire had already begun to spread whispers about his mistress.

Jack squeezed her elbow. 'Do not make a scene, sweet-heart, for that is what they all hope for. It is the nature of the servant beast.'

Jon set his ale aside and faced them. His face gave nothing away, although he sketched a bow of sorts. 'My lady. My lord of Lincoln.'

'Sir Jon.' Jack returned the bow with more generosity.

Cicely gazed at her husband, unable to do anything else but stand there. The coolness in his eyes told her all she needed to know. He did not seek to restore harmony.

The hall was utterly silent, and Jack cleared his throat awkwardly. 'I trust you had a good journey?'

Jon glanced around at the watching servants. 'Get about your business!' he ordered gruffly. Everyone obeyed, but still kept glancing at the trio by the fire. Then his eyes swung to Cicely, indicating quite clearly upon whom he really wished to vent his anger.

She went a little closer. 'Do you intend to speak to me, Jon?'

'Not unless I have to,' he replied.

She gazed at him, her chin coming up in a way he should have recognized. She was Plantagenet again, and not about to permit him to make her look foolish in a hall filled with curious servants. Without giving him time to see what was coming, she went close enough to kiss his cheek, and then whispered in his ear. 'I am resisting the temptation to sink my teeth into you, sir. Welcome home.' She smiled sweetly, knowing that to onlookers she appeared loving, and then she walked away towards the door that gave to the staircase. Her train hissed over the floor and her headdress veil streamed regally behind her.

Jack watched her go. 'You have a job on your hands, Jon.'

'I can deal with it.'

'One does not *deal* with Cicely.'

'If I want your advice upon my marriage, Jack, believe

me I will ask for it. Where have you been with her?'

'The queen summoned her to Greenwich, and Henry instructed me to escort her home again.'

'Home? I hardly think it is that. More should she have stayed at Greenwich. Wherever the king is, my wife clearly belongs as well.'

'You do her an injustice.'

'Do I? I could sense the cloves upon her, Jack.'

'Did you actually smell them?'

'I did not need to.'

'She has been in my company, Sir Jon, so you should be able to sense thyme on her as well. And if you were to have embraced her just now, I do not doubt she would now be imbued with—' Jack leaned closer and sniffed. 'Woodruff,' he finished.

'No doubt at one time or another she has lain with most of the scents we men favour.'

'That was a mean remark, and totally without foundation.' Jack gazed at him. 'You do not seem well.'

'There is nothing wrong.' But Jon's tone was unnecessarily defensive.

'You have lost weight and you are hardly glowing.'

'Which is my concern, not yours,' Jon snapped.

'You are angry, I can see that, but . . . regarding Cicely . . . do not raise your hand to her. If you do you will have me to deal with.'

'Do not fear for her safety, Jack, for she is safe enough from me. I do not intend to go near her.'

'Do not insult her either.' Jack was pricked by the other's attitude.

'You have appointed yourself her St George?'

'Yes, if needs be.'

'Has it not crossed your mind that *she* is the one who has insulted *me*? I no longer respect her, and I certainly do not respect the king.'

'But do you still support him?'

'You think to recruit me?' Jon gave a short laugh.

'No, Jon, I merely ask what the king himself is bound to wonder. So take care. You may not have time for your wife, but she has time for you. She loves you, and would not wish to see you fall into danger.'

'She is Henry's whore, Jack, and he is welcome to her.'

Jack looked at him. 'Do not judge her too harshly, for she is loyal to you. She defends you and thinks of you constantly.' He glanced away, wanting to tell Sir Jon Welles *exactly* what his wife had been doing to protect him, but he knew that it was the last thing Cicely would wish. Especially now. So instead he said, 'I tell you this, Jon, if she was my wife, I would *never* let her go.'

'So, *you* want her as well? My God, and you have a nerve saying it to my face!' Jon was provoked.

Jack held his eyes. 'There is a palfrey in the yard, Sir Jon. Did it convey your mistress from Lincolnshire?'

Jon paused. 'What business might that be of yours?'

'I am Cicely's cousin and the heir of her House. She *must* be my business. Well? Is your mistress in this house?'

'Yes, my lord of Lincoln, she is.'

Jack was appalled. 'Dear God, you would actually install your leman in the same house as your wife? I thought you had more honour! Henry will have your neck, if I do not have it first!'

'Perhaps you—and my nephew—should consider the fact that I really did not expect to find Cicely here. I believed her to be somewhere cosy with him. So do not lecture me. Least of all will I take it from a man who has cuckolded more husbands than he can even remember!'

'I have not broken any marriage, sir. You are doing that.'

'I think enough has been said, sir.'

Jack was about to leave, but then looked at Jon again.

'And know this too. If I could make Cicely mine, openly and without shame, I damned well would. Yes, I love her. Clearly much more than you do. But she is *your* wife. Send

147

your mistress away and pay attention to your marriage bed. You have been granted the warmest, most utterly captivating woman in all England. Try not to lose her, for you will *never* find her again, because I will have carried her off.'

'So, *you* have been bedding her as well? I begin to feel pure and innocent.'

'Do not allow yourself that false luxury, Jon. And do not play the cur in the manger.' Jack turned to leave, but then hesitated. 'Strange to say, I do not wish this to destroy our friendship. Our dealings should not suffer because we both love the same woman.'

'I do not love her.'

'Yes, you do, Jon Welles. So, can we remain civil in all other respects?'

Jon nodded. 'Yes, damn you, we can.'

Jack bowed again and then left Pasmer's Place.

When Cicely went up to the bedchamber she still regarded as hers, she heard raised female voices through the open door. One was Mary's, the other of someone Cicely did not recognize.

Mary was indignant. 'You have no right to come in here and inspect my lady's wardrobe!'

'Why not? It is now my wardrobe too.'

The second voice was haughty, insolent, and was an echo of Lucy Talby. So, Jon's mistress was as arrogant and bold as her dead sister! 'We will see about *that*!' Cicely breathed, and swept into the room like an avenging angel.

She only glimpsed Judith Talby, who was statuesque and appeared to possess sufficient bosom for three lesser women. The creature had the same flaxen hair as her sister, and wore an appropriately wanton red gown. Her face was beautiful but disdainful, and her manner was, if possible, even more assured and brazen than her sister's had ever been. She was, Cicely guessed, about twenty years old, and clearly considered herself mistress of Pasmer's Place. And of Sir Jon Welles!

Cicely gave her no time to think, but seized her arm and bundled her forcefully from the room, along the passage. Judith struggled and screamed, taken completely by surprise, but then she recovered and a fight commenced, during which Cicely pulled the flaxen hair as hard as she could, succeeding in ripping out a handful. Judith shrieked with pain, tottered at the top of the staircase, lost her balance, and fell backwards down it.

Mary came running, as did servants from the hall, and then Jon appeared as well. 'What in God's own name is going on?' he demanded, halting on seeing his mistress sprawled at the foot of the staircase, her gown up around her waist, her nakedness on full display.

Cicely raised her chin and tossed Judith's hair aside contemptuously. 'The second Mistress Talby appears to have lost her way, sir. She actually believed she was entitled to be in *my* room to use *my* property. From whom did she gain *that* notion, I wonder?'

'Not from me, madam!'

'Well, unless you wish for more undignified scenes such as this, I suggest you lodge her elsewhere!'

'You could have killed her!' he answered, relieved to see Judith sitting up, shocked, bruised and confused, but well enough. He was about to help her up himself, but then seemed to think better of it and gestured to a nearby manservant.

'What a pity I failed,' Cicely replied icily. 'I must be losing my unerring touch!' With a toss of her head, she stalked away to the bedchamber and slammed the door. Mary bent to retrieve the torn flaxen hair, tucked it swiftly in her purse, and then followed.

Hardly had the maid joined her mistress than the door was flung open again to admit Jon. He glared at Mary, who hurried out again. Then he faced his wife.

'That, madam, was an appalling display!'

'Do not speak to me of appalling displays, sir! I found her in *my* chamber, going through *my* belongings. I pushed her out, we struggled and she fell down the stairs of her own volition, not mine. Although on reflection, it would have been good to have actually pushed her. And now here *you* are, having brought your harlot into this house, accusing *me* of appalling displays!' She had never lain with Jack here, out of respect for this man!

'Well, one harlot should surely feel affinity with another!'

She ran at him and hit him as hard as she could on the cheek. 'How *dare* you!' she cried, and tried to hit him again, but he managed to seize her wrist. She could smell woodruff on his clothes, strong and fragrant. Why? Was it to ward off evil? Could it be that he feared his whore's black arts?

'It is *my* house, madam, leased and paid for, and you would do well to remember it!' He still held her.

'Oh, I do not forget it is your house, Jon Welles, for I have rattled around in it alone since October, like a lentil in a pan. But I *am* your wife, and have our marriage vows to prove it.'

'Marriage vows? Are you *quite* sure our union stands in law? As I understand it, the matter is open to question.'

She drew back, for the words cut deep. 'I was *never* married to Ralph Scrope, and you know it, Jon.'

'Do I?' His vivid blue eyes were cool and so very hard.

'So, that is what you really believe after all? That I married you bigamously, as my father did my mother?'

'Why not? There is clearly a family precedent. Besides, what reason have you given me to hold you in any regard?'

She gazed at him. 'No reason at all,' she answered quietly. 'Very well, if that is what you wish, I will not stay beneath your roof. Your whore may sleep wherever she chooses, especially the privy, but she will *not* do it in my finery and jewels. I have been requested by the queen to join her household, and I will do so tonight instead of waiting.'

'Well, I am sure Henry will move over in the royal bed to accommodate you.'

'That will be for you to wonder.'

'I will not waste my thoughts. Or perhaps you will go to Jack? He clearly desires you.'

'Jack? Yes, I well might go to him. I know the way well, and already have my name carved upon his bedpost. He and I do *such* things. You liked those things too, did you not? Perhaps I should give your creature a few tips, for I doubt she is very inventive. I will warrant her lips do not know their way around your cock. You will *never* get those sweet attentions from her; she has no imagination.'

'Have you finished?'

'Unless you wish me to have you standing even more than already.'

'I do not stand for you, Cicely. Not now. '

'Liar,' she whispered. 'Call me whore if you wish, for it shows you for the fool you are. You have no idea why I have done anything. If you did, you—' She broke off.

'If I did?'

'Please have someone escort me to Three Cranes,' she said, turning away. 'I will send for my belongings when I have been given accommodation at Greenwich. Do not let your hag near what is mine. She can have *you*, of course, because you are not my husband, are you? And you never have been. I have been bigamous.'

'Cicely—'

'The matter is settled, Sir Jon. I will no longer dishonour you with my presence, nor need you concern yourself with me. Our acquaintance, for it was clearly no more than that, is at an end. We will leave each other alone from now on.'

'There is no need for this.'

'Oh, but there is, sir, and if your damned witch-hag

comes near me again, I will do more than simply watch her fall down the stairs, I will stick a knife between those great wobbling breasts that must surely hang down to her knees when she is naked. No doubt you have to fight for breath. Now, please leave, before I forget myself again.'

He gazed at her, and then turned towards the door. She spoke again. 'You will keep me informed of Leo? Or should I look direct to Master Kymbe?'

'You may do both, for I will not forsake any promise I made concerning Leo.'

'You have already permitted your strumpet near him. Please tell me she did not hold or even touch him. Tell me she had no reason to overlook him, as her sister would have done.'

'Jesu, Cicely, what do you take me for?'

'I no longer know.'

'Judith Talby did not touch your child. She believes him to be Tom's son and the Kymbes have made sure that is what the rest of the world believes as well.'

'Thank you.'

He turned to go again, but then remembered something and fished in his purse as he returned. He took out a little lock of dark chestnut hair, tied with a green ribbon. 'Leo's first trim,' he said.

Her fingers trembled as she took it. Her baby's hair. Richard's hair. 'What is he like, Jon?' she whispered.

'His father,' he answered.

For a moment she thought he was going to put his hand to her cheek, but instead he left her.

She kissed the lock of hair and then sat on the edge of the bed, sobbing silently.

Barely fifteen minutes later, as the afternoon light faded, Cicely left Pasmer's Place escorted by a small party of Jon's men to see her to the palace in safety. She made no attempt to see Jon before she left, nor did he attempt to see her. The escort had waited for her in the courtyard and there was nothing she could do to prevent them from accompanying her down towards the river. Mary came too, carrying a large leather satchel that contained what would be needed overnight. Everything else would be sent to Greenwich the following day.

The sky was dark grey now, and rain scattered through the streets that descended to the wharf, where the wooden cranes were busy unloading wine. She had no intention of permitting her husband's escort to remain with her all the way to Greenwich, because she wanted *nothing* more from Sir Jon Welles, only what was hers by right. She had removed her wedding ring and left it on the small table in the bedchamber. If he did not regard her as his wife, she would not regard him as her husband. She was Lady Cicely Plantagenet again, and proud to bear the name.

But as she and Mary threaded through the busy wharf to the stairs, she saw a familiar figure waiting. Jack. She ran to him and he caught her close as she burst into tears. He held her tightly, stroking her cheek. It was so caring, and told so much about him. He was a rock amid shifting sands, and Cicely did not know what she would do without him.

'He says we were never married,' she sobbed, hiding her face against him, unable to retain the control she so desperately wanted.

Jon's men still hovered close by, and Jack waved them away, but they hesitated, incurring his wrath. 'Be gone, damn you! My lady wishes nothing more from your master!'

They backed away, glancing at each other. They knew who Jack was, and decided he had to be obeyed before Sir Jon Welles. As they hastened away to tell Jon what had happened, Jack returned his attention to Cicely. 'What exactly happened?'

She told him, and he was startled. 'You caused his

153

mistress to fall down the stairs? That must have been worth seeing.'

'Do not make fun of it, Jack. It was horrible. Jon and I said such cruel things.' She pulled away to take the kerchief he offered.

'A raw moment, sweetheart. He will regret it.'

'No, Jack, nor do I think I care. I did not believe he could be like this. We meant so much to each other, but now it is as if I imagined everything.'

'Godforsaken numbskull,' Jack breathed. 'Cicely, I wanted to tell him *why* you have been going to Henry.'

'I am relieved you did not. After what he said to me today, let him think what he wishes.' Somehow she managed to say it firmly, as if Jon's trespass was simply too great, but she wept inside. She was able to make herself meet Jack's eyes. 'Why are you still here?'

'I knew by his attitude that you would not stay. It did not seem wise to wait within view of Pasmer's Place, and so I came here, which was the way I knew you would use. You go to Greenwich?'

'Where else? I have nowhere, Jack.'

'Do I take you to Bess?'

She hesitated. 'No, I cannot face her now, not when I tried so hard to persuade her to turn to Henry. He behaved badly, and now he wants me to return to him.'

'Then where? I would offer you the use of my rooms at the palace, but I do not think Henry would appreciate such thoughtfulness.'

'I would not accept anyway, Jack.' She gazed at his lips, wanting to kiss them. Here, in the middle of the crowded Three Cranes wharf.

'Then will you go to Henry himself?'

'No! It has to be more discreet than simply going to him, before my chambers are ready. Or he is prepared.'

'He will always be prepared for you.'

'That is as maybe. No, take me to his mother.'

Jack's lips parted. *'Margaret?'*

'She knows about Henry and me, and will help. If she does not, I will threaten to go openly to him and permit him to set me up as his mistress. *That* will move her! It will only be for a day or so anyway, but I must have somewhere.'

Jack kissed her on the forehead, just a tender little gesture, warm and reassuring, nothing that could be mis-understood by any watcher. Then he hailed a skiff, before adding, 'Sweetheart, I will take you to Margaret, but then I will have to tell Henry. He charged me with escorting you, and so I have no choice. You may yet find yourself in his bed tonight.'

# Chapter Twelve

HENRY'S ICY MOTHER faced Cicely. They were in Margaret's rooms at Greenwich. It was now dark, and candles had been lit. The windows were boarded against the night outside, and there was a smell of spices from an open bowl in the hearth, among them cinnamon, which brought Taleisin ap Gruffydd to mind.

'You seek *my* protection, Lady Welles?'

'I believe you will find I am Lady Cicely Plantagenet again, my lady, or perhaps even Dame Scrope, which is what Sir Jon Welles now chooses to believe. Yes, I seek your aid for a day or so, until my rooms are prepared.'

'Are you not to be in the queen's household? Why do you not go to her?'

'It is better I do not.'

Margaret did not notice the significance of the answer. 'You leave my half-brother and then come to *me*? If there is a side to be taken in this, I take his.'

'Your half-brother has installed his common mistress at Pasmer's Place and would have permitted her to wear my clothes and jewellery had I not returned and discovered it. That may be acceptable behaviour to you, but it is not to me. He can have his witch-hag if he wishes, but not if by doing so he gravely insults the queen's sister. I am prepared to go to the king about this, to accept his offer.'

'Offer?'

'He wishes to make me his mistress, and not secretly. He it is who is issuing instructions concerning my accommodation here.'

Margaret was dismayed. Set a king's daughter, Henry's own sister-in-law, up as his paramour? Yorkist opinion would be up in arms. Was *he* mad too? She paced up and down, her funereal robes making the candles flutter and smoke, but then she halted. 'Very well, Lady Cicely, I will protect you until such time as your accommodation here is ready. But on one condition.'

'Name it.'

'That you do *not* become my son's mistress. I will not allow *you* to be the cause of rebellion.'

'I fear I cannot meet your condition, my lady. I have no desire to be anyone's mistress, Lady Margaret, but if I am dealt insults and punishment of any kind, I *will* go to the king in whatever capacity he chooses to take me. And I will be all to him that he could possibly want. Believe me, I can secure his love forever if I choose.'

Margaret looked away and fell silent.

Cicely curtseyed politely, and withdrew.

While seated at Margaret's crowded board that evening, apart from being subject to constant glances and whispers, Cicely had a very sharp and disagreeable reminder of unpleasant events in the past. She was seated close to Margaret, as was bound to be, given her high rank, when a manservant poured her some wine. She would have drunk it had not something—she knew not what—made her sniff the cup. Spearmint!

In a trice she was back at Wyberton, the new Lady Welles, heavy with child and beset by the witchcraft of Judith Talby's elder sister, Lucy. Mary discovered spearmint in her wine, and knew it to actually be pennyroyal, a very poisonous and dangerous herb intended on that occasion to induce miscarriage. Tonight the smell was far stronger. What else could pennyroyal achieve? Grave illness? Death?

Suddenly fearful, she put the cup down audibly, and several people looked towards her. She tried not to show anything, but her mind was racing. It could not have anything to do with Margaret, who would be as shocked as she was. No, Cicely had a good notion with whom the blame lay. She turned to the manservant. The ewer he carried was small, and clearly intended only for her. 'Who gave you this wine?' she asked.

He was startled. 'Why, a woman newly employed, my lady. I do not know her name. She said she had been told this was your preferred wine and to give it only to you.'

'Was she tall, with flaxen hair?'

'Yes, my lady.'

'The wine is spoiled. Have it poured away. Do not drink it yourself, or permit anyone else to drink it, because I fear it will make you ill.'

'My lady?'

'Do as I say. And be *sure* to do it. Do you understand?'

'Yes, my lady.' He took the cup and the ewer away.

After that, Cicely was careful to drink only what others were drinking.

Later she told Mary what had happened, and they resolved to be especially careful from now on, because Judith Talby was clearly intent upon revenge—or maybe even ridding herself of her protector's inconvenient wife—and was enterprising enough to get herself employed at Greenwich Palace.

That night, when Cicely was trying to sleep in the small but comfortable chamber that had been found for her in Margaret's apartments, Judith Talby had the temerity to actually enter the chamber and come to the bedside stealthily, a mere shadow against the glow of firelight. Cicely pretended to be asleep, but watched from half-closed lids.

How the woman had found her way in was a mystery, for the door was bolted. Or so Cicely believed.

Judith did not touch her. Instead, she stretched up to tie something beneath the bed's grey damask tester, in a corner where the curtain gathers were most generous. Then she stepped back from the bed and whispered something—a chant—several times, before moving towards the door to leave as silently and ultimately invisibly as she had come.

Skin crawling, Cicely slipped from the bed, lit a candle at the small fire, and then went to look at what had been tied to the tester. It was a charm of ill intent, consisting of a dried frog, dried monkshood, other unidentifiable items of disgusting appearance, and finally two small, neat locks of hair, both dark chestnut colour. One had been cut from the head of whosever hair it was, the other had clearly gathered from a hairbrush. The whole was tied with thin black ribbon, and cast a monstrous shadow in the swaying candlelight.

Cicely's pulse raced as she removed the repellent thing, but then, about to hurl it on the fire, she looked again at the two lots of hair. That from a hairbrush was her own, she was sure, while the other ... She hurried to her purse for the little bag containing Leo's hair, and examined both locks by candlelight. They were the same: colour, length, texture, everything! Jon's witch of a mistress had been able to take a lock of Leo's hair! But how did the creature even *know* that Leo Kymbe was connected to Lady Welles?

Shaking, she replaced Leo's original lock of hair safely back in her purse, and then hurled the offensive charm on to the fire, using a poker to be sure it burned completely. What should she do? She could not let this happen without doing anything at all! She had to speak to Jon. The last thing she wished to do was contact him, but she could see no alternative. The bitch was his whore; *he* had to deal with her!

Still trembling, she placed the candle on the small table, where there was paper, quill, ink and sealing wax. The note, to be sent to Pasmer's Place at first light, was brief, simply requesting him to meet her at the palace steps at noon. There was no need to say anything else, because she knew he would respond. No matter how rancorously they had parted, he would know she had very good reason to make such an urgent and direct request.

It was windy and raining heavily the next day as she waited at the steps, wrapped in a cloak, her hood raised. The river was choppy, the air icily cold, and everything was bleak and cheerless. She did not know if Henry's spies were watching, nor did she really care. Lady Welles would merely be speaking with her husband, for which surely not even Henry could find fault. If he did, she intended to say it concerned a missing jewel that she suspected Jon's mistress of taking. She would tell Jon to say the same. Blackening Judith Talby's name was immaterial.

Another skiff approached, and she recognized Jon's huddled figure. He was hooded and cloaked, but she knew it was him. The boatman manoeuvred the skiff through the throng of vessels at the congested steps, and Jon alighted. She saw him instruct the boatman to wait, before he came up the steps to her.

'My lady?' He inclined his head.

'My lord.'

'I trust your clothes and other belongings have been safely delivered? Yes, I see by the hem of your gown that they have. Can we at least converse out of the rain? Or is the harangue to be fairly brief?'

'Harangue? I merely wish to tell you something important. Well, important to me. I cannot speak for you.'

He took her elbow before she could protest, and ushered her just inside the palace entrance, where they were clearly visible to the stream of people passing to and fro. Not that anyone gave them a second glance. There was such a concourse at the entrance, and the weather caused such inconvenience, that paying attention to two particular cloaked figures was not of prime importance.

Jon placed his gauntlets on a window shelf and threw his hood back, so that the turquoise on his finger caught the pale light momentarily. 'Well? Did you spend last night with my concupiscent nephew?'

'No, but I did spend part of the night with your evil hag.'

'Judith was with me.'

'Not all the time. I imagine you slept inordinately well, helped by some draught or other she prepared for you. Please hear what I have to say before you dismiss it out of hand.'

'As you wish.'

First she reminded him of everything that had happened at Wyberton with Lucy Talby, and then said what was happening now, with the poisoned wine and the charm. 'It was Leo's hair, Jon,' she finished, abandoning the formality that really had no place between them. 'Mary Kymbe knows of these things, because of her aunt, Mistress Kymbe, of whose knowledge and experience you are well aware. Mary assures me that *this* charm has now been thoroughly destroyed by fire, and that *I* am safe from her because I destroyed my own hair, but that does not mean Leo is as well. He would have to burn his own hair, you see. Your hag can still try to hurt him again, and again. And when I look at you, and see how unwell you are, I cannot help but think that somewhere she has put a charm directed upon you.'

'That is nonsense.'

'Is it? Have you refused her something she really wants? Does she wish to be Lady Welles? She certainly wishes to be rid of the present holder of the title. You should really look in a mirror long and hard. You are her victim, Jon.'

He ignored her. 'You are *sure* it was Leo's hair?'

161

'There is no doubt. You think I would not recognize it after you gave me another lock? This second lock is exactly the same in every way, even to the length and the manner of being cut. It was purloined when you took your evil hag to Friskney. You swore to me that she had not been near Leo.'

'I am aware of what I said, and believed what I said. But she did *not* know he is your son. How could she? Tom Kymbe certainly did not tell her, and no one else knows, except Mistress Kymbe.'

'Nevertheless, she knows. I thought, perhaps . . .'

'Jesu, Cicely, I may fuck her but I do not *confide* in her, least of all such a dangerous secret!' He was irritated. 'If she has learned that Leo is your child, I do not know how.'

'She has to know. Why else would his hair be with mine in the charm?'

'What do you wish me to do, Cicely?'

'You need to ask? Get rid of her. For your own sake as well as Leo's. I would have her dead, but no doubt you will balk at that. Keep her away from Friskney, instruct Tom Kymbe not to let her on his land, and tell Mistress Kymbe to protect Leo with every charm and incantation she knows. And to protect *you*. Get rid of the creature for your own sake, Jon. Fucking her will be dangerous to you until you cast me aside for her, do you not see it?'

'I am merely taking longer than expected to recover from an ailment.' Had he said it was the shock of what had happened at Winchester, he could not have been clearer.

She took in the greyness of his complexion, his loss of weight, and the overall change in him. 'This has nothing to do with my failings, Jon. For pity's sake, take care. Do not eat or drink *anything* she has prepared for you. Please, Jon, for we may be apart at the moment, but I have no wish at all to be your widow.'

'What a cheering thought.'

'Widowhood will not suit me.' She tried to smile. 'You

know I am right about her, Jon. Yes, of course you do, for why else do you suddenly wear woodruff? Protection? Mary says it is. *Why* are you still keeping the hag so close?'

'Because I cannot be rid of her,' he answered.

'Cannot?'

He met her eyes. 'That is what I said, and it is what I mean. But I *will* remove her from Pasmer's Place.' He glanced towards the river. 'And I will see that Tom Kymbe takes every precaution possible with Leo.'

She was confounded. What else could she say to him? 'Jon, you rescued me at Sheriff Hutton, and I have always appreciated and loved you for it. Now, *please*, let me rescue you.'

He smiled, straightened from the wall, and then took her wedding ring from his purse to push it back on her finger. 'There, that is more proper, I think. For now, however, I must return to the city. Henry has found a long list of duties for me to attend to. *Anything* to prevent the possibility of me having you back in my bed. In the meantime, you have my word that I will do all I can to protect Leo.' He bowed over her hand, his lips not touching, and then went out into the winter cold.

She gazed after him, and closed her fingers to keep the ring tight.

It was noon a few days before Christmas when Cicely was commanded to go to the king. She had spent a number of nights with him, but this was a daytime command, and not to his bedchamber, but to the official audience chamber.

Greenwich Palace was crowded, and the command was formal. She wore a leaf-green velvet gown, and her hair was hidden beneath a delicate butterfly headdress from behind which floated a fragile gauze veil. There were pearls at her throat and looped down over her bodice.

The announcement of her name was a matter of surreptitious but definite interest. What was this about? The great chamber was thronged with courtiers, even though Henry had dismissed much of the court again for Christmas, as he had at Hallowtide. He was in an inner chamber, and as she sank to her knees she understood the interest in her arrival, for Jon was there too. The three of them were alone.

Henry was seated at a table, leaning back in his chair, his elbows on the arms, his fingertips together, tapping his lips. He was in unrelieved black, the circlet his only adornment, except for two rings, ruby and emerald. Jon wore indigo, and stood with a stony expression, not acknowledging his wife with even a glance. She was dismayed, because at least they had been able to speak civilly when she asked him to come to the palace. Something had happened.

Henry acknowledged her, however, getting up to come to raise her by the elbow. 'Be seated, Lady Welles.' He conducted her to a chair. Jon he left standing. She was glad of his hand, and of the gentle squeeze of his fingers before he released her, because the change in Jon was a blow.

Henry resumed his seat and leaned back in his chair again, this time resting his hands on the table before him, as if testing whether it lived or not. 'So, Uncle, we have a pretty state of affairs, do we not?' he said at last.

'I do not wish to embroil you, Your Majesty.'

'I am already embroiled, which I am sure you have not forgotten.'

Jon did not respond.

'I am given to understand that you have insulted my sister-in-law—your wife—by permitting your common mistress to take liberties. Sir Jon, you are my uncle, but your wife is a princess of the House of York, a highborn Plantagenet, and closely connected to me through my marriage. I will not have her treated in such a way, do you understand?'

'I do, Your Majesty.'

She sat forward hastily. 'May I speak, Your Majesty?'

Henry nodded.

'There was a misunderstanding. I am no longer as greatly estranged from Sir Jon as was at first the case. I cannot assign the blame entirely to him. And he has assured me that the matter has been resolved. The woman is no longer at Pasmer's Place.'

Henry looked at Jon. 'Is that so?'

'It is.'

For a long moment Henry continued to look at his uncle, and then his gaze returned to Cicely. 'Your wish is to forget about this?'

'Yes, Your Majesty.'

'Uncle?'

'Yes, Your Majesty.'

Henry held Jon's eyes for another long moment, and then nodded. 'The matter would appear to be settled then, but there is one thing more, Uncle. I need to be sure of your loyalty.'

Jon gazed at him. 'You really need to ask?'

'I fear so. Under the circumstances.'

'The ... circumstances make no difference to my allegiance, Your Majesty, and I am insulted you should even question it.'

Henry raised an eyebrow. 'Then forgive me, but it seemed you had every cause to abandon me, because my part in this sorry state of affairs is not innocent. I was not trapped or tricked, I did what I wanted to.'

Cicely fixed her eyes on the floor, wishing for invisibility.

'That is all, Uncle. You may go.'

Jon bowed low, and withdrew.

Henry came to her immediately, taking her hand and pulling her up into his arms to kiss her. 'You are sure you do not wish him to be properly reprimanded? I will *not* have you insulted by his whore.'

'I insult him with you, and you know it. I wish to forget it, Henry. The creature has now been removed from Pasmer's Place, and—'

'He has installed her close by. My spies have their uses. Knowing that, do you still wish to let the matter lie?'

She nodded. 'Yes. I do not live with him now, nor do I wish to.'

'Yet you wear his ring again? You discarded it, but wear it again.' He caught her left hand and held it up.

'Yes. I—' She did not know what to say.

'Well?'

'I . . . do not know, Henry. I left the ring when I left Pasmer's Place, but when I asked him to come here to speak to me—'

'To speak? What about?' he interrupted.

'I believed his mistress had stolen something, and wished to have it returned. He had found the ring and brought it with him. He said that we were still man and wife, and that it was appropriate that I should remember I am Lady Welles. He put the ring back on my finger, and I have not removed it. Because I *am* Lady Welles, Henry.'

'In the eyes of God, but not in my eyes.'

'Yes, in your eyes too, Henry. You know it to be so.'

He turned away. 'Take the ring off and put it in your purse.'

'But—'

'In your purse. It displeases me to see you wearing it. You will *not* wear it in my presence, do you understand?'

'Yes, Henry.'

He paused, and then closed his eyes. 'I *ask* you not to wear it when you are with me. That is all. I do not order you. Forgive me. Again.'

He put his hand out, and when she took it, he drew her gently to him again. 'Cicely, you have made a slave of me. I have always tried to hide everything I feel and do whatever I must to keep what I have taken. I will strike down anyone who is a threat to me . . . But I am so afraid of forfeiting what I have of you that I cannot sleep at night.' He paused for a long, eloquent moment. 'I try not to succumb to my

166

irrational, unreasonable jealousy, but it is not easy.'

She put her hand on his sleeve. 'I know, Henry.'

'I am the leopard that wants to change its spots but may never quite succeed.' He caught her face in his hands suddenly, his eyes direct and intent upon hers. 'There is something on my conscience. I am sorry for so many things, sweetheart, but especially for the cruelty of showing you that blood-stained kerchief. I knew you must have given it to Richard, and I deliberately caused you pain. I so wanted to hurt you because I desired you so very much that it twisted my emotions. It was not the first time I have been affected that way. There was another woman for whom I felt similar desire. Not as great as the feelings I have for you, but close. I have tried to forget she ever existed.'

'Who was she?'

He paused, but then shook his head. 'No one I wish to speak of.'

'Did she hurt you so much?'

'She did not hurt me, Cicely, I hurt her. By leaving her.'

Was this mysterious woman the one who had taught him so much about making love?

He drew himself together. 'Now you had better leave, before it is wondered if I pump you on the floor.' He looked into her eyes again, 'Can you try to understand me, sweetheart?'

'Of course I can. I do.'

He moved away. 'Please come to me tonight.'

'I will.'

'Then go now,' he said softly,

She hesitated, because she could feel something about him. 'What is wrong, Henry?'

'Nothing, I swear. I am well enough.' He smiled.

By the time she opened the door to the crowded room beyond, he was seated again, toying with a quill as he waited for the next person who had been granted the inestimable privilege of a private audience with the king.

167

# Chapter Thirteen

AT DUSK ON Christmas Eve, Cicely walked quietly with Jack in the walled garden at Greenwich. They were alone, and had come outside openly, making sure everyone saw they did not seek secrecy.

Warmly wrapped, they strolled beside the stark winter flowerbeds, where evergreens gave the only bright colour in the light of wall lanterns. Sounds of the seasonal merriment carried out from the palace, where they had left a scene of great festivity, with minstrels, waits, acrobats, puppets, fools, and a fine Abbot of Misrule. The evening was cold, with an abundance of stars that heralded a frosty night.

Rumours about Lambert Simnel were now multiplying across the land. Fears of imminent invasion and blood-shed were everywhere, even in the depths of winter, and the people expected daily to hear of Henry's overthrow. It was also now known that Simnel no longer claimed to be Edward IV's younger son, but the Earl of Warwick. Strangely, when such rumours seethed through London and across the land, Henry showed a calm face to the world. Tonight he even seemed in good spirits, putting himself out to be amiable towards Bess.

Cicely so wanted to hold Jack's hand. Even more, she wished to be in his arms. She needed the physical reassurance, having only been alone with him twice since coming to Greenwich. She was in her old rooms again now, but Henry had instructed a guard to be placed not far from the entrance, which made it virtually impossible for Jack to come to her.

'Cicely, you have to be reconciled with Jon if you are to see your son,' Jack said suddenly. 'You cannot go to Friskney on your own, for you have no reason that will convince Henry, not least because it is my manor. If you attempt to leave London, Henry would know of it almost before you made the decision. He will suspect something, *anything*. We are being watched even now, I can *feel* the eyes. Thankfully, not even his cursed imp can read lips in the dark.'

'I know it, Jack, but returning to Jon, even supposing he wants me, will mean accepting Judith Talby. He has removed her from Pasmer's Place but she is still nearby. He still goes to her bed. And if I return to him, it may also mean returning to Wyberton, should Jon request it and Henry permit such a thing. I am particularly disliked there because of my father's victory at Losecoat Field. So many Lincolnshire men were killed that day, including a number from Wyberton. Lucy Talby—Judith's sister and his then mistress—subjected me to a cruel campaign of witchcraft, abuse and tricks to make *me* seem to be the hag. And it was believed. She also overlooked Tom Kymbe's baby and its mother. They both died.'

'Sweet Jesu. And where was good, noble Sir Jon during all this?'

'Rockingham. He is constable there. He had to leave Wyberton urgently the morning after we arrived. I was heavy with child and could not travel again. He was right to make me stay behind to rest. Lucy Talby was no longer his mistress, but wanted him back and so set about me, just as her younger sister now also sets about me, and Leo as well. She eventually conspired with my so-called "husband",

Ralph Scrope, whom Henry had sent to Wyberton to spy upon me.'

'Scrope seems to have been omnipresent.'

She nodded. 'He claimed to the end that I was his wife, but all we ever shared was a smile when I was only fourteen. He and Lucy practised witchcraft out on the marsh around Wyberton. They are dead, but now there is Judith. My little boy is in danger, Jack.' She mentioned the pennyroyal and the charm with the locks of hair.

'Sweet God. *I* will see to it that she is stopped from now on! I will confront Jon and if he does nothing, I will do it for him. Make no mistake of it. But, sweetheart, Leo is also in danger from Henry.'

She looked away. 'Yes, I know.'

'And the only one who can help you even to *see* your boy is your husband. You *have* to settle things with him.' They fell into step again as he continued. 'There is something else I must say, Cicely, for I am concerned that no matter how great Henry's feelings for you may be, when I flee the country, he may think you are involved. Everyone knows we are close, and right now we confirm the fact by walking together like this. Henry's mind is so finely balanced that I fear for you.'

'He is afraid of himself. It is sad, Jack.'

'Does he still suck his thumb? Sweetheart, Henry Tudor is a grown man, fully responsible for everything he does. I do not give a fuck how sad he is, because he is also cruel, manipulative, selfish, avaricious and supremely indifferent to the suffering of others—except you. Feel sorry for him, if you wish. I certainly do not.'

'That is clear, nor can I blame you.'

'Sweetheart, you will receive a note after I have slipped over the wall. It will be vaguely termed, but will bear my seal and signature, and will state that I have kept everything from you. I want you to go to Henry with it.'

'No!'

'Yes. I want him to read it. Please let *me* shield *you* this time.'

She nodded reluctantly. 'Very well. I will do as you ask, Jack.'

They continued to stroll around the garden, and then Jack leaned closer. 'The new summerhouse is not far ahead of us,' he whispered.

'And?'

'With suitable craftiness, we might be able to steal a few kisses. Only kisses, I fear, but there are kisses and there are kisses, mm? I was not thinking of a peck on the cheek.'

'You tempt me, as always,' she replied, excitement kindling, 'although it might be  foolhardy.'

'All the more stimulating. So, some tears, if you please. You must appear distressed enough to be taken into the summerhouse to recover.'

'You have done this sort of thing before, Cousin.'

'Once or twice,' he replied modestly.

They walked on at the same leisurely pace as before, and she pretended to be in tears. Jack offered comfort, made his anxiety plain, cast around at the summerhouse, and ushered her into the shadows inside.

The increasing chill of the night no longer touched either of them as they embraced and kissed. Such delicious kisses, that made their hearts race and their flesh melt. She found gratification just from holding him and feeling how hard and ready he was. She tasted his mouth, dragged her lips over his cheek and throat, and luxuriated in the rich sensations of twining his hair through her fingers. The scent of thyme infused her as for these few stolen moments they were in each other's arms again.

But they dared not linger, and after one last, deeply loving kiss, they emerged from the summerhouse again, she still pretending to be in tears, he with a protective arm still around her shoulders. He was solicitous and concerned, she so very much the weak, reliant female, and all

171

for the benefit of Henry's hidden creatures.

The path at last took them back to the palace, and Jack spoke again. 'Cicely, if Henry asks you about the summerhouse, which he probably will, tell him that you were upset because you love him.'

She halted. 'But I do *not* love him,' she breathed, keeping her voice low. 'I will not say that, Jack!'

'Can you think of a better way to reassure him?'

She gazed at him. 'No, I suppose not.'

'Then say it.' He smiled. 'Those three words are easy to say, but when I say them to you, they come from my heart. I love you, Cicely. You have no idea how much.'

'And I love you, my lord. *You* have no idea how much either.'

Henry had learned of the walk in the garden within minutes of it commencing, and then within several minutes of the brief adjournment to the summerhouse. He wasted no time about taking Cicely aside in the great hall, in front of everyone. His agitation and changed mood was clear to all, even though he struggled to hide it. The Christmas merriment went on all around, but everyone watched.

Bess, swathed in orange brocade and silks, with a pearl-stitched gauze headdress, observed with dismay, while Margaret pretended nothing was happening. Jasper, needless to say, simply scowled. Jon was not present, having yet to arrive from the latest of Henry's incessant errands and duties. Perhaps he would not come at all.

Cicely sank into a very deep curtsey when Henry approached her, and he was obliged to raise her. He was resplendent in purple cloth-of-gold and ermine and could not conceal his distraction.

'You went into the summerhouse with Lincoln?'

'Yes, Henry, I did. It was not a secret.'

'What did you do in there?'

'Please do not make this into a scene, Henry,' she begged, while trying at the same time to appear as if they discussed the weather. She could feel Jasper's loathing and disapproval boring into her from the dais.

'Do not tell me what to do,' Henry replied sharply.

'I am not, I only worry for you. Look kindly at me, please. I went into the summerhouse with my cousin because I needed to sit down. Because I was crying, Henry ... should I call you Henry? Maybe you wish me to be formal?' She spoke gently, soothingly.

'I care not what you call me right now, only that you explain yourself. Why were you crying?'

She loathed herself for what she knew she had to say next. 'Please do not sink back into this, Henry. Please, for I do not want you to be unwell again. I will tell you why I cried. It was because I love you.'

He gazed at her, and then rubbed an eyebrow, trying to retrieve his scattered composure. 'Do you mean it?'

'Yes.' And for a moment she did. The look in his eyes, and the change in his manner was so marked and almost charmingly confused that she felt a great deal for him. Yes, it was possible to love him, but she had only to remind herself of all he had done for that spark to fade again.

'I would give my crown to have you, Cicely. Tell me again. Tell me you love me.'

'I love you, Henry.'

'You already know that I love you.' He smiled. 'Dear God, I want to kiss you now. Your hand will have to do.' He raised her fingers to his lips, and kissed them with such tenderness that a pin could have been heard to drop in the great hall. There was not a sound.

'We draw attention,' she said gently, pulling her hand from him.

'If I had my way now, we would more than draw attention. Please come to me tonight, sweetheart.'

'I will.' She smiled ... and looked forward to him, because tonight he would be *such* a lover.

*

173

Midnight passed, and it was Christmas Day as Cicely still waited in her room for Henry to send for her. At any moment she expected to hear his page at the door, and indeed someone *did* tap, but it was Jon whom Mary admitted.

He wore mustard velvet, clothes she had seen him wear before, and there was an emerald brooch fixed to the soft black velvet hat he removed as he entered. His piercing blue eyes swept over her. 'There is no mistaking where you are about to go at this late hour,' he said, placing his hat and gloves on a table.

'And by your pallor, there is no mistaking that you are still bewitched.'

'Oh, please have done with this, Cicely.'

'I will drone like a great bumble bee until you do something sensible to help yourself. You look dreadful . . . and woodruff does *not* suit you. Rosemary. Yes, you should smell of rosemary. Why did I not think of it before?' She looked at him again. 'You have not banished the creature completely. Why?'

He sighed resignedly. 'She is not at Pasmer's Place, which is all that need concern you. I have come here because, believe it or not, I have your best interest at heart. I had thought of it already, but have now had a visit from Jack. Such a visit. We almost came to blows, but he made it clear that unless I sent Judith well away, she is likely to meet a bloody end in the dark. He reminded me that his skill with a dagger is almost second to none.'

'Jack said that?'

'Oh, yes. He loves you a great deal. Enough to kill for you. But then, I have done that as well, have I not? I saw in person to the extinction of Lucy Talby and Ralph Scrope. Jack also reminded me that you and I must speak of Leo.' Jon smiled thinly. 'The Earl of Lincoln shines when he speaks of you, sweetheart, so he clearly knows you in the biblical sense.'

'I admit it. So I am a doubly adulterous wife to you. Do you find fault? How many Talby sisters are there, Jon? Is the next one coming up to a suitable age to be fucked by the Constable of Rockingham, Bolingbroke, and wherever else?'

'I would have to commence upon their cousins, the eldest of whom is nine, and no, I do *not* consider that to be a suitable age.'

'So, you will have to make Judith last a while yet.'

'I fear so. I will be sure not to wear her out. Which I cannot do if she has been despatched back to Wyberton. Which she already has been.'

'Truly?'

'Truly.'

'And you have warned Tom Kymbe of her?'

'I have done everything I should and can.'

She smiled. 'She should count herself fortunate, because if you were fit and well, you would make a limp rag of her.'

He inclined his head. 'Thank you.'

'But as you now are, sir, you will not survive long enough to wear her out. *She* will have killed *you* off long before that happens. I wonder you have the strength to get it up at all.'

'Thank you,' he said again.

She studied him, her glance lingering on his long, well-shaped legs and the height of his thigh boots. 'Thin and grey you may be at the moment, Jon, but you still cut a fine figure.'

'Another warm compliment? I grow suspicious.' He held her gaze. 'Cicely, you and Jack must be very careful indeed, because Henry will be barbarous if he learns.'

'I know. He does not like it that he agreed with my request that he called you back to London.'

'*You* asked him to summon me? Why?' He was clearly surprised.

'Because you are my husband, and because in spite of

175

everything I still want to be with you.'

'Even though I am sullied goods?'

'I asked before I knew about your hag.'

'Ah. Of course. Well, I am astonished Henry granted your request. It cannot have escaped your notice that he is hardly a well-balanced man.' Jon leaned back against the table, arms folded. 'Tell me why in the name of God you went to him in the first place.'

'It does not matter why.'

'It does to me, because I foolishly believed our marriage was happy.'

Tears filled her eyes. 'Please do not ask me, Jon, because I have a very good reason for my silence.'

He gazed thoughtfully at her. 'Does he threaten you?'

'Me? No.' She did not lie, for the threat was to him and Jack.

'Well, you are tangled with him now, sweetheart, and I cannot see how you will ever *un*tangle yourself. He has been in love before, but certainly not to this degree.'

'I know, and it is something he wishes to forget.'

Jon remained silent.

She watched him. 'You know about it, I can tell. Who was she?'

'I do not *know* anything.'

'Yes, you do.'

'It was someone in Brittany, and it was over long before he came to England to confront Richard. He was only about seventeen, eighteen maybe. It was a boyish matter, and if you think he loved her as he loves you, you are in error. You are everything to him, Cicely.'

'You were with him in Brittany; you *must* know more than you have just said.'

He spread his hands. 'Would I lie to you? I am the personification of sincerity.'

'Discretion, more like. Henry has a secret.'

'Oh, Henry has *many* secrets, sweetheart, but this is one

you will *not* hear from my lips. Take my urgent advice, forget all about it. I mean this warning, Cicely. Do not probe or try to question him. Believe me, it is *not* something he will ever divulge, nor will he risk anyone else discovering. And that will include you. So leave it well alone. Well alone.'

'It is *that* important?'

'Oh, yes, sweetheart. Look at me. Leave—it—alone.'

He was in deadly earnest, and she stared at him.

He changed the subject. 'Now, we were speaking of Leo. I do not wish to stand by and see you deprived of your son, so I suggest we make an outward appearance of being husband and wife again. We have pretended before. I married you to protect your good name and attempt to ensure your child's legitimacy. We pretended a great deal in public. To me the situation now is the same. We can pretend to be together again, and I will be able—Henry being persuaded—to take you with me when I attend to my duties and my lands. I am prepared to find any reason to visit Friskney. My squabble with Jack over that watermill will suffice, whether he is still here or has gone over the wall. Oh, do not put on such an air of innocence, sweetheart. He is going to make an escape soon.'

'He does not confide in me.'

'Yes, he does. He is in love with you! And he trusts you, which he can, because one thing you will *always* do is support York.'

'It can never be otherwise.'

'So, if Henry can be persuaded, do you agree to my offer? I will not expect a husband's rights, which will reassure Henry.'

'Perhaps *I* want a wife's rights, Jon.'

'You wish to juggle *three* lovers? Do not embroil me in your capers between the sheets. I would not share you with Richard's memory, and I certainly will not share you with Henry and Jack de la Pole, who are very much alive and capable. So no, there will not be a cosy marriage bed. Now, do you accept?'

'There is just one thing. I spent long weeks alone at Wyberton at the hands of Lucy Talby. If I go to Lincolnshire again with you, or to be with you, I will *not* countenance the same with her sister.'

'I will see to it that when you are on my lands, you will not see Judith. She will not be with me or near me. You will not be humiliated, insulted, distressed or hurt in any way. I will keep you close and not leave you behind. I cannot say more, Cicely, and under the circumstances I consider my offer to be more than fair.'

'It is an offer I accept. I do still feel love for you, Jon, no matter what you think.'

'Not enough to keep you only unto me.'

'Nor have you kept yourself only unto me,' she pointed out.

'If we are to pluck nits, Cicely, I think you broke the vow first.'

There was a tap at the door. This time it *was* Henry's page.

Jon swept a gracious arm. 'Do not let me detain you, Lady Welles.'

Cicely lay in bed with Henry, They were naked, curled close, he behind her, his face in her hair, his arms around her. The unremarkable room was at the end of an outer wing of Greenwich Palace, and the door was locked upon their privacy. The bed curtains were drawn, and a little firelight glimmered through a crack between them.

He had made such exquisite love to her that she was still warm from it. Warm from him. It had been beautiful, more beautiful than anything they had shared before, and she knew why. He believed her lie, and to salve the pangs of regret that beset her now, she had shared his kisses with all the fervour of which she was capable. If he had still feared

178

her insincerity, he could not possibly fear it now, and the way he held her as he slept was proof of it. He was completely relaxed, as if cares had been lifted from him, and it was because he was convinced she loved him. She wished she did, for it was so very good to please him. He was a joy when his senses were liberated, and now, in his sleep, he seemed happy for the first time.

His hands were clasped around her waist, and he stirred as she wrapped her fingers around them. 'What is it, sweetheart?' he murmured, still not entirely awake.

There would probably never be a better moment than this to ask him if she could return to Jon. 'Henry, you know Jon came to see me earlier?'

'Mm?' He moved his face against her hair.

'Jon came to see me tonight, not long before I came here to you.'

He awakened a little more as he began to understand. 'My uncle?'

'My husband. Yes.'

He sat up and leaned back against the carved headboard, his eyes alert, his pleasant languor banished. His pale auburn hair was tangled about his shoulders, and he pushed it back with both hands. 'It would appear I am not as well informed as I thought. You have my attention. Did you request him to come?'

'No.'

'Then why did he come?'

'He seeks a reconciliation.' She moved around on the bed to rest her head on the soft mound of his loins.

He played with her hair. 'I sense I am not going to appreciate where this is leading.'

'I also wish for a reconciliation, Henry.'

His hand paused. 'What has brought this about?'

'His desire to restore my reputation . . . and yours. He has reconsidered Winchester, and wishes to please his sister, your lady mother, by taking me back. He feels that

179

as the king's sister-in-law and aunt-by-marriage, I should appear above reproach. As should the king.'

'I see.' He drew a long, thoughtful breath. 'And you really do wish to proceed?'

'Yes. He is content that I should continue to come to you, and he will seek his pleasures elsewhere. It will be a marriage in name only.'

'And you expect me to give it my blessing?'

She smiled up at him, the beam of firelight shining in her eyes. *'Blessing?* Hardly, but I do hope for your consent, no matter how grudging.'

'Plague take it, Cicely, your marriage has always been a blight upon me.'

She caught his hand tightly and pressed it to her lips. 'I do not wish to court notoriety openly, Henry. I hate it so. By being together as we were in the great hall this evening, we kept Winchester alive. You know it too. But if I am with my husband again, appearing happy to be so, the sting will soon go. Jon wishes to fully restore my respectability, and I am grateful to him.'

'So, my uncle restores the respectability that I have stolen?'

She reached up to touch his face. 'Yes, if that is the way you wish to express it. We were caught, Henry. Our guilt could not be mistaken. But remember, Jon is your half-blood uncle. You need his loyalty as much as you need the Duke of Bedford's.'

'So, I need the two Js, Jasper and Jon?'

'Three. *Jolly* Jasper and Jon.'

He smiled. 'Have it your way.'

'You know I am right about Jon. Close family is not something you possess in abundance. And you will still have me, so honour Jon. Please. I know you would protect me properly if you could, but it can only be as your mistress, and I really will *not* do that.'

'That point has been effectively drummed home,' he

murmured in his old dry tone.

She gazed up at him. 'I love to make love with you.' If ever there was an unwelcome truth, it was this one, but he knew her 'treacherous little muscles'.

'So you do, as you have just proved from every angle known to this human's carcass. I know you speak good sense about my uncle, sweetheart. Very well, what else can I say? I do not want you to return to him, but I know it must be allowed. To make a fuss will be to turn a light shower into a cataclysm.'

'I am sure you will always find a reason to order Jon back here again if you wish.'

'And reasons to keep him here in London.'

'Would you do that to him?'

He met her eyes, but then shook his head. 'No.'

When she thought of how icily controlled and frightening he had been the first day she met him, it was difficult to believe how very different the real man was. Henry Tudor had no inner peace, and had to face all the things he himself had imposed upon Richard. *All* of them, as well as whatever dark secrets of his own he had to hide from the world. But tonight, because he was sure of her love, he was contented.

He watched her face. 'What are you thinking?'

'Of how you have to confront so much.'

'Well, I made myself a king, and so have to fucking well get on with it. Is that not so?'

'Yes.'

'And to console myself through the misery of winter, I will not let you leave London with your husband until the spring.' His tone was almost challenging, and yet not quite.

'The spring will do, Henry, and even when I do go, I will only be a few days away.' Always she had to reassure him. Always. She moved a little on his lap, and pushed her face into his loins, which did not remain soft and sleepy for long.

He closed his eyes as her lips played with him. 'Tonight

should go on and on, sweetheart, for I do not look forward to tomorrow,' he murmured.

'Tomorrow?' She slid her tongue and lips over him, capturing, playing . . .

His breath caught. 'I must receive a tiresome legation, and deal with so many documents and legal points that my head aches to think of it.'

'Do you need to do it all in person? You have secretaries and advisers.'

'No, I must attend to it. I must be sure of everything. Once it is in my head, I will not forget.' He looked down at her. 'I check all accounts as well, every last farthing, but I do not imagine that will surprise you.'

'No. Those moths wax fat, I imagine.'

'Every one a behemoth.' He smiled, and sank his fingers into her hair. 'Love me forever, sweetheart, but never hate me. I can bear anyone else's hatred, but yours would surely kill me.'

She stroked and kissed his erection, breathing the scent of him and stealing such wicked pleasures from the familiarity. Her lips idled lovingly along his shaft, and then her tongue flicked over his gleaming tip as she drew it into her mouth. How she enjoyed it. *How* she enjoyed it.

He closed his eyes. 'Oh, sweetheart, you take me to heaven.'

# Chapter Fourteen

Two MONTHS PASSED, and it was on a cold evening of freezing fog in late February, 1487, that Cicely was to lie with Jack for the last time before he fled the country.

The court was now at Sheen, upstream of Westminster, and the threat of invasion had fast reached an almost feverish pitch. Henry had summoned his Great Council—of which Jack was a member—to discuss the situation, and the sense of alarm and danger suffused everything. There would eventually be a battle, at which Henry Tudor would have to defend his crown, as he had once forced Richard to do. Cicely knew how aware Henry would be of following the same path; perhaps the same destiny.

Falsehood followed fabrication, hearsay upon hoax. There were stories that the Earl of Warwick had escaped from the Tower, that a great fleet was assembling off the coast of Holland for a planned invasion of East Anglia, and that a huge ransom had been offered for anyone who could kill Henry. A general pardon was issued, to persuade the disaffected not to join any planned invasion and rebellion, but still the unrest increased. Beacons were ordered to be made ready along the east coast, for it was there the danger was anticipated.

Henry found it hard to counter the resultant uncertainty

and confusion. But he always managed to appear controlled and confident, except when alone with Cicely, at which times she was aware of how much the stress really affected him. She knew how very much harder he would have found it had he not felt so certain of her love. He had always been formidably resolved to hold his crown and his realm against all challengers, but at the same time his inner struggle continued. The strain was written in his eyes even when he was with her, as it had been in Richard's eyes at Nottingham in the fatal summer of 1485.

She could still hear Richard's voice. 'What shall I do, Cicely?' Raw isolation had been in his grey eyes.

She had been so moved that she could only whisper, 'Do? You have to be king. There is nothing else.'

'And when everything I touch turns to dust?'

She had not hesitated to embrace him and rest her cheek to his. 'You touch *me*, but I have not turned to dust.'

That had been before they became lovers, before she understood what her feelings for him really were. And now Henry believed he would soon face his own Bosworth Field, where he would be cut down by Richard's ghost in the form of Jack de la Pole. And this before Jack had done anything to indicate his intentions; indeed, he still appeared all that was loyal. Cicely knew that Henry's sleepless nights, tossing and turning, fending off bad dreams, pacing endlessly to and fro, were because he dared not sleep: it would mean confronting more demons.

In spite of it all, Henry still allowed her to be Jon's wife again, although she did not know when it would be possible for her to see Leo. Only if Jon was sent to his duties, and only then if Henry actually permitted her to leave London. However, in the meantime she was sometimes at Pasmer's Place, where she and Jon did not share a bed but were amicable. He continued to see Judith, and nothing Cicely said would prevent him. His health did not improve, nor, she supposed, did it worsen, but she was still very anxious for him.

During one of her very brief sojourns at Pasmer's Place, she received a message from Jack. She was alone because Jon's weekly duties at the Tower would keep him away until the following day. He had hardly left when Mary brought her a newly delivered note. It bore a seal she did not recognize, but the writer identified himself:

*My lady, your cousin begs that you come to him. All is well. Come secretly. I await you in the lane. Destroy this.*

*T.*

It was Tal. She threw the letter on to the fire, made certain it burned to a cinder, and then told only Mary what she intended to do. The maid protested, and begged to accompany her, but Cicely was determined to be as secret as the message requested. Wrapping herself in her cloak and hood, she went out into clammy fog that was laden with trapped coal smoke.

Lanterns and torches were dimmed and haloed in the gloom, and church bells echoed eerily. Sound carried a long way, although from which direction it was hard to tell, except for the wavering horns of ships on the Thames, which could only come from one place. The atmosphere was fanciful and unsettling, and she hesitated as she emerged into St Sithe's Lane. No one seemed to be there, but then a cloaked man moved out of the slowly swirling murk.

'My lady?'

'Tal?'

He came close. 'Did you destroy my note?'

'Yes, I burned it.'

'Good. Come, I will take you to him. It is not far, only around the corner in Budge Row. The sign of the Red Lion. You know of it?' His Welsh accent seemed more pronounced tonight.

'Yes.' She fell into step beside him, and they soon reached Budge Row, where the only sounds appeared to emanate from the inn, but Tal paused before reaching it.

'I trust you will forgive the familiarity of my arm around your shoulder? And the further impudence, if not to say insult, of it appearing as if you are, well, paid for?'

She hesitated. He was so serious, without even a small smile to lighten the atmosphere. 'Is that necessary?' she asked.

'It is convincing and will not attract a second glance. The Red Lion is often used for such, er, encounters.'

'Then . . . by all means.'

'No liberty will be taken, I swear. Please pull your hood well forward, your face should be in as much shadow as possible.'

She obeyed, thinking he wore reserve like a suit of armour, and she was again conscious of the crucifix and Catherine wheel she knew he would be wearing beneath his cloak. As he put his arm around her, she could smell cinnamon again. The Holy Land in the midst of a bitterly cold London night.

The Red Lion was busy, even if the street outside was quiet. It got its name from the great carved wooden lion by the entrance to a large courtyard full of shops, among which was the inn's main doorway. No one paid attention as they went in, except for one or two suggestive comments. The innkeeper nodded at Tal, who conducted her upstairs to the first-floor bedrooms at the rear of the hostelry, and then halted before one of the doors. 'I will return you to Pasmer's Place in due course, my lady.'

'You disapprove, do you not?' she observed suddenly.

'It is not my business to approve or disapprove, my lady.'

'What you wear around your neck tells me what I need to know of you.'

'No, my lady, you know nothing of me. Absolutely nothing. And the beliefs to which I hold do not prevent me from understanding love. I know my friend is completely devoted to you, as I am sure you are to him.'

'We break the Commandments.'

He smiled at last. 'Not all ten, my lady, at least I trust not.' He knocked briefly on the door and then went back to the stairs.

Jack admitted her, and then stretched past her to lock the door. Richard had once leaned past her to do the same—so long ago, it seemed— and now both worlds seemed to collide within her. Memories blended with the present, and both so sweet and beloved that she would gladly have given up her life in them.

Then he removed her cloak and embraced her as life itself. Their hearts beat wildly together and they just stood there in each other's arms. No words, only silent love. Then his parted lips caught to hers in a gentle kiss that was at odds with the ferocity of his embrace. Thyme caressed her, but she knew this was to be a farewell. He was going to leave and needed to be with her one last time.

Her heart was rent in two, half to go with him, the other half to sustain her until he returned. If he returned. Oh, the parallels. She had parted from Richard like this, and he had not come back, except in her imagination. Please do not let the same thing happen again. *Please.*

Jack's lips trailed kisses from her mouth to her cheeks, to her forehead, to her eyes, where he tasted the tears she could not restrain. 'Oh, please do not cry, sweetheart,' he breathed.

'I know this is goodbye.'

'Yes, but only for now. I will return, sweetheart, and so will the House of York.' He took her face in his hands, stroking her tears with his thumbs.

She gazed at him, committing him to memory. He wore russet stitched with tiny white leaves, and his gold collar of sapphires and pearls caught the firelight, reflecting in her eyes. He meant so much to her. To be granted such love once was more than many ever experienced, but she had now been granted it twice, with Richard and now with Jack.

He took off her headdress and allowed her hair to cascade over his waiting hands. 'I have been miserable without you, Cicely. A brief kiss at Sheen, and then a week of not even *seeing* you! And all the while knowing that Henry Tudor has you in his bed every night!'

'He believes I love him.'

'I am supposed to sympathize with him?'

'No. With me, Jack. With me. I know what he is and how you despise him, but it is very hard indeed to deceive him about such a thing. He loves me so very much, and I have led him to believe I return his feelings. I do not admire myself.'

He put his hand to her cheek. 'You are right to think I feel absolutely nothing for Tudor, and right to accuse me of not thinking of you. I am sorry, sweetheart. I did not think it would affect you that much.'

'Men have no idea, do they? It is all so simple in your eyes. Henry is no different. You use us, even as you need us so very much.'

He gazed at her, and she saw the remorse in his eyes. 'Forgive me, Cicely. I did not think, and I should have. But even so, I defy you to say the ruse did not work. In the midst of war and threatened rebellion, Henry Tudor is a happy man. Would you rather he were not?'

'You, sir, are being guileful.'

'True, but I want your forgiveness. And your love one last time before I leave.'

'That was even more guileful.' She smiled a little, but was then serious again. 'When do you go?'

'Imminently, sweetheart. The deliberations of Henry's Great Council alert me to the preparation of a noose or scaffold for the heir of Good King Richard. I sit there with the rest of them, *knowing* they are aware a dire fate awaits me. My rebellious Yorkist neck already feels the strain.' He paused. 'Today it was decided to punish your mother by banishing her to Bermondsey Abbey. Did you know?'

'No. Why?'

'It is being said that she requested isolation at a House of God, but the truth is that Henry is punishing her for imagined involvement in Lambert Simnel. If she *is* involved, I certainly know nothing of it.'

'Mother would not do anything to help put Clarence's son on the throne. She could not abide him. Nor he her. And she still has every reason to believe my brothers are not only alive but have been made legitimate again. She would *never* support Lambert Simnel. As she is at present, she is mother-in-law to the king, the mother of the queen and the grandmother of Prince Arthur. She would be mad to endanger all that.'

'Nor has she endangered it. I believe Henry is finally punishing her for coming out of sanctuary to Richard. He cannot forgive her because he feels he was made to appear a fool when she left sanctuary with her daughters *after* he had taken a vow to marry Bess and unite York and Lancaster. Henry never forgets, and always punishes in the end. He has not only forced your mother to Bermondsey but has taken her lands and property as well. She is to have accommodation and a small pension, but will live a frugal life, believe me.'

'Has Bess tried to prevent this?'

Jack glanced at her. 'No. Nor did she do anything to help Dorset. She will not raise a finger for anyone but herself, because she is so unsure of Henry. You did not expect otherwise, surely?'

'Thomas the Tub has been arrested too?' Had she been asleep? How had all this happened without her knowing? Thomas Grey, Marquess of Dorset, was her elder half-brother, from her mother's first marriage. Her mother doted upon him as upon none other of her children.

'Dorset is being detained as a precautionary measure, according to Henry. Another such measure is Robert Stillington.'

'The Bishop of Bath and Wells?'

'The same.' Jack ran his fingers sensuously through her hair, closing his eyes for the pleasure of it.

Robert Stillington was the priest who had once over-seen, if not conducted, the secret marriage between Edward IV and Lady Eleanor Boteler, born Talbot. Unfortunately, Edward had then proceeded to 'marry' Dame Elizabeth Grey, born Woodville, and became a bigamist. It had apparently been through Stillington that Richard had learned of his brother's first marriage, and thus that the second marriage was not legal. That Stillington, now a bishop, might concern himself with this new plot to restore the House of York was more believable than the Queen Dowager or Thomas the Tub.

Jack continued, 'Henry has decided to have the supposed Earl of Warwick, the boy in the Tower, paraded through the streets of the capital, to prove that the Duke of Clarence's son has not escaped. Henry also decided today to make a progress through East Anglia, to show himself to the people, remind them of his strength, and to make them understand that he takes nothing lightly.'

He moved behind her to unfasten her green gown and ease it from her shoulders and thence to the floor. Then he undressed and kissed her naked shoulders before leading her to the bed, where they lay down together. He was leisurely, allowing every small pleasure, and taking his own, and she closed her eyes with the ecstasy of it. Whispered endearments brought them even closer, and they moved in unison. They both knew how to give and to take, how to experience everything as one. She gazed at his face as he gave himself to her. It was an image to hold forever and *never* relinquish.

And when they lay in each other's arms afterwards, she

studied his dark-lashed, dark brown eyes, the firmness of his lips and the strong line of his clean-shaven jaw. Oh, how striking his eyes were, shining with love and humour, with kindness and thoughtfulness. And his hair was so tangled and wayward that she just had to touch it, separating the strands between her fingers.

'You are perfect, my lord of Lincoln,' she whispered.

'And you are more than perfect, sweetheart.' He brushed one of her nipples with his fingertip. 'We must remember tonight for some little while now, dearling,' he said then.

'I am so frightened for you.'

'I know, sweetheart, but justice will triumph, Tudor will pay for destroying Richard.' He smiled a little, holding her gaze. 'A week without you seemed like a lifetime, God alone knows how even longer will feel from now on.'

'Then we must make use of this time together,' she whispered, putting her lips to his again.

# Chapter Fifteen

CICELY WAS TO encounter Jack once more, at sunset on the eve of his flight. They had a chance meeting at the thronged river steps by Sheen palace. The sky was blood red and the air was very cold as he arrived at the very time she was leaving to return to Jon at Pasmer's Place. Jack was preoccupied, huddled in his cloak as he paid his boatman and then hurried up towards her, his head bowed beneath his hood.

She was escorted by two of Henry's men, who drew back discreetly as she paused to draw Jack's attention. 'Cousin?'

He started, and then realized who she was. 'Lady Welles.' He smiled and drew her aside from the busy steps and smoking torches. 'How are you, sweetheart?' he asked.

'The better for speaking with you. I have missed you so.'

He gazed at her, the sunset shining in his eyes and finding glints in his dark hair. 'Believe me, sweetheart, if I thought I could pleasure you here and now, I would, but even my notorious skills would not pass unnoticed with Henry's escort watching like hawks.' Then he leaned close to whisper. 'I go tomorrow, sweetheart.'

'I will miss you so very much, and worry about you even more,' she whispered, her face turned from the guards.

'You will see me again, sweetheart. I vow it. How is

Jon?' he asked then. 'His health, I mean?'

She was surprised. 'Not well. His witch is still in the offing and he says he cannot be rid of her. I do not understand him.'

'If she is doing evil to him, sweetheart, he may indeed be unable to cast her off.'

'You know about witchcraft?' She was astonished.

He smiled. 'Not exactly, but I once made love to a rather tempting sorceress. Well, maybe more than once. She was really quite innovative. However, she gave me this . . .' He searched in the leather purse at his waist, and took out something small, round and blue. 'Give this to Jon.'

It was a blue marble, perhaps half an inch in diameter, very beautiful, and cold enough to be felt through her glove. The torchlight flickered over it, catching colours: bluebell, lavender, rose and azure.

'It is a charm to protect against witchcraft,' Jack explained. 'My sorceress once gave it in gratitude for my stallion services.'

'Your ladies pay *you*?'

'Certainly not, nor do I pay them. Give the bead to Jon, and *tell* him it will help to protect him. It will help more if he knows he carries protection. My sorceress knew her art, and it is important that Jon knows this. It will hearten him. It was given to protect me from the jealousy of others of her kind, whom she said would all wish to lie with me.'

'Good heavens, Jack, you must have been exceptional that night.'

He grinned. 'I am always exceptional.' He became serious again. 'I have to go now, sweetheart.'

'No—'

'Until we see each other again, Cicely.' He kissed her cheek, and then hurried on to the palace. She gazed after him until he disappeared through the entrance. Maybe she would never see him again at all.

She struggled with tears as, still under escort, she was

conveyed downstream to London, and to the steps at Three Cranes. More steps, more memories of Jack. Tears could no longer be denied as she hurried uphill through the narrow, overhanging streets towards St Sithe's Lane, forcing Henry's men to hasten after her.

Jon had just ridden into the torch-lit courtyard ahead of her. He was alone, and saw her as he dismounted. 'Cicely?' He had come from his mistress's arms. She, his wife, knew him so very well, certainly she knew when he had made love. Except he had not made *love*, he had fucked his witch-hag!

She halted, a thousand expressions upon her face. She could not speak, she could only struggle not to cry in front of him. But he saw anyway, and handed the reins to a waiting groom before coming to her. He nodded at her escort that they could leave, and to her relief they did.

'What is it, Cicely?' Jon asked then.

'I am being foolish, Jon.'

'Has something happened at Sheen? Has Henry—?'

'It has nothing to do with Henry.'

'Sweetheart, surely you know me well enough by now to know that nothing you tell me will go further? So, what is the matter? Is it Jack?'

'He is on the point of fleeing,' she whispered, for not only did she not wish to be heard, but saying it aloud would make it all the more final.

'Fleeing the country?'

'Yes. He suspects Henry of intending to arrest him.'

'Come inside, for it is too cold out here.' He ushered her into the house.

'I am so happy we are together again, Jon.' Realizing she might sound inviting, she added quickly, 'Do not fear I am making overtures.'

'I would not dream of it.'

'Not that it would be worth my effort anyway,' she added.

He raised an eyebrow. 'And what does that mean?'

'That you are still spent from your exertions in Judith Talby's bed. The prospect of the infinitely greater exertion in mine would probably kill you. Do not deny anything, for I am your wife and we once shared a rewardingly physical marriage. I recognize all the signs with you, Jon Welles. She will be the death of you yet.'

At noon the following day, Cicely and Jon were about to leave for Sheen when a messenger arrived with a note for her. Jon was with her as it was brought, and she knew it would be from Jack. One glance at the seal was confirmation.

Without opening it, she dismissed the messenger and turned to Jon. 'Jack.'

'Are you not going to open it?' He watched her face.

'It will be to tell me he has gone.' She bit her lip and dug her fingernails into her palm to prevent more tears as she handed it to him, still sealed.

He glanced shrewdly at her, and then broke the seal to read aloud.

*'My dearest Cousin. There is no time to say goodbye in person, and so I do it in writing. My secret plans I have never divulged to you, for fear of your implication, but my silence has never been an indication of any lack of regard. Think of me. I pray to see you again in more fortunate circumstances. Loyaulte me lie. Jack.'*

Jon lowered the note. 'And the inclusion of Richard's motto makes his purpose plain enough. He intends to restore the House of York, for himself, I fancy.'

'No. Jack seeks only to be Lord Protector.'

'I trust you are not actively involved?'

'No, only in as much as Jack is my lover. But then you already know that.'

'He has not embroiled you in more? Cicely, if you have supported him in any way, Henry will—'

'I helped him once, by warning him that one of Henry's spies was watching, but that is all. Except that I have held my tongue, of course. Jack would not have permitted my inclusion in anything. Unless matters became so extreme that he needed to speak with Henry in person. For that he would have asked my help.'

He looked at the note again. 'Why has he chosen his words so carefully?'

'Jack fears my closeness to him may prove dangerous to me, so I am to show the note to Henry.'

'He is right. So, will you? Show it to Henry?'

'Yes. Jon, I do not want to put you in an awkward position.'

'You do not. In spite of his impudence in purloining my wife and issuing high-handed commands concerning my mistress, I think a great deal of your cousin.'

She looked at him. 'Could you support him?'

He did not answer.

'Jack told me he thought you were no longer strong for Henry.'

'Did he? How very sharp of him. No, Cicely, it is not open for discussion. What I may or may not feel is for me alone to deal with.' He changed the subject. 'I imagine Henry does not yet know Jack has taken himself off, so we should waste no more time, but get the note to him.'

'We?'

'I intend to be there, to defend you should it be necessary. I opened the note, and I will say that you did not know what it contained before I read it out to you. As for what lies ahead for Jack, you must be prepared, sweetheart. He has committed himself now, and his fate is in the lap of the gods.'

*

196

They arrived at Sheen to find Henry and his Great Council still waiting upon Jack's presence. It was Jon who sent word in that Lady Welles felt it most urgent that the king should speak to her. Cicely knew her name would bring Henry, who came quickly to the crowded anteroom where they waited. He wore black again, tight and perfect, with an elaborate golden collar and the circlet.

He dismissed everyone else, and they both began to make obeisance, but he bade them stop. 'There is no need for ceremony, I think.' His eyes swung to Cicely. 'Why do you wish to see me, my lady?'

'I have word of the Earl of Lincoln,' she replied, and held out Jack's note.

He read it quickly, and then screwed it into a ball and hurled it into the fire. 'So, his true colours at last,' he breathed. 'Where has he gone? To the north? He sent money, his horse *and* his white fucking falcon there some weeks ago.'

'I do not know where he has gone. Truly, Henry, I do not. This note was delivered as we were about to come here.'

'It is the truth,' Jon said. 'I broke the seal and read it first.'

Henry's glance encompassed him for a moment and then returned to her. 'Lincoln's choice of words appears to clear you of any involvement.'

'Because I am *not* involved. Nor is my husband. The Earl of Lincoln is my cousin, that is all.'

Henry gazed at her, and then turned apologetically to Jon. 'Uncle, forgive me, but I wish to speak to your wife alone. I *do* seek your understanding, and I mean you no insult.' He extended a hand as a mark of respect.

Jon met his eyes for a moment and then bowed to press the hand briefly to his forehead. Then he withdrew.

Henry turned to Cicely again. 'Is this the truth, sweetheart? Did you hand the note to him?'

'Yes.'

'You did not trust my reaction?'

She smiled ruefully. 'Henry, there is so much happening now, and you have to deal with it all. I feared you might not be as understanding as might otherwise have been the case.'

'You should have been a damned ambassador,' he observed.

'I have come straight to you.'

'You made a hard choice, did you not?'

'I love you, but I also love my cousin and my House.'

'And Lincoln even chose to use Richard's motto. *Loyaulte me lie.*'

'With all due respect, Henry, I think you and Richard have a lot in common at the moment.'

'Not least you. But yes, I now fully appreciate his dilemmas.'

'And you do not have grief to contend with as well.' Richard had lost his queen and his son before Bosworth.

He touched her cheek. 'Have you lain with Lincoln?'

'No. Would you prefer me to say yes?'

'I accept your word, Cicely, because I do not think you would have come to me this morning if I could not trust you.'

Another guilty knife twisted in her heart. 'I am still the wrong House, and even though I love you, there may come a moment when I am torn just a little too much.'

'I cannot ignore treason, sweetheart, not even from you. I know what Lincoln means to you, but treason is too great an offence.'

'He has not done anything as yet,' she reminded him. 'Do not put him to death unless you have no choice. Please.' She was begging for her love. She had to.

Henry pulled her closer and rested his cheek to hers. 'I do not wish him dead, Cicely, not least because I want to find out exactly what this monstrous plot is all about and who is mixed in it. Nor will I do to him what I did to John of Gloucester. Never think that I would. That is my past, not my present or future. If it comes to a battle, I will issue orders that he is to be taken alive.'

'Do not leave for your progress to East Anglia without sending for me. I must be with you again before you depart,' she said.

'You will be.'

She gazed at him again. 'Then return to your Great Council, and do what you must.'

'I wish Lincoln had remained true to me, sweetheart, but he has made his choice. I think you will need some moments alone, to compose yourself again, and will forbid anyone to come in. Leave when you are ready. I will send for you as soon as I can.' He drew her hand to his lips, then thought again and pulled her near to kiss her on the lips. He had drunk wine, and she could taste it. Wine and cloves, a reminder of Christmas.

Then he had gone, and within moments she heard the uproar as word of Jack's flight spread through the palace. Her love for her cousin was so immeasurable that it seemed to pull at her from all directions. Jack was York, and first and foremost, he was the man she loved, but it was *Richard's* arms she needed around her now.

'You summon me again, sweetheart?'

He did not speak within her, but was present in the room . . . behind her. She turned, and went to him without a word. His arms folded around her once more, and she was where she belonged. But it was all false.

'You do what you have to, sweetheart,' he said, his lips moving against her ear, sending erotic shivers over her entire body. 'You cannot do right by everyone, no matter how you wish it. You love Jack, and you unfailingly do right by him. He could not ask for more, and to him you give all the love you gave to me. Well, almost all of it.' He smiled.

'But to shield him I must continue to soothe Henry,

whom I still do not dislike as I should. I cannot hate the good side of him. And I have lied to him that I love him.'

He drew back, his hands upon her upper arms as he looked into her eyes. 'I know everything you think. You do not need to explain to me. Not about Henry, about your husband, or indeed about Jack, who has taken my place. I am still in your heart, I know it, as I know I will always be there. I ask no more of you. Wish no more of you.'

He took her face in his hands. 'Face the facts about Henry Tudor. He adores you, and is filled with joy that you love him at last, but he is still constantly filled with mistrust and suspicion, always watching for you to make an error that will finally prove he has been a fool with you. That is the truth, sweetheart. Part of him *wants* to be proved a fool, because that will pacify his insecurity. After that he will feel justified in *never* trusting again, and never placing himself in the arms of so much emotion and happiness that he is frightened by it. His constant suspicions comfort him. He knows how to deal with suspicion, but not love. Do you understand? So never, ever be taken in by his charm and smiles. *I* am telling you this, but it is only what you know— fear—in your deepest heart.'

'I wish so much that you still lived, Richard.'

'But I do not. I am dead, utterly, completely and irredeemably. I am your past, and you have three other men now. A king you must fear, a husband you will always honour, and a cousin for whom you feel so much love that it dominates you. That is your life now, and I have no place in it. Jack is my successor in every way, sweeting, and you know it.'

'Kiss me again, Richard,' she begged and closed her eyes as his lips claimed hers. She held him tightly, afraid that he would go from her again.

The door opened, and he was suddenly not there anymore. She turned to see Jon entering. 'I came to be sure you are well, Cicely. Henry said you were not to be disturbed, but I need to be sure nothing is wrong.'

She smiled. 'I am well, Jon, very well indeed. I have been with my king.'

'I think I do not need to ask which one.'

# Chapter Sixteen

A FEW DAYS after Jack's escape, Jon was instructed to take up his duties as Constable of Bolingbroke castle, which lay north of Boston in Lincolnshire. Its position made it essential to the defence of the east coast, Lincolnshire being considered almost as likely a place for invasion as East Anglia. Jon's responsibility was to strengthen the defences and rally as many men as he could to the royal standards. Cicely knew the invasion would not come from the east, but she did not say anything, not even to Jon.

Bolingbroke was also only about ten miles north-west of Friskney, which remained Jack's until the moment he landed back in England at the head of a force intended to topple Henry from the throne. From then on he would be a traitor, all his lands would be confiscated by the crown, and he would be attainted. Only victory in battle would save him after that. Which could also be said of Henry.

Jon departed for the north on his own, because Henry would not permit Cicely to leave the capital until he himself had set out on his progress into East Anglia. Such a progress necessarily took longer to arrange, it being required to make a pageant of the sovereign's appearance to his people. He would leave on 20 March, the Feast of St Cuthbert, the northern saint so favoured by Richard. It was also her eighteenth birthday.

Cicely had not seen a great deal of Bess in recent weeks, but they managed to see each other when Jon had departed. The first thing Bess said was, 'Do not mention Mother. I will not speak of her.'

'I . . . was not going to.'

Bess paced angrily up and down. 'I have had Henry lecturing me about her, interrogating me, as if *I* know what she has been doing. I do not care what she has been doing, Cissy. I loathe her.'

'Please sit down, Bess, you are in such a state that it has made you look quite unwell.'

'I am not unwell, I am simply with child again.'

Cicely's lips parted. 'Why, that is happy news!'

'Is it? All it proves to me is that Henry's prodding around has had the desired effect. I will not be bothered by him again until after the birth, when I have been churched and am again considered ripe for the royal cock!'

'Bess!'

'Oh, he makes me so *angry*!'

'So I see. I thought at Christmas that things were better between you.'

'They were. In a manner of speaking. But as soon as he realized he had succeeded in his purpose, he stayed away again. I feel like a breeding mare!'

'Bess . . . there is something you probably do not know about Henry.'

Bess halted. 'More advice from one who knows him far better than his wife? Well, why not? I really do not care anymore.'

'It has nothing to do with knowing him better, rather that he once said something to me that I have not forgotten. Bess, he will not lie with a woman who is with child. It is because his mother was so small and young when she bore him. It matters to him. He is afraid to do anything that might cause harm.'

'His father was an odious molester of children, forcing himself on a twelve-year-old child,' Bess replied acidly.

'Well, you will not hear anything bad of Edmund Tudor from Margaret. She loved him then and still does now.'

'Really?' Bess was startled.

Cicely nodded. 'So she tells me.'

'Even *she* confides in you? You amaze me, Cissy.'

'I amaze myself. Believe me, I do not enjoy being confided in. I'd rather mind my own business and get on with my own problems. Of which I have plenty.'

'Not least being Jack's disappearance.'

Cicely nodded.

'I am so sorry, Cissy. You love him very much, do you not?'

'Yes.'

'And I suppose my husband still summons you? Oh, these men, how they impose themselves upon us.'

'And how we love them.'

'I do not. I cannot abide Henry!'

'Liar,' Cicely replied softly. 'You have now glimpsed the pleasant side of him, and it affected you more than you like. When next you see him, ask him to sleep with you. Just that. To sleep and be together.'

'After the loathing and anger that has passed between us, he will think I am mad.'

'I do not think so. But Bess . . . be careful of him.'

Bess's blue eyes met hers. 'Sometimes, just sometimes, that darker side of him excites me.'

Cicely stared at her.

'Do not look at me like that, for it is true.'

'Then you are certainly *not* indifferent to him. Persevere, Bess, for I know that in the end you will be happy.'

'Unless Jack de la Pole puts an end to him this coming summer. You see, while part of me is excited by Henry, the other part wants his sly head sliced from his shoulders with his severed cock shoved in his mouth!'

Cicely began to laugh. 'Oh, Bess, you really are with child! I have never heard you being so contrary.'

Cicely spent the night with Henry on the eve of his departure for East Anglia, very secretly, at an ancient manor house a mile from Sheen. There were hardly any servants, and those there were had been paid handsomely for their discretion. Henry arrived cloaked and hooded, and so did she. Thus very few even knew where the King of England was that windswept March night.

They made love as the gale gusted and whined around the eaves, and the firelight flickered over the otherwise unlit room. The draught sucked down the chimney, and then clouds of sparks fled up into the night as the wind changed.

Henry fell asleep in her arms. She wanted to sleep as well, but her mind was too busy. She wondered where Jack was, and if he was safe. And whether she would ever see him again.

The gale continued to bluster, and the firelight gradually faded to a soft glow as she cuddled close to Henry in the bed with its rich wine-red velvet hangings. She had only slept once with Richard. Truly slept. And that had been at the hunting tower near Sheriff Hutton. It had been the last time she had seen him alive. The very last time.

'You cannot sleep?' Henry asked sleepily.

'I am content to just lie here with you. When you leave in the morning it will be after Easter before I see you again. In Huntingdon,' she added, for that was where he wished them to meet next. Huntingdon was where his route from East Anglia to the heart of England crossed hers as she rode north to Lincolnshire. She could not leave London until then, he had forbidden it. After that he intended to wait in Coventry for Jack's invasion, as Richard had waited at Nottingham for Henry himself to invade.

He turned to pull from her arms and take her in his

embrace instead. Then he rested his cheek against her hair. 'I know you wish to join my uncle, although God knows why, but I have to spend Easter in Norwich and Walsingham, and then go across country by way of Huntingdon. I cannot pass through that place without seeing you. I need you too much.' He kissed her hair. 'I hope to be there on the twentieth or twenty-first of April. Somewhere thereabouts. I wish to spend a day or so there, but it will depend on many things. I only know that I will be glad if you are there. Just an hour or so in your arms and I will be restored.'

She looked away. How often had she wanted to restore Richard? Especially at the hunting tower near Sheriff Hutton, where his weariness, his wretched exposure, his despair, his haunting masculine beauty and appeal had almost destroyed her soul. Just a few minutes with her had lightened his heart so much.

Henry drew a long breath. 'It all depends upon when your cousin chooses to make his move. God damn him, I wanted to be at peace with him, not to have this.'

'You killed Richard, and men like Jack will never forgive you for that. When Richard took hearts, he never relinquished them. His influence reaches out still, and I do not doubt it will for many years to come. There was something in him. I do not say this to anger you, Henry, just to help you to understand what it is that you must battle with. Richard Plantagenet was not an ordinary man, he was extraordinary, with a charm that was akin to magic. I do not exaggerate. And like you, he was not born to be king. And like you, he was capable of being a great king. You still can be if only you will be true to yourself, not to the notion of what you think you *have* to be. The face you show to the world can be quite horrible.'

'Thank you, you are too kind.'

She kissed his mouth, dwelling upon the moment because it was pleasurable, and then she looked at him again. 'Well, it is true. You *can* be horrible.'

'As you have been at pains to tell me on more than one occasion. Have you no sympathy for my wretchedly crippled nature?'

'None at all.'

He smiled. 'So, you will not let me be Poor Little Henry?'

'Well, you can be Bad Little Henry quite convincingly, and Royal Big Henry. Occasionally you manage to be Good Little Henry, but *Poor* Little Henry . . .' She pursed her lips and shook her head.

He chuckled. 'Well, I fully intend to be *Rich* Big Royal Henry.'

'Yes, well, the royal purse strings are notoriously hard to undo, and those behemoths are still unable to escape. So, rich you will definitely be.'

'I am not *that* mean,' he protested.

'Yes, you are.'

'Then let me prove you wrong.' He slipped from the bed, his lean body pale, flushed with the moving firelight. He went to his purse, took something from it, and brought it back. 'Not that you deserve it after being so rude to me,' he said, taking her hand, pressing a small velvet bag into her palm. 'For your birthday.'

She gazed up at him. 'I did not know you realized.'

'The Feast of St Cuthbert? Yes, I rather think I do. The significance is not lost upon me.'

She sat up to open the little purse. There was a ring inside, and as she took it out, he caught her hand suddenly. 'I do not do this for any poisonous reason, sweetheart, I give it to you because I know how much it will mean to you.'

He released her again and she saw that he had given her Richard's ruby ring. She gazed at it. How often she had seen Richard toying with it as he listened to conversation . . . or music.

'It will fit, because it has been altered for you.' He took the ring and pushed it on her right middle finger. 'It is yours now, Cicely. No doubt he would have wished it.'

She was struck with emotion. 'I do not know what to say, Henry,' she said softly, 'except, thank you. Thank you, so much. Yes, it does mean a great deal to me.' The ring was warm already, but not from Richard. Not from Richard. She gave Henry a wicked look. 'When it is my birthday again next year, I have a fancy for that handsome emerald you often wear.'

He looked at her, taken in for a moment, but then he laughed. 'For your impudence, you damned well *shall* have it.'

'And it must be warm from your finger.'

'That can be arranged. If I thought I could ever get it off again, you could have it warm from somewhere else.'

'I can vouch that you would never get it on *that* in the first place, let alone off again.' She smiled at him. 'You can be *so* endearing, Henry Tudor.'

'So, you do not only pursue me for my rings?'

'Certainly not.'

He slid lithely into the bed with her and lay back, his arms folded behind his head. 'What were you and my queen laughing about?'

'Laughing about?' For a moment she did not know what he was referring to. 'Oh, *that*! You really do try to confuse people, do you not? Believe me, Henry, you do not wish to know why we laughed. You are a man, and it was a *very* female joke.'

'So, being male, I am incapable of understanding?'

She gazed at him. 'On this occasion, yes, you are.' She continued to gaze at him, remembering when Richard had happened upon an awkward scene in his queen's apartments. The scene concerned bolts of cloth for Christmas gowns, and had happened at the height of Bess's public infatuation for him. Poor Richard had made matters worse by unwittingly choosing the one bolt of cloth that would provide Bess with a gown so similar to Anne's that it could only add to the unwelcome speculation.

'Cicely?'

She came back to the present. 'I was remembering something, when Richard arrived on a scene as you did with Bess and me. He did not have any idea about it either. Nor did anyone explain.' She smiled, having no intention of telling him anything more. Reminding Henry of the rumours about Bess and Richard was never a good idea.

'He will never be finally in your past, will he?'

She could feel his suppressed torment. 'Henry, to put him finally in the past would be to forget him.' She softened the response by taking his hand and kissing the palm. 'You would think less of me if I could forget those who have meant so much to me. If I could do that, you would believe me capable of forgetting you as well. Which I will never do.'

His fingers closed around hers. 'But will you ever speak of me with such love? I know you will not.'

'You are my king, Henry,' she answered softly, 'and I am your lover. To be a lover, one must love. Is that not so? You already know that I love you.' She diverted him by moving to sit over him, her knees on either side, her secret feminine parts resting warmly over his slumbering loins, which very quickly slumbered no more. She rubbed herself to him, and as he grew, so she was able to take him inside her.

'How impressive you are, Your Majesty.'

His breath caught and he arched a little as she enclosed him completely. 'Dear God, just how many muscles do you have in there?'

'Ten for every year of my life.'

She relished his pleasure. Being joined to him now was to want to love him. But she could not, and never would, even though she had told him she did.

She clenched her muscles again, but in a very certain way. He gasped. 'Sweet God above, Cicely, how do you do *that*?'

'Practice.'

'I will not ask with whom, for I believe I know already.'

'Whoever it was, sir, he did not have *your* pleasure in mind at the time.' She stretched down to kiss him.

He closed his eyes as she continued to move on him, but then ended the kiss on another gasp. 'Holy bells of Hell, lady, you will stop my heart if you continue this.'

'Will you come to me at Huntingdon wearing your crown?' she asked playfully.

'Certainly not. I will enter Huntingdon with all pomp and majesty, but I will enter *you* a little more discreetly.'

'I believe you wished me to thank you for my birthday gift,' she said softly.

'So I did. How very ungallant of me. You have already fucked me to the brink of insanity, and it is actually *your* birthday, not mine,' he said, and pushed her gently on to her back. His long hair fell forward as he moved to kiss the inside of her thigh. She lay there, luxuriating, as he made love to every inch of her, and when at last he penetrated her as she lay beneath him, the gratification was considerable. He thrust so deep she felt he sought to touch her heart. But Richard and Jack had touched that heart before him. And would always bar his way.

He left her before dawn to return to Sheen, where the preparations were well in hand for his departure later that morning. She was asleep, and did not see him dress or hesitate by the bedside. Her hand rested on the pillow, Richard's ring plain to see. Henry gazed at her for a long moment, and then left.

The road to East Anglia took the royal progress right past the manor house, and Cicely was at the window as it approached. She knew Henry would look up to see her. The huge cavalcade reached the manor house and was a splendid sight, with banners and heralds, livery colours and badges, rich clothing, fine trappings, dazzling clothes and all the splendour of the monarchy. Henry rode a black horse caparisoned in gold, and he wore emerald green, not black for which she was thankful, because on such a day as this he needed colour and display. There was a shining brooch on his soft black velvet hat, his russet hair shone in the sunlight, and he was all that a king should be, she thought. Except that he was unsmiling and reserved, for he simply could not help it, but when he looked up and saw her, he did smile.

'Oh, Henry,' she murmured, 'if *only* you would do that more often.' But why did she care? Why care whether he was liked by the people, or hated by them?

He removed his right gauntlet to raise his hand. He wore the emerald ring she had teased him about, and she knew it was a promise.

She returned his smile, and watched him ride on until he was lost to view. Then she turned back into the room to go to the fire, and the new flames leapt and danced as she raised Richard's ring to her lips. The light flashed and flooded through the ruby, as if giving it life.

# Chapter Seventeen

EASTER WAS OVER, and Cicely had reached Huntingdon, where she waited for Henry. Mary accompanied her, of course, and they were both under the protection of a small party of mounted men-at-arms Jon left behind for her protection. Henry's great procession was near now, for his riders had already preceded him into the town, shouting as they heralded his approach. Richard's ring was on her finger, she wore lavender brocade, and her hair was loose, as Henry would wish it to be. It would not be long now before he was here.

Huntingdon stood on the great road from London to the north, and was always thronged with travellers. The Crown was one of the most important inns, and was never quiet. It fronted both the High Street and Germyns Lane, and the galleried courtyard was reached from the latter. The streets of the town were crowded now, and fanfares were heard from the south, just beyond the fine bridge over the River Ouse.

It was 20 April, and the weather was beautiful. On such a day it seemed impossible to think that England was once again preparing for invasion. From her window she could look across the gallery and down into the yard to the archway, through which she knew Henry would come to her. Not as the king, of course, but anonymously. He would be hooded, even on such a day as this, and would give his name as Sir Jon Welles as he requested the room in which Lady Welles was accommodated.

Word had been sent to Jon that she would be here for possibly several days, and that she would tell him when she had arrived at Wyberton. After that, within a day or so, she would see Leo at last. The prospect made her nervous and thrilled at the same time, because she knew that when she touched Leo, it would be like touching Richard again.

She sat with an open book, her wandering thoughts anywhere but on the page before her. She had not heard anything from Jack, but so wished to. To be able to put her arms around him again now would be to enter heaven again. Instead she waited for Henry, towards whom she did not really know how she felt. Of one thing she was certain ... she was not indifferent to him, nor did she hate him as her conscience bade her. And at this moment, she was ashamed to know she was looking forward to being on a bed with him again. Did that mean she loved him after all? Sometimes her feelings were so strong and almost protective that she feared love was indeed not far away.

She did not want to think of such a betrayal of a lineage and past she had always honoured, and turned her thoughts to Jon instead. How would he be when she saw him again? She was worried for him, and bitterly disposed towards the hag who would rather see him dead than married to another. Surely she, Cicely, the obstacle in the witch's path to Jon, should be the sole object of the evildoing, not Jon himself?

Mary had offered an explanation. 'She hopes to frighten Sir Jon into giving you up, my lady. She did try to overlook you, my lady, but you found her spell and destroyed it, so she failed. Now she *cannot* harm you, but she *can* harm Sir Jon, because he will not set you aside, or worse. Judith Talby is ignorant, and blind with jealousy, and only when she has ended Sir Jon's life will she realize she has left herself with nothing at all. She knows spells, but that is all. And, my lady, she can and *will* harm Master Leo, because he could not burn his hair himself. If he had, he too would be as safe as you. There is only one thing to be done. She must die, my lady. That is the only way to be certain of his safety.'

Cicely remembered being completely shocked by the calm way in which the usually gentle maid had said it. But Mary Kymbe had been in deadly earnest.

More fanfares sounded, in the town itself now, and soon she heard cheering and hooves, and knew how close Henry was. She set aside the book, of which she had read not a single line, and then waited for him to come to her. It was an age before she recognized his tread upon the gallery. She opened the door and he stepped swiftly inside, turning back the hood of his light summer mantle. 'My lady?' he said softly, teasing off his gauntlets and dropping them one by one.

'Your Majesty.'

She would have curtseyed, but he held out the hand with the emerald ring, and she went to him instead. He kissed her palm and then held it to his cheek. 'I have missed you so,' he breathed, his gaze steady and even, his expression so warm and loving that she wished she could truly understand what she felt for him. And then follow that truth.

She was among cloves again as she reached up to brush his lips with hers and then brush them again before finally capturing them in a truly urgent kiss.

He returned everything with honest passion, and then moved his lips sensuously against her ear. 'Sweet God, I have been longing for this moment,' he whispered, his fingers twining into the silken warmth of the hair at the nape of her neck to pull her head back gently to expose her throat to his kisses.

Then he stepped towards the bed, lifting her in his

arms and then putting her down on the coverlet. She caught his hand and pulled him down on top of her, wrapping her arms around him and holding him in a kiss that spread richly through them both until feeling her beneath him made his desire mount unstoppably. There was little finesse in the way he hauled her gown up and then undid his laces. 'I have no gallantry now, sweetheart. I beg you to forgive me.'

'I do not seek gallantry, only to be joined,' she said, excited by his urgency.

He entered without further ado, almost ramming himself into her. The sensations were riotously pleasing. He abandoned himself in the welter of his desires. It was such lovemaking, the quenching of a thirst that had begun from the moment he last left her. She knew he had not lain with anyone else. He was the King of England, young, potent and skilled in bed, yet he only lay with her, and sometimes Bess. But he gave himself to his sister-in-law, and even if rebels were to storm the house now, it seemed he might finish making love to her before facing his enemy.

He came quickly, almost ferociously, and his breath snatched as his body jolted with protracted gratification. She shared his pleasure, because his emotion was so very eloquent and compelling, and then, when the last wavelet of his climax had washed into a voluptuous but calm warmth, he sank down gently against her to link her fingers and stretch her arms above her head. He pressed his face into her hair to lose himself in the aftermath of love, kissing her throat occasionally, and drawing her into his private paradise.

At last she moved a little to kiss his forehead. She did it gently, tenderly, and with great feeling, because these moments with him were always so rich and rewarding, so very close and tender.

He opened his eyes. 'Something concerns you, does it not?' he asked perceptively. He was always alert to her, seeming to sense every small thing.

She was honest. 'How can it not be? Two men who mean so very much to me are to face each other in battle.' It was painful honesty.

He released her hands and sat up, leaning back against the bed. 'It is Lincoln's fault, sweetheart. I treated him well, he swore fealty, and now he has broken his word.'

'*Were* you about to have him arrested?' She sat with him, pushing her skirts down a little over her thighs.

He held her eyes. 'No.'

She looked at him.

'No, sweetheart. I actually *trusted* his word. He is a prime example of why never to trust anyone.'

'But why should *he* trust *you*, Henry?' She knelt up, facing him. 'You have deprived my mother of her freedom and her lands. You have locked up Dorset, and the Bishop of Bath and Wells, to say nothing of the countless others of lesser prominence you have seen fit to put away. Do you *honestly* believe my mother and half-brother would have anything to do with a plot to put the Duke of Clarence's son upon the throne? She is Bess's mother and your son's grandmother. The only reason she would ever enter such a plot would be if the leader of it were to be one of my full-blood brothers.'

'The only worthy thing your mother has ever done is give birth to you. She is a tiresome, interfering bitch, and I am not the fool Richard was. I intend to keep her in seclusion to prevent her from even thinking of dabbling.'

'And you have taken her property for yourself. I was thinking of Greenwich.'

'You think I do not have a right to it?'

There was a perceptible change in him, a subtle shade that made her wary. She met his eyes and knew a truthful answer would not be appropriate. 'I would not presume to say.'

'Yes, you would, you have simply thought better of it.'

He searched her face. 'Your family will always be between us.' He said it quietly, and not lightly.

At that unnerving moment came the sound of female footsteps hurrying along the gallery, then Mary spoke urgently at the door. 'My lady? My lady? Sir Jon is here!'

Startled, Cicely drew back from Henry, whose fingers immediately gripped her chin as harshly as they had done once before. 'What trap is this?' he breathed, his eyes cold, wary and . . . dangerous.

She tried to pull away, but his fingers tightened. 'What are you up to, madam? Have you thrown in your lot with Lincoln after all? You intend to do away with me?'

Her eyes were huge. 'No! No, Henry! There is no trick! I do not know why my husband has come here.'

'Then how is he even aware that you are here?'

She gazed at him. 'Because I wrote to him that I would break my journey here. Oh, Henry, *please* do not think I have planned this! I would not do it, not to you, or to Jon. This town is filled with your men; only a complete fool would attempt to do anything to you under such circumstances. Or perhaps you think I have my cousin and a conquering army of Yorkists surrounding the town, about to fall upon you like ravening wolves? Perhaps my husband is here to face you in single combat for his marital honour?'

'I do not believe you!' he breathed, his fingernails digging into her chin until they drew blood.

Tears flooded her eyes and she was so afraid that she could not speak. She was with the other Henry, the one who was barely in control and who might be capable of anything. 'You are hurting me, Henry,' she whispered.

He relaxed his hold, but not by much. 'What a fool you make of me, madam.'

'Is this how you destroy love, Henry? Is this what you did to the lady of whom you will not speak?'

She did not see the blow coming, she only knew a pain so ferociously delivered by the back of his hand that it jerked her head aside and made her fall back upon the bed. He raised the hand to strike her again, but stopped himself, gazing down as she curled into a protective ball, trying to hide her face, where the emerald had left a scratch. 'You go too far, Lady Welles,' he breathed with icy control. 'You are *never* to mention her again, do you understand?'

'Yes,' she whispered, even more terrified by his iciness than his rage. Finally she had been physically confronted by his uncontrollable flaws, by the demons he could not drive away.

Mary knocked again. 'Forgive me, my lady, but I believe it to be urgent.'

Henry got up calmly, almost as if nothing had happened, and as he began to straighten his clothes, Cicely was able to slip from the other side of the bed. 'One moment, Mary!' she called as she shook out her crumpled gown and then went tentatively around the bed, not knowing what to do. Henry was a complete stranger, and she was frightened of him.

'What am I to say to you now, Your Majesty?'

'There is nothing I wish you to say, madam.' His eyes were like frost. 'Should you not elicit what is so very important that your husband has deemed it necessary to neglect his royal duties at Bolingbroke?'

'You do not know that he has neglected anything.'

'Do not answer back now, my lady, for believe me, it is the wrong time.'

She searched his eyes, and then thought it wise to sink into a curtsey. 'I crave your pardon, I meant no discourtesy.' What was happening? She had not done anything, and yet suddenly it had come to this.

'Attend to your maid, madam, before she attracts even more attention.'

'May I rise?'

'You *have* to if you are to obey my instruction, madam,' he pointed out sarcastically.

She went to the door and slipped out discreetly. Mary waited anxiously, her eyes widening as she saw the marks on her mistress's cheek. 'Forgive me, my lady, forgive me, but I encountered Sir Jon as he arrived. I think you should see him without delay. Something is wrong.'

The fear sprang into Cicely that Leo was dangerously ill. Or worse! What else could it be? Jack? 'Where is Sir Jon?'

'I bade him wait in the private parlour.' Mary pointed across the courtyard. 'I told him you were indisposed with a headache. He seems a little better himself,' the maid added. 'Maybe the earl's blue bead has helped.'

'Thank you, Mary. Please tell him I will be with him directly. I—I cannot simply leave my room. Do you understand?'

'Yes, my lady.'

'Not a word to Sir Jon about the king. Just tell him I will not keep him waiting.'

As the maid dashed away again, Cicely went slowly, reluctantly, back into the room to face Henry.

He was endeavouring to straighten an obstinate fastening at the throat of his doublet. His face was set with suspicion and wariness, and he did not look at her.

She took the liberty of going closer. 'May I speak, Your Majesty?'

He looked at her then, his manner indicating consent.

'Before leaving London I sent word to Jon, and said I would halt here for a day or so, then at Peterborough and Boston, with maybe other stops if the weather was adverse. I do not know what is wrong, please believe me. There is no plot, I do not mean you any harm.'

'You have always meant me harm, madam.'

Seeing how he still fumbled with the fastening, she dared to go close enough to do it up for him, and then spread her fingers on his chest. 'Please do not go from me in anger. Whatever you suspect, you are wrong.'

He glanced at the fiery mark he had left upon her

cheek and the bloody dents of his fingernails on her chin. 'Wrong to suspect a daughter of York? A woman who has openly told me she loves and supports my enemies? Why in God's own sweet name would I suspect such a woman of anything?'

'Please stop, Henry,' she whispered.

'Do not presume.'

'Presume? We have just made love!'

'I serviced you, madam. That is all.' He was cold, remote, unfeeling. And cruel.

'If you wish to hurt me, Your Majesty, then you succeed well, both physically and mentally. I am glad that being in my arms has restored you as you wished, because Henry Tudor restored is clearly the real Henry Tudor.'

He met her eyes again, and then snatched up his light mantle and raised the hood to conceal his long russet hair, which would not stay obediently out of sight.

Once she would have tucked it away for him, but not now.

'I will summon you if I ever require you again, Lady Welles, which is unlikely, and I warn you to not even *think* of approaching me uninvited. You are no longer of any consequence to me, is that clear?'

'Perfectly. But I must ask if you mean to punish your uncle.'

'I am considering it.'

Anger blurred her common sense. 'Then you confirm how paltry you really are! Not only do you strike women, but you punish your own innocent kin. No *wonder* there are so many who would rise against your reign. How low you have sunk, so much a victim of your own dreads that you cannot even make a rational judgement. I no longer love you, I *despise* you. There, is that not a fine example of how spirited and direct I am? Of how I will tell unwelcome truths to your face?'

Silence hung. She knew the enormity of such audacity,

and awaited his violent response. She felt sure he would hit her again, perhaps more than once, but her Plantagenet pride allowed nothing less than confrontation. The savage change in him had been too arbitrary, too disturbed and disturbing. From being loving, in the space of a heartbeat he was the personification of hatred and mistrust. And it was due to something entirely innocent and beyond her control or causing. Well, she would not pander to him. By doing this today he made her adherence to Jack so very much easier.

When he did not move, she sank into a deep, insulting obeisance, from which she did not want him to raise her. Let him strike her again if he would, let him do whatever he wished, *she* would not try to soothe or comfort him. He could go to the Devil.

His hesitation in those seconds sucked all the violence from him. She knew that if she said one gentle word, he would gather her to him again. It was in his eyes, but now that he had laid his hand upon her so brutally, she wanted him gone. Never to return to her. 'I believe you were leaving, Your Majesty,' she said, outrage still ruling her.

He strode to the door and left it swinging wildly as he departed. He was still all around her, though, as were the cloves, the fading warmth, and the memory of how he could make love to her.

That was all it would be now. A memory.

Minutes later, Cicely paused at the door of the inn's private parlour, where Jon awaited. She still wore the lavender brocade, and Mary had pinned her hair beneath a head-dress. The door was slightly ajar and she could see him lounging wearily in a chair, his head flung back, his eyes closed. He still looked unwell, but Mary was right, there was a slight improvement. Only a little, but it was there.

She went to him. 'Jon?'

He started to his feet, and had to steady himself on the

back of another chair. 'Cicely?' His gaze flew to the marks on her cheek and chin. 'Jesu, sweetheart, what—?'

'You seem a little better,' she interrupted. 'The bead has helped?'

'I believe so. Cicely, who did that to you? Henry? Is *he* the reason for your headache? I know he is here in Huntingdon.'

'I . . . cannot speak of it yet, Jon. Please.'

He nodded. 'Well, *now* you know him, I think. I despise men who lay violent hands upon women. And do not say again that he is excused because he is unwell.'

'I was not going to.'

'Why did he do it?'

'Because he thought your arrival was a plot to kill him.'

Jon stared at her. 'You jest!'

'No. Well, I have now discovered how justified everyone has been to warn me against him. A late lesson, but one well learned all the same.'

He indicated Richard's ring. 'Well, he has certainly left you with a very handsome bauble.'

'For my birthday.'

'*Richard's* ruby? I would have thought that the very last thing Henry would give to you.'

'I would have thought so too,' she replied 'Nevertheless, he gave it to me.' She lowered her eyes, remembering how loving Henry had been on that occasion.

Jon came to put his arms around her. 'I am so sorry, sweetheart, for my unwitting part in it *and* that my nephew has been such a brute.'

'It is not your fault, Jon,' she replied, returning his embrace, which always felt good. And right. What she felt for this man was different from her love for Richard and Jack, but still very strong.

He touched her scratched cheek. 'Sweetheart, there is an important reason for me to come in person like this. It concerns a matter that is confidential between us.'

222

A sudden chill swept out of the hitherto warm air. 'Leo?' she whispered.

'He is ill.'

Her mouth ran dry and she found it hard to speak. 'How ill?'

'Mistress Kymbe *fears* it may be the plague. Only fears, I hasten to emphasize, for she is not certain. He shows the symptoms, and there are always agues and intermittent fevers in the area because of the low land. But there *is* plague around Grimsby, on the coast further north. We should leave for Friskney as quickly as may be done, sweetheart.'

She was stricken, but then felt another dread. 'Perhaps it is not the plague, but your hag's work?'

'Mistress Kymbe believes his ailment to be of natural causes, Cicely, but nevertheless has him protected with every beneficial agent known to wizard or witch. I have even left the blue bead beneath his mattress. But your presence is required, which is why I came here in spite of risking Henry's finding out. Some things are too important.'

'Thank you, Jon. Thank you so much.'

He kissed her cheek. 'I will stay with you at Friskney if bad news awaits, but if it is good news, as I trust, then I will have to leave again almost immediately. I would be mad to desert my duties for too long at a time like this.'

She tried to assemble her thoughts. 'What . . . what will you tell Henry? He has mentioned your apparent neglect of your duties.'

'Along with my treasonous intention to kill him? His terrors are not confined to the dark, mm? I will deal with whatever he says or does, when he says or does it. In the meantime, we should prepare to set off, sweetheart. Leave Henry to me. And to Margaret.' Jon smiled. 'She is my great weapon where Henry is concerned.'

'Henry will want to know why you came here,' she warned.

'To intercept you and prevent you from going to Wyberton, where I have been told the plague has broken out.'

'And has it?'

'No.'

'What a pity.' She was thinking of Judith. 'And if Henry decides to verify the claim?'

'Why, then I was told it in error. Mistakes are made.' He smiled.

A little later, accompanied by his small company of mounted men-at-arms, and followed by Mary and the escort from Pasmer's Place, Sir Jon and Lady Welles rode out of Huntingdon. Their route took them past the royal progress, which was already preparing to leave. Cicely glimpsed Henry, stern-faced and remote. She knew he saw her at the last moment, and that he paused to watch her leave. Did he regret allowing his fear, temper and jealousy regain such an upper hand? Did he wish he had not struck her? Perhaps he was indifferent.

The seventy miles to Friskney could not be accomplished in a day, and one of the halts along the way was Peterborough. The weather had changed to a fine drizzle that soaked everything, and Cicely was glad to reach the Cross Keys, a welcoming hostelry in the shadow of the great church of St Peter's. She and Jon had separate chambers, at his insistence, although she wished it were otherwise, because it would have been a great comfort to sleep in his arms. Just for the consolation.

But if she had been with Jon in his room at the rear, facing towards St Peter's, she would not have heard the drunken but excellent singing in the street, or looked out to see who owned the fine voice. The song was 'The Ballad Of Good King Richard', all about the Lionheart and Robin Hood, but such a title drew her to the window like a magnet. It was late evening, the light was fading, and the continuing drizzle turned everything to a dismal monotone.

The man who sang was Jack de la Pole! At least, she was sure it was Jack. Hooded against the soaking drizzle, he had Jack's wild tumble of dark curls to his shoulders, and he moved like him as well. And when he looked up at her and raised a hand, she was *convinced* it was him. Who else did she know with such hair? Who else would wave to her like that? Who else would sing of 'Good King Richard'? Why was he here? Why was he not in Ireland?

Collecting her summer mantle from its hook behind the door, she ran from the room, down through the inn and out into the wet street. The man was just disappearing down a narrow alley between two buildings opposite, and she did not hesitate to follow. Steps echoed in the confined space, and she could hear him ahead. He was only humming now, but it was the same song. She gave no thought to danger, so certain was she that Jack was only just ahead, but as she reached a high garden wall where a willow overhung the alley and thick, unrestrained ivy rambled thickly, someone stepped out at her, clamping a hand over her mouth and pinning her to the wall.

She was terrified, fearing rape or robbery, perhaps both, but then a voice she recognized spoke softly. 'It is all right, my lady, it is only your friend from Shropshire.'

*Tal?* She stopped struggling and he released her slowly. Smiling, he threw back his hood to snatch off the wig that had given him Jack's hair. For a moment she saw his topaz ring in a dim slant of light from a window that overlooked the alley. 'Forgive me, my lady, but I had to lure you out. I have been following you since you left London, waiting for a chance to catch your attention. I almost came to the Crown at Huntingdon, but decided not to risk Henry. And then your husband went there as well.'

'I am relieved you stayed away. Henry was angry enough about Jon coming to see me.'

'I saw him leave in a fury.'

'Do not ask me to explain, for you would not believe it if I told you.'

He smiled. 'I know of Tudor's, er, oddness, my lady.'

'So do I. Now. I fear I may no longer be of use to you and Jack, for I will not have Henry's ear, or any other part of him,' she added, again feeling the urge to shock this enigmatic Welshman.

Tal gazed at her. 'I saw his face as he left you, my lady. It bore the anguish of a man still in love with you. You will hear from him again.'

'Is it your Welsh feyness telling you so?'

'No, my lady, just the knowledge of a man who has been exactly where Tudor is now. I recognize it only too well. Although the lady in question was not you, of course.'

'Of course.' His answer surprised her, for she could not imagine him in a towering emotion about anything, let alone a woman. She glanced along the alley. 'Is Jack somewhere nearby? Please say he is.'

Tal kept his voice low. 'No Red Lion this time, my lady. Jack will be in Dublin by now. I was put ashore in Pembrokeshire, to make my way back across England on various fund-raising errands, twisting wavering arms, securing Welsh support, and fomenting rebellion wherever I can. I am rather good at that. Then I go to Calais. But first, I have a letter from Jack to deliver into your hand. It is not an urgent matter, nor is anything wrong, he has merely taken the opportunity to write to you. A love letter, I would imagine.'

Shoving the wig into the depths of the ivy, he reached into his mantle for the letter. Even in the fading light she could see the seal had been pressed with Jack's amethyst ring; she recognized the shape and size.

She took it, and then looked at Tal. 'How is he?'

'In excellent spirits, my lady, save he misses you. A great deal. It does not do for him to have a little wine, for then

226

he misses you even more.' Tal smiled. 'He loves you very much, my lady.'

'As I love him.' She paused. 'I have spoken like this once before, with Sir Robert Percy, about King Richard, whom I still love so very much. Richard did not return from battle with Henry Tudor.'

'But Jack *will* return to you, my lady. Never have a doubt of it.'

At that moment they both heard footsteps approaching from the other end of the alley. Male footsteps, with a chink of spurs. Tal considered ushering her back towards the street, but there was no time, and so he pressed her into the ivy, put his arms around her with mock passion, and pretended to be kissing her passionately. He acted instinctively, as did she, for she did not struggle or protest, but went along with him.

The man to whom the footsteps belonged faltered on seeing them, but then walked on. Tal glanced at him over his shoulder and saw him to be elderly, stout and nondescript. Whoever it was did not look back, and clearly accepted having happened upon lovers.

Tal drew quickly away from her. 'Forgive me, it was all that came to mind.'

'I see only Sir Galahad, sir.'

'Thank you. Now, I must see you safely back to the Cross Keys and then be on my way.'

Raising his hood, he ushered her back towards the inn, and on reaching the lantern-lit courtyard he took his leave. She slipped back up to her room, took off her damp mantle and then lit a candle to read Jack's letter.

*Sweetheart,*

*I have to write this in a hurry because our mutual friend is about to depart. It was a last minute decision and so I have not had time to compose a poetic tribute to my love for you. I miss you so much that I cannot sleep for thinking of you, and the obnoxious fellow who forces you to his will. If I can soon end your torment, I will. Believe me. You are all that really matters to me. I pray I could have you as my lady before God, but we have obstacles. Always there are obstacles, and it is made worse because I hold your lord in high regard. And so I must yearn for your kisses, and take them as I can. Know that I worship you, my dear love, and the world is only sweet because you are in it. Be sure that when we next meet, I will make such love to you that you will know you are the only woman in my life. The only one. Be safe for me, and pray for me. My heart is forever yours.*

*J.*

Tears were wet on her cheeks as she read it a second time, and then a third. And then, as she had countless times with the letter Richard had given her at the hunting tower, she kissed this one too, before folding it carefully and putting it in her waist purse, along with the other souvenirs of Richard and the past that she always kept close. She had not always dared to have them with her because Bess, in a fit of jealousy, had threatened to burn everything. But they were loving sisters again now, and the purse and its contents were safe once more.

How she wished Jack were with her now, and they were about to share the bed that seemed so very empty and lonely. Another night in his arms was all she asked. Instead she would curl up alone, unhappy, anxious and fearful of the coming months.

# Chapter Eighteen

THE WEATHER DETERIORATED the further into Lincolnshire Sir Jon and Lady Welles rode until finally, as they attempted to reach Boston for their final night before reaching Friskney, it became impossible to continue. They were in a flat landscape of marshes—called fens hereabouts—meadows, pastures, small clumps of woodland, decoys and fisheries—and a great deal of it would be inundated throughout the winter. The sea had once ventured further inland than it did now, and there were salt works, some of which dated back to the Romans.

As light began to fade there was torrential rain, and a blustering wind that roared across the low land from the south. The road was such a quagmire that Jon eventually felt he had no choice but to order a halt at nearby Wyberton. He did not wish to do this because Judith was in the village, but he told himself that she was confined to the cottage where she had once lived with her parents and older sister, but where she now lived alone. She had been forbidden to venture anywhere near the castle, which stood in a moated enclosure half a mile to the east of the village.

And so Cicely returned to the fortress where Richard's son had been born, and where she had once been branded a Yorkist witch by the trickery of Judith's elder sister, Lucy. Across the marshland beyond the castle lay the dangerously tidal River Witham, beyond which, only thirteen miles as the crow flew, was Friskney.

There was no word of plague in the area, or indeed in Boston, although it was learned that the fishing town of Grimsby was still affected. Cicely could only pray that whatever ailed Leo, it was not witchcraft or the true plague, just something that would run its course and permit him to recover.

That night, as the rain continued, Mary came to Cicely. 'May I speak with you, my lady?'

'Of course, Mary.' Cicely had just lit another candle, which she placed on a table so the flame illuminated her face from below.

'Do you remember I told you that when you burned the charm at Greenwich, you not only broke its power but made it impossible for Judith to overlook you again?'

'Yes, I remember.'

Mary continued. 'There is another way to destroy her powers forever, to make it certain that she can never again turn her evil upon anyone. I have said it before, my lady. She has to die and by the same means she herself has used upon others.'

Cicely recoiled. 'Die? I know what you said before, but—'

'It has to be, my lady, or she will continue to harm others, including Master Leo and Sir Jon.'

'What are you saying, Mary?'

'That possessing another's hair gives great power. She cannot be allowed to continue.' The maid placed something on the table in the pool of candlelight. It was another charm, just like the one Cicely had found, only this one had a roughly gathered knot of flaxen hair tied to it.

Judith's hair! Cicely stared at it. 'How did you get—?'

'I collected it from the floor when you struggled with

her at the top of the stairs in London, my lady. I knew its value and collected it, in case it might someday be useful. Well, it is useful now. She must die, and soon. Her hair and this entire charm must be consumed by fire, and *you* must toss it there because she has tried to kill your baby and works her wickedness against your husband because he has chosen you. There is power in you now because she failed to harm you with her magic. When she sees her hair and these other things ablaze in the fire, she will lose all her skills and strength. She will die within moments, my lady, and then *everyone* against whom she has set herself will be freed. Those others of whom we do not even know.'

Cicely gazed at her, wishing she did not believe every unbelievable word.

'I will help you, my lady. We will go to her cottage and force it upon her. There will be two of us; together we will be too strong for her.'

'But will *you* not be at risk?'

'Oh, no, my lady, for I found and destroyed her spell against me a long time ago, and Lucy's before her. You and I are safe from her, which is why we can do this.'

'You appear to know a great deal about these things, Mary Kymbe.'

'I do, my lady. My aunt has taught me well, and one day I will return to Friskney as her successor.'

Cicely took a very deep breath. 'But how does Judith even know that Leo is my child?'

'I have learned that one of the ladies in attendance at the birth was suspicious, my lady. She expressed a view that the dead child in the cot—my brother's child—was a changeling, and that when Tom and my aunt left here before dawn, they took your living child with them. It is a whisper, no more, but Judith Talby is known to have spoken of it with this lady. Then, when she was at Friskney with Sir Jon, she must have taken some of Master Leo's hair when it was cut.'

There was such a ring of truth about it that Cicely began to pace, the draught setting the candle swaying. Then her mind was made up. 'When can we do it, Mary?'

'Now.'

Cicely's heart seemed to falter. 'Now?' she whispered.

Mary nodded. 'We can slip out to the village in the dark and the rain, and go to her cottage.'

'Then let us to it, before my courage fails.'

The wind and rain were relentless, and both women were soaked through, their hems and shoes thick with mud, as they entered Wyberton village. They had left secretly, on foot, because to take horses would have been to draw attention, and Jon would soon have prevented them from their purpose.

It was a cold night, and the wind tore wisps of smoke from chimneys, including Judith's. So there would be a fire onto which to toss the charm. The Talby cottage was a little aside from the other dwellings. Candlelight glowed in the single window, where a piece of cloth had been draped to conceal the room inside. It was a small, ivy-covered dwelling, very low, the eaves overhanging and dripping profusely.

The scent of rain-soaked herbs assailed the nostrils of the two women as they paused in the little front garden before approaching the door. There was an unpleasant atmosphere about the place, as if something was hidden there, something to be feared.

Cicely shivered, bracing herself for the coming minutes, and Mary looked at her. 'Are you ready, my lady?' She took the charm from her purse. 'Remember, she must see the charm and know exactly what it is, and then you must throw it into the fire. I will see to it that she cannot rescue it. But it must be thrown by *your* hand, my lady. So come, let us attend to what should have been done some time ago.'

Giving Cicely the charm, Mary went forward to thrust

the door open without warning. Cicely followed her swiftly into the single room beyond, swept along by her bitterness and need for revenge. The room was shabby and cluttered with all manner of things that a witch would need: dried herbs, jars, pots, dishes, and caskets, and something that bubbled and stank in a pan over the small fire. A wooden ladder led up to a small gallery, where presumably there would be a straw bed.

Judith had been kneeling by the fire, using a poker to force something small, dead and furry into the heart of the flames, but she leapt to her feet in alarm as the two women burst in. Seeing Mary, her eyes sharpened warily, because she knew whose niece she was. Then, recognizing Cicely, she backed away, brandishing the poker.

'Get out!' she cried.

Mary advanced. 'Your time has come, Judith Talby. You will do no more evil, threaten no more lives.'

'You think *you* can overcome *me*?'

'Oh, yes, because I have been taught by my aunt, who has knowledge.' Mary glanced at Cicely and nodded.

Cicely held up the charm so that Judith could not help but see exactly what it was.

The witch's eyes widened and she swallowed, but then she leapt forward, swinging the poker as she tried to reach Cicely to get the charm.

'Throw it, my lady! Throw it now!' Mary cried.

But Cicely froze, incapable of doing anything. Triumph grimaced across Judith's face, until Mary hurled herself at her, shoving her forcefully off balance and then dragging Cicely towards the fire, prising her fingers open and jolting her hand so powerfully that the charm was catapulted into the fire.

Judith began to scream and scrambled to rescue it, but it was already curling up and disintegrating into a glittering cascade. Still screaming, the witch collapsed to her knees, whimpering.

Cicely stared at her, riveted with both dread and revulsion, but Mary was relentless as she bent to whisper in Judith's ear. 'You are no more, witch! You will go to torment and damnation, to burn in Hell for all eternity. I do not wish any pity on your evil self. The world is rid of you, and I do not know a single soul who will mourn your passing.'

Judith summoned the last of her draining strength to turn terrible eyes upon Cicely. 'Your husband and child will die, my lady, and *I* will have them then, wherever I may be.' Her voice was weak but filled with infinite hatred and menace. 'Jon Welles is mine, he will *always* be mine!'

The words banished Cicely's physical imprisonment. 'You will not have *anyone*, witch-hag. I have no child, and Sir Jon Welles is *my* husband—my *loving* husband!— and he always will be. He will lie with me again tonight as we celebrate your death, and he will be so ardent, virile and rewarding that you could only have ever dreamed of him that way.'

But Judith was already beyond hearing. Her fleeting defiance evaporated before their eyes, and she seemed to shrivel, although Cicely knew it was not so, unless it was her evil spirit that shrivelled. Then, as the last of the sparks were scattered, she sank slowly to one side and lay still, her eyes open and staring.

Mary calmly prodded the witch with her foot. 'She is dead,' she remarked in a matter-of-fact tone.

'We have actually *killed* her?'

'No, my lady, we merely turned her own spell upon her.'

'But—'

'We must leave now, my lady. She will be found soon enough, but there must be no trace of us. Raise your hood fully, to hide your face.' Mary pulled her own hood up again.

'She . . . she cannot simply have died! Not in those few seconds!'

'She intended you and your son to die slowly, wretchedly and horribly. *She* died with merciful swiftness. That is the only difference. There is a charm somewhere that is directed against Sir Jon, and it has been killing him gradually, day by slow day. It cannot work now because she is dead, but if she still lived, we would need to find it to save him. He believes, you see, and while that is so, her evil will affect him. She has probably placed such a charm wherever she has been with him. There will certainly be one here at Wyberton. Now, though, he will start to improve, and then return to his true self again. So do not feel any guilt for this heartless hag, my lady, she does not deserve it.'

Mary hurried Cicely out into the darkness and rain, and they trudged back to the castle through mud and mire. Cicely was alternately exultant and frightened, and had to remind herself over and over that she and Mary had saved Jon and Leo, and probably a number of Judith Talby's other victims. They were glad to reach shelter once more, and were able to slip in past the gateway guards the same way they had left. Most guards were less aware in the hours of darkness, often pausing to talk to each other. That was when two shadows moved stealthily past them.

After washing and changing, and seeing Cicely warmly seated before the fire, Mary went down to the kitchens for some hot milk. When she returned, she found her mistress fast asleep.

Cicely hurried to Jon's apartment early the following morning. The stormy weather had drifted away to the west, but clouds remained. They were to leave for Friskney immediately after breaking their fast, and could reasonably hope to arrive at journey's end before darkness fell again. But before then, she needed to see how Jon was. *Please* let him be feeling better!

He was surprised by her visit, but readily allowed her to

be admitted. 'To what do I owe this singular honour, Lady Welles?' he enquired, turning for one of several attendants to adjust the shoulders of his black leather doublet.

She gazed at him, her bluebell gown a brilliant splash of colour in the sunless room. 'How are you today, Jon?'

He had begun to reach for a sealed, unopened letter on the table, but paused. 'Well . . . to be truthful, I feel better than I have. Almost as if a weight has been lifted.'

Seeing the tears of relief in her eyes, he immediately dismissed those around him. 'Cicely?'

'I have been so worried for you, Jon, and now, at last, I know you will soon be well again.'

'Sweetheart, while I am flattered that you still care, I have to point out that one small improvement does not mean complete recovery.'

'But it does, Jon.' Suddenly she knew where to look for the charm the hag had set against him. Hastening to his bed, she looked up beneath the tester, and there it was, as ugly and malevolent as the others, this time with a lock of Jon's hair. She beckoned him. 'See? Behold, the reason for your ill health. Mistress Talby's handiwork. The bead helped you a little, but it is the ending of the magic that has released you.'

The letter forgotten, he came quickly to look, and snatched it down. 'Dear God!' he breathed, and then looked at her. 'Ending?'

'Yes. There will be other such charms at your other residences, but they cannot work now. Dame Fortune did not forsake you after all, because if I had not fought with the Talby creature at the top of those stairs, and pulled out some of her hair, she would still be casting her evil upon you.' Cicely put a hand on his sleeve. 'She is dead, Jon.'

He gazed at her, lips parted. 'What do you mean? How—?'

'She was frightened out of her own life because her own craft was turned upon her.'

'Can you explain a little, sweetheart?' He threw the spell on to the fire, and then ushered her to sit on the side of the bed, where he joined her. 'Now then, remember that I am a mere man, and need to be spoken to in simple language.'

She told him everything that had happened since they arrived at Wyberton. 'So you are free again, Jon,' she finished. '*She* is the weight that has been lifted from you.'

Jon regarded her. 'Jesu, lady, I hardly know you.'

'Oh, yes, you do. You know there is *nothing* I would not do to protect those I love. Which would seem to include you, sir, because I am certainly protecting you, in more ways than you can possibly imagine.' No sooner had the words been uttered than she wished them back in her mouth again, for he was upon them in a moment.

'Right, I *will* have this from you, my lady. What is it that you are so loath to explain?'

'I do not want to say, Jon.'

'I am prepared to stay here in Wyberton for however long it takes to loosen your pretty tongue.'

'You would not! I have to be in Friskney!'

'Test me.'

She looked away. 'You will not like what I say.'

'Allow me to decide.'

'Very well. I did not go to Henry's bed voluntarily, but because he made threats to Jack's life. And to yours.'

He gazed at her as if he had not understood.

'Did you hear, Jon?'

'My nephew has been *forcing* himself upon you? I wish him in Hades, his fucking cock on fire and a red-hot poker up his tight little arse!'

It would have been amusing had he not meant every word. Agitated and upset, he paced up and down, running a hand through his hair. 'Sweet God above, Cicely, why did you not *tell* me?'

'To what purpose? To bring about the very reaction I

see before me now? But perhaps when Henry was within a few minutes' reach? To have you set about him and end up imprisoned for treason? Perhaps executed? Oh, yes, I should have told you that, Jon. I was trying to *protect* you, not see you dead of misplaced honour!'

'*Misplaced?* Mother of Jesu, Cicely, I am your husband and he is my fucking nephew! He shares my blood and has been blackmailing you into submitting to his filthy desires!'

'You may think of yourself as my husband, but I think of myself as your wife. I was able to protect you, and so I did. I have no sword or dagger, no armour or warhorse, I have my body, and I know how to use it.'

'I will not argue with *that.*'

'You know I have not been punished in his bed. I am prey to my appetites, Jon, and cannot help but find pleasure with a lover who knows as much as he does. But even had he been a perverted monster, I would still have gone to him to shield you. And Jack. You both mean so much to me. I would lie in the Devil's own arms if I had to.'

He closed his eyes, and then exhaled slowly. 'Oh, Cicely . . .'

She got up to go to him. 'Hold me, Jon. Tell me you understand.'

His arms moved swiftly around her and he held her tightly, his lips moving against her hair. 'I understand, sweetheart, of *course* I understand, but that does not mean I have to like it. Does Jack know?'

'Yes, and likes it as little as you. I made him promise not to do or say anything. I begged him to let me do all I could for him, and for you. I wrung that promise from him, Jon, as I now wish to wring it from you. Besides, it is over. With Henry. He hates the very sight of me, and may well hate you as much. You may find yourself banished to the wilds of Lincolnshire for evermore.'

'First he fucks you, then he hits you, and I am to do *nothing*?'

'Yes. Leave it be, Jon. He is not worth your life. Please, sweetheart. If you wish me on my knees to beg you, then I will.'

'If you are on your knees before me, sweetheart, *I* will be the one begging.' He smiled.

'And I would gladly grant your plea. You know that.'

'Dear God, you have me rigid just to think of it.' He released her and moved away to lean his hands upon a table and gaze at nothing in particular.

'You will not confront Henry, will you?' she pressed anxiously.

'No, sweetheart. Or Jack de la Pole,' he added.

'Does my affection for Jack make a difference to your regard for him?'

'You know me better than that. I will be honest, my loyalty to Henry was wavering before hearing what you have said today. Now I waver much more. Before I left Bolingbroke to find you at Huntingdon, I received word from Henry that I was to raise ten thousand men from London and the surrounding counties, and rally them to his standards. I can raise them without difficulty, but I now find it very difficult indeed to think of rallying them to *him*. There is a choice to be made, between conscience and principle on one side, and family loyalty on the other. I now bear such a grudge against my nephew that I do not know if I *can* support him.'

'Then support Jack.'

'How simple it is to you.' He glanced around with a wry smile.

'Yes, I know.' She paused. 'I am sorry for everything, Jon. I have brought the House of York into your life in a way you could not possibly have foreseen.'

'I foresaw well enough when I decided to offer you marriage, sweetheart. I may be a numbskull in many ways, but not in all of them.' He gazed at her steadily. 'I was once in your father's household. Did you know that?'

She was surprised. 'No. Why have you never mentioned it?'

'It was of no consequence.'

Puzzlement entered her surprise. Of no consequence? How could he think that? 'Jon, I know that I was seldom at my father's court because I was so young, but even so—'

'I was merely one of tens of others, sweetheart.'

'Were you there when he died?' The question came suddenly.

'Yes, along with God knows who else.'

'Was his death natural, Jon?' The second question followed swiftly upon the first.

He met her eyes. 'I do not know. Possibly, possibly not. His symptoms could have been identified as just about anything. He was far from fit, he had given his latter years up to almost every vice you can think of, and he was barely able to leave his bed. He relied completely upon Richard, who—'

'Who was in the north and could not possibly have had a hand in anything!' she said quickly.

'Jesu, sweetheart, I was not about to accuse *Richard* of causing your father's death! If anyone did it, we have to look in an entirely different direction.'

'Where?'

'I do not know, just that it was *not* Richard, who was caught completely off guard when it happened. He certainly would not have been far away in Yorkshire if he had a hand in it.'

She watched him keenly. 'Jon Welles, I recognize signs with you.'

'Signs?'

'That you are keeping something from me. You have done it too many times for me not to be alert. You know something about my father's death.'

'You have been with Henry too much, sweetheart, and have become as suspicious as him. No, I do *not* know anything.'

'You have heard the story of the three wise monkeys?'

He smiled. 'Yes, my love, I know it. And no, I do not consider myself to be one or all of them.'

'If I promise not to press you about my father's death, will you at least give a little ground on something else? You owe me, sir, now I have rid you of a vile hag.'

'That is unfair, my lady.'

'No, it is not. Tell me about Henry's lady in Brittany.'

'Cicely, you have now seen both sides of Henry Tudor's coin. He has always been the same, charming, sweet and engaging, and then quite suddenly he changes into someone you do not know at all. He is sharp and shrewd, single-minded and resolute to the exclusion of all else, and more than capable of keeping his hold upon the crown and of ensuring the peace he vowed would replace decades of civil war. But he will do it through fear and intolerance. He unsettled me in Brittany, for I could *feel* the imbalance in him. Now, however, that imbalance can make a monster of him. You have been a beneficial influence on him, but if there has been a rift, God alone knows how he will react. Believe me, I now regard Richard as a tragic, truly irreplaceable loss. If Bosworth were to be fought again, I would be with him, not my nephew.'

'You are not answering my question.'

'Because I dare not.'

She drew back. 'Dare not?'

'The less you know the better. Please, sweetheart, leave it alone. I will answer about your father instead. Yes, I believe he was poisoned, but I do not know whose hand administered the draught, or whatever way it was done. Or *why* it was done. There were whispers, but no more than that. I cannot tell you anything more. Now, please, can we leave both topics?'

'I will return to them, Jon.'

He raised an eyebrow. 'You think I do not know it?'

He reached again for the sealed note he had been about to pick up earlier. 'In the meantime, perhaps this is of much more importance. It arrived moments before you did, and I was going to open it in your presence as soon as I was dressed. It is from Tom Kymbe. His rider saw my banners raised here. If he had not, he would have ridden on to Huntingdon, and we would surely have reached Friskney without receiving it. Forgive me for not giving it to you the moment you entered. You may open it, if you wish.'

Her hand shook as she took the rolled sheet and broke the seal. She read aloud.

> *'Sir Jon – I am glad to let you know that Master Leo is no worse, and my aunt believes he is going to recover with no lasting ill effect upon his health.'*

Her breath caught and she looked at Jon, her eyes alight with joy and tears. 'He is going to be all right, Jon!'

'Finish it, sweetheart, to be absolutely sure.'

> *'It was not the plague, but some ague. Please be so good as to relay this to Lady Welles, whose anxiety must be weighing heavily upon her. Come gladly to Friskney, for bad news will not await you.'*

The note slipped from her fingers and she hid her face in her hands, sobbing her relief. Jon went to her, gathering her close to stroke her hair. 'All is well after all,' he said gently. 'I should have given it to you immediately, but the conversation's direction rather confounded me.'

She clung to him, her face buried against him. 'Leo is going to be well, Jon! He is not going to die!' The words were muffled and barely comprehensible.

'I am so happy for you, sweetheart.'

She drew back quickly. 'You will still take me to him?'

'Of course.'

'This is a moment for a kiss, Jon. Do not deny me now. Not now.'

She raised her lips, but he released himself from her arms. 'No, sweetheart.'

'But why not? Is it not plain that we still love each other?'

'I love you, Cicely, but whatever it is you feel for me, it is not enough. I could accept that Richard would always come first with you, because he was dead. I can force myself to accept Henry, because I now know the truth of it, but Jack de la Pole is very much alive. I will not share you with him.'

'He is not your rival, Jon. What I feel for him and what I feel for you are two very different things. You own a very special part of my heart, and you always will. You are my husband, and the only man with an undeniable right to my body. It is not a right that I resent; indeed I welcome it because *you* matter so very much to me. And if I am yours, then you are mine. We belong together.'

'Oh, Cicely, how sweetly you juggle words.'

'And how elegantly you begin to think of surrender,' she answered softly, smiling. 'You are about to make love to me again, and you know it.' She moved closer and began to undo his doublet. 'It is such a shame to take off the clothes in which you have just been so patiently attired.'

'I feel I should be protesting now, my lady.'

'Resistance is pointless,' she answered, standing on tiptoe to kiss him.

And as he responded at last, her eyes closed with the bliss of it. She had missed this husband of hers, for he had a particular and subtle command of her affections. He was her friend and lover, her calming influence and conscience, and she was aware of the honour of having his love.

But Jack possessed her passion and blood, and Richard, the beloved, grieved-for uncle would never be truly dead to her. These three men illuminated her life like the panes of a magnificent stained-glass window, shedding spangles of light over everything she was. She was blessed. The most blessed creature that ever drew breath.

# Chapter Nineteen

THE MUDDY ROADS were drying fast in the brisk breeze, and the final miles from Wyberton through Boston to Friskney took all day. It was nightfall when Tom Kymbe's 200-year-old moated house appeared ahead, with torches alight at the top of the single tower in the south-west corner. The land was low and mostly marshy, fens that in winter suffered from flooding, as did Wyberton and a great deal of east Lincolnshire. There were areas of cranberries, of peat moss, countless small waterways and some small clumps of woodland. Profitable decoys were much in evidence, trapping wild duck, widgeon and teal, as well as many other waterfowl that brought a good price at market. Friskney itself was a prosperous village, relying upon its wet but fertile terrain.

This was where Richard had instructed Jack to bring her brothers in 1483, to the late Yorkist supporter, Thomas Kymbe, and where her boy was now under the protection of Thomas's Lancastrian son, Tom Kymbe, whose devotion to Jon was such that he was prepared to guard such an important Yorkist boy. It was also where Jack had warned her she would see him if things went against his cause. Three important trails led to this village in the middle of the Lincolnshire lowlands.

Cicely was delighted that Jon was clearly getting better, and being in his bed again was such a longed-for comfort to her. To them both. They were together again as man and wife, and she wished to mark the reunion in a way that was very personal to her. She associated the men of importance in her life with certain scents and precious stones. Costmary, mint and rubies for Richard, thyme and amethysts for Jack, and cloves and emeralds for Henry, although she could no longer think well of the latter. Now there would be rosemary and turquoises for Jon. She would request Mistress Kymbe to provide her with some oil of rosemary, and Lord Welles would find himself being smoothed all over with it by his attentive and deter-minedly seductive lady.

They drew nearer to the house, where the moat was spanned by a wide, three-arched stone bridge, illuminated with lanterns. The entrance to the torchlit courtyard was through a gatehouse beneath a large arched window, its coloured glass lit from within. The house was not impressive, except for the tower, nor was it particularly beautiful, but it was solid and defended well by the moat. The tower would give an unrivalled view for miles over the surrounding fens.

She reined in suddenly. 'Jon, do you really have to return to Bolingbroke soon?'

'Yes, sweetheart. As quickly as possible.'

'When . . . when you see Henry, will you have to tell him where I am?'

'If he asks, yes, of course. I will say that you are unwell and wished to be in Mistress Kymbe's excellent care rather than Bolingbroke.'

'Can you not say I am at Wyberton? I do not want him to know I am here.'

He leaned over to squeeze her fingers. 'Sweetheart, with Henry it is always best to stick as close to the truth as pos-sible. Lies can lead to more lies, and thus to pitfalls, and my nephew will pounce upon each one.'

'But he may think I am here because of something to do with Jack.'

'Who happens to hold the manor? Yes, I am well aware of that, and so, no doubt, is Henry. He will have made sure of all your cousin's lands, with intent to seize them the moment he can. Other than that, Henry will only be interested in Friskney if he wishes to see you himself, and then he will send for you, not come here in person. So be easy, sweetheart. You will be with your son for some time, which I am sure will gladden your heart to the exclusion of all else.'

'No, not to the exclusion of all else, Jon. There is so much danger ahead for you, and I know how divided your loyalty has become.'

'It is all in the lap of the gods, sweetheart, and fate has already decided who will live and who will die.' He leaned across to draw her hand to his lips. 'You must be strong, there is no other way. The men do battle, the women have to wait. Even Lady Welles.' He smiled.

Watchmen looked down from the tower as the riders approached, the yellow and black colours of Sir Jon Welles becoming plainly visible as they crossed the bridge and into the courtyard, where the surrounding walls were welcome protection from the stream of unexpectedly chill air from the sea. Torches flickered and smoked, servants hurried to attend the tired travellers, there were voices, and the tired horses stamped and snorted.

Tom Kymbe came out to welcome them. He was a little younger than Jon, although not by many years, and was good-looking, weatherworn and sturdily built, with a mass of brown curls and light brown eyes. He was very like Mary, both in looks and, as Cicely knew since Judith's demise, in character too. There was steel in the Kymbe siblings, hidden within an amiable exterior. His clothes were good, but not rich, and he had a calm manner that Cicely knew concealed a ferocious ability to defend whatever and whoever he had to. She trusted him implicitly.

Mary beamed to see her brother again, for the two were very close, and he winked at her as he came down a shallow flight of worn stone steps to greet Jon. 'Sir Jon, welcome to Friskney. My lady.' He bowed to Cicely.

She smiled. 'Master Kymbe.'

Jon dismounted, and clapped him warmly on the shoulder, a sign of true friendship. 'We arrive to good news, I think, Tom?'

'Indeed, Sir Jon. May I say that you look better than when I last saw you?'

'I *am* better, Tom. The source of my problem is now extinct.'

'I know, Sir Jon. My aunt realized the moment it happened.'

Jon smiled ruefully. 'Ah, yes, Mistress Kymbe has the craft. I should never forget it.'

Then Tom looked at Cicely again. 'My lady, I am truly glad to be able to tell you that Master Leo is recovering.' He spoke from the heart, because he had suffered great bereavement—his lady and his baby son—at the hands of the elder Talby sister.

She smiled as Jon helped her down from her tired palfrey. 'I am so glad, Master Kymbe. Thank you for sending the message, I was so grateful.'

'I believed you would be, my lady.'

'May I see my little boy?'

'Of course, my lady, but will you not wish to take refreshment first?'

'I have waited since February last year to see my child, Master Kymbe, and will not delay a moment more. He was a few hours old when he went from me, now he is fourteen months. I *must* see him.'

He smiled. 'Then allow me to escort you myself.' He glanced at Jon. 'With your permission, sir?'

'I would not dare to refuse.' Jon took Cicely's hand quickly, and raised it to his lips. 'You will be proud, sweetheart, for he is a fine boy.'

Richard's name was in the air around them as he released her hand again and she followed Tom into the house. Inside, in the candlelit screen passage that led through to a walled garden at the rear, servants came to relieve her of her outdoor clothes, revealing the bluebell gown beneath.

Tom led her up to the great hall on the first floor, where lamps shone, and thence into the private apartments beyond the dais. The rooms were brightly lit by candles, and his aunt stood waiting. Then he left the two women together.

Mistress Katherine Kymbe was a small, almost wizened figure in a grey kirtle and gown, her hair hidden beneath a wimple. Like Henry's imp, she had not always been deaf, and communicated by reading lips, which she did very well indeed. She began to sink into an awkward curtsey, but Cicely prevented her.

'No ceremony, please, Mistress Kymbe. Oh, I am happy to see you again.' She hugged the old lady. 'Thank you for caring for Leo for me. I am so very indebted and thankful.' She spoke clearly, the better to be easily read.

'We do it for you and Sir Jon, my lady, and—forgive my forwardness—I am pleased that you and he are in accord again. It was so sad that you were estranged.'

'How do you know we are reconciled? We have only just arrived and I have come straight up here.'

The old lady smiled. 'I know these things.'

'As you knew of Judith Talby's demise?'

'Of course. And I know by the lightness of your tread that you have lain with your husband again. You have been brought together because the hag is dead. Do you deny it, my lady?'

'There would be little point.' Cicely smiled.

249

'Nor would there be any point in denying that you love another more. Your cousin, Lord Lincoln.'

Cicely recoiled. 'How can you possibly know *that*?'

'I just know, my lady. He is in your soul as was your uncle, King Richard. I can sense the bond between you and these two great men. You mean no hurt to Sir Jon, whom you love greatly, but now it is Lord Lincoln who holds your heart, and for whom you feel great anguish.'

'It is true, Mistress Kymbe, but I am resigned to having to wait to learn if he is to live or die. I so want to see him again. I *long* for it.'

'Do not give up hope, my lady. I am sure you will see him again. He is a very comely lord. I remember when he came here with your brothers, and can see so very well why you love him. If I were many years younger, why, I might even try to take him from you.' The old lady smiled like a little pixie, but then became more serious, searching Cicely's face. 'You will wish to learn of your brothers' time here.' It was a statement, not a question.

'Yes, Mistress Kymbe, I would very much like to know of them.'

'I will tell you all. I am the only one here who knows their identities. And Mary, of course. If any others are aware, they can be trusted to hold their tongues. Tom only knows two boys were brought here by your cousin and then taken away not long before Bosworth Field.'

'The Kymbe family has been invaluable to my family.'

'We do as our hearts direct. Now then . . .' Mistress Kymbe indicated a drawn arras curtain. 'Master Leo sleeps in the nursery beyond, my lady. I will leave you now, but Mary will be within hearing, should you need either of us.'

As the old lady withdrew, Cicely turned towards the curtain, suddenly afraid to step beyond it. How she wished Richard could be with her now.

'I *am* with you now, sweetheart.' He took her right hand and smiled at her.

She closed her eyes and lifted his fingers to her lips. Why did he feel so warm and real? He was a figment of her mind's longing, but even so he made everything sweet again. 'I will always love you most of all, Richard,' she whispered, and for a moment his arms enfolded her again. She could smell the mint on his breath and the costmary on his clothes. Oh, such scents, so evocative, so heartbreakingly beloved.

He raised her hand to look at the ruby ring. 'It is good that *you* have it now,' he said, drawing it to his lips.

'Put it on again, Richard. Please. Let it come direct from you, that I see it on your finger and then on mine. I know you are not real, but I want to imagine it so very much.'

'It is that important?'

'Yes.'

He took the ring and slipped it on the shortened little finger of his right hand. He left it there for a few moments, and then returned it to her finger. 'There, now it is direct from me to you.'

'I miss you so much, Richard.'

He put his hand to her cheek and caressed her with his thumb. 'You have living lovers now, sweetheart, Jack and your husband. Leave me in the past, where I should be allowed to stay.'

'But not at times like this, when I am to see Leo again. You are the only one who should be with me now.'

'Yes, I believe so too. At least, my second self should be with you now.' He took her hand again. 'Come, we will see our son together.'

He held the curtain aside for her to go into the nursery, where a fire burned in the small hearth, and more light was shed by a night candle on a small table. Leo slept in his cot, his dark hair tousled, his plump little cheeks flushed.

Tears welled in Cicely's eyes. 'We did well, did we not?' she said softly, as Richard had said to her on the night Leo was born.

'Yes, sweeting, we did.' He glanced down at Leo again. 'Pick him up, hold him a while.'

'Do you think I should?' she asked nonsensically.

'You would come all the way here and *not* hold him?' Richard smiled, loving her with his eyes. Those wonderful eyes, so grey and expressive.

She bent to gather the sleeping child into her arms. He was warm and cosy, stirring a little and stretching, but he did not awaken, instead he snuggled closer, his little face turned towards her, his long dark lashes resting against his cheeks. He was delicately made, like his father, and could not fail to be in the same image.

Richard put his arm around her again, so that Leo was almost between them, and then he rested his forehead to hers. 'He is well cared for, Cicely, because he is surrounded by those who love him.'

'But I am not here with him, Richard. *I* am not here.'

He kissed her forehead. 'Who can say what will transpire?'

'What do you mean?'

'Only that we do not know what the future holds.'

She closed her eyes. 'Not even what will result from this rebellion.'

He put his hand to her chin. 'I think you do know, sweetheart, you simply do not want to confront it. That is why you speak of it to *me*, so that *I* will tell you.'

'Then do not say it, please.' She had been refusing to face it, but now she had to.

'You do not think Jack will succeed in this, Cicely. You felt it at the outset, and in your heart of hearts nothing has changed. You are desperately afraid for him, but nothing you could have said or done would change him from his course. Look at me, sweetheart. You *know* this. Tell me you do.'

Her lips remained firmly closed.

'Say it, sweetheart,' he said gently.

'I know it,' she whispered, fresh tears running down her cheeks. Yes, she had only put her own fears into Richard's mouth. She *did* fear her cousin's defeat. Henry appeared to live a charmed life, and would remain in the ascendant. 'I love Jack so, Richard. Henry will overcome him, and I will lose another man who is precious to me.' She held Leo even closer, her body trembling as she tried not to sob aloud and awaken him.

'The wheels turn, Cicely. Fate has already brought you here to Friskney, and Jack *will* come here. He felt it too, or he would not have made such a point of telling you. He will be a defeated man, in danger of his life, sought by Henry's men. There is nothing that can change it. Jack has thrown the dice and must now play the game. All you can do is wait here for him.'

'But what is there that I can actually *do* for him?'

'Help him to leave the country.'

She gazed at him over Leo's head. 'But it may not happen, Richard. Jack may overthrow Henry.'

'Do you believe it?'

'Henry is the Devil's own.'

Richard nodded. 'Do I not know it,' he said softly.

She felt him begin to alter . . . to fade. She always felt it. 'You *will* come to me again?' she whispered.

'Yes, because you need me.'

She gazed at him. 'Kiss me,' she whispered.

His lips were warm and pliable, tender and loving, and she slipped into his matchless spell, but then, gradually, she could no longer feel him. Or see him.

She cuddled Leo, and after a moment began to hum a little lullaby. Her eyes were closed as she rocked gently. She was holding her son, Richard had been with her, and for a few moments they had been parents with their child. Oh, such brief conjured moments, but incredibly important to her. Leo stirred again, and slowly opened his big grey eyes. Then he smiled, made a little cooing sound and stretched up a plump little hand to touch the rich embroidery on her gown.

Jon slept with her that night, for the first time in months. He held her lovingly, his arms closed around her, his face against her hair. They were together, tender and filled with affection. Just that. They did not make love, they simply lay lovingly together. She was as glad of him now as she ever had been. His breathing was steady and deep, but she knew he dreamed. Of what? The coming conflict? Unable to stave off her fears, she wriggled around to face him, hold him tightly, and breathe the male scent of him. He drew her near instinctively, not awakening.

At daybreak, as the morning sun fingered subtly into the room, casting the first beams of muted light across the colourful tapestry on the wall, Sir Jon and Lady Welles made love again, slowly and sweetly. They did not know when they would be together next, because he and Tom Kymbe would be leaving for Bolingbroke as soon as everyone had broken their fast.

She watched from the solar window as they rode out of Friskney at the head of the large group of mounted men-at-arms that Tom had raised in the villages around. Hooves clattering, Jon's banners streaming, they passed beneath the gatehouse, over the bridge, and away towards the north-west, where Bolingbroke was a mere ten miles as the crow flew.

She was afraid for them, and for Jack, whose devotion to Richard and the House of York had led him into what she dreaded would be utter folly. She lowered her eyes, because she above all creatures understood what it was to be devoted to Richard Plantagenet, King of England and France, Lord of Ireland.

Her conscience would always weigh that she had complied with Richard's order to go to Sheriff Hutton. Her place had been at his side, and she should have defied everything to be with him on the eve of Bosworth. That same cruel guilt and emotion filled her again now. Her place was with Jack, but here she was in Friskney. Another Sheriff Hutton, where she endured new anguish for a beloved Yorkist prince.

# Chapter Twenty

NEWS OF THE approaching conflict only trickled to Friskney, always arriving many days after it had happened. They learned that Henry had been at Coventry, but then moved to Kenilworth, where, clearly intending to indicate to the populace that he was relaxed and not in a state of panic, he had summoned his wife and mother. No, Cicely thought wryly, it would be his mother and *then* his wife.

Jack, Francis Lovell, Robert Percy and their forces had reached Ireland to join forces with Irish lords and supporters, who adhered to the House of York. The mysterious Lambert Simnel was lauded, for he was handsome, courteous, knowledgeable and poised, and gave every impression of being lordly and highborn. He was also said to greatly resemble his 'father', the Duke of Clarence, who had been only slightly less tall and attractive than Cicely's father, Edward IV.

Certainly the boy did not seem to be the son of an organ-maker or joiner from Oxford, or whatever was the latest fame according to Henry's stratagems. He was convincing enough for there to be a coronation at the end of May, where at Dublin Cathedral he was crowned Edward VI, King of England and France, Lord of Ireland. Jack was present, together with all the other English lords and gentlemen who had joined the conspiracy. When the rebel army crossed to England, many, many more would join them. The question was, would there be enough?

On first learning that his enemy was gathering in Ireland, Henry mustered his closest forces and marched swiftly to Leicester, and then to Nottingham, where he was joined by Lord Strange, the son and heir of Margaret's husband, the Earl of Derby. Strange brought six thousand men. These were not the only forces to flock to the royal banners, or the only forces still expected, which included Jon's ten thousand. Henry Tudor would have a superior army, as Richard had at Bosworth, but would he also suffer the same devastating defections?

Cicely could only imagine the horrors of the sleepless nights Henry endured now, but somehow he would show a calm face to the world. Even feeling about him as she now did, Cicely had to admire the fortitude and determination she knew he would find from somewhere. He had been hunted for much of his life, evading Yorkist foes, and he would continue to survive.

After the Dublin coronation at the end of May, the invading Yorkist army landed on the Lancashire coast on 5 June and immediately began to march east into Yorkshire, Richard's heartland. They reached Masham on the 8th, from where letters were sent to gather further support. From there Jack also sent a brief letter to Cicely, whom he knew to be at Friskney because on the day that Jon and Tom left for Bolingbroke, a man from the village had also left, to join the rebels, apparently fully aware where they intended to land in Lancashire. On reaching them, however, he became involved in a brief skirmish with Lancastrian supporters and received injuries that rendered him incapable of fighting. He had no option but to make the long journey back to Friskney, but before leaving he was well questioned by Jack about the defences and activity on the land he had passed through. Thus Jack learned that Lady Welles was at

Friskney and Sir Jon gone to support the king.

Jack's note to her was necessarily hasty:

*It has begun, sweetheart, and I am confident of victory. I wish I could be in your arms, but perhaps ridding England of Henry Tudor must be given precedence. We will be together again soon, that I swear to you. I need your kisses, and to hear your sweet voice. My only consolation is that my route must necessarily bring me south and there-fore closer to you. No doubt my forces will converge with Henry's somewhere in Nottinghamshire. Instinct tells me it will be somewhere near Newark, although I confess this is no more than a feeling. Wherever it is, it will not be near enough for me to steal some time with you. But I will be with you in my heart, never think otherwise. Please, always love me as I love you. Loyaulte me lie.*

*J.*

Then he added: *Francis and Robert require me to extend their warmest greetings.*

She tried not to cry as she folded the letter and then kissed the broken seal. How she wished she could give him those few longed-for hours. Not to do so would surely be to repeat the guilt of the past.

Her distress was evident as she went to the nursery. Mistress Kymbe was there, and spoke kindly. 'You must not grieve for what has yet to happen, my lady. Here, take your son and find solace in him.' She lifted Leo to give him into his mother's arms.

Cicely gathered her baby close, and smiled as he reached up to touch her face. 'Good morning, sir,' she said, kissing the tip of his nose. It always made him laugh, a funny little trembling laugh that seemed to come from his very toes. He looked up at her with Richard's eyes, and the likeness was a reminder so acute that she knew she had to go to Jack. Somehow. She could not stay away from him as she had from Richard.

Mistress Kymbe watched her face closely. She knew from whom the recently delivered letter had come, and could interpret so much from simply observing. 'You wish to go to Lord Lincoln, my lady?'

'Yes, even though I know I should not. But I do not know where he will be or when he will be there.'

'It will be dangerous, too. Had you thought of that?'

Cicely nodded. 'He needs me, Mistress Kymbe, and I will not be able to forgive myself if I do not go to him. What if history should repeat itself? My uncle—Leo's father—died when I was far away from him. Now the same may happen again. I could not bear it.'

'Then go to him.'

'How?'

'This morning, when you broke your fast in the great hall, I made it my business to examine the crumbs on your plate. Do not tell me the name, just whether or not Lord Lincoln mentions a town.'

'Yes, he does.'

'Is it Newark?'

Cicely gazed at her. 'Yes. How did you know?'

'The breadcrumbs spelled that name, my lady. They also revealed an arrow pointing to the west, and the word "stay". I believe they foretell that you will find him west of Newark, at a place that includes "stay" in its name.'

'Do you believe such things really foretell the future?'

'I do, my lady. They foretold your brothers' arrival here, and that Good King Richard would be betrayed. Now they foretell that you will find Lord Lincoln somewhere west of Newark.'

'Do they foretell his victory?' Cicely asked, afraid to hear the answer.

'Only that there will be a terrible battle. The outcome is not shown.' The old lady looked earnestly at her. 'My lady, if you wish to see the earl before that battle takes place, you must leave today. It is a long ride to Newark, and then you must find the place to go. You cannot go alone. Mary will accompany you, and so will some of the men Tom has left behind. It will be dangerous where you go, and you must have protection.'

Cicely knew the sense of the advice, and nodded. 'Very well. Please see that preparations are made.'

'My lady.'

When Cicely and her small party reached Newark, there was news of Jack's progress from Lancashire. Although York was still faithful to Richard's memory, Henry's bribes had secured the city against Jack. He had been refused entry or succour, even though he was Richard's loyal nephew and heir. It was a blow, but Jack did not waste time trying to coax the city fathers, instead he marched on south towards Tadcaster. On the 11 June, he came upon the forces of Henry's supporter, Sir Henry Clifford, and there was a decisive skirmish from which Jack, Francis and Robert emerged victorious. It was not news Henry wished to hear, but as word spread like ripples in a pond, it gave great cheer to all Yorkists.

Newark heaved with alarm and unrest because the king's army would advance up the river from Nottingham, which lay south-west. The rebels were on the other side of the river, approaching through Southwell to the west. Henry had reinforced Newark, and the bridge over the Trent was garrisoned, which meant that Jack and his host would not attempt the crossing there. Jack's intended destination was unknown, but when Cicely heard mention of a small village named Staythorpe, west across the Trent, she knew where he would go.

And so it proved. The rebel army camped at Staythorpe while Henry was still near Nottingham, but the king despatched an advance force towards Newark, under the command of the formidable Lancastrian commander, the

Earl of Oxford. The forthcoming battle seemed so close now that it could almost be heard in the still summer air.

Late in the evening of Thursday, 14 June, in perfect weather, Cicely crossed the Trent by a rope ferry not far south of Newark. The raft was large enough to accommodate her, Mary, and two armed escorts from Friskney. One was named Daniel Green, a burly forty-five-year-old with a shock of red hair and a beard, the other was Rob Haydon, in his thirties, long, lanky and already balding. Both were guards at the Kymbe house, and were considered by Mistress Kymbe to be well capable of protecting Lady Welles. They were all, with their mounts, taken easily across to the far bank.

Now Cicely was only a mile or so from Jack. And Francis and Robert, whom she longed to meet again. The landscape was wide and low, undulating slightly, except on the eastern bank, where wood-cloaked contours rose along the river. There was a huge sky, flawless and blue, and wild flowers were in full bloom, filling the air with their scent, especially the honeysuckle that blew so freely in the hedgerows. Whitethroats and dunnocks sang their hearts out, and it seemed so very beautiful and peaceful that Cicely found it very difficult to believe she was actually caught between two great armies that were on the point of battling to the death.

On reaching the other bank, she was dismayed when the ferryman made haste to haul his cumbersome craft back again. He was not about to wait and risk the means of his livelihood being commandeered. The closer she drew to the village of Staythorpe, the more she knew Jack was near as well. The glint of sunlight on weapons was ahead, and she could hear the noise of countless men and horses as the great force he, Robert and Francis commanded prepared for the night.

Staythorpe manor belonged to the Cistercian Abbey of Rufford, and there was a large and prosperous grange, but otherwise it was little more than a small gathering of cottages on the road to the larger villages of Rolleston and Fiskerton, further to the south-west. On the flat, open land beyond, the rebel encampment seemed to stretch for well over a mile.

At last she encountered scouts who halted her party, demanding to know who she was and what purpose she had. She lowered her hood to face them, revealing not only her face but her costly headdress. 'I am Lady Lincoln, and have come at my lord's request,' she said clearly, having decided this to be an almost certain way of being taken to Jack himself, without revealing her true identity. Daniel and Rob had been advised of her intention, and although they had exchanged glances, they had said nothing more. They were to look after Lady Welles, and if she wished to say she was the Countess of Lincoln, they would support her.

The scouts were startled by her title, but neither of them knew the real countess by face. One of them, more aggressive and suspicious than his companions, demanded proof, and she removed Richard's ring. 'Show this to Lord Lincoln, and if he is not able to be contacted, then show it to Lord Lovell or Sir Robert Percy.' They would certainly recognize Richard's ring.

He took it and then examined it.

'Do not be foolish,' she warned, 'because your neck will be forfeit if anything should befall such a jewel.'

The man shoved the ring in his purse and then rode swiftly away towards the encampment, while she and her little party remained where they were, effectively under close guard. Just when she feared the scout had thought stealing the ring too profitable to resist, he returned, and jerked his head at his comrades.

'She is Lady Lincoln, and we are to take her to his lordship.'

Relief flooded her as her horse was released and she was

able to ride behind the scout towards the vast encampment. Her three companions came along as well. The new arrivals aroused great curiosity, for it was clear to one and all that she was not a camp follower, or indeed any sort of whore. She saw men, weapons, pavilions, makeshift tents, horses, armour, mail, banners and coats-of-arms, camp fires, and cannon. Irish warriors had joined the rebels, and she knew their simple clothing would give them little protection in battle; their ferocity was their great weapon. There were two thousand German mercenaries, all armed and clad for the business of shedding blood, and there were English troops as well, less disciplined than the Germans but much more disciplined than the Irish.

There was no sign of Jack, Francis or Robert, until she suddenly saw—or thought she saw—Jack, in the distance, mounted on Héraut, whom he must have retrieved as his army marched through the north. She reined in to watch the rider, who wore armour, except for his helm. He was the same age as Jack, the same build, and had the same long dark curls. He even wore Jack's colours on his surcoat, but she realized he was not Jack.

One of the scouts manoeuvred his mount alongside. 'It is not Lord Lincoln, my lady, but a gentleman named Paul de Wortham. He has been advised to ride a different horse and change his appearance, but refuses. So, to the enemy, there will appear to be two earls of Lincoln, but the real one has wisely chosen not to advertise himself to the extent of his famous white horse. He will be target enough without that as well.'

The tents of the leaders had been erected along the edge of a small wood, where a little shade could be had. Jack's was blue-and-white striped, with his standard curling lazily before it as an evening breeze crept up from the river, about a mile away.

He heard the hooves outside and emerged immediately. He was in his shirt, hose, and thigh boots, and had clearly been washing, for his hair was wet and he was wiping his hands on a towel, which he gave to a waiting page. He was tired, but clearly well, and the smile he gave her was worth a thousand such hazardous journeys.

'Lady Lincoln?' He came to take her hand, kiss the palm and slip the ruby back on to her finger.

'It is so good to see you, my lord.' She held his hand tightly.

'You should not be here, you know that.'

'I received your note from Masham, and knew I had to find you.'

'I must scold you, but your presence pleases me more than you can possibly know.' He waved the watching men away, and turned to Mary. 'If you go to that green tent over there, you will find some ladies who will welcome you . . . wives, so do not fear the worst. Tell them I directed you to them.' He smiled and the maid, already half in love with him, all but melted.

Then he helped Cicely from her mount and held her close. She clung to him, filled with such passion and love, such tremendous need to hold and protect him, that tears stung her eyes.

'Oh, sweetheart,' he whispered, aware of her trembling.

'I love you, Jack, so much that I can hardly breathe of it.'

'Perhaps the privacy of the tent is best?'

She nodded. 'For several hours at least, I hope?'

He smiled again. 'I think I can manage that. We have halted for the night. The men need a rest before pushing on to the confrontation. Henry has yet to skirt Nottingham, and is also settling for the night, although I gather he himself does not intend to suffer the rigours of a tent.'

'How do you know what he is doing?'

'He has his imps, I have mine.'

He conducted her into the cool, blue-and-white striped tent, which was furnished in accordance with his rank, including a portable bed of reasonable comfort. He dismissed his page and another manservant. 'I am not to be disturbed unless Henry Tudor himself is hauled before me in chains, is that clear?'

They bowed several times and then hurried out, being sure to close the tent flaps behind them. He relieved her of her mantle, revealing the apple-blossom silk gown she had chosen to please him. He was immediately appreciative. 'I have not seen this gown before.'

'It was made just before I left London. I knew you would like it.'

'I will like it even better on the floor around your sweet ankles.'

'I know that too.'

He gazed at her. 'I love you so,' he whispered, and pulled her into his arms again to just hold her. He did not say or do anything more, he simply held her, one hand to the nape of her neck, the other around her waist.

She could feel how he drew upon her strength and love, just as Richard had done at the hunting tower. The emotion was the same, the intense devotion and understanding was as fierce and binding, and the need to be together as poignant and imperative. Neither of them could move; it was enough to be in an embrace, to feel each other's warmth and life. The scent of thyme was on him, faint, but it could be breathed in and almost tasted.

'There has not been a minute when I have not thought of you,' he said softly. 'I have slept with you every night, and woken up with you every morning. I almost have my arm around your waist to steady you before me when I ride out. You are with me all the time.'

'Would that I could be, always. It is what I want so much. I fear for you when we are apart, but seeing and touching you is to know you are safe and well.' If only . . . if *only* she had been with Richard like this on the eve of Bosworth. But she *was* with Jack now, and she would not leave.

He tilted her face towards his, and kissed her gently. It

was a moment of sweetness and romance in the heart of an army encampment, where the symbols and sounds of coming battle were all around. They were protected from everything, with each other.

'I still cannot quite believe you are here, sweetheart,' he said softly, easing her headdress off and setting it aside before loosening her hair and enjoying its liberation.

She slipped her hands beneath his shirt to slide them lovingly over his naked skin. 'I am here, and I will not leave unless you make me.'

'I will have to send you away, sweetheart, for I cannot possibly keep you where there will soon be so much threat. No, do not argue. I know how keenly you still feel your separation from Richard, and that this means the same to you now. I am glad of it, so glad, and we *will* have some time together, but then you will go.'

'But, Jack—'

'No, sweetheart. Not only will your life be at risk, but there is a very real chance of Henry finding out you are here. As I said, he has his imps. You might easily be recognized. Jesu, you came here unhooded. You certainly will not leave in the same exposed state, my lady. And if you claim to be Lady Lincoln, then you must obey Lord Lincoln. Is that not so?' He smiled, looking teasingly through half-closed eyes.

She considered resistance, but then smiled too. 'Yes, it is so, if only for the honour of being considered your wife. Make love to me, Jack, that I will know it for certain.' She drew back and looked down at his thigh boots. 'And please do not remove anything you wear at this moment, because I feel sinful desire for you as you are.'

He laughed. 'Then you shall have me, boots and all. You, however, I wish to see undressed, completely, except for the wearing of a tempting smile. Not that I need tempting, for I already stand at the thought of all this exquisite brocade lying on the floor. But . . .'

'But?'

'I have been weeks without you, sweetheart, so patience may not be too evident the first time, but I promise all the skill and pleasure you want after that.'

Her smile did not falter, but she was reminded of what Henry said at Huntingdon. She turned for him to unfasten the gown, and as it whispered down to the reed rug that was one of several placed upon the grass, she turned for him to see all of her. 'Love me now, Jack. Love me however you wish, for I will exult in every moment.'

'Do not let me suddenly awaken and find this is merely a dream. A blissfully erotic dream, but a dream nevertheless,' he whispered, as she took his hand and led him to the bed, which was really only meant for one.

'How cosy we will be,' she said, lying down to present herself to him. 'Do as you will, my lord of Lincoln, for I will most certainly follow your lead.'

He undid his laces and lay down too, and as he leaned over her his long, damp curls brushed her skin. There was no longer an ounce of spare flesh upon him, he was fit, agile, strong and perfect, and there was not, after all, any undue haste as he began to make love to her. The ampleness of his loins was a gift of intense reward, pleasuring her in an entirely different way. It was sumptuous enjoyment, rich and potent.

He was as attentive and passionate as ever, rushing nothing, adoring everything. Having him inside her again was such joy that her entire existence focused upon him. Her mouth was pliant beneath his, her body as soft and yielding as his was hard and demanding.

The climax was gratification and happiness of such power and concentration that it exhausted them both. He gathered her to him as the almost enervating warmth and satisfaction settled into a haze of love. It was several minutes before he spoke, and when he did, it was not of something she expected.

'Please do not tell me you went to Friskney to wait for me, sweetheart. Please tell me you went because of Leo. If I thought you went for me, it would mean you have no faith in my cause.'

She managed to smile, and hide the doubts and fears that lurked so deep within. 'Leo was ill.' Omitting Huntingdon for the moment, she told him everything, ending with Mistress Kymbe and the breadcrumbs.

He laughed a little. 'So I have the crumbs of your daily bread to thank?'

'Yes. And she was right. I did find you west of Newark, at a place with "stay" in its name. She also said it would be a mighty battle, Jack, but she could not tell the outcome.'

'Victory will be ours, sweetheart. We may not have acquired quite the hoped-for force, but we have more than enough. Plus the advantage of high land once we cross the river. Well, as high as it gets in these parts, for the Trent meanders here, and not through hilly terrain. I will take what advantage there is.'

'Where is it to be?'

'We go a mile or so further south-west to Fiskerton, where my scouts have found a good ford. The river is only just over two feet deep there at the moment. We will ford it before first light tomorrow, and assemble on the other side on a rise called Burham Hill. The height, such as it is, will place us where Henry will least want us, our backs protected by the river. His main encampment is about twelve miles away, although my scurriers report the Earl of Oxford's vanguard to be closer. He is a seasoned battle commander, so we know we will not have an easy time of it. We will confront each other tomorrow or the day after. Not beyond.'

'I cannot bear to think of it.'

'Sweetheart, I want you to leave again soon. This is *not* a suitable place for you.'

She sat up, anxiety suddenly pounding through her. She

would not be sent away so quickly. She would *not*! 'I will stay tonight, Jack. We sleep together, not apart.'

He put his hand gently to her cheek. 'That you have come to me at all is enough, my love.'

'No,' she whispered.

'You have to go. I will have you taken to safety beyond Newark, and you will set off for Friskney immediately.'

'No,' she said again. 'I will sleep in your arms tonight, Jack de la Pole, and only tomorrow will I let you send me away. I am here for *you*, and here I stay until my presence becomes a danger, or a worry that weighs too heavily upon you. Which I cannot possibly be at the moment.'

He sat up as well, and smiled resignedly. 'I have not the heart to argue more, because in truth I want you with me.'

She hugged him tightly, tasting the salt of his throat and then his cheek.

'Tomorrow it is,' he whispered, closing his eyes for the pleasure of her lips, 'but you will leave before our force sets off for Fiskerton, and you will ride with all haste to be well east of Newark. Is that understood? I want you away from here before armies come close to deployment. Argue with me now, and I will be obliged to make you leave immediately. So, please, sweetheart, do not force me to that.'

'I will do as you ask, Jack.'

'I will have to inform my companions you are here, at least two of whom will recognize you.'

'Francis and Robert?'

'Yes.'

'I will like to see them again.'

'No doubt it will be mutual, although what they will think on learning that you are now *my* lover, I do not know.'

'They will understand. Richard himself would understand.'

Jack smiled. 'Maybe. I trust you do not intend to summon him in order to find out?'

She lowered her eyes. 'No. I am getting better, truly.'

'Good.' He reached up to smooth her hair. 'You can meet your new king as well.'

'Lambert Simnel?'

'Your first cousin, Edward of Warwick, now King Edward VI,' he corrected.

'You still believe in him?'

'Yes.'

'*You* would be the best king for England, Jack. If you had only risen against Henry in your own name, you—'

He interrupted by changing the subject. 'Cicely, you have not mentioned Huntingdon. Tal wrote to me, so I know that matters are at an end between you and Henry. For the moment anyway. What happened?'

She hesitated.

'Sweetheart?'

And so she told him.

Jack's face changed. 'He *hit* you?'

'Yes.'

Jack gazed at her. 'I will have his life, sweetheart. I will tear out his miserable gizzard.' He stroked her cheek, as if by so doing he rubbed away the memory of Henry's violence.

Now she changed the subject. 'Tal said he was on his way to Calais.'

'Yes.'

'Why?'

'To secure it against Tudor.'

'How can he do that?'

'And how is good Sir Jon?' he asked, once again diverting the subject.

She smiled. 'You and I are adept at evading matters. Jon is well on the road to recovery. He is no longer hag-ridden, because she is dead.' She explained Judith's demise.

'Sweet God, lady, I cannot turn my back without you are in some new scrape.'

'You were right about his loyalty to Henry. It was

uncertain even before I told him how Henry made me go to him, and then it became far worse. I do not know what he had decided when he left to go to London and the surrounding counties to raise ten thousand men to Henry's standards.'

'Those ten thousand men might come over to me? That would be very helpful.' Jack got up, straightened his clothes and reached for his doublet. 'Come, we will make ourselves respectable and you must meet—'

'Oh, no, sir, not yet. You must bed me again before I meet Francis, Robert, or your new King Edward VI. Nor am I ready to meet your double.'

'Ah, you have seen de Wortham. He is an obscure supporter who joined us in Lancashire. He had the white horse with him, and nothing would induce him to change it for something less conspicuous. With that and his undoubted resemblance to me he is a prime target to my enemies, but he will not listen to reason. It may cost him his life.'

'So he is not another intentional double?'

'Certainly not. Nor does he sing in the streets of Peterborough.' He smiled.

How she loved his smiles. 'Jack de la Pole, I fear you must love me at least twice more before I will set foot from this tent.'

'I am that good?'

'Oh, yes. And so am I,' she added.

'So I recall,' he said softly, and began to unfasten his doublet again.

# Chapter Twenty-One

IT WAS BEFORE dawn the following morning, with a thick mist rising from the river, when Cicely left Jack to return across the Trent. She was hooded, with no chance at all of being recognized as he and an armed escort rode with her to the rope ferry. The raft glided silently towards them out of the vapour, the ferryman only lured by the promise of a fat purse. Jack's escort waited at a discreet distance as he helped her down from her horse for one of the Friskney men, Daniel Green, to coax it onto the sturdy raft, where his friend Rob Haydon waited with Mary and the other horses.

When Jack embraced her one last time, she held him as tightly as she could. A thousand and more fears span through her. This might be the last time—the very last time—she ever held him. One of three things could happen in the coming hours: he could be victorious, he could be taken prisoner or he could be dead. Or—there was a fourth—he could escape with his life to Friskney, hunted by Henry.

Her tears were wretched, and her fingers clawed his doublet, for he had yet to don armour. 'Do not send me away, *please*,' she begged again.

He put his gauntleted hand beneath her chin and made

her look up into his eyes. 'Please, my love, just go. Do not make my pain even worse. I will be with you again soon, as Lord Protector of England. I swear it.'

'I love you so much, Jack. Be victorious. Defeat Henry and restore York to its rightful place.'

He smiled. 'You give me all the strength I need, Cicely.'

From her purse she took a lock of her hair, cut before leaving Friskney. Together with a sprig of sweet cicely, it was tied with silver satin ribbon. She kissed it and then gave it to him. 'Now I *know* I will be with you.'

He bent to kiss her softly on the lips, and then released her gently. 'Go now, sweetheart.' He turned her towards the waiting raft.

She was almost blinded by tears, and even as she stepped on to the ferry she almost ran back, but when she glanced over her shoulder, he was remounting his large dun horse. Their eyes met for a long moment, and then he smiled one final time before turning his mount and riding back towards Staythorpe. His escort followed, and even though they disappeared into the mist, leaving it swirling behind them, the drumming of their hooves seemed to take forever to dwindle into eventual silence.

The raft was hauled across the Trent, and the vapour was damp on her face as she continued to look back. Jack was still not far away. If the raft returned to the Staythorpe side, she would be able to follow him back to the camp and *make* him keep her with him.

Mary came to her side and put a comforting hand on her arm. 'He will be safe, my lady.'

'I pray so. How I pray so.' Cicely bowed her head, biting her lip as she struggled to control the urge to cry.

From the other bank they rode east towards the Fosse Way. The brilliance of the rising sun was already beginning to burn the mist away, and to the south, towards Nottingham, they could see the campfire smoke, and the shimmer and occasional flash of weapons where the Earl of

Oxford's vanguard had camped overnight.

They reached the Fosse Way and soon learned from local people that the battle was expected to take place just to the south-west of a nearby village called East Stoke, the church tower of which could be seen behind some trees. Beyond it was Burham Hill, the only place in the area that offered advantage, and where Jack intended to take his position.

Daniel and Rob began to cross the Fosse Way, meaning to strike further east for Friskney, but Cicely remained where she was and called them back. Mary halted with her, looking curiously at the expression of her mistress's face.

'My lady?'

'I cannot leave, Mary. I *will not* leave.'

'But Lord Lincoln wishes you to be safe.'

'And I wish him to be safe. I cannot do this, Mary. I may have resisted the urge to follow him back to Staythorpe, but I will not ride any further away than this.'

'What do you wish to do?'

'We must find a hiding place, somewhere from where we can watch the battle. I must be able to see he is not harmed. Or worse. There must be *somewhere* in East Stoke.'

Daniel was dismayed. 'You cannot do that, Lady Welles. Every building will be searched by the earl's men, and will probably be secretly searched by Oxford's yeoman-prickers as well. They are bound to be sent in about now to be sure there is no ambush being prepared, or longbowman put in place. It may be that the king intends to take his host past us to the east, to come upon Lord Lincoln from this side. If you are caught up in it, I cannot speak for what may happen to you. Blood will be hot and excitement at a pitch, my lady. You are very beautiful, and men will be men.'

'There will be somewhere safe,' she declared, so certain that she might have been quoting from the Bible.

He looked unhappily at Rob, who was equally unenthusiastic.

'I will not go from here,' Cicely said again, levelly. 'You two can return to Friskney, and you as well, Mary, for I cannot expect you to assist me in this.'

Rob shook his head. 'We will not desert you, my lady. Our task is to guard you well, and that is what we will do.'

Mary was indignant with Cicely. 'You cannot believe I would leave you now, my lady!'

'I give you the opportunity, Mary. All of you, because my reason for staying is purely selfish, as was this entire journey.'

'We will not leave you,' they all three replied.

But as they rode slowly towards the little lane that led into East Stoke, a third of a mile in the direction of the looping Trent, the threading mist closed in again, obscuring the distant view of the royal army. With the closing of the mist, there was an exaggeration of sound, and thus they heard other hooves, muffled, of horses being led towards them from the direction of the village. The party from Friskney halted warily and drew quietly out of the lane into a field and the shelter of a hedgerow.

The other horses came slowly on, and as they passed Cicely clearly saw that the men walking them wore the blue boar badge of John de Vere, 13th Earl of Oxford. Whoever they were, and whatever their purpose, it was plain they wished to leave East Stoke as anonymously as they had entered.

When they had gone, Daniel looked at Cicely. 'Oxford's yeoman-prickers, my lady.'

'So you were right.'

He nodded. 'Well, they will not have found anything yet, for Lord Lincoln will not have stationed anyone. Maybe Oxford has a fancy to pitch on Burham Hill as well, although somehow I think not.'

All was very quiet again as they continued along the lane. East Stoke was a hamlet more than a village, and most of the inhabitants had wisely chosen to flee ahead of the battle. There were two Fosses, the main Fosse Way itself, the other a lesser route that passed across the breast of Burham Hill and was called the Upper Fosse. Both led north-east to and past a ruined Roman fort that had once guarded a long-gone wooden bridge over the Trent.

Cicely and her small party were almost at the church when she saw the perfect place to conceal themselves to watch everything that took place on Burham Hill. There was a narrow track only yards long that led up the sharp slope from the lane, to a moss-covered stone barn that seemed on the point of collapsing into the wide pond with which it was now surrounded. The barn was disused because a land slip had made it too dangerous. A solitary old sycamore grew against the walls, and the shift of the land was where the pond had now formed. Walls leaned, part of the roof had collapsed, and much of the stone had been taken away to be used again, but it offered enough concealment for the fugitives' presence to remain undetected. Daniel thought it would not be of much interest to Jack or the Earl of Oxford because although it gave a view over the expected battlefield, it gave no more than was to be seen on the hill itself. Certainly Oxford could see more from the other side as he approached from the direction of Nottingham.

There had been a door at the arched entrance, but it was now attached by a single hinge, and pitched half hidden among weeds and shrubs. The four horses waded slowly across the pond, disturbing billows of mud and rotting vegetation from the bottom, and on reaching the land where the barn stood, the riders dismounted to lead them around the collapsed door and into the shadows beyond. Behind them the disturbance in the water was already subsiding.

The horses were concealed towards the rear of the barn. A dividing wall was still partially in place and a pool of rainwater had collected where the foundations had started to sink. Then they all climbed up a rickety ladder to what had once been a hayloft. Daniel and Rob hauled the ladder up behind them. There was still some old straw, overgrown with grass and moss where part of the roof had given way, and a narrow slit window that faced directly on to Burham Hill, upon which the first outriders of Jack's army had begun to appear.

Concealed and silent, Cicely and her companions watched the arrival of the rebel army. Thousands of men from England, Germany, Ireland and Switzerland spread down the slope in front of the village, straddling the two Fosses and commanding the route to Newark. More men were drawn up on the crest of Burham Hill, where Jack's standards were raised, as well as the colours of Francis Lovell, Robert Percy and the boy king, Edward VI. Numerous horses were brought down to the edge of the village to be tethered until needed. The English way of battle was to fight on foot, and horses were only used by leaders, commanders and other knights, or for charges.

Suddenly voices sounded near the barn entrance, and there was splashing as men waded noisily through the pond. Those hiding in the loft kept very still, until, to Cicely's alarm, someone addressed her.

'Lady Lincoln?'

The voice was familiar, and although Daniel and Rob gestured for her to stay silent, she got up and went to the edge of the loft, holding a rotting rafter for balance. The men were Jack's, and they were led by Paul de Wortham, whose likeness to Jack was so astonishing that for a split second Cicely again thought he *was* Jack. The man who had spoken was none other than the scout who had taken her to Jack at Staythorpe.

'How did you know I was here?' she asked de Wortham.

He sheathed his sword and gestured towards the hidden horses. 'Your mounts were recognized, my lady. The maid and your two men are up there with you?' At least his voice was not like Jack's, but had a heavy Lancashire accent.

'I should not be here, sir,' she said, 'and my lord will be angry if you tell him, so I beg you to forget you have seen me.'

'My lady, it is my duty to report—'

'I am not of interest to my lord's battle plans, sir, but I can tell you that the king's yeoman-prickers have been here. They came when the mist was still heavy and my lord's men had yet to appear on the hilltop. That is all I know. Certainly Lord Oxford must now be aware that the village is almost empty. Maybe the king—Henry, that is— knows as well, and I do not know if he can send a force around to come at you from the Newark direction as well, but you should tell my husband you heard this information from a woman in the village. No names need be given.'

'I should still tell the earl of you, my lady,' he insisted.

'I love my lord, sir, and cannot leave when I know he is in danger. All I ask is that you allow me this small boon.'

De Wortham hesitated, undecided, but she had appealed to his chivalry, and so he nodded. 'Your presence will remain secret, my lady, but I beg that you defend me should I be blamed by Lord Lincoln.'

'I will tell him that I called upon your honour and that you have been gallant. I trust you can rely upon the discretion of your men?'

'I can, my lady.'

'Why do you go so far out of your way to appear as my lord?' Even at such a moment she was curious to know.

'I was born with these looks, my lady, and I wear the earl's colours because I am heart and soul his man. The horse was a gift from my father. I am merely being myself, my lady, Paul de Wortham, gentleman of High Wortham. '

'But you make yourself so conspicuous. A good long-bowman might well pluck you from your saddle.'

'If I draw enemy attention away from the earl, then that cannot be a bad thing.'

She had no answer to that. 'At least be sure to leave as

278

little trace of your being here in this barn as we were of ours.'

'I will.'

'I wish you well, sir. May the day go with my lord.'

He inclined his head. 'God will be on our side, my lady.'

They withdrew, splashing back across the pond to where they had left their mounts. Soon they had gone.

Cicely breathed out with relief, and moved to the window to see if de Wortham went straight to Jack, but he did not. She gazed towards the standards, and was sure she could see Jack with Francis and Robert, and even the boy king, who wore a small suit of gilded armour. She had met them all the evening before, and a happy reunion it had been with Richard's old friends. The boy king had been disturbing, for he looked so like her uncle the Duke of Clarence that she could not doubt he was as much her first cousin as Jack. The boy was poised, educated, knowledgeable on family matters and certainly knew who she was when Jack presented her. He even told her how like his uncle Richard she was because of her hair. Someone must have told him of this similarity, of course, for he had never met Richard. When she had left him, she felt no cousinly bond at all. Nothing. Nor had he glanced after her. She had wished him well. He said nothing.

The small party in the barn loft settled for a long wait. They had water, and a little food for their journey back to Lincolnshire, but it was not much and they had to make it last, because now it would be far too dangerous to leave the barn. Jack's men were on the lookout for anyone who might support Henry, and were likely to strike first and ask questions later.

All the sounds Cicely had heard at Staythorpe she heard again throughout that day and long night. Campfires danced, sending their uncertain light through the barn's slit window. There was singing and laughter, but the atmosphere was charged, as if a thunderstorm were in the offing. Which in a manner of speaking it was.

The rebels aroused at first light to eat and hear mass, then Jack's scurriers galloped to him to say the Earl of Oxford's army was about to march. Cicely did not need to hear the message to know what it was, for the scurriers waved their arms towards Nottingham, and the only force that was within reach was Oxford's. Drums rang out to battle stations, and the army began to deploy, six men deep for three-quarters of a mile, north-west to south-east, across the two Fosses, with East Stoke village behind them. It consisted mostly of men-at-arms, supported by archers and billmen, with horsemen in readiness at the rear, to bear down upon the enemy once the initial advance and conflict was well in hand. There was still no sign of Henry's forces, only Oxford's, which was smaller than the rebels.

The boy king was prominently displayed on the hilltop, with royal standards and all the trappings, while Jack, Francis and Robert rode up and down the lines, exhorting their men to fight for the true king. They instilled heart, courage and the belief that God was on their side. Jack's head was uncovered as he passed, his dark hair streaming loose, and as he rode close to the barn, Cicely could hear him quite clearly as he bolstered his men with the will to defeat the anointed King of England. Just as Henry had done before Bosworth.

Oxford's force of mostly Englishmen was beginning to arrive on level ground a quarter of a mile to the south, and he had still to properly deploy when Jack and companion commanders saw that attacking before he was ready was their best chance of swift victory. Just before nine, with Jack in the lead and fully helmed, the signal was given to advance in orderly but relentless manner, in the hope of throwing Oxford's forces into complete confusion, which initially they were.

Cicely hardly dared to watch as she watched Jack in

the heart of the fighting, lunging and slashing, riding men down and stabbing whichever part of them he could reach. He was as a man possessed. She had never seen this side of him, just as she had never seen Richard in battle. She was not shocked, or repelled by his violence, rather was she proud that he was such a courageous and skilled son of York that he would hack his way to victory.

The German mercenaries, under the command of their fearsome leader, Martin Schwartz, moved forward to the shrill thunderous racket of fifes and drums. It was the first time this frighteningly military sound had been heard in England, and it must have been carrying for miles, maybe even to Henry, wherever he lurked out of the thick of battle. Arquebuses were fired, arrows flew like driving hail from both crossbows and long bows, and there was shouting, screaming, the awful clang of metal upon metal, and the terrified whinnying of horses caught up in the fray. The ground was soon soaked with blood, with numerous bodies cluttering the path of their living comrades.

Two and a half hours of slaughter passed, but so grindingly slowly that it seemed to Cicely she would hear it in her head until her last breath. It was so awful that at last she could not watch at all, until Mary touched her arm.

'Lord Lincoln is returning to the hilltop, my lady.'

'Is he. . . ?'

'He is well, my lady. Wounded somewhere on his left shoulder, I think, for I see some blood. But he is still able to ride well and to command again. Look, you will see.'

Cicely gazed at the hilltop again. There was fighting there as well, as a group of Oxford's mounted men broke through to the standards. Her hands were pressed tightly to her mouth as she saw Jack and others fight back and drive the attack away. She saw how he tried to ease his left shoulder, where blood still found its way between the plates of his armour. He waved his physician and attendants away, and remained mounted, still overseeing the battle and issuing commands.

Sir Robert Percy was in the midst of the fighting further down the slope, and Cicely watched in dismay as he was cut from his horse and fallen upon by Oxford's men. He could not possibly survive such an onslaught. For a moment she was back at Sheriff Hutton, and he was speaking softly. *'I have a message for you, my lady.'* The message had been from Richard, who was waiting for her at the hunting tower . . .

Mary squeezed her arm gently. 'It will have been quick for poor Sir Robert, my lady,' she said comfortingly.

Of Francis Lovell there seemed no sign, not even his riderless horse. He was not on the ridge either, where his tent and standards were alongside Jack's, and after the battle the rumour would spread that he drowned while trying flee on horseback across the Trent having unfortunately chosen a reach where the opposite bank was too steep for his mount to clamber up. If this was so, his body would not be recovered.

Gradually and inexorably the tide was turning in the rebels' favour. Henry's force had yet to arrive from Nottingham, and Oxford fought alone against great odds. Then Paul de Wortham appeared on his white horse, carrying a heraldic banner that displayed Jack's arms and colours. The stir he caused showed that Oxford and his men clearly believed it was Jack himself they saw within reach. He was immediately surrounded and hauled from his horse, and Cicely saw one of Oxford's men kill him by forcing a rondel dagger through his visor, using both hands and all his weight. He did it more than once, until his companions dragged him away. But Paul de Wortham was dead, and Cicely could tell by the manner of the men who had been in at the kill that they were frightened because, she guessed, Henry had indeed ordered Jack's life to be saved.

But the shout had gone up that Jack of Lincoln was

dead, and the effect upon the rebel army was electrifying. From fighting courageously towards victory, they suddenly broke ranks and fled in all directions. It was a rout, and yet Jack himself was still on Burham Hill, clearly in view. Cicely saw him shouting orders to rally them again, but the panic was too great for them to even hear, let alone obey.

Oxford's men pursued the routed rebels, horsemen coming through from the rear to gallop after the fleeing men, killing without quarter. Jack raised his visor and watched for a long moment, his whole attitude one of dejection and utter disbelief. Paul de Wortham had not only thrown his own life away, but the battle itself and the lives of hundreds of his comrades-in-arms as well.

Jack recovered his wits, lowered his visor again for fear of an accurate longbowman picking him off from a distance, and then gestured to his attendants to make good their escape while they still could Then he shouted at the boy king's guards to take him to safety as well, but those craven fellows saved themselves and left the frightened boy behind.

The fleeing rebel army streamed towards the Trent, where a way through the woods to the lower land beyond formed a funnel, concentrating them into a narrow cleft where they fell and were trampled upon. Henry's army gave chase and the ensuing massacre was so terrible that the cleft ran with blood, and would ever after be called the Red Gutter.

Some of Oxford's knights were now galloping up the long slope towards the standards and tents at the top. Jack tried to make the little king escape with him. The boy's small horse in its royal caparison was tethered nearby, and there was even a fallen tree trunk upon which to stand to mount easily in armour, but instead King Edward VI sat down on the grass and hid his face in his hands.

Cicely watched in huge dismay. Jack had no choice. If he stayed he would be captured, but if he left now, he had the chance to fight another day, and so he was faced with a decision. He could not carry a boy who wore full armour, or rescue one who did not wish to be rescued, and so he turned his horse towards the hanger wood and kicked his heels, disappearing into the trees just before Henry's men saw him. They believed the Earl of Lincoln was already dead, and were more concerned with securing the person of the pretender to Henry's throne.

Jack rode swiftly through the trees towards the slaughter of Red Gutter. Cicely glimpsed him now and then and was filled with dread that he would ride straight into it, and be cut down anyway, but before he reached the hellish cleft his horse suddenly shied at something. She could not see what it was, only that Jack was unseated and hurled into some thick shrubs at the very edge of the battlefield. The shrubs sprang back, covering him completely, and he made no movement at all, whether from caution or inability, Cicely could not tell. Please let it be caution. Some of Oxford's men came along almost immediately, and caught his horse, which although richly garbed, did not actually bear his arms or colours. They searched all around for its knightly owner, for only a knight or greater nobleman would have such a horse. They prodded and poked likely hiding places, but they did not investigate the shrubs, which they must have deemed too dense for an armoured man to hide in. It cannot have occurred to them that the rider might have been tossed into them from above.

When the men had moved on, Cicely watched the shrubs for any sign of movement, but there was none. Was Jack all right? More of Henry's men then scoured the wood for survivors, but although they found some unfortunates, who were immediately put to death, they too failed to discover the Earl of Lincoln, whom Henry wanted most of all.

There was continuing slaughter as the royal troops roamed the battlefield, putting to death those who had survived, albeit with terrible disfigurements and injuries, or those who were on the point of death anyway. Thousands of bodies lay on the sloping land, with abandoned weapons, wounded horses and scattered banners and pennons. Discarded armour lay everywhere, helmets, breastplates, and various other costly items that were gathered eagerly by the conquerors. The Battle of Stoke Field had been a far longer, more savage and utterly ruthless battle than Bosworth.

The king's divisions arrived at last, and Cicely noticed with scorn that Henry, wearing armour and Richard's circlet, was to the rear of his men, not prepared to endanger himself. How like him, she thought contemptuously. Those kings before him, her father and Richard, had been brave commanders and skilled fighters who had led their men into battle, as had Jack. Not so this Tudor.

As she watched, he and Jasper Tudor were conducted, still on horseback, to where 'Jack de la Pole' lay dead. De Wortham's body was one of the few untouched by looting, because the Earl of Oxford's men had been guarding it for the king to see. The armour had been removed, however, for Henry to see the bloodied, gashed face and wounded body. It must be impossible to identify, she thought, save that so much about him in general pointed to his being the Yorkist leader Henry so wished were still alive. Without dismounting, Henry indicated a nearby soldier to raise the dead man's right hand. He was looking for Jack's amethyst ring! Not seeing it, Henry instructed that the other hand was raised. There was still no ring. He exchanged some words with Jasper, who shook his head, as if he too doubted the body's identity.

Henry continued to look down at the lifeless body, and she knew he was really unsure if it was the Earl of Lincoln. Or if Jack's body had been looted after all. Cicely could feel the way his mind was working. She knew him that well. Yes, the body before him resembled Jack de la Pole in many ways, and had even worn Jack's colours, but *was* it Jack de la Pole? Then Henry nodded, and men came to carry the body downhill and over a slight rise to pass out of her sight. She would later learn that there was a shallow valley down there, where a spring overhung with willows rose at the side of a lane. Two graves were dug there, the other for the German commander, Martin Schwartz, who had also fallen. Both bodies were buried hastily, and when the graves were complete, fresh willow staves were driven into them, to mark the resting places. The staves would take root, and new willows would grow, but they would not mark Jack de la Pole's final resting place.

As Henry and Jasper returned to their forces, Cicely's attention went to the shrubs where she had last seen Jack. Everything was perfectly still. Daniel came to her side. 'We will wait until dark, my lady. If the earl is there and still alive, we will find him and take him to safety at Friskney.'

Where Jack had always felt he would go, she thought.

# Chapter Twenty-Two

THE SMELL OF death and blood hung like a pall over Burham Hill as the occupants of the barn crept out into the shadows of nightfall. Daniel and Rob had tried to make the women stay behind, but Cicely would not hear of it. She *had* to be there when they found Jack. They left the horses in the barn, and waded through the pond before scrambling up the small slope to the battlefield. Some geese from a village yard set up a clamour, but no one seemed to be aroused.

Fires flickered on the battlefield, and the night was warm and sticky. Oxford's men still examined the fallen for anyone still alive, and occasionally Cicely heard screams as such poor souls were found and despatched to the hereafter. The fugitives slipped along behind the village, from tree to shrub to dip, desperately trying to remain unseen, and at last they reached the edge of the wood, which seemed to be quiet now. There was still activity in the blood-soaked gully where hundreds of mutilated corpses choked the way, but Cicely and her companions managed to hurry past the opening to the cleft without being detected. Now she could clearly see the shrubs where Jack had fallen, and at last they were able to hide behind them and knew no one had seen anything.

It was Daniel who pushed into the thick foliage. 'My

lord? Lord Lincoln?' he called quietly, but there was not a sound.

Then Cicely wondered if Jack might think it was a trick. 'Jack?' she said. 'Are you there? Can you hear me, sweetheart?'

'Cicely?' A weak voice responded.

Relief rushed through her, and she pushed urgently through the dense leaves and resistant branches, careless of scratches or tears to her clothes. There he lay, his armour removed so that he only wore the protective padded garments beneath. The off-white of the clothing over his left shoulder was badly stained with blood, and there was more blood on his forehead, for he had lost his helm and knocked his head badly during the fall. His face was ashen, as she could see even in the darkness.

She knelt beside him and gathered him on to her lap, where she cradled his head and smoothed his knotted hair. 'Oh, Jack, my dear love,' she whispered.

'Why are you here?' he managed to whisper, but weakly.

'You think I would leave you? You do not know how stubborn I can be, my lord of Lincoln.'

'Is . . . there word of Francis?'

'No. I heard Oxford's men say they thought he had drowned trying to escape across the Trent.' The words sounded so flat and hard, and she bit her lip.

Jack closed his eyes. 'And I saw Robert fall in the fighting. I suppose Henry now has our failed king. Today was humiliation, sweetheart. An unnecessary rout caused by that fool de Wortham. I still had my mounted divisions to send forward! But suddenly it was as if I had ceased to exist.'

'He thought he helped by drawing attention from you, and I am sure did not imagine for a moment that he knew the effect he would have.'

'Has Henry had the guts to arrive yet? I think he shrinks from a little blood.'

'Yes, he has been and has now gone again, toward Newark. He did not even set foot on the battlefield, except by the hooves of his horse. As for striking a blow in his own cause, he did not come near enough. He is so craven.'

Daniel suddenly reached down to put a hand on her shoulder. 'Hush, my lady, for horsemen come towards us. A patrol, I think.'

They all fell silent as the riders approached at a leisurely trot. The men wore Oxford's blue boar badge and talked of the lucrative looting they had done, and of their hope to return to their homes soon. Then they had ridden by.

Daniel was urgent. 'We must get from here, my lady. Rob and I will help Lord Lincoln. It will be difficult to get past the gully, but if we take every precaution, we should manage it. Rob spotted a stray horse close to the village, saddled and unclaimed as yet. We will use it, otherwise we will not have enough mounts between us.'

Cicely scrambled reluctantly to her feet, and pressed back as the two Friskney men helped Jack from the ground. He was very weak, and being suddenly upright made him lose consciousness, but Daniel and Rob had him firmly, an arm beneath each of his, supporting him easily as they pushed out of the shrubs' ferocious grip and began to go back in the direction of the barn.

A column of men-at-arms was just emerging from the ravine, blood-stained and grim, not a word being uttered from seeing the atrocities that had been done there. A brief draft of air breathed up from the Trent, and suddenly the stench of the cleft was so powerful and cloying that they all four gagged of it. Only Jack remained unaware.

As soon as the soldiers had gone and the gully was quiet, the four fugitives hastened across the open area between the two parts of the wood, and then held close to the perimeter of the trees again.

Rob found the abandoned horse, and with Daniel's help they lifted Jack on to the saddle. He was aware again, and as soon as they had fitted his feet firmly into the stir-rups, was able to take the reins and manoeuvre the horse himself, although not a great deal, and for how long could only be guessed. The two Friskney men then went to bring the horses out of the barn, and soon they were all mounted.

There was hardly anyone about, no villagers, of course, but no sign of Oxford's triumphant army either. The lane to the Fosse Way was completely deserted, and they even managed to get across into its counterpart on the opposite side of the main way between Nottingham and Newark. They did not encounter even one of Oxford's men in the lane that led to the Fosse Way. Soon they were moving slowly carefully away from the carnage of Stoke Field. To move swiftly would be to attract attention.

They needed to be further away from East Stoke before risking speed and clatter, even supposing Jack was capable of strenuous riding. He did not look it. As they passed a lighted cottage window, Cicely saw how white his face was, and how fresh blood spread over his shoulder and down from his forehead, even though Daniel had tied a make-shift bandage around his head. But he was alive. He was alive. Nothing else mattered now but that he be cared for and then sent safely to the Continent, where their aunt would give him all the protection he needed.

But as they rode south-east, thinking themselves well away from danger, and with Daniel and Rob about ten yards in front of the women and Jack, the two men heard something and suddenly reined in. Daniel managed to wave the other three from the roadside into a small copse that grew right up against the roadside.

As they drew out of sight, Cicely was able to see through the trees that armed men barred the way. They were uni-formly clad and carried colours and a badge that she knew so very well. They were Jon's men! She recognized two of them from Wyberton.

She watched as Daniel and Rob rode up to the leader

and spoke quietly. The man's surprise was evident, but he nodded, bade his companions to stay where they were, and then he turned to ride away at speed.

Jack swayed in the saddle, exhausted by his loss of blood and bruises. Cicely dismounted quickly, and she and Mary managed to pull him down from his horse and prop him against a tree. His head lolled, his dark hair falling forward to brush his cheeks. Cicely knelt beside him and pulled him into her arms, rocking gently as she kissed his hair and stroked his face. The scent of thyme was still there, but faintly, and mixed with blood and sweat.

He roused a little. 'Still disobeying your lord, sweetheart?' he whispered, smiling.

She kissed his lips, her heart so full that she could not speak.

Hoofbeats returned, two horses this time, and she knew it would be Jon. Gently she eased Jack against the tree again, and then got up. She heard Jon order his men away, and Daniel and Rob, and then he dismounted. He wore light armour, although without a helm. 'Cicely?'

She stepped out from the trees and then ran to him. 'Jon?'

He caught her in his arms and held her for a long moment, but he did not kiss her, nor did he take her hand. Instead he was cool. 'Why are you here? Mm? I am told you have a third man with you. Who is he?'

She drew back. 'Before I tell you, I wish to know why you are here and not at the battlefield?'

'I am resting my men, all ten thousand of them, having been obliged to come by a roundabout route because Huntingdon is flooded. I sent a scurrier ahead to tell Henry what had happened, and now he orders—somewhat tersely—that I am to go back to London to quell the unrest Jack de la Pole's clever Yorkist rumour-mongering has caused. Half the country believes Henry is defeated, even dead.'

'Would that were so.'

'Have a care, Cicely, for there are sly ears everywhere. I know the battle is over, and that Jack is dead. I am sorry.' He watched her face. '*He* is the other man with you?'

'Yes, but he is wounded. I am trying to take him back to Friskney, from where he can go to the Continent.'

'Jesu, Cicely, have you *any* idea of the risk you take? If Henry finds out, he will not be lenient.'

'Henry will not find out,' she replied firmly.

'He will if you continue on this road. My encampment is just out of sight over there, and the road passes right through it. Henry's messengers are there as well. Believe me, you do not want to take Jack this way.'

'Then help him, Jon.'

'You ask a great deal of the husband to whom you so clearly continue to be unfaithful. How long have you been with him? Since I left Friskney? Did you go to Lancashire to meet him?'

'No, Jon. I have come here from Friskney because . . . I could not endure the thought of him dying as Richard did. Without me.'

'And what of me?'

She gazed at him. 'I did not for a moment feel you were in danger, Jon. I *knew* you would return to me.'

'How convenient a belief.'

She was dismayed that he should even think it, let alone say it. 'Jon, please—'

'Just take me to him.'

'Jon? You do not mean to—?'

'Put an end to him? No, damn it, I do not, although to be sure I would be justified. Where is he?'

She led him back to the trees, where he tethered his horse and then crouched beside Jack, who managed a smile.

'Well, now, if it is it not good Sir Jon.'

'How are you?'

'In the shit.'

Jon smiled. 'True. Can you manage the ride to Friskney? It is a cursed long way, and will take several days.'

'I have to make it there, Sir Jon. It is where I am meant to be.'

'So I understand. I do not appreciate sharing my wife with you, sir.' He had lowered his voice that Cicely would not hear.

Jack met his eyes. 'I love her, Sir Jon, and while that is not an excuse, it is the only justification I can give. That, and the knowledge that you are far higher in her love and estimation than you ever take credit for. Stand by her, and she will stand by you.'

Jon straightened and spoke of something else. 'Well, my late appearance did not go down well with my nephew, but there was nothing I could do about it, and . . . I would not have thrown in with him anyway.'

'With me?'

Jon nodded. 'Even if you are fucking my wife.'

'If you had arrived in time, England would now have a new king.'

'Fate decreed otherwise.' Jon explained that floods had halted him at Huntingdon. 'But for that, yes, there would be a new king. I would rather it had been you, not that boy.'

'You are not alone. Perhaps I made an error after all.'

'You did. *You* are the leader York looks to, not a boy. You would have raised far more support for yourself.' Jon straightened. 'I will do what I can for you now. You had best stay here, or perhaps go deeper into the trees. I will station some guards to close the road, and also see to it that your wounds are cleansed, you have food and drink, and then given more guards to see you to Friskney. I think it best if your hair is cut. You are too damned recognizable.'

'Make a Samson of me?'

'I am sure the loss of your pretty locks will not incapacitate your overactive cock. And curls will grow again as

293

much in Burgundy as here.'

'My gratitude knows no bounds, Jon, and if I am ever in a position to do anything for you, be sure that I will.' Jack held up a hand.

Jon seized it. 'In the meantime we keep faith with each other.'

'Until another time.'

'Now, rest a while. You will receive all the help you require.'

'But no escort, I beg of you. We will travel better if we remain as we are. Unless you would prefer Cicely to be under your separate protection.'

Jon laughed. 'Dear God, man, do you honestly imagine she will return to London with me and let you go off without her? Her injured, beloved Jack de la Pole? *I* know her, even if you do not.'

With that he left again, pausing only to speak briefly to Cicely. 'Well, my lady, you have saved him, and so will I. See that his damned hair is cut to disguise him a little. I will send some of my clothes. At the moment he is too clearly a knight without his armour.'

'Thank you, Jon.'

'I do not do this for you, but for him. I was on my way to join him. But as far as you and I are concerned, well, I was wrong to think I could endure your love for him, for it bruises me too much. I should have known better than to let you in again. You are his, Cicely. I relinquish you.' He removed his gauntlet and the turquoise ring she had given him. 'Take it back, for I think the wrong finger wears it.'

'Please, Jon, do not do this.'

But he walked away, remounted his horse and rode back the way he had come.

Two days later, at dusk, the tired little party was within half a mile of Friskney when a strange feeling came over Cicely. It was nothing she could have identified, just a wariness that told her it would be very unwise to go on.

Jack, his hair now unbecomingly shorn, clung to his pommel, for he was very weak and weary, in need of Mistress Kymbe's attention and a good sleep. 'What is it, sweetheart?' he asked.

'I do not know, Jack, just that I am afraid to take you to the house. I need to see that all is well.'

'What could be wrong?'

'Anything where Henry is concerned.'

'My imps told me that if Henry triumphed, he would commence a triumphant progress to the north, so he is hardly likely to come here. I heard some of the searchers mention it as well. His lack of presence on the battlefield was not appreciated by those who risked their lives for him.'

'Nevertheless, I must be sure. I could not endure it if, after all this, you fell into his hands anyway. He knows I am here, because Jon will have told him.' She turned to Daniel and Rob. 'Is there somewhere safe to hide?'

'There is a hut at the decoy a quarter of a mile over there.' Rob pointed.

'Then go to it and stay with my lord of Lincoln. Mary and I will go on to the house.'

Jack was uneasy. 'Two women alone at dusk? Sweetheart—'

'Are you in any position to stop me?'

'I could make a damned good try of it.'

'And open your wounds again? Go with Daniel and Rob. Do as you are told, my lord.' She looked at the two men. 'Take what food and drink we still have, and see to it that my lord is comfortable and safe. And make certain the horses cannot be seen from the road. We have to be very cautious.'

Daniel took the choice away by leaning across to take the bridle of Jack's horse, and the three men left the road.

Cicely turned to Mary. 'Something is wrong. I *know* it. Come, we will find out.'

They rode quickly on, and soon the village and the Kymbe house was ahead. Everything seemed quiet and peaceful, but the feeling of anxiety and trepidation grew worse the closer Cicely rode. She and Mary rode unhindered over the bridge into the quiet courtyard, where torches were already alight and grooms came out to attend their horses.

'Is all well?' she asked one.

'Why, yes, my lady.'

'You are sure?'

'Yes, my lady.'

She waved him to take the horses away again, and then hurried inside, to her apartments, where an astonished Mistress Kymbe soon came hurrying.

'What is it, my lady?'

'I do not know, but I have a very bad feeling. Mary, I must change quickly, and wash as best I can.'

'But, my lady—' the maid began to protest.

'Quickly, Mary. I just *know* that if it has not happened yet, something is about to.'

She washed by candlelight, in cold water, scented herself with a little rose oil, put on a simple grey gown, and then sat for Mary to attend to her hair. 'Leave it loose,' she said then. Instinct was driving her now. Every nerve was jangling, every heartbeat filled with fear, but she knew she looked as if she had been here at Friskney all day.

She went down to the courtyard again, and as she emerged at the top of the steps she heard the drumming of a dozen or more horses approaching at speed along the very road Jack, Daniel and Rob had quit to go to the decoy.

Armed men rode out of the gathering dusk. They carried no banners, nor wore any colours, and had clearly been riding hard for some time. Their horses were flecked with sweat and breathing heavily as they clattered noisily into the yard.

Only one man dismounted. It was Henry.

# Chapter Twenty-Three

DREAD PLUNGED VICIOUSLY through Cicely as she froze on the step, staring at Henry. How right her intuition had been! Thank God above she had not allowed Jack to be brought to the house. But why had Henry come *here* at such an important time? He had won a great victory—not that he could be aware she knew of it yet—and should be attending to great matters of state, keeping the peace and embarking on his royal progress. Instead, he had ridden to an unremarkable house in a remote Lincolnshire village.

Henry paused, tossing his reins to a groom who hurried to him. He wore simple tan leather, and she could not tell by his eyes what his purpose might be. Removing his gauntlets, he came slowly up the steps towards her. 'Lady Welles?'

She sank into a belated but very deep curtsey. 'Your Majesty.'

There was a startled stir among the watching Kymbe servants, because Henry was not known here, and his non-descript clothes and small party of unmarked riders had given no indication that he was the king. Several men and maids ran to spread the word, especially in the kitchens.

He bent to raise her by the elbow. 'So, my lady, we meet again after all, it would seem.'

Cloves. 'I . . . I am honoured, Your Majesty. Please, I extend the hospitality of this house.'

'Of which you are not mistress.'

'That is true, but I know not what else to say or do, Your Majesty.' She looked up at him. His eyes were not entirely in harmony, so she knew he was tired or feeling stress. Or both. Why was he here? *Why?*

'I accept the generosity, Lady Welles.'

She led him into the house, where he was divested of his outdoor clothes. 'May I offer you some refreshment, Your Majesty?' she enquired nervously.

'Nothing formal. Certainly a little wine.'

She nodded at a hovering servant. 'Some wine and a little supper. Only the very best you have. In the solar,' she added. Her mind was spinning as she looked at him again. 'Please . . . come this way.'

He followed her up to the solar, where servants hurried to light candles. Wine and refreshments were brought, and also towels and water, that the king could wash his hands. They almost fell over themselves trying to be all they should be, and she dismissed them the moment she could, indicating that the door should be firmly closed behind them. Whatever Henry had to say, she knew he would not wish anyone else to hear.

Henry hardly seemed to notice anything as he calmly dipped the corner of the towel into the water to cleanse his face as well. Then he ran both slender hands through his long russet hair, pushing it well back from his face.

Cicely could not help watching him, because everything he did was paced and thoughtful, and above all dignified.

He looked at her at last. 'Will you not serve your king some wine, my lady?'

Tom Kymbe's Rhenish was not of royal quality, but was probably palatable enough for a thirsty man, even a king, she thought as she obeyed. She hoped her hand did not shake too much as she presented the cup to him.

'Drink with me, Lady Welles.'

'Your Majesty.' Again she obeyed. Huntingdon had destroyed the affection she had been able to feel for him. His gentle side was nothing more a distant memory.

'You are well again now?' he asked. 'My uncle told me you had to stay here because you were ill, and Mistress Kymbe is skilled with medicine.'

'Oh. Yes. I am well now. As you see.'

He gazed at her. 'Yes. I see. I have been most concerned about you. My uncle also told me he came here due to some dispute with your cousin Lincoln?'

'Yes, Your Majesty. A mill, I believe. It is ongoing.'

He gazed at her, and she felt he was trying to gauge her truthfulness. She had to say something. 'You have ridden a long way, Your Majesty?'

'From Lincoln. The city, that is. Small light horses, a constant swift trot, with a few sensible rests. About forty miles using back lanes and marsh crossings with a local guide who knows every inch of the terrain. The weather conditions are as good as they are ever likely to be.' He spoke almost absent-mindedly, but his eyes told her he was still assessing her.

She knew something was weighing heavily upon him, but could hardly press the King of England to explain himself. He was not Henry to her now.

At that moment Leo began to scream with temper in his nursery. The solar door was closed, but still the piercing sound carried. Another door was quickly closed, and the crying was muted.

Henry glanced towards the disturbance. 'Whose child is that?'

'Tom Kymbe's son, Leo, Your Majesty.' She was the very model of calm collectedness, but it took a huge effort.

'Ah, yes, the inestimable Tom Kymbe. On your cousin's manor but loyal to my uncle and, I trust, to me.'

'Yes, Your Majesty.'

'It cannot please you too much to be in a Lancastrian house, my lady.'

'I am Sir Jon's wife, and adhere to his wishes.'

'Indeed? That will be the day. You are York, my lady, and always will be.'

'May . . . I enquire why you are here, Your Majesty?' she ventured at last.

'No, you may not.'

She lowered her eyes quickly, feeling so much at a disadvantage that she could not summon even one small smile of the charm that had served her so well in the past. She was so aware of him, of his closeness, of the cloves and the sound of his voice, that she felt like a cornered hen, waiting for him to put an end to her with a quick twist of her neck.

He drained his cup and put it down on the table next to him, indicating he did not wish to be offered more. 'Do you have de la Pole's ring?' he asked suddenly.

'His . . . ring?' She was startled.

'The amethyst. Do not pretend you have never noticed it. Every woman in the land notices that amethyst, just as they notice the size of his dick!'

'I do not have the ring, Your Majesty.'

'So, if I search your purse, I will not find it there?'

No, but he would find much more! The letters from Richard and Jack, for instance. And the little lock of Leo's hair. She removed the purse and placed it boldly on the table beside her. 'Search if you wish, Your Majesty, but I swear I do not have Jack de la Pole's ring. If I had it, you can be sure that amethyst would be on my finger.' She held up her hands to show that she only wore Richard's ring. She was playing with fire by inviting him to examine the purse, but she felt he would not, because he was in control of himself and would not wish to appear foolish if the purse revealed nothing.

The seconds hung, and then he waved the purse away.

Relieved, she returned it to her belt.

He glanced again at Richard's ring. 'So, what is the ruby to you now? No doubt it is still Richard's ring, not a gift from me.'

She gazed at him. 'It is both things, Your Majesty.'

'Liar.' He said the word so softly it was almost an exhalation.

'Please . . .' His first name was so nearly on her lips, but she knew she could not say it. 'Have you come to torment me?' she asked then, finding enough courage for that at least. But it was only a whisper.

'No, Cicely, I have not.'

Her name at last? She looked at him. 'I do not know how to speak to you, Your Majesty, and even if I did, I would not know what to say. I am at your mercy, and I think that is what you seek.'

'I seek many things, Cicely, but having you at my *mercy* is not one of them.'

There was a note in his voice, almost an echo of something that was itself unheard. It rested its sad little fingertip upon her, gentle, invisible, but there all the same, and she felt it so keenly that he might almost have touched her physically.

'What is de la Pole to you?' he asked then.

'Only my cousin, Your Majesty,' she answered, noticing that he used the present tense.

'As Richard was *only* your uncle?'

'Please, Your Majesty, I really do not feel able to spar with you.'

'Stand up to me, Cicely.'

'I cannot.' She met his eyes.

'Why?'

'You surely do not have to ask?'

He paced a little, linking his fingers and tapping his mouth. 'I do have to ask, Cicely, because I need to know what is in your mind at this moment.'

301

'You would not like it if you did know.'

'Really?' He stopped pacing. 'Pray tell.'

'I do not wish to provoke you.'

'You will not.'

Now *she* gauged *him*, and decided to take him at his word. 'At Huntingdon you said such vile things, made terrible accusations and struck me so hard that I fell. You said I was plotting against your life and that I was never to come near you again. You said you were considering punishing Jon, and that . . . Well, it does not matter what else you said. You spurned me, and—'

'In the end *you* spurned *me*, Cicely. You know it. In that final moment, you could have stopped me from leaving, but you did not. I did not want to go. I had said so much and done so much, but I did not want to go from you.'

She looked at him. 'You hid it well.'

'No, Cicely. You knew the precise moment I realized what I had done. I needed you to extend your hand.'

'To permit you to save face?'

He did not answer.

'I was not going to spare you, Henry, I was *afraid* of you, and did not want you to stay. You had shown violence before, at Winchester, when you also accused me of that treasonous letter, but you had never struck me. Can you not understand how I felt at Huntingdon?'

'Yes, I understand, but I hoped . . . needed you to turn me from it. You know me, Cicely, and—'

'I knew you were violent, but had never thought you would hit me.'

He gazed at her. 'To have done it at all was monstrous. To have done it to *you* . . . I seek your forgiveness.'

'You do not have it.'

'Cicely—'

'No, Henry. I do not wish to be close to you. I do not wish to spend every minute wondering when you will explode into fury again, when you might strike me . . . or worse.'

'Jesu, Cicely, I am *not* a violent man.'

She looked at him, askance.

He paced a little. 'Very well, yes, I can be violent. Yes, I have struck a woman before. And yes, I craved her forgiveness too.'

The woman in Brittany? 'And did she give it?'

'Yes.'

'Well, I will not. I bore the mark of your fury for some time, and have not once regretted being estranged from you. Now you come to me like this, mysteriously, without explanation, questioning me about my cousin's ring and not even mentioning the rebellion, when it is clear *something* has happened. Do you think I am reassured by this?'

'You know I did not mean what I said and did at Huntingdon.' He ignored the mention of the rebellion.

'You astound me, Henry. How can you stand there, looking so sorrowful, and pretend you did not mean it? Of *course* you meant it! The result is that while I respect you as my king, I have no respect at all for you as a man. If you wish to strike me again for my temerity, then go ahead. I cannot prevent you.'

'You must still be the only person in England who dares to deal with me in this fashion.' He glanced away towards the window. 'You consign me to Hell, do you know that?'

'You do not burn enough.'

'Always you have a pin with which to prick me.' He gave a slight laugh. 'And yes, I know it, I have a prick with which to pin you.'

'Why have you come here, Henry? I do not believe you wish to mend things between us, so why?' A thought occurred. 'Has something befallen Jon? Please tell me it is not that.'

'You ask about him before your cousin? You surprise me.'

'Is Jon safe?' she asked again.

'As far as I know, although he failed to join me when

303

I ordered it. Ten thousand more men might have been useful.'

'Might have been? The battle has taken place?' Was she innocent enough?

He did not reply.

'He certainly intended to join you, Henry. That I *do* know.'

'Cicely, your husband turned craven. Or traitor.'

Her lips parted. 'Craven? Jon? No, never! And you know it, Henry.'

'Then perhaps he turned traitor.'

'I do not believe *that* either,' she replied, without a flicker.

'Would that I had your faith.'

'You are *bound* to suspect. Your nature leaves you no option.'

He inclined his head. 'So kind.'

'Is it because of Jon that you are here?'

'No.'

'Then why? Surely not to ask about my cousin's ring, for I will not believe it.'

'I needed to know about the ring, and I needed to see your face when I asked you about it.'

'Well, you have.'

'Do you know where he is?'

She was cautious. 'Has a battle taken place, Henry? Yes, I can see that it has, and I believe you have won, because no matter how furtive this visit may be, you do not have a hunted look. So how do you not know where my cousin is? Did he escape? Is that it?' Her mind's eye saw Henry on the battlefield, looking down at Paul de Wortham's lifeless body.

He came suddenly to put his hand to her chin and make her look at him. 'You know nothing? Is that the truth?'

'Yes, Henry, it is. Please, you are hurting me!'

He released her as if stung, and so many emotions

flitted through his wintry eyes that she could almost share his distress. Distress? Yes, that was what he felt now, and the emotion was so powerful that it almost daunted him.

'I never wish to hurt you, sweetheart. Never. Yet I know I do.' The words were uttered on an oddly subdued note, as if he confronted himself for the first time. Or so the thought occurred to her. An unseen clock seemed to tick in the silence that fell between them. The air was still, and yet teemed with his unspoken thoughts. He wanted to say so much, but could not.

'Tell me what it is, Henry,' she said, as always caught up by his struggles with himself.

He closed his eyes, and she saw him surrender to whatever it was that weighed upon him. 'Being without you is crippling me.'

'Please do not do this to me.'

'I have to, *cariad*, because you are the only one to whom I can turn. I know that today I prey upon your warmth and love, but I must, because if I do not, I may lose you forever.' He indicated Richard's ring. 'You cannot *begin* to know how much affinity I feel with him. He needed you, he turned to you and could not do without you. It fractures me, Cicely, because he haunts me. I cannot rid myself of him, because *he* has you. His legacy is all around me, all the time. I stole his throne, and I accuse him of crimes he did not commit. I paint him black, when I am the man in black, am I not? Now he is reborn as Jack de la Pole. Over and over I fight Richard Plantagenet. Will it never stop? Will I ever know peace, my own peace, within *me*?'

'You stole Richard's throne, murdered him through treachery, and come to *me* for comfort and understanding? I loved him, and can *never* forgive you!'

'Yes, I come to you. I always will, because you mean everything to me. Richard has his revenge, for I am bereft without you. Only half a king.' He smiled wryly. 'I know, in your eyes I have never been much of a king anyway.'

'You are my enemy, Henry.'

'And you are mine, but that does not prevent me from loving you. If you think I say it lightly, then you have never understood me.'

'I know you mean what you say.' He was finding his way through her barriers again. God curse him, he was reaching her . . .

He saw the breach and lifted her hand to kiss the palm. 'I love you, Cicely, but know I do not deserve a single kind thought.'

'Humility does not suit you.'

'I wear it anyway.'

'As you wear the crown?'

'Yes. The crown is mine now, Cicely, and will remain mine. I have defeated your cousin, and the House of York is in disarray. Now you can hate me even more.'

'Is Jack dead?' She already knew the answer, but was curious to know what Henry would say.'

He released her and moved away. 'The Earl of Lincoln is either dead and buried on the battlefield, or he is alive and free. I do not know which.'

So, her judgement had been right, he really was not sure.

'I cannot help you, Henry. Jack has certainly not come to this house.'

He glanced at her. 'He may yet. If he lives, of course.'

'Why are you unsure? If he is dead, you will have his body to prove it.'

'Which proves that I have a body, but am not sure it is his. I am told it is him, and yet I have also been told the body may be that of a certain Paul de Wortham. If it is de Wortham, then the Earl of Lincoln has yet to be found, dead or alive. I swear, Cicely, that I issued orders that he was to be spared. I did *not* break my word to you.'

She knew it was the truth. 'I believe you, Henry. So, Jack may still be alive?'

'You are probably delighted to know it.'

'Yes, of course I am. I love him as I loved Richard. Lying about it would be pointless.'

He gave the ghost of a smile. 'Do you wish to know about the battle?'

'Yes.' Would he continue to tell the truth?

'It was at Stoke Field, by the village of East Stoke, just south of Newark. I was not actually there until afterward, but it has been described to me.' The account he then gave was accurate, even to Paul de Wortham's death. 'His demise sent everything into chaos. It was a moment of utter lunacy. If he was your cousin, why then did he *suddenly* appear? The battle had been in progress for several hours before he appeared, and Oxford told me that Lincoln had been on a dun horse, unmarked, and fighting in the midst of it all. Then, all of a sudden, he wears every identification imaginable, carries his colours and rides his damned white horse as if in the lists? It is not tenable, and yet his forces believed it. They fled and were slaughtered. Now all I have is a dolt named Lambert Simnel, a tool in Lincoln's hands, and I have consigned him to the royal kitchens.'

If Henry had sent 'Lambert Simnel' to the royal kitchens, he made the real Earl of Warwick into a cook-boy, and was keeping a changeling in the Tower.

Henry spoke again. 'I still believe your cousin wanted the throne himself. Well, that little dream is at an end now, and if Simnel sits any throne, it will be in a privy.'

'What of Lord Lovell and Sir Robert Percy?'

'Percy is dead, killed in battle. As for Lovell, I do not know. Some say he drowned in the Trent, I say he could be anywhere. He has escaped capture too many times for this to be any different.'

So, Francis might still be alive as well. She prayed so. 'What has my cousin's ring to do with it?'

'Simply that it was not on the body that was shown to me as de la Pole's. Its absence leads me to suspect he lives.'

'I cannot help you, Henry.'

'Nor would you if you could.'

'Nor would I if I could.'

'I admire you so, Cicely. You still confront me, still defy me. You are the king the House of York should have had.' He took her face lightly in his hands and kissed her lips.

It was the sort of kiss that resurrected so much that was sweet about him, so much that was good and gentle. She was still trapped, but no longer feared his hands around her throat. Instead she feared her own weakness, because this was Henry Tudor at his most irresistible.

'Please, Cicely,' he breathed. 'Please . . .'

His arms slid around her, his kiss warmed into an urgent desire that provoked a response she wished was not there. But it was there, because she would always find pleasure with him, and her body always craved pleasure. She was with a powerful man, a king who was crippled by his own self, and his appeal in those moments was so intense as to be impossible to withstand.

'Let me love you, sweetheart,' he whispered.

She could not prevent herself from being swept along. He was Henry the man, loving and needing her, and she had to twine with him, because it was impossible to twine against him. She could feel his gratitude that she did not spurn him now, when he knew she had every reason to do just that. There was no artifice, nothing to suggest he manipulated her or used her. But she knew that something slight could ignite him again, and these gentle new moments would be destroyed.

And she knew that he feared being the way he was, that he did not know how to counter it, and that even though he had turned upon her, she remained the only person to whom he could look for reassurance.

'Love me,' he whispered again, 'for I need you so.'

She kissed him, her arms linking around his neck, and he lifted her to the table, easing her skirts up to expose her to the apex of her thighs. He moved his hands lovingly over her skin, venturing partly between her legs, but then he looked deep into her eyes. 'I will stop now if this is not what you want. I do not wish to do anything at all to alienate you again. This matters too much to me, sweetheart, and I know how much you have to forgive.'

'I forgive you for hitting me and saying such terrible things, but do not expect me to forgive you for Richard, or for defeating Jack de la Pole. Those things I cannot and will not forgive, but when you are like this, I can feel for you the way you want me to. If that is enough, then do not stop now.'

'It is enough, sweetheart.'

She gazed at him. He was the King of England, triumphant from battle, and safe on his throne, at least for now, yet he begged for her love. Slowly, and without any more hesitation, she reached to the front of his hose to undo his laces.

He closed his eyes as she touched him, and his lips parted on a soft gasp as she stroked him, but when he finally pushed inside her, it was Jack of whom she thought.

Jack was making love to her now, knowing her, possessing her and promising her a devastatingly ecstatic peak of pleasure. And that was what she had. Henry came, but it was Jack de la Pole that she received.

# Chapter Twenty-Four

IT WAS INEVITABLE that Henry would remain overnight, and that Cicely would sleep at his side. What else could she do?

But she was still Plantagenet and Yorkist enough to take any measure to protect what she held dear. She knew Tom Kymbe kept Lancastrian banners, including the red rose, which would certainly be all the warning Jack would need to keep away from Friskney. There were always lit torches on the tower, so the banner would be visible even in the darkest hours, and Henry could surely not find it suspicious that the badge of the House of Lancaster was draped from the residence of a Lancastrian supporter. Could he?

Please let her be doing the right thing, because she had used banners this way before, but unwisely, and with unfortunate results. She had raised Richard's colours at Sheriff Hutton after Bosworth, to show defiance when Henry's representatives, including her husband-to-be, Sir Jon Welles, approached Sheriff Hutton to secure the persons of Richard's heirs. All she had succeeded in doing was convincing John of Gloucester his father had won. He had ridden into the castle, and been taken prisoner. It had been her fault. All her fault. Now she did all she could to prevent Jack de la Pole from suffering the same fate.

But something happened during the small hours of that

night that might easily have put Leo in the utmost peril. The room where she slept with Henry was close to the nursery, and a strong breeze had sprung up, blowing freely from the sea across the flat Lincolnshire landscape. It found its way into the house, and opened a creaking door with its draught. The sound groaned through the silence, and the draught rattled the door of their firelit bedroom as well, making her sit up with a gasp.

Someone was coming in! But then she realized it was no such thing. The draught sucked through again, and then she heard a little cooing sound in the passage. Leo? There was no nurse's voice, only another little baby noise. Getting out of the bed, she put on a robe, for she and Henry were both naked, and hurried to open the door. A wall lantern cast a dim glow as she heard little pattering steps from the direction of the staircase. Pulling the door to upon Henry, who still slept, she hastened towards the sounds.

There her little boy was, alone in a nightshirt, rubbing his eyes and then gurgling with pleasure as he saw her. He staggered towards her, arms outstretched, and she lifted him. Laughing and squirming, he played with her loose hair, and she held him close, indulging in the delight of it. He was part of her, and part of Richard, and her love for him knew no bounds, for it was a mother's love, even though she could not acknowledge it.

She carried him back towards the nursery. 'What are you doing out here, sweetheart?' she said softly, but the draught had crept strongly through the house again, and she had not completely closed the door of the room where she slept with Henry. The creaking hinges had awakened him, and on seeing her absence and the open door, he got out of the bed, his body pale and lean in the borrowed light from the passage.

He saw her and she halted, for she dared not do anything else, but her arms were so very protective of her baby.

Henry came towards her and looked at Leo, who

gurgled again and instinctively held out his arms to be taken. Henry took him, and not awkwardly. 'Well, little Master Kymbe, and what are you doing wandering around in the middle of the night, mm?'

Cicely's heart tightened unbearably. Henry Tudor was holding Richard's child, *her* child, and he had no idea of it!

Henry glanced at her. 'Do not look so terrified, for I do know how to hold a child. I am a father twi—' He broke off, and returned his attention to Leo, who seemed to find him fascinating, grabbing at his hair and tugging it.

She wondered what Henry had almost said. A father twice? She tried to smile, and hoped she seemed natural and unconcerned. 'This is a draughty house, and the wind has blown doors open.'

'In my Garden of Eden nakedness, I am well aware of draughts,' he answered with feeling, still amusing Leo by offering his little finger. The little boy tried to chew it, and Henry smiled. 'Ah, he teethes.'

Cicely watched his face. He was genuinely pleased to hold the little boy, and his fondness for children was evident in everything about him. But what if he were to realize whose child *this* was? 'I . . . I should return him to his nurse,' she said.

He did not immediately take the hint. 'Children are so pure and innocent, with no hint of the slyness that comes with age.'

'Are you saying that Prince Arthur will be sly?'

'Well, perhaps sly is not the word. I was thinking of the less agreeable traits that come with adulthood, and with which you will no doubt say I abound.' He gave Leo back to her. 'And tell the nurse to take more care or *I* will see she is punished. That should cure her of future neglect.'

His concern was so kind and honest that it plunged a knife through her. 'Perhaps you should go back into the bedroom, for you have the royal jewels on full display.' She smiled at him.

'So I do. Well, at least it proves I have some.' He went back into the room.

She breathed out with relief, and held Leo close as she hurried to the nursery, where the maidservant who replaced Mistress Kymbe at night slept on, unknowing. She was awakened by sharp words and the threat of royal displeasure, and then Cicely hastened back to Henry, being careful to close the door and wedge it.

He was lying back against the pillows, covered to the waist, his hands behind his head. 'The child might almost be yours,' he said then, his eyes reflecting the firelight.

'Mine?' She froze.

'His hair and something in his face. The eyes, maybe.'

'I assure you I have not lain with Tom Kymbe.'

Henry smiled. 'I did not for a moment think you had. I was merely commenting.'

'Leo has his father's colouring,' she said, without thinking.

'Really? I thought Kymbe was a lighter brown than that, and very curly. Still, what does it matter?' He held out his hand, the one upon which he wore the emerald. 'Come to me again, Cicely, for I cannot look at you without needing to hold you, at the very least.'

She removed her robe and went to the bed beside him, to link her fingers through his. 'Cicely, I must leave at daybreak. I should not have come here at all, but I had to, for my own sake.'

'I will warrant Jolly Jasper did not approve.'

'Jolly Jasper does not know where I am. I endeavour to avoid arguments with him. His Welsh is far cleverer than mine.' He smiled, but then sighed. 'I really do not wish to leave you. Right now I believe the life of a Lincolnshire squire, with you as my wife, and ten children like Leo Kymbe would be pure heavenly bliss, but I am not a Lincolnshire squire, and must continue on a triumphant progress of sorts. I have to show my face around the land, make my victory plain and distribute reward or punishment wherever either is warranted. I have to weed out all those who supported the rebels.'

'The obligations of a king.'

'I know. Please, do not say anything now that will raise ghosts between us. There are things I must do to consolidate my hold upon the throne, and I know how it places me on the wrong side in your eyes.' He put a gentle palm to her cheek. 'It grieves me, truly it does, because I love you so much. Although you no longer love me, do you? Huntingdon put paid to me.'

She had to put her hand over his, but she did not say anything to contradict him. And she saw the disappointment in his eyes. No, it was more than disappointment, it was ill-concealed distress. And hurt.

'Cicely, I may not be back in London until late autumn, but when I am . . .' He paused. 'I will have to consent to my queen's coronation; in fact, I already have. I have sent word that preparations are to be put in hand for the twenty-fifth of November. I am secure on the throne now, I do not need her birthright for anything, and so am able to allow this without any accusation of reliance upon the House of York.'

'Such indisputable logic.'

'I am known for it.'

'Are you still cold with Bess? Did you send for her at Kenilworth out of affection?'

'Yes and no. I do my best by her, Cicely, but it is not easy when I feel nothing for her and she feels the bloodiest of hatreds towards me. I know she wishes me dead. The role of Queen Mother in Arthur's minority clearly holds great appeal.' He drew a long breath. 'I have tried imagining she is you, but although it enlivened me for a few nights— during one of which I appear to have impregnated her again—I can no longer hoist anything with her.'

'Not that you will attempt to until she is delivered of the child and churched.'

He smiled in the candlelight. 'You remembered that, mm?'

'Yes. Of course.'

'Mind you, it would be very difficult indeed to observe such a rule if the lady in question were to be you.'

'You resisted well enough that day at Pasmer's Place.'

'You have no idea how close I came, sweetheart.' He held her hand and smoothed the palm with his thumb. 'Things must be as they were before, you know that? I will want you to be in London—yes, at Pasmer's Place with my uncle, if it so pleases you—but I *must* be able to send for you whenever I need you. Which will be often. I do not care if I put my uncle's nose out of joint, for he failed me at Stoke Field. I made an agreement with you before—apparently with his consent—that I could send for you whenever I needed you. That must hold true again now.' He smiled a little ruefully. 'I do *ask* you, of course.'

'I will do as you wish, Henry.' She could not be sure what Jon would say. Their last parting had not been exactly warm and loving, and the turquoise ring was in her purse to prove it.

'My wish is to have you as my queen, to take you away from all other men, living and dead, to cherish you as my own. I cannot have that wish, but I *can* make love to you again, now.' He pulled her hand to his lips and kissed it tenderly.

Henry rode away from Friskney at barely daybreak, intending to return to the city of Lincoln as swiftly as he could. He took his public leave of Cicely with every formality, except in his eyes and the way he squeezed her fingers. As another king had once done, in another courtyard.

When he and his riders had gone, disappearing into a low morning mist, she ordered the red rose to be removed from the tower. The sky was almost grey, but not quite, and the dawn chorus of birds was shrill across the countryside.

Barely half an hour later, Daniel and Rob brought Jack into the courtyard. He was weak and had lost more blood from his shoulder. His complexion was almost white, and he looked strange without his long hair, but his smile was still the same as he saw Cicely coming down the steps to greet him. 'Well met, Coz,' he murmured as he was lifted down from his horse.

She hugged him as best she could without hurting him. 'You are safe now, sweetheart,' she said, kissing his sweat-dampened cheek.

'You have had royal company?' He met her eyes. 'I trust I served my purpose?'

She smiled. 'Yes, Coz, I thought of you all the time.' But it was not entirely true, because there had been a point when it was only Henry she held.

'How did you know Henry would come here?'

'I did not, I only knew something was wrong. I cannot explain it.'

'Do not try, for your instinct was timely.' He drew a long breath. 'I trust there is a good bed here?'

She turned to Mary, who waited at the top of the steps. 'Please tell Mistress Kymbe that a gentleman requires her attentions.' She deliberately did not use Jack's name or title, for the fewer who knew who he was the better, and he *did* look different without his long curls. 'And see that he is taken to a suitable room,' she added.

The maid was uncertain. 'The one that you and the king—?'

Jack gave a wry smile. 'Any bed will do.'

Mary hurried away to find her aunt, and Daniel and Rob helped Jack into the house. He knew very little as he was carried upstairs to the first room they came to. Maids were already laying the bed with fresh laundry, and within moments the two men had placed Jack carefully on the mattress. He was barely conscious now, and more blood, thick and dark, oozed from his shoulder and forehead. His head lolled sideways.

Mistress Kymbe hastened in with her caskets of medicines, balms and herbs, and waved Daniel and Rob away. 'Get to your duties, whatever they may be.'

Cicely detained them a moment. 'I am in your debt, both of you. Thank you.'

Daniel smiled. 'We will do it again, should you require us. Lord Lincoln may not be of Lancaster, but he is a gallant and good lord.'

Rob nodded. 'Aye, and he would have been a better king than the bastard we have now.'

Daniel nudged him. 'We have committed treason enough already, without your great mouth adding to it. Come on.' He shoved his friend out.

Mistress Kymbe began to examine Jack, and then looked at Cicely and Mary. 'I think you two should go now, for I must cut his clothes away.'

Mary went out without a word, but Cicely stayed. 'I have seen all there is to see of my cousin, Mistress Kymbe, as I think you know. It will be better for him if we both attend to his clothes.'

'You have power over men, my lady.'

'So it would seem.'

The old lady studied her face. 'And it is to protect Lord Lincoln and Sir Jon that you lie with the king.'

'Is there anything of which you are not aware, Mistress Kymbe?'

'Oh, a great deal, but I feel close to you. Close enough to sense things. Very well, my lady, take this knife and begin to cut away these quilted undergarments, but carefully, or you may cut away the source of a great deal of gratification.'

Soon Jack lay naked, the amethyst ring his only adornment. The stone gleamed purple against his pale finger. The old lady looked down at him approvingly. 'Good heavens, what a *very* comely fellow. I ceased to be a maid a very long time ago, and with such a man as this. Dashing, handsome, winning, and more able to make love than was decent. A nobleman, too. Oh, yes, I know a little more of life than you have realized, Lady Welles.' She smiled mischievously and patted Jack's genitals. 'This part of him will certainly give women much pleasure again, you mark my words.'

'I certainly hope it pleasures me.'

'Oh, it will. It will. Now then, dip that towel in the bowl of water over there and wash him carefully, while I prepare the best salve I know for his wounds. He will soon be well again and able to cross the sea to Burgundy, my dear, so do not fret for him. Yes, I know that, too. Little passes me by.'

# Chapter Twenty-Five

THAT NIGHT CICELY remained with Jack, sitting beside the bed, trying to read, but not succeeding. She thought he was still asleep, until he spoke suddenly.

'Are you about to read me a story for bedtime, Coz?'

She smiled. 'So, you are back with me again, my lord.'

'So it would seem, and feeling better than I did, although I stink of some vile herb or other. What is it?'

'It is not an "it" but a "them". Mistress Kymbe has mixed a salve that has been applied to your shoulder and forehead, and then bandaged.'

'So, no thyme?'

'Maybe, there were so many leaves that she pounded with a pestle. All I saw then was a smooth green cream.'

'Delight upon delight.' He gazed at her, and then took her hand. 'Did Henry treat you civilly?'

'Yes. More than civilly. But he strongly suspects you are still alive.' She told him everything Henry had said. Well, almost everything, for she did not disclose any of the very private things he had told her, of his feelings and how he viewed his situation. Having lain with him again, been drawn into his spell again, she could not betray such things. Even to Jack. Perhaps especially to Jack.

'Was this before or after you let him make love to

you again?'

Her lips parted and she looked away.

He smiled and put a finger to her cheek. 'It does not matter, sweetheart. Ignore me. I confess to jealousy. How could I not?'

'I have always been able to make love to him, no, *with* him.'

He nodded. 'I know.' He glanced at Richard's ruby, and then removed the amethyst. 'Your hand, sweetheart.' When she did not extend it to him, he took it anyway, and slipped the amethyst on her middle finger, but it was still too big. 'There, now you *do* have it, but for pity's sake, do not wear it anywhere near Henry.'

'Oh, Jack . . .'

'See how beset by generous lovers you are? You have Richard's ruby and my amethyst, soon you are bound to have Sir Jon's splendid turquoise, and Henry will give you that emerald I know you covet.'

She bit her lip, and then took the turquoise from her purse. 'It was my father's, and I gave it to Jon, but he has returned it.'

'Why?'

'Because he finds it too hurtful that I love you so much.'

Jack gazed at her. 'Oh, sweetheart . . .'

'I can understand it. He is a proud man, and I do wrong by him.'

'So do I, and yet he helped me at great risk to himself. I am so sorry, sweetheart. I did try to make him understand . . . about you.'

'He does understand, he just cannot accept everything. It is not your fault, but mine. I should be faithful to him now, but I love you. And I have permitted Henry to lure me into his arms again.'

'But you love Jon too,' Jack reminded her.

'Not as much as you, and he knows it. He has always known it, first with Richard. He deserves better.'

'You cannot help it if you wreak havoc with male genitalia. We men should pray and brandish our rosaries instead of brandishing our knobs.'

She smiled. 'And how strong is your knob right now, Lord Lincoln? Strong enough to enjoy assault by kisses?'

'It heard you, sweetheart. See how excited and eager it suddenly is.'

'Indeed. Totally irresistible,' she whispered, moving closer to caress him and make love with her lips. All he had to do was lie there, and be satisfied as only with her.

She was soon weak with the joy of it. Mistress Kymbe had been right. This part of Jack de la Pole *was* pleasuring her again, and it took her to the same paradise that she took him.

Late that night, as the racing clouds fled to make way for clear skies and a good moon, and all was quiet, Cicely slept in the bed she had shared with Jon that one night before he and Tom Kymbe left to raise men for Henry. A sudden clatter awakened her, and she sat up with a start. Something had fallen, or been knocked over!

She sat up in alarm, listening as she had the night before, but this time heard nothing else. There were no little baby sounds to suggest Leo had wandered out again. But then . . . was that struggling and footsteps? Slowly and nervously she got out of the bed to put on her night robe, and then listened again at the door. There was a scuffling sound, from further away now. Towards the stairs.

She opened the door and looked out. Leo's door was closed, so it was not him. But Jack's door was wide open! She hastened to it and halted in the entrance. The bedclothes had been dragged to the floor, a small table had been toppled against the wall near the bed . . . but of Jack there was no sign at all. The pillows were askew as well. He had not simply got out bed, he had been *dragged* from it!

'Jack? *Jack?*' She cast around. There was silence now,

until she heard the clatter of horses in the courtyard. Swift horses, being urged towards the gatehouse. She ran to the window and was in time to see four cloaked, muffled horsemen riding swiftly away from the house. One of them had something slung over the horse before him. It was pale and looked like a naked man. Jack!

As they galloped away to the west, along the same road Henry had taken, she dashed out into the passage and raised the alarm. 'Help, someone! Help!'

The whole house was disturbed by her screams, and both Daniel and Rob came running. They were fully dressed, having fallen asleep while sharing some relaxing ale in the kitchens. Daniel seized Cicely's arms to calm her. 'What is it, my lady?'

'They have taken Lord Lincoln!' She gestured towards the open door, and the two men went to investigate. 'I heard something fall,' she explained, and then told them what she had witnessed.

Daniel turned and ran down through the house, followed by Rob, and they roused every man they could. But no one admitted to having seen or heard anything. Then it emerged that the night guards had all been knocked unconscious or tied and gagged, although someone had to have opened the gates to the bridge, because the horsemen had entered the courtyard and been able to slip into the house undetected.

Daniel and Rob took parties of armed riders to try to follow the trail, but the culprits were long gone. Who had they been? They must have known the identity of their victim, and yet who could possibly have known that the Earl of Lincoln was in hiding, not only in Friskney, but in the Kymbe house?

Cicely waited anxiously in the solar for the search party to return. Mistress Kymbe and Mary were with her. At last, long after sun-up, the horsemen returned and Daniel came up to speak to Cicely.

Mistress Kymbe poured him some wine, which he accepted gladly. 'There is no trace of them, Lady Welles, and no one around about seems to have seen anything. Except one man who did not want to say anything because he had been poaching. In the end he said he kept out of sight when four horsemen halted in a clearing in the marsh wood, near the small decoy. They had a naked man with them, young, dark haired and bandaged, but bleeding from the forehead and shoulder. It had to be Lord Lincoln. He was conscious—just—and his hands and feet were tied. They had stuffed something into his mouth to keep him quiet. They forced some clothes on to him and then flung him back over the horse. They rode on again, directly to the west.'

Cicely bit her lip. *Oh, Jack, what do they mean to do with you?*

Daniel could not offer comfort. 'There is nothing more we can do, my lady. We cannot even raise an alarm, because to do so will mean risking his identification, *and* the fact that he received succour here. He is surely the man, proof of whose death, the king wants most in all the land.'

Henry? 'Do you think the king might have ordered his abduction?' she asked.

Daniel spread his hands. 'How can I say? As far as we knew, no one was aware of Lord Lincoln's presence. Well, there are those here who know, of course, but they would never betray anything.'

'But someone inside admitted those four men,' Cicely pointed out.

He nodded. 'I know, my lady, and if I discover who it was, he or she will not be long for this world.'

'But it might yet be the king's work?'

'He has reason enough to want to be rid of your cousin, my lady, both as a Yorkist prince, a rebel, and as someone close to you.'

'The king wanted my cousin alive to question him,

and . . .' She stopped, because if Henry was indeed behind this, then he had Jack alive after all, and in spite of all his promises, the spectre of John of Gloucester rose before her. 'I cannot bear to think of what might happen to my cousin if the king has him. I truly cannot.'

Daniel made so bold as to touch her shoulder. 'You need Sir Jon, my lady. Rob and I can take you to him in London, if that is your pleasure.'

'You would do that?' Whether or not there was another rift in her marriage, it *was* Jon she needed now.

'Of course, and it is what he would wish, I am sure. You should not stay here now. There is nothing you can do anyway. If there is any news of Lord Lincoln, it will be sent to you, but—'

'Yes?'

'Do not hope too much, my lady. Remember, as far as the world is concerned, he is a dead man already, buried at Stoke Field.'

Tears welled from her eyes, and Mary rounded on him. 'Have you no tact, Daniel Green? Can you not see how upset my lady is?'

'But it has to be said. I saw him the night before the battle and during the battle. He was brave, gracious, natural, knew how to give heart and lighten spirits, and he was a fine military commander. If he had not been believed to have been killed, I am not at all sure we would still have King Henry. And that could also have been said of Good King Richard, whom the Lancastrian in me would not have been ashamed to serve.'

Cicely got up shakily from her chair. 'Forgive me, but I must be alone.' Her voice was choked as she caught her skirts to hurry to her room.

It was time to leave with Daniel and Rob, and a dozen other horsemen, to see Lady Welles safely to Pasmer's Place. The horses were waiting in the yard, and Mary was ready too, standing outside to say farewell to her aunt.

Cicely had just had a final long play and cuddle with Leo, and found it very difficult. She loved her little boy, and parting from him again was a hard thing to do. If only she could be his mother openly, but any suggestion of such a thing would endanger him, and he had to be put first. And so she kissed him goodbye, and then gave him back to the maid who looked after him in the mornings.

To go down to the courtyard Cicely had to pass the room where she had slept with Henry, and then the room where Jack had been. The door of the latter still stood ajar, and she paused to look inside. It had yet to be tidied, and the bedding remained scattered on the floor. She went to take one of the pillows and hide her face in it. She inhaled the mixture of herbs from Mistress Kymbe's salve, but not thyme. Suddenly she feared so much that she really had seen Jack de la Pole for the last time that she hugged the pillow tightly, as if it were Jack himself.

Richard's voice was sharp behind her. 'Do not wallow, Cicely!'

She whirled about. He stood at the foot of the bed, and his grey eyes were disapproving.

'Richard?' Confusion drove everything else away.

'You are wallowing in self-pity, and I will not have it!'

'Wallowing? I am not!' She began to find her tongue.

He came around the bed to her. 'Yes, sweetheart, you are. You think of all that you have lost and you let yourself sorrow for it. By all means be sorrowing, but for Jesu's sake do not let it rob you of your wits! You have consigned Jack to the grave, yet you have no real reason to believe he is dead.'

'No real reason?' Her eyes began to flash as brightly as his.

'You *know* he is not dead. Not yet, anyway.'

'*How* do I know that?' she demanded.

'Because I do, and I am you.'

She gazed at him. 'I do *not* know it,' she answered.

'Where is your common sense? Well? You summon me, albeit unknowingly, because you need *me* to point out the obvious. If Jack was abducted, it was because someone wanted him alive. If they wanted him dead, they would have killed him here, in this bed. Why go to the trouble of carrying him off? Why risk being seen, or even apprehended? A few sharp stabs as he slept, there would be no sound, and they would have been able to leave as silently as they came.'

Her lips parted. It *was* obvious. 'They may mean to torture him. *Henry* would take him and torture him, to learn who else might have been involved in the rebellion.'

'Do you believe Henry is behind it?'

'I . . . do not know.'

'He has to be a suspect, sweetheart, but there may be others, of whom you know nothing, men with as much reason as Henry to interrogate Jack de la Pole. Did Jack say anything to you? Hint at anything?'

'No.'

'You are sure?' He put his hand to her cheek, and spoke more gently. 'You need me now to help you assemble your thoughts. This kidnapping has shaken you and your thoughts are everywhere at once. Jack is not yet dead, of that I am sure, although he probably *is* in danger.' He searched her eyes. 'You do not believe it is Henry, do you? Not deep in your heart.'

'No.'

'Why?'

'I do not know, it is simply how I feel.'

'Be careful, sweeting, do not allow yourself to be completely lured back into his web. Yes, he loves you, with all his heart, but it is his head that will rule in the end. You now know he is irrational. For Jesu's sake, tread on eggshells.'

She gazed at him. 'I have been so blessed, Richard. First

to have you, and now Jack. Two such great men, two such great loves.'

'You are also blessed to have Sir Jon Welles, lady, and do not forget it. My sympathies lie with him, because he loves you so truly and yet never comes first. I know the sorrow of that.'

'I know, and I bear such guilt, but I cannot stop loving you, or turn away from my love for Jack.' She smiled wistfully. 'How good it would be to spend a night with you again.'

She looked at his face, those features that were sculpted upon her memory, and she reached up to take some strands of his hair between her fingers, parting them slowly, as he had once parted hers. 'Richard, whenever you come to me, and I see and talk to you, you put everything else into perspective.'

He pulled her into his arms, into the embrace that was totally unlike any other man's, and he kissed her. There was mint on his breath, and his lips were as dear to her as ever. She closed her eyes and enjoyed him again. He was the personification of first love, the essence of every good feeling and thought, of everything that was right and true. She did not care that theirs had always been, and would always be, forbidden, because it defied the words of the Bible. So much of her still belonged to him, to her uncle, to Richard III, the most captivating and incorruptible king ever to reign over England.

But there were voices from the yard as the party bound for London prepared to leave Friskney. She could hear Mary hurrying upstairs, calling to her.

Richard smiled again. 'Go now, sweetheart, and do not give up hope for Jack. He may yet need you.'

'I love you, Richard.'

'And I love you,' he replied softly.

Mary was at the door, and Cicely was alone when the maid entered.

# Chapter Twenty-Six

THERE WAS STILL tension in the streets of London, although it had now become clear to all that Henry had won the battle and was secure upon his throne. Jon's ten thousand men had helped to restore calm, and now he awaited further commands from Henry, who was somewhere on his way north towards York.

No commands came, and Jon had no option but to wait. He happened to be at Pasmer's Place when Cicely arrived, and he came out into the yard on hearing the horses. His face changed on seeing her. 'Cicely?'

She gazed at him, biting her lip to stop even more of the foolish tears that had flowed so freely since Jack's disappearance.

'What is it? What brings you here?' Jon asked, hurrying to lift her down from her palfrey, and then holding her tightly as she clung to him, her face hidden against the gold-embroidered bronze cloth of his coat. He looked enquiringly at Daniel.

'By your leave, Sir Jon, we should speak in private.'

'As you wish.' His arm tight and reassuring around her shoulder, Jon ushered her inside and shouted orders. Then they adjourned to the parlour where they could not be overheard. He made her sit down, and then pressed a small cup of wine into her hand. He poured larger cups for himself and Daniel. 'What has happened?' he asked.

Daniel told all, and Jon's face changed. 'Abducted?'

'Yes, Sir Jon. I have told you everything we know. I have no idea who might have been responsible for it, what their ultimate purpose, or whether, indeed, the earl is still alive.'

Cicely closed her eyes again, gripping her cup in both hands. Now she was no longer with Richard, it was so hard to cling to the hope that Jack still lived.

'And the king was at Friskney? Do you suspect him?' Jon asked Daniel.

'Well, he came because he knew Lady Welles was there, not, I believe, because he knew Lord Lincoln was there as well.' Daniel was careful not to meet Jon's eyes.

'Yes, he knew *her* whereabouts from me. Damn it, sir, I know all there is to know about my nephew's dealings with my wife, but clearly seeing her may not have been his sole purpose. You say he doubts Lord Lincoln was killed at Stoke Field?'

Cicely answered, and held up her hand to show Jack's amethyst. 'Henry was suspicious because the dead man was not wearing this ring. He thought I might have it. If I did not, then someone else clearly did, and that someone else might be the real Lord Lincoln.'

'And clearly you *do* have Lincoln's ring,' Jon replied.

'Jack gave it to me after Henry had left Friskney, not any time before then. I will not wear it when I am with Henry.'

'Damn it, you will not wear it at all!' Jon cried. 'Has Jack lost his senses?'

'No, Jon, he warned me not to wear it when Henry might see.'

'Well, *I* do not want to see it either! I reminds me how many horns I wear! Please, sweetheart, put it away somewhere and leave it there. That ring, like Richard's, cannot be mistaken. The world knows it was Jack's.' He paused, and then looked at Daniel again. 'This whole thing has the

329

feel of the king's work. It cannot be coincidence that he was there at such a time. As if he knew Lincoln would go there. And I cannot believe he actually chose to do that instead of remain where he should have been after victory in battle. What was he thinking of?' He turned to Cicely. 'How was Henry when he departed? Did you notice anything amiss?'

'No. He was all that was natural and courteous, without hint of suspicion or animosity. Yes, he wanted to know about the ring, but he was also very anxious to make amends with me.'

Jon studied her for a moment and then dismissed Daniel. 'All is quiet here now, and I have no further need of you. If you wish to stay, by all means do, you are welcome to my hospitality. But if you wish to return to Friskney, you may.'

'By your leave, Sir Jon, I will go home again in the morning.'

Jon nodded. 'As you wish. See that your entire party is accommodated and the horses taken care of. There is room enough here.'

When Daniel had gone, Cicely looked guiltily at her husband. 'I have always brought you such trouble, Jon, and have *never* been worth it.'

'Life would be intolerably dull without you, Cicely.' He smiled.

She took the turquoise ring from her purse and went to him. 'Will you wear it again? Please?'

He held out his hand, and she slipped the ring back where it belonged. Then she hugged him tightly. 'I do love you, Jon, please do not ever think I do not.'

'I know you do, sweetheart. I was upset, that is all. I find it harder to accept everything than I believed I would. But I am myself again now. I know I will never have all of you, and that you are true in your way.' He pulled her close for a moment. 'Take heart now, your scoundrel of a cousin is most likely still alive. You must not give up hope. Whoever took him must want him alive, otherwise they would have put an end to him at Friskney, in his bed. By taking him, they made it clear they have some other purpose.'

Richard's words, she thought. No, her own common sense in disguise. 'If Henry is behind this now, I fear what he will do with Jack. He will torture him for information, and if Jack gives up that information, will Henry make another John of Gloucester of him?'

'I do not think so. You and he have clearly smoothed things, and if he has you back, the last thing he will wish is to do something that is bound to lead to losing you again. Perhaps irredeemably.'

'He will see to it that I do not find out.'

'Please do not see only clouds. We do not know anything for certain, not even that Henry's finger is in the pie. Come now, tell me how Leo is.'

'Well. Flourishing, in fact. Henry held him in his arms,' she added. 'He even commented how like me he is.'

'So, he saw *you* in the boy, but not Richard?'

'He gave no sign of it, but then he only ever saw Richard as a demon in armour and then as a blood-soaked corpse, not as the living man.' She remembered something. 'Jon, Henry started to tell me that he was used to children, because he was a father twi— Just that, a word beginning T-W-I, and then he broke off. I can only think he meant he had been a father twice. Am I right?'

Jon drew a long breath. 'I will tell you, Cicely, but only on your vow never to repeat it.'

'You have my word, but why such secrecy?'

'Henry has an illegitimate son in Brittany. I doubt the boy will be acknowledged openly. Not after all the furore about kings and their bastards that we have endured since 1483.'

'Why is Henry not open about it? He was not married to my sister then. High-ranking men mostly acknowledge their bastards, do they not?'

'Cicely, my half-nephew's mind twists like woodbine. Who in God's own name knows what he is thinking? Leave this whole thing alone, or you will find your damned ring returned again. Is that clear?'

'Yes, Jon, it is, but I will say only one thing more. It does not press you for information, it is merely my own conclusion. I think this Breton lady must have meant a great deal to him, Jon. I am sure she is the one who taught him about lovemaking, for he certainly knows a great deal. He learned from someone he loved very much. He told me he had been violent to a woman before me. I think it was this same lady.'

'Conclude as you wish, sweetheart, for I am more concerned with *our* marriage. Henry wishes us to renew our vows, in front of him, after the queen's coronation.'

'Do you wish to renew them?'

He smiled.

The remaining summer months passed in a haze of dreamy sunshine, but without any word at all of Jack. The unrest and unease of the earlier part of the year had lifted, and Henry's progress was a great success for him. But in his absence his queen lost the baby boy she had been carrying. It was the result of stumbling while taking a morning stroll with Cicely in the gardens of Westminster Palace, but she had fallen heavily. Her pains began an hour later, and by the evening she had given birth to a stillborn son. Henry did not even hear the news until well over a week after it had happened. Preparations for the coronation continued, because Bess would have recovered by the end of November.

It was the beginning of that month when Henry returned to his capital, entering in triumph. He was proven as king, but there was no way of knowing it as he rode through the streets. He was magnificent, bejewelled, elegant and regal, but still he did not smile. Cicely watched him ride past, and could not help imagining the difference if it had been Richard or Jack, who knew how to win hearts with smiles.

Within days of Henry's return, Jon was ordered north again, to Rockingham, and it was made clear he was not to take his wife with him. His obligations did not allow for protest or disobedience, and the orders were of sufficient import to warrant complete and immediate attention. And so Sir Jon Welles rode out of the capital at the head of a large force, to be certain of subduing any lingering Yorkist support around Rockingham. Uriah had been sent away, and Bathsheba waited to go to King David's bed.

The summons came quickly enough. Henry lodged at Westminster, even though his wife and the court were at Sheen, and he received Cicely alone, saying nothing as she sank into a very deep curtsey. She wore primrose silk, and her only jewels were Jon's wedding band and Richard's ruby.

Henry wore black, and no jewels at all, but he smiled, and as he raised her she was amid cloves again.

Should she mention the lost baby? It would be wrong not to. 'I . . . am so sorry about your son, Henry.'

He paused. 'Such things happen. I have offered words of sympathy.'

*Words* were not what Bess needed! 'Henry, would words suffice if it were me?'

'You know they would not. No more, Cicely, for I will not speak of it.'

'But—'

'Jesu, lady, do you think I *enjoy* the loss of my child?'

She gazed at him. He was truly upset! 'Forgive me, Henry, I did not wish to cause you pain.'

'Your sister sent word to me in the curtest of terms and made it clear she did not wish to see me. I observed her wishes. That is the truth of it, so do not lecture me. Even a king can be put in his place by his wife.' He lowered his eyes for a moment. 'Sweetheart, if you were to lose my child, I would be heartbroken. You once told me that if you carried my baby, you would not go full term. Do you still feel that way?'

'No. I would carry your child and cherish it, Henry. I saw you with Leo Kymbe. I know you love children.'

He pulled her closer for a moment, to kiss her forehead. 'Thank you for saying that, sweetheart. It means much to me. Now, however, I think we should talk of your cousin. I know he was at Friskney when you were. I am not such a fool that I did not realize the significance of the red rose banner that suddenly appeared on the tower.'

She could not speak.

'Do not fear me, sweeting, for I am not about to do as I did at Huntingdon.'

'Why? Surely you have every right. I would have helped him to escape.'

'I forgive your deceit, but that does not mean that I will not hunt him down.'

'You do not have him already?'

Surprised, he stepped back to look at her. 'No, I do not have him. I would have told you if I did. But I know he has been abducted. My agents discovered the poacher of whom you must already know, and he repeated to them what he told Daniel Green, which I believe is your fellow's name? I do not have Lincoln, Cicely, nor has his disappearance anything to do with me. And no, I do not know who *does* have him.'

'What will you do with me now?'

'Lock you up in the Tower and seal the door until the day of doom.' He smiled, but then became serious. 'I will keep this throne by whatever means I need, Cicely, I will cut out anyone who challenges my authority or my crown, and I will found my own dynasty. Make no mistake of it. The white rose will not stand in my way again, for I intend to rid myself of it. All of it. Every York male will suffer at my hands, just as I would suffer at theirs. I would not expect otherwise. If Lincoln had won at Stoke Field, I would not be here speaking to you now. It has all changed now, sweetheart. I *have* to be harsh, and I will be.'

He came close again. 'Hold me, Cicely, for I need you.'

When she drew him into her arms, she could feel his distress. 'Henry?'

'I have had enough of conspiracies, plots, rebellions, invasions, Cicely. Enough. I am thirty years old, and I feel as if I am forty-five. My health is so indifferent that I must be careful every winter, and the only time I sleep well is if you are with me, because it is only then that the nightmares are kept at bay.'

His confidence seemed to have deserted him completely. He was a victorious king, returned to his capital after defeating his greatest enemy and having made a triumphant progress around his kingdom, and yet he seemed as if *he* were the defeated leader. His mind's uncertain balance was close, and her distress for him was tinged with unease.

'Henry, if knowing my cousin was at Friskney has caused you this pain, I—'

'I am simply weary, Cicely,' he broke in, 'and Richard's shade is always upon my shoulder. I did not think I would *defeat* him at Bosworth. I was swept along by idiocy and the ambition of others, and then Richard lost. Can you imagine it? He fucking well lost, and there I was, the new King of England, wondering how in God's own name I had managed it.'

'You . . . did not think you would win?'

'I expected to suffer as your cousin has. I expected to be the one bundled naked over a horse and carried ignominiously into Leicester. Except, do not say it, Richard would not have inflicted such an indignity on the corpse of a fallen enemy.'

Cicely did not answer.

He moved away, 'And I have been trying to deal with

the aftermath ever since. I have no choice now but to cling to my throne. And cling to it I damned well will. It is mine. The wind has been sown, and now I reap the whirlwind. I *must* rid myself of the House of York, because until I do, there will always be pretenders.'

She was shaken by his utter resignation to fate, coupled with the ferocity with which he would cling to what he had taken. The paradox within was killing him, as slowly and inexorably as his health already did. He would never be an old man.

'*This* is what I am. Cicely. *This* is what has cowered within me since Bosworth. Mostly I am able to hide it, and I appear cold, hard, in control, relentless, devoid of feeling, call it what you will. But I cannot hide from you any longer. Here I am, in all my ignominy. A frightened man who has no choice but to rule.'

She went to him and held him as tightly as she could. He was so unutterably vulnerable and in need of her that he tore her heart. Henry Tudor intended to annihilate her House, and yet she could still hold him close.

His arms went around her, and there was a truly haunting tenderness in the way he kissed her, a sense that he feared she would suddenly disappear and he would find it all to have been only smoke amid the shadows.

They swayed together again, as if to the faint music of minstrels, somewhere in a distant part of the palace.

It was snowing as Lord and Lady Welles—Jon having been elevated to the rank of viscount—took their vows again in the upper chapel of St Stephen's Chapel at Westminster Palace. The upper chapel, crowded today for the wedding, was only used by the royal family, and could only be reached from the royal apartments. It was richly adorned, with an azure-blue ceiling that was liberally scattered with gold stars.

Cicely wore dark green velvet, with a golden gauze

headdress, and Jon wore a charcoal doublet and grey hose. They held hands as they repeated the words that had already united them once before, but now they had royal consent. Henry was present, and so was Bess, now truly the Queen of England. Margaret was there too, smiling benevolently. Cicely was in her favour again, as if nothing had ever happened.

Jasper Tudor and his duchess were also present. Jasper's face seemed set in a permanent sneer, and he did not look at the bride at all. He was clearly there under duress. Henry, Cicely thought.

Henry was splendid in purple cloth-of-gold, and his face was thoughtful throughout, giving nothing away until Cicely caught his eye and he smiled. Such a warm smile, filled with longing and regret for what might have been.

The wedding band was upon her finger again, and she raised her lips to Jon's, before taking his hand, kissing the palm and whispering, 'Now we have another marriage night to enjoy, Viscount Welles, and I trust we will make better use of it than last time.'

'You may count upon it, Viscountess Welles,' he said softly in return.

Henry came forward. 'You are now, without question, Lady Welles,' he said softly, and in front of everyone he pulled her closer and kissed her on the lips. Then he released her and smiled at Jon. 'What a pity the days are gone when I could have claimed feudal rights to the bride.'

Bess caught Cicely's dismayed glance, while Jon looked his nephew in the eyes. 'Do you wish to claim such a right of your aunt and sister-in-law, Your Majesty?'

A hint of amusement crossed Henry's face. 'I think not. It was but an idle remark.' He glanced at Cicely again, and his eyes gave the lie to the words. Then, in front of everyone, he took off the emerald ring, which now fitted his little finger, not the index upon which he had always worn it before, and pushed it on to her finger, where it fitted snug, warmed by the blood flowing through his veins. 'It is a lady's ring now, because I have had it made so.'

There was something of a commotion among the guests as Jasper left, almost dragging his Woodville wife with him. Cicely heard him say something foul in Welsh for Henry's benefit. Henry's smile froze, but he said nothing as Jasper stomped out of the chapel like an avenging angel.

Cicely hoped attention had been drawn away from the ring, but Henry would not allow it. 'I trust you are pleased to now possess what you have coveted for so long?'

The hush and interest descended in a moment. She did not know how best to react to a gift that must seem to everyone present to be a lover's gift. A lover's very costly and personal gift. The emerald was so magnificent, the light slanting through it in rays of such exquisite greens that its beauty caught her breath. 'You honour me greatly, Your Majesty.'

The continuing rustle of whispers was silenced immediately as Henry glanced around. Then he looked at Cicely. 'You have a winning hand, Lady Welles. One wonders what fabulous trophy you will acquire next.' He met her eyes, his love so blatant that it could not be misinterpreted. Those in the room could only believe that the notoriously intimate kiss at Winchester had not been the last the apparently chill, undemonstrative King of England had shared with his wife's sister.

There was reproach in the look that Cicely returned to him, for this was not well done at all. Such a gift should have been given in private, certainly not in front of everyone when she had just repeated her vows to his uncle. And certainly not in front of his queen. Henry knew it as well as she did, but there was no repentance in his response. He had not forgiven Jon for Stoke Field, or Bess for all the insults she had dealt him.

He spoke again. 'Well, my lady, I believe you and my uncle do not wish to linger, but return to Pasmer's Place without further ado. It would seem the marriage bed beckons.'

'It does,' Jon replied, perhaps a little more bluntly than he meant to, for it made his feelings as plain as Henry had made his.

Henry returned the look, and in the same vein. 'It is a little chilly today, I think,' he murmured, and then offered his arm to Bess, whose face was devoid of any expression at all.

Jon watched the king and queen return to the royal apartments. 'Plague take him,' he muttered.

'I am sorry, Jon.'

'It was hardly your fault. He made it far too public.'

They left through the crowded royal apartments, for there was no other way. Cicely saw Henry standing alone before a fireplace, his hands clasped behind his back, making it plain he was taking a moment or so to himself and was not to be approached. However, when a messenger brought him a sealed document that seemed to be of some urgency, Henry's attention was suddenly fully engaged upon its yellow-wax seal, which he touched for a moment between his finger and thumb.

Cicely halted, watching, making Jon stop too. She was sensitive to everything about Henry, and knew he had seldom been more guarded or tense than in this moment. The impression increased as he broke the seal and read the document. It was brief, because almost immediately he crushed it into a ball and threw it on the fire. As he did so, the broken seal was dislodged and fell to the floor, striking his foot before rolling on to the hearth, where it lay in two pieces. Henry did not notice, for he was suddenly beset by coughing.

The whole room turned to look as he struggled to control himself. For the splitting of a second his eyes met Cicely's, and she felt the force of feeling that suddenly gripped him. Then he mastered himself, turned on his heel and strode from the room. There was a startled stir, because many people present had hoped to secure his attention the moment he indicated he could be approached again. Instead, he had left.

The document was burning, shining and twisting into nothing on the blazing coals as Jon went swiftly to the hearth to retrieve the seal. He shoved the halves into his belt purse and returned to usher Cicely from the royal apartments.

They hurried to the accommodation that had always been Cicely's here at Westminster, and where their outdoor clothes waited, but as the door closed upon them, Jon immediately removed the pieces of yellow seal and pushed them together again on a table.

For a moment, fleeting but very poignant, she thought it was Jack's seal. But it was no more than a brief impression, gone in a moment. She pressed her lips together as her emotions threatened to grip her again.

Jon understood, and squeezed her hand. 'Jack will be safe, sweetheart. Look again. It is nothing like his seal. See? His seal bears a Moor's head, this is a mythical creature of some sort.'

Something in his voice caught her attention. 'You know whose it is, do you not, Jon?'

'No.'

'Liar,' she breathed. He *did* know, she could see it on his face. 'Well, it certainly means something very important to Henry. He was as if struck by lightning.'

Jon nodded.

'It means trouble, does it not?' she observed softly

Jon nodded again. 'Do not ask me about it, sweetheart, because it is, quite literally, more than my life is worth to tell you. Come, let us return to Pasmer's Place. I want to kick my heels free of my cursed nephew.'

But as they hurried through the palace, she remembered leaving her hood behind. Jon would have gone back for it, but she told him to wait by the entrance, and hastened back herself. Then, clutching the hood, she retraced her steps, but as she passed an open doorway she heard a beloved voice.

'Coz?'

She whirled about, her heart leaping. 'Jack?'

He moved into sight within the doorway, and held out his hand. She ran to him, flinging herself joyfully into his arms and losing herself in his kisses. He held her to him, devouring her with his lips and making love to her with his caresses. They were moments of ecstasy, of a dreamed-of reunion that was suddenly wonderful fact. Tears soaked her cheeks, and her mouth trembled to his. Her whole body yearned for him, and so did her spirit.

He had to hold her away gently. 'Sweetheart, I cannot stay. I saw you and had to speak.'

'Why are you here? It is perilous for you to be in the centre of Henry's—'

'It is the last place he would expect to find me.'

She gazed at him. He wore a nondescript cloak over . . . she did not know, for the cloak hid his other clothes. But he did not wear the thigh boots. He was thinner, and the wound to his forehead had left a scar. His hair was growing again, but was far from the length it had once been. His dark eyes were filled with love, and his smile touched her heart.

'I love you, Jack de la Pole,' she said softly.

'And I love you, Viscountess Welles.'

'What happened to you?'

'Believe it or not, I was taken at Tal's behest. The men he engaged thought they were apprehending an escaped felon. Which, I suppose they were. I am safe, and that is all you need to know.'

'No, I deserve to be told a little more. Stoke Field was not the end of it for you, was it? There is something else set to happen. Please tell me, Jack. I may as well worry for

341

what I do know as what I do not.'

He hesitated, and then nodded. 'Henry has a great secret, Cicely, one of such import that if it should become known, he will of a certainty lose the throne. Every Yorkist in the land will rise against him, and so will many Lancastrians Well, he now knows that this secret is in the wrong hands. All we lack is evidence, but we *will* obtain it. And soon.'

Her mind raced. 'Have you sent him a letter with a yellow seal?'

'Yes. How—?'

'Jon and I were there when he received it. He was utterly shaken.'

'As well he might be.'

'What is the secret?'

He shook his head. 'It is too dangerous for you to know, Cicely. I have already endangered you by speaking to you now, but I could not be so close and not even touch you.'

'Hold me,' she whispered, wanting it to seem he would never release her . . . or go from her again.

He crushed her to him, and she lifted her lips for another kiss. Thyme surrounded and filled her. Oh, how she worshipped him, how she needed him and wanted to stay with him. She had to end the kiss, for it invaded her too much. 'Why have you not sent word to me?' she whispered, not without accusation.

'To protect you, sweetheart. Henry knows I am alive and his weasels follow me everywhere.'

'He is having you followed? He said he did not know anything of you.'

'Another Tudor fibling. At least . . . so far Tal and I have been one step ahead all the time. Henry is afraid, and understandably, given what he has to hide.'

'Jack—'

'I will twist the throne from beneath him yet, Cicely.' He caressed her cheek with soft fingers. 'He has you again?'

She held up her hand.

'Ah, the emerald. Did I not tell you?'

'Please stay away from him, Jack. Henry will do *any-thing* to keep the throne. Believe me, I know how iron a will he has. I *know* him. Corner him and he will fight viciously. Leave England, be safe somewhere across the sea. I can exist if I know you are safe from him. Please, for I love you so much.'

He kissed her softly, playing his lips to hers. 'I *will* be safe, sweetheart. But now, if I stay with you, *you* are the one who will not be safe.'

'Send me word, somehow. *Anything* to tell me you still live.' More tears welled from her eyes. There was so much feeling within her now, so much devastating emotion that she had to grip his cloak. 'Please,' she whispered. 'Please.'

There were tears in his eyes too, and he kissed her again. 'I will. You have my word.' Then he released her. 'I must go. Tal is waiting at the steps.'

She could not turn to watch him leave, but stood there, head bowed, trying to compose herself. At last she mastered her tears enough to follow him towards the entrance, where Jon waited, and by his agitation she knew he had seen Jack.

'Cicely? What in God's own name. . . ?'

'I did not know, Jon. Truly.'

He looked at her tear-stained face. 'Oh, sweetheart. Damn his hide!'

'Did you see him, or did he. . . ?'

'He spoke to me. I would not have known otherwise, for his hood was raised.'

'What did he say?'

'He told me to care for you. Damn his impudence. That is all. Why is he here?'

'The message Henry received was from him.' She moved even closer, and told him what Jack had said. 'You know this great secret. What is it?'

343

'I only know some of it. Sweetheart, I will *not* tell you, and so I ask, seriously, for you not to question me again.' He took her arm and made her walk towards the river steps. There was a press there, of people and craft, and everyone was huddled to keep out the winter chill. Christmas greenery was being unloaded from a large skiff — holly, mistletoe, ivy — and torches smoked and flickered.

She saw Jack and Tal waiting near one of the torches, but only knew them by Jack's cloak and the fact that he had said he was with Tal. Jack turned as Tal pointed her out, and although most of his face was in shadow, his lips were not, and she saw him smile.

Jon's fingers tightened on her elbow, to be sure she did not do anything foolish. 'He is mad to come here,' he muttered. 'Who is he with? Do you know?'

'He is Jack's friend, called Tal. His full name is Taleisin ap Gruffydd.'

'How well do you know him?'

'Not well. He has brought me messages from Jack. He has something to do with Calais.'

'Indeed?' Jon looked thoughtfully at Tal.

A large party of young courtiers and pages disembarked from a barge, and as they streamed noisily past, Jack and Tal hastened down the steps to enter a small vessel that had just arrived to one side of the stairs. It was a costly craft, clearly private and yet oddly anonymous, and as it was manoeuvred away from the steps, Jack stood at the stern, gazing back at her. He raised his hand. A small salute, but a huge acknowledgement of everything.

More tears shimmered in her eyes as the vessel disappeared into the flying snow.

Jon put his arm lovingly around her shoulders. 'Take heart, sweetheart. He is alive and clearly well. There is *nothing* you can do. Do you hear me? Nothing. And I want you to keep out of it. If you receive *any* communication from him, you are to tell me. Please tell me you understand, and that you will do as I ask.'

'I understand, Jon, and will do as you ask.'

Jon drew her hand over his to descend the steps as a skiff became available. They climbed into the rocking craft, and as the boatman poled it away from the steps, she toyed with the emerald ring and looked back at the palace. The breeze caught the falling snow for a moment, lifting it like a curtain, and she saw Henry's standards and red dragons flying from the roofs. Then the snowy curtain fell again, and everything was obscured from view.

Jon put his arm around her shoulder again. 'Leave the past where it belongs, sweetheart. We have our future to look forward to now. Ours, no one else's.' He removed his gauntlet to put his hand to her chin and raise her lips to his. They kissed, and the snow eddied around them as the skiff skimmed downstream towards Pasmer's Place.

# Author's Note

As with the two previous books in the Cicely series, this is also a work of fiction. I have used history and actual people to weave a story that 'might' have happened.

Bearing this in mind, when I give Cicely her royal lovers, I am inventing such affairs. I am a staunch supporter of Richard III, and will remain so until it is proved beyond all doubt that he was a monster. As far as I am concerned, he was an honest and honourable man caught up in events from which he had no escape. Were it not for treachery, he would have won the Battle of Bosworth. That he did not was, in my opinion, a tragedy for England. Given the chance, I truly believe he would have been a great king. But he was not given that chance, and now we will never know how his reign might have developed.

Richard was Cicely's uncle and I do not think for a moment that he really did share an incestuous love with her. There were rumours about his oldest niece, Bess, who is supposed to have loved him in such a way, but rumours were all it was, and he strenuously denied it. That his nieces held him in high regard, in spite of being declared illegitimate when he became king, I base on the fact that they never once, throughout the reign of Henry VII, said anything to criticize or blacken Richard's name. They certainly had the opportunity, and I do not doubt that Henry would have been pleased if they had used it. They did not.

It is therefore pure conjecture that Cicely may have had a child by Richard III, who would probably have been appalled to know that all these centuries later someone would still be perpetuating the calumny that he liked his nieces a little too much. But it is not unknown for an uncle and niece to love each other in such a way. That does not make it right, but perhaps more understandable if true love really is involved. As far as I know, there was no such child as Leo Kymbe, or any child at all of Cicely's by her uncle. Leo is fiction.

Nor do I have any basis at all for the continuing love affair between Cicely and Henry. But why not? Why should he not fall in love with his wife's sister? From all accounts, he was not an easy man, and certainly he was damaged by the circumstances of his upbringing. He spent a large part of his early life in hiding in exile, staying out of the way of the Yorkists, who would prefer to have been rid of him. He was highly intelligent, with a secretive, cunning nature, and would eventually succumb to tuberculosis (consumption) at the age of fifty-two. His illness had affected him off and on for many years, seeming to be seasonal, and I have chosen to introduce this aspect of his life a little earlier than it is mentioned in historical sources. But that does not mean he was free of it in 1486/87. The early signs may well have been in evidence when he was a young man. In his later reign Henry became a terrible tyrant, cruel, avaricious, indifferent to his subjects and much hated. He was never a popular monarch, and his nature played against him. He died a very rich man . . . and his son, the truly monstrous Henry VIII, promptly squandered it all.

I must be clear that although Richard III's illegitimate son, John of Gloucester, was supposedly kept at the Tower until his believed execution in 1499, I have no justification at all for claiming he was tortured by Henry VII. This is my fiction.

So too is the suggestion that Ralph Scrope turned coat against Richard III or claimed falsely to have been married to Cicely. There is evidence that a marriage of some sort took place, but it was set aside by Henry VII so that she could be given instead to his half-uncle, Sir Jon Welles. The real Ralph Scrope did not die horribly on the marsh near Wyberton, but lived to become 10th Baron Scrope of Masham, dying in 1515. I apologize to his memory for turning him into such a scoundrel.

Taleisin ap Gruffydd is an invented name for an actual historical person, whose real identity will be revealed in the next book in the Cicely series, as will that of the woman who 'introduced Henry Tudor to lovemaking'. This latter aspect of Henry's character is yet more invention. He may have been a great lover, or he may have been very dull between the sheets. He was certainly complex enough to be just about anything. History does not tell us about this side of him, except to suggest that he was not 'uxorious' towards his wife. Nevertheless, he fathered a number of children with her, so either he was uxorious after all, or his marriage bed was a case of getting down to business! Wham, bam. So, I have fashioned him as I wish. Such is the power of a writer of fiction.

The man at the heart of this book is, of course, John (Jack) de la Pole, 1st Earl of Lincoln. He and Cicely could have been passionate lovers, but that they were is another of my flights of romantic fancy. And yet again . . . why not? In spite of his importance as Richard III's nephew and chosen heir (never formalized and so not known for certain), Jack de la Pole was mysterious in many ways. So little is known about him as a man, only where he was and when he was there. He was shrewd and intelligent, and named as 'a good lord'. There seems to be no record of what he looked like or his personal views on anything. But he was a proud Yorkist nobleman and had every intention of returning his House to the throne. He supported Lambert Simnel, but his actual intentions remain a mystery. I have chosen to make his aim to be Lord Protector during the boy-king's minority, but he could very easily have intended to take the throne for himself.

There is a story of the Duke of Clarence having secretly sent his son to his sister, the Duchess of Burgundy, and substituting another child here in England. It may be true, it may not. If it is true, then it could explain the identity of Lambert Simnel, and thus Jack de la Pole's willingness to support the 'pretender' instead of promoting his own strong claim. Attainders could be reversed, and if Simnel really was the Earl of Warwick (the title Clarence's son had held before his father's death), then he was from a senior line to Jack, and more importantly, a male line. He was therefore likely to win support against the might of Henry VII, although whether he would have drawn more than Jack de la Pole is not so certain.

The real Jack de la Pole died at the Battle of Stoke Field, and legend has it that he was buried near a spring on the battlefield, with a willow stave through his heart. This is just a legend, but Jack has no known resting place. Henry did indeed issue orders that he was to be taken alive, and was furious when he was killed in battle. Paul de Wortham is fiction. If a man of that name did actually exist, it is pure coincidence, because as far as I am concerned, I have invented him. That he might have been misidentified as Jack de la Pole, who then escaped, is therefore my storytelling.

These books about Cicely Plantagenet are not meant to be taken for fact. They are stories woven around fact, but with the addition of romantic and other imagined events. Please do not forget this. Historical fiction is for entertainment; history itself is for serious study. Never mix the two.

Sandra Heath Wilson
Gloucester, 2014